Redeeming
THE Rogue

DONNA MACMEANS

B

BERKLEY SENSATION, NEW YORK

THE BERKLEY PUBLISHING GROUP
Published by the Penguin Group
Penguin Group (USA) Inc.
375 Hudson Street, New York, New York 10014, USA

Penguin Group (Canada), 90 Eglinton Avenue East, Suite 700, Toronto, Ontario M4P 2Y3, Canada
(a division of Pearson Penguin Canada Inc.)
Penguin Books Ltd., 80 Strand, London WC2R 0RL, England
Penguin Group Ireland, 25 St. Stephen's Green, Dublin 2, Ireland (a division of Penguin Books Ltd.)
Penguin Group (Australia), 250 Camberwell Road, Camberwell, Victoria 3124, Australia
(a division of Pearson Australia Group Pty. Ltd.)
Penguin Books India Pvt. Ltd., 11 Community Centre, Panchsheel Park, New Delhi—110 017, India
Penguin Group (NZ), 67 Apollo Drive, Rosedale, Auckland 0632, New Zealand
(a division of Pearson New Zealand Ltd.)
Penguin Books (South Africa) (Pty.) Ltd., 24 Sturdee Avenue, Rosebank, Johannesburg 2196,
South Africa

Penguin Books Ltd., Registered Offices: 80 Strand, London WC2R 0RL, England

This is a work of fiction. Names, characters, places, and incidents either are the product of the author's imagination or are used fictitiously, and any resemblance to actual persons, living or dead, business establishments, events, or locales is entirely coincidental. The publisher does not have any control over and does not assume any responsibility for author or third-party websites or their content.

REDEEMING THE ROGUE

A Berkley Sensation Book / published by arrangement with the author

PRINTING HISTORY
Berkley Sensation mass-market edition / August 2011

Copyright © 2011 by Donna MacMeans.
Excerpt from *The Casanova Code* by Donna MacMeans copyright © by Donna MacMeans.
Cover art by Aleta Rafton.
Cover design by George Long.
Cover hand lettering by Ron Zinn.

All rights reserved.
No part of this book may be reproduced, scanned, or distributed in any printed or electronic form without permission. Please do not participate in or encourage piracy of copyrighted materials in violation of the author's rights. Purchase only authorized editions.
For information, address: The Berkley Publishing Group,
a division of Penguin Group (USA) Inc.,
375 Hudson Street, New York, New York 10014.

ISBN: 978-0-425-24267-4

BERKLEY® SENSATION
Berkley Sensation Books are published by The Berkley Publishing Group,
a division of Penguin Group (USA) Inc.,
375 Hudson Street, New York, New York 10014.
BERKLEY® SENSATION and the "B" design are trademarks of Penguin Group (USA) Inc.

PRINTED IN THE UNITED STATES OF AMERICA

10 9 8 7 6 5 4 3 2 1

If you purchased this book without a cover, you should be aware that this book is stolen property. It was reported as "unsold and destroyed" to the publisher, and neither the author nor the publisher has received any payment for this "stripped book."

ACKNOWLEDGMENTS

I don't think it would be possible to write a novel without the collaboration of many generous and talented individuals. I'd like to take a moment to thank them here.

Thank you to my editor, Cindy Hwang, who suggested the original concept go in a different direction. Thank you to my agent, Cori Deyoe, for her unfailing support. My husband says everyone should have someone like her in their life. I think he's right.

While I wish to thank the Romance Bandits for their constant support and friendship, I'd like to single out Jeanne Adams, Nancy Northcott, and Cassondra Murray for brainstorming plots with me amid copious wine and chocolate. My thanks as well to wordsmith Jo Robertson, who helped me over some early hurdles, and to my fabulous historical writer–sisters in the MR-Debut loop who kept me pushing forward.

Thank you to my daughter, Jessica, for giving me the nonfiction book that inspired this story, and thanks as well to my son, David, whose enthusiastic support for his crazed mother brought new readers to my stories.

And as always, thanks to my husband for being there through these many, many years.

Prologue

LOVE SHIMMERED AS BRIGHT AS A BEACON AS HER brother, the Duke of Bedford, exchanged vows with his new American heiress wife. Arianne's heart lifted. Both of her brothers had found devoted wives who made them happy. She almost laughed. Some might say her work here was done.

"Arianne," her brother Nicholas called before she could leave the Deerfield Abbey chapel. "William and I need to speak to you before you leave for some distant country."

She smiled, her penchant for travel well known but perhaps not as well understood. While she had lived at Deerfield Abbey in her childhood, she never considered it home. William's recent renovations to the abbey failed to rid it of painful memories. Indeed, it was her intention to go to Vienna immediately after her brief stay at the abbey.

"Surely it can wait till later." She glanced over her shoulder. "Look at him. I've never seen William so happy. I doubt he even knows I'm here."

"He knows," Nicholas assured her. He linked his arm in hers and walked with her outside. "It gives us the perfect opportunity to speak with you about some surprising news on a recent discovery."

"News?" She tried to pull back from her brother to better see his face, but he kept her arm tightly linked in his. That more than anything lifted the fine hairs on the back of her neck. She looked at him askance. "William has been quite free with news in his letters. Why should this be different?"

For a moment, her marvelously talented, handsome rapscallion of a brother dropped his rakish demeanor. "Because some things, dear Sister, should not be committed to paper."

SHE AND NICHOLAS WAITED IN WILLIAM'S LIBRARY, THE windows bearing witness to the new vast improvements made in Arianne's absence. The last time she was here, the abbey seemed to be crumbling about her ears. How serendipitous that while traveling in Switzerland, she had met a wealthy American matron searching for a titled husband for her daughter. Who would have envisioned that today's festivities would result from that chance meeting?

William entered the library in high spirits, flushed and grinning widely.

"Arianne," he said, "you grow lovelier every time I see you. Thank you for joining our celebration. You will be staying with us awhile, will you not?"

"Your wife extended an invitation for two weeks," Arianne said, leaning forward to accept her brother's kiss on her cheek. "There should be plenty of time for us to speak privately if this is keeping you from—"

"No," Nicholas interrupted. "It is precisely because you're staying that you need to know about certain individuals who you might encounter."

Her two brothers exchanged a glance. "Yes. I'm fairly certain he's going to want to meet you," William added with an air of mystery.

Arianne glanced from one to the other, confused and a bit angry that they were obviously keeping secrets from her. "What are you talking about?" She addressed Nicholas, then turned toward William. "Who am I likely to meet?"

"Our father," William replied, with brows raised. His eyes studied her face.

After a moment of shock, she laughed. Obviously, her brothers had conspired to play a trick on her. "That's ridiculous. Our father is dead. In case you've forgotten, that's precisely why you're the new Duke of Bedford."

Neither Nicholas nor William joined in her laughter. Met with silence, her smile died and faded away.

"We've recently discovered that the old Duke did not provide the seed that produced us," Nicholas said softly.

Arianne shook her head. "No. Our mother was not one of those women. She was good. She was faithful." Her brothers didn't offer a word in protest; they just waited. "Look at you two," she continued. "In spite of the age difference, you are mirror images of each other. Surely the same man—"

"Our mother was faithful," William explained. "Just not to the old Duke. We've learned that due to an infection in his youth, he could not provide needed heirs. He found someone else to take his place in that regard. Someone who has maintained his silence all these many years."

The air fled her lungs; blood drained from her face. All these years, she'd believed a lie? Her fingers fumbled in the air; her glance darted between her brothers while she struggled to breathe. "Is there . . ."

"Proof?" Nicholas supplied. "Yes. We've seen the proof."

William nodded his head. His voice dropped to a compassionate pitch. "Think, Arianne. It explains so much. Father's anger. His moodiness."

His abuse of her mother. Arianne's fingers dug into her gloved palms at those resurrected memories. Her head throbbed. Her gaze settled on William, on his quiet dignity, on his pride. "But you're the new Duke of Bedford," she said, breathless. "How can that be?"

"Legally, we are his heirs." William's lips moved into a gentle smile. "That's why the old Duke took such drastic measures. He acknowledged us as his children, and in the eyes of society and the law, that's all that matters."

"But we're not," she whispered. Her eyes narrowed in concentration. Such a simple concept, yet it shook all her beliefs.

Who was she? Whose blood flowed in her veins? Her life had been defined by her father's title. If he wasn't her father, then who was she?

"And," Nicholas added, his face launching into a grin, "we've met our real father. He's a marvelous chap, Arianne, and he can't wait to meet you."

"He's here?" Her head was still swimming with the implications of William's revelation. Her mind raced to recall the titled gentry present in the chapel. Which one provided the seed? Did he know of her existence before this day? Surely, he must look familiar in some regard.

"He's been here all along," William said quietly. He, more than Nicholas, seemed to understand her shock. "He watched us grow from afar."

"Watched us?" How was that possible? Her father was never known for his hospitality. Few visitors came to the abbey. Which could only mean . . .

"Thackett," Nicholas supplied. "Do you remember him?"

"Lord Thackett?" She frowned, trying to put a face to that name.

"Farmer Thackett," Nicholas corrected with a grand smile. "I suppose that's where you get your knack for flowers and things."

"*Farmer* Thackett? Not a lord or a sir or even a squire?" Her shock must have shown on her face, as even William started to grin in response. They apparently had eased into accepting the different husbandry, but then they were no longer participants in the marriage mart. They weren't rated on their bloodlines like a brood mare. At least, not anymore. Not like herself.

"So you see, Anne," Nicholas said, his face flushed with humor. "You truly are the farmer's daughter."

Fear of the old Duke had once bound them together. Now the bond dissolved a bit. She felt estranged, adrift, her shock at odds with their easy laughter. What would be the result of this revelation? An anxious thought slipped into her mind. "Who knows about this?"

"Our wives, of course. Fran, after all, uncovered the connection." William's pride for his wife beamed from his face.

"I think Emma was actually pleased by the news." Nicholas

hugged Arianne's shoulder. "Wait till you meet him, Anne. You'll like him immediately. We all do. You'll see."

William looked at her sympathetically. "I'm sorry, Anne. Once the genie has left the bottle, we can't very well push him back in."

She smiled for her brothers' sake. As William had mentioned, it was a relief to understand the old Duke's anger. His tendency to abandon her at school, even over school holidays, made sense in light of this discovery. But even that knowledge didn't lessen her lingering sense of foreboding.

· One ·

WHILE UNEXPECTED ON A HIGH-CLASS MAYFAIR street, the press of a knifepoint to the base of Michael Rafferty's spine proved annoyingly familiar.

"Your valuables or your life," a guttural voice hissed. "I reckon a couple of swanks like you two have nice fat pockets."

Rafferty glanced at his colleague. After receiving his slight nod, Rafferty turned abruptly, rapping the miscreant's hand with his walking stick. The knife flew from the robber's grasp and slid harmlessly along the street. Deprived of his weapon, the thief resorted to his fists but quickly discovered he was outclassed there as well. Rafferty soon had the man's face pressed to the side of a well-appointed Mayfair town house with his arm twisted in a painful hold.

"Well done." Rafferty's companion applauded. "You didn't need my assistance at all."

Rafferty winced, feeling the sting of a cut on his lip. The bloody bugger had landed one lucky punch. Blast that it had been the fist with a ring.

"Some of that famous sleight of hand would have been appreciated," Rafferty said, shaking his hair clear from his eyes. "Or is that only for the stage?"

His friend, the renowned Phineas Connor, Master of Illusion, laughed. "My performance onstage is limited to cards and doves. You're the one, Rafferty, known for his fists." He glanced at Rafferty's captive. "At least among the Irishmen who should know better."

The man squirmed. "Rafferty? Is that you?" He swore like a seaman, which—based on his filthy rags—he could have been. "I swear I didn't know."

Rafferty tugged the crook's arm higher and heard fabric rip. "Check his pockets."

While Phineas rummaged through the man's clothing, Rafferty glanced around the corner of the building to a line of hansoms in front of a stylish town house. Such an elite gathering might offer temptation for the kind of criminal he held captive. "This is a dapper neighborhood for a wharf rat like you."

"I was minding me own business until you two came along," the thief muttered.

Silver glinted in Phineas's hand, the contents of the thief's pocket. Rafferty gave the man a shake. "A half crown? Who else did you rob tonight?"

"I didn't rob nobody. That was for a message. Half now and half when I brings the reply."

"What sort of reply did you expect to a knife in the back?" Rafferty tugged the arm, earning a squeal from the thief.

"The message weren't for you. I was to hand deliver it to a lady, I was. I thought you two was easy pickings while I waited for her to show."

Phineas retrieved an envelope from the crook's jacket. No name or address was noted on the front, but a blob of red wax sealed the back. He bounced the letter off his fingertips. "Nice quality stationery. Too nice for the likes of a gutter rat."

"Who's the lady?" Rafferty asked. When an answer wasn't immediately forthcoming, he tugged the twisted arm higher. "Tell me before your arm leaves its socket."

"I don't know her name," the man bellowed, his eyes squeezed shut. "All I know is she's dressed in green and she's going to that party of swells." He slid his face on the limestone to point the way with his chin. "Barnell said . . ." His eyes widened, and his mouth clamped shut.

"Barnell?" Rafferty glanced at Phineas, who nodded in recognition. "James Stuart Barnell from the House of Commons?" Lord Henderson, Rafferty's superior at the Home Office, had suggested Barnell would be attending the diplomatic reception at Countess D'Orange's town house. Rafferty had supposed that was the reason he'd been ordered to attend in spite of a spirited vocal protest. An evening spent in the company of haughty, preening, supercilious diplomats was an even greater insidious torture than the stiff starched collar currently pinching his neck. Now that intelligence listed Barnell as chairman of the Home Rule League, a group advocating violence in pursuit of Irish independence, the British government monitored his every move. Thus Rafferty had to attend the stuffy reception rather than spend a pleasant evening with the accommodating colleens at Brannigan's Tavern.

Phineas retrieved the knife and handed it to Rafferty, who slipped it temporarily into the waistband of his trousers before releasing the thief. "What exactly did Barnell tell you?"

"I ain't saying nothing more," the man grumbled.

"You're in luck." Rafferty smiled. "I happen to be going to that particular gathering. I'll be happy to convey your message to Mr. Barnell's mystery woman."

"She's expecting the likes of me, not you," the hooligan complained. "How's I'm supposed to get my other half crown if I don't bring back her reply?"

"Be content you're still alive," Rafferty said, already pondering the identity of the woman. "Now be off with you. Don't let me see your nose up here again or you'll be returning to Kerry without it."

The man began to slink down the road but turned after he'd traveled a safe distance. "It's a sad day"—he snarled—"when the Irish turn against their own."

Rafferty's jaw set, his fingers curled into fists. Had it not been for Phineas's restraining hand on his arm, he'd have chased the boggler down to make him eat his contemptuous words.

"Easy, Rafe," Phineas counseled. "It's a fool that's talking. Remember who pressed a knife to your back." They watched until the thief blended into the shadows.

"How can they think I'm not doing my part to fight for Irish independence?" Rafferty grumbled. The insulting moke hadn't been the first to taunt him about loyalties, and most likely he wouldn't be the last. "Killing innocent people isn't the right way to gain home rule."

"I know, I know." Phineas slapped him on the back. "It's true what Samuel Johnson said—the Irish, we're a fair people. We never speak well of one another."

In spite of his lingering disgust over the lout's taunt, Rafferty found his spirits lifting. Phineas was right. The man was a fool. Best to focus on the recent plum that had fallen in his lap . . . the message to a mystery woman in green. His lips twisted into a smile. History had proven that even the most fiery of politicians had a vulnerability where beautiful women were concerned. Could she be the key to the elimination of the violent Fenians? He pulled the paper from his jacket. "This message could prove a stroke of good fortune. Do you think Barnell is establishing a tryst?" He contemplated the red seal. "We should read it before it's delivered."

Phineas examined the envelope. "I can't lift the seal without the woman knowing it's been read. If we had the time to go back . . ." He glanced at Rafferty. "Maybe we should just deliver this and follow her. I can always finger the message later." He smiled. "My sleight of hand may prove useful yet."

Rafferty pushed his hair back from his face. The long, shabby cut allowed him to blend in among the criminal underbelly where vital intelligence accumulated for those who knew the treacherous route. Rafferty knew it well.

"So, Mr. Connor, master of feats of wonder and illusion." Rafferty bowed in a mimicked salute. "Can you use your powers to foresee this woman? That information would be helpful if every woman is dressed in green."

Phineas laughed. "Even if I had such abilities, I wouldn't tell you. Locating her should make the reception much more appealing."

Rafferty was tempted to argue. His experience with the hoity-toity sort of woman likely in attendance suggested they would not be interested in dallying with the likes of him.

The clop of hooves and the jangle of a carriage brought his attention back to the town house. Another diplomat arriving for idle chatter and secretive glances. Phineas tapped Rafferty's elbow. "I'll watch the outside while you question the ladies inside."

If he had his druthers, Rafferty would have preferred that Phineas play the role of gentleman diplomat and he be the outside lookout. After all, Phineas was the stage performer. But Lord Henderson had been explicit that Rafferty alone was to attend the reception. He started to cross the street.

"Wait."

Rafferty glanced back. "What's wrong?"

"Your jacket is ripped." Phineas pointed to the deep rent under Rafferty's arm. "And your lip is bleeding on your silk. You won't get past the doorman looking like that."

A matched set of black horses pulled another liveried brougham to the entrance. The streetlights caught a shimmer of green on the skirts of the woman emerging from its depths.

Rafferty cursed under his breath and glanced at Phineas's frock coat. He tugged the end of his own bloodied white cravat. "Quick. Exchange with me."

"Hell, you say!" Phineas shook his head, but Rafferty had already shed his cravat and was shrugging out of his ripped coat. With a sigh, Phineas loosened his black neck cloth, then removed his jacket. "You're too broad for this to fit properly, you know."

Rafferty accepted the garment with a smile, then slipped one arm in the sleeve. It was a little short, but it would suffice. He tugged the jacket across his back to secure the other arm.

"That's my best performance coat," Phineas cautioned. "Have mercy on the seams!"

The fit was tight, but it would have to do. He moved the knife from his trousers to his boot, the purloined letter to an inside jacket pocket, and tied the cravat in a four-in-hand knot.

Phineas shook his head. "All you need is a black mask and a swift horse and you'd pass for a highwayman. You won't look at all like the other swells."

"That, my friend, is a compliment," Rafferty replied, then started across the street.

Phineas called after him. "There is one thing you should know . . . The last time I wore that coat—"

"Tell me tomorrow," Rafferty yelled back, anxious to track down the woman who had just entered the town house. "Lord Henderson's residence at three."

"CUPID'S MISTRESS!" THE BACHELOR'S JAW DROPPED AND trembled like a fish gasping air. "I didn't realize you were the matchmaker."

Before Lady Arianne Chambers could explain that those arrangements were purely accidental and not something she consciously practiced, the frightened man vanished into the chattering crowd of diplomats and their spouses gathered in the Italian ambassador's salon. Ever since word had spread of Arianne's success at suggesting successful matrimonial matches, bachelors had run shrieking the moment she entered a room. Two years ago, such rejection would have startled her. Now she'd come to expect it.

"I'm sorry, Anne." Lady Cardiff's gaze held that special pity married women reserved for those less fortunate. "I thought Crenshaw would be different."

"It matters not. I'm resigned to spinsterhood." Arianne patted her best friend's arm before fluffing the lace attached to her green satin sleeve. "I'm bound to be happier that way."

Lady Cardiff frowned. "Not all men treat their wives as did your father. It's possible to find love and companionship within the bounds of matrimony."

Arianne did not correct her friend's mistaken assumption, for no amount of explanation would convince her otherwise. Kitty had not lived in the Chambers household and therefore had not witnessed her mother's decline. Abuse was neither pretty nor easily forgotten.

"I wish, though, they hadn't assigned me that awful name." Arianne glanced toward the string quartet whose vibrant chords were lost in the noisy crowd. "I'm afraid it will become my epitaph. Cupid's Mistress . . ."

"The one who coined that phrase never witnessed your lack of ability on the archery field," her old schoolmate taunted. "If so, men and women alike would run with fear for their lives."

Arianne chuckled at the mental image of the bejeweled ton seeking shelter from her arrows. "Perhaps then society matrons would be hesitant to trot their daughters forward for an introduction." Though she imagined that would cease soon enough for another reason, but she pushed that thought aside. Tonight, she intended to concentrate on her childhood friend. After all, as long as Arianne's secrets remained hidden, she could socialize at receptions such as this.

She turned toward Lady Cardiff. "Have you received word of Lord Cardiff's posting?"

Kitty turned with her lips poised for reply, then stopped and sniffed before leaning closer. Her nose wrinkled. "Anne, is that another of your scent concoctions?"

"Have the florals failed?" Arianne gasped. "I thought to substitute the white wine in my summer formula with something stronger. I hoped it would draw more of the oil from the petals." She sniffed at her own wrist. "Perhaps I should have used more water for balance?" Blessed Saint Christopher. She smelled less like the sister of a duke and more like a distillery maid. She snapped her fan into motion.

Kitty shook her head. "Don't be alarmed. It's too faint for anyone to notice unless they stand unusually close. I'm quite sure Crenshaw disappeared due to your reputation, not your scent."

Arianne's eyes widened. Had gossip already started?

"Oh!" Kitty laughed. "That did not sound right. What I meant to say was—" Her expression shifted. "Good Lord, who is that man? The one speaking with Lady Trembel."

Arianne followed Kitty's gaze. A man, fascinating in his total unsuitability for a gathering of this nature known for strict adherence to convention, mesmerized Lady Trembel with his attentive smile. Long black hair dangled low on his forehead. Lady Trembel's gloved hands clenched at her side, causing Arianne to think she was having difficulty not brushing the dark strands aside. Yes. Arianne suspected she might feel a similar strain, if only to gain a better view of those engaging eyes. He looked as disreputable as a buccaneer, yet something about him hummed along her skin, scattered her thoughts, and sent a tremor down her spine. She wished he'd glance her way so she could see his features more clearly.

"Some people should not wear that pale shade of green. It does nothing for Lady Trembel," Kitty groused beside her. "She has managed to capture his interest, though. Do you know him?"

Arianne shook her head, noting similar reactions repeated behind a multitude of quickly fluttering fans. Apparently he'd been noticed by every female in the room. Did they feel that same invisible force that prickled her skin?

"His jacket is wrong for this affair," Kitty observed. "And entirely too small."

"Or his chest is too big," Arianne replied absently. "I wonder if the rest of him—"

Kitty lightly smacked her with her fan. "An unmarried woman shouldn't make such observations," she scolded. "Even one with a notorious artist brother."

Either Kitty's playful gesture or Arianne's fervent wishes caught the stranger's attention, as his gaze swept the room for a moment.

"If I remember correctly," Arianne said, observing Lady Trembel tap his arm with her fan to regain his attention, "such things interested you before you married."

Back in their schoolgirl days, Kitty had joined Arianne at her brother's Yorkshire residence. When Nicholas wasn't about, they had sneaked into his studio to peruse his sketches of scantily clad figures.

"Well, I'm married now," Kitty said with a smug smile. "Look! He's caught the Countess's notice. Perhaps we can garner his credentials from her."

Countess D'Orange, the wife of the Italian minister assigned to London, had sponsored the reception in honor of some new envoy. A purpose was always stated on the invitation but rarely needed at these affairs. Diplomats loved to talk and needed little incentive to congregate and swap pleasantries. Due to her extensive travels, Arianne knew most in the room and enjoyed the opportunity to renew acquaintances.

"He is a handsome devil, even with his questionable attire," Lady Cardiff observed. "If I weren't a married woman . . ."

"Kitty!" Arianne scolded. They hid soft laughter behind their gloves. Both knew the observation was in jest. "He can't possibly be a diplomat; he's too . . . different. I wonder what he's doing here?"

Fascinated, she watched a dimple form in his cheek as he

smiled at something the Countess said. His visage transformed to one with a shy flirtatious charm. "I believe the Countess D'Orange has considerably improved his demeanor," Arianne said. "He's lost some of his menacing aspect."

"Menacing?" Kitty's brows lifted. "Whatever do you mean?"

Was it not obvious? Arianne was about to reply when both the Countess and the stranger turned toward them. Quickly she averted her gaze, embarrassed that he might recognize her curiosity, but then her pulse slowed. Of what consequence could that knowledge bring? Once he discovered her identity, he was bound to retreat to the distant wall to join Crenshaw and every other bachelor in the room.

She glanced at that very group as they tried to hide their sidelong glances at the stranger. The newcomer made them uneasy. There was justice in that.

"They're coming this way," Lady Cardiff said with exuberance. "Perhaps we won't have to wait till the end of the reception to learn his identity."

Oh dear! Arianne's heartbeat hastened. Even though she had chosen spinsterhood, she wasn't immune to male attention. Perhaps she'd been hasty in believing this man was an unlikely negotiator, for at this moment, under his dark perusal, she felt robbed of protest.

"Lady Arianne Chambers, Lady Cardiff"—the Countess nodded to each of them—"allow me to introduce Mr. Rafferty, a recent addition to the diplomatic corps."

A quick doubt crossed her mind even as she and Lady Cardiff nodded acknowledgment. A fresh cut on his lip confirmed this man spoke as much with his fists as with a diplomat's clever words. She should be wary of that proclivity given her mother's experience, yet something about this man called to her, something that defied common sense.

"Mr. Rafferty," Kitty said. "You must be newly come to London. I do not believe I've seen you at any embassy functions."

"Perhaps you weren't looking in the dark corners," he responded with a faint Irish brogue. A mischievous sparkle lit his watchful eyes.

"Lady Arianne." His sudden attention robbed her of breath. "I expressly requested an introduction so that we might share a private word."

Kitty's expression twisted into one of shock, while surprise rattled Arianne's bones. Men simply did not seek her out, especially dangerously handsome ones. Her mouth dried to ash a moment before she realized her jaw was agape. Dear heavens, she must resemble Lord Crenshaw!

"I'm not sure there is such a thing as privacy in this salon," the Countess teased. "Come along, Lady Cardiff, I have someone you should meet." Kitty hesitated, then reluctantly followed their hostess.

"Perhaps we might move away from that popular punch bowl?" Mr. Rafferty clasped his hands behind his back as if to reinforce that he posed no threat, yet every nerve in her body tensed. Sensing a current of envy from the feminine eyes that followed their progress, she led the way toward a grouping of potted palms where the crowd thinned.

"Lady Arianne." His voice purred as soothing as the violin's lilting refrain. "I believe I carry a message intended for you . . ."

A fringe of black hair dipped just below his eyebrow. Arianne clenched her fan more tightly to avoid smoothing it aside.

". . . But I find I'm hesitant to deliver it." His lips curled in a pleasant line at odds with the alert assessment in his eyes.

"Why is that, sir?" Her chest expanded, pushing forcefully against her stays. Christopher! She, of all people, should know better than to fall victim to stirring accents and seductive smiles.

"I fear as soon as you read this note, you will rush from the salon, denying me further opportunity to share your company."

While she accepted the false flattery as a social staple, the unexpected delivery of a note lifted the fine hairs on her neck. Only bad news carried such urgency. Her pulse quickened. "Is it a message from my brother?" she asked with due gravity. "His wife is expecting their first child. If something has gone awry, I must leave immediately!"

"No." Mr. Rafferty's fingers grasped her arm as if to stop her immediate departure. A ribbon of tingling awareness raced to her shoulder. Shocked, she searched his gaze, surprised at the disdain she noted there. What had she done to earn such derision?

"I apologize if I alarmed you," he said. "The note is not from your family." Yet he still held her captive. She stared pointedly at his inappropriate touch. Recognizing his error, he released her, but without apology.

"It was meant to be delivered by another." He reached inside his coat and removed an envelope. His gaze narrowed on her face, almost in accusation. "As you can see, it lacks identification." He leaned close, pausing a bit overlong in that tight proximity. "I had to be certain it was intended for you."

Curiosity rippled through her. She accepted the envelope, broke the wax seal, and unfolded the paper, scanning the contents.

Wrap the dog in wool and loosen him on the Yanks. The day approaches and death draws near.

B.

Christopher! She scanned the cryptic words again. "This is nonsense." She frowned. "Are you certain the message was intended for me?"

"Nonsense?" Mr. Rafferty ripped the paper from her hands and read the contents. "This isn't an assignation," he murmured.

"An assignation!" she exclaimed a trifle too loud. Her cheeks heated. Lowering her voice, she snapped her fan to flutter at a furious pace. "As the sister of a duke, I assure you I am not accustomed to complete strangers maligning my reputation. Whatever made you think that message was intended for me?"

His eyes narrowed, his jaw set. "I admit I assumed the message was to establish a rendezvous. When I overheard a reference to you as 'mistress,' I believed you were meant to be the intended recipient." He stuffed the paper and envelope in his jacket and scowled. "A simple mistake."

He thought she was someone's mistress! Her fan fluttered so violently, the palm fronds shook. She chose her words carefully and enunciated them clearly for his apparently impaired faculties. "The difficulty with eavesdropping, Mr. Rafferty, is that one almost never hears the full context. I believe what you heard was a reference to my talents as a matchmaker."

She really didn't need to expound. With his inappropriate attire and freshly injured lip, he was most likely a gate-crasher to this elite gathering of diplomats and certainly not someone she would ever see again.

But that unspoken censure in his eyes rankled. Even to this man, she felt it important that her reputation was not needlessly besmirched. That would happen soon enough.

"Some call me Cupid's Mistress," she explained in a rush, before embarrassment could further stain her cheeks. "I imagine you overheard a portion of that most ridiculous name."

"A matchmaker?" His lips quirked in humor for just a moment, before he straightened. Arianne thought she heard a seam rip. "My apologies, Lady Arianne. Obviously this note was intended for another. I hope the true recipient—"

"So on the basis of a nickname, you decided I was ripe for a tryst?" She wasn't sure why she couldn't let the matter drop. Perhaps his apology seemed insufficient for the affront to her honor. She should let him make a hasty departure like Crenshaw and the others.

His eyes narrowed. "There were other considerations . . ."

"Please tell me of these considerations. I wouldn't want others to be under the delusion that I'm available for illicit sport." Her sarcasm hit its mark.

He hesitated as if debating the wisdom of saying nothing or defending his unconscionable behavior. His eyes raked over her, then a faint smile bloomed on his lips.

"I was told the recipient would be wearing a green dress. As I assumed the sender was interested in a tryst, I simply looked for the most attractive woman in the room wearing the proper color. I chose you." He bowed his head. "Now if you'll excuse me, I'll—"

She ignored his transparent flattery. "There are several other women in green. I saw you speaking to Lady Trembel earlier, yet you gave the note to me . . ."

What began as an attempt to correct his foolish assumption festered into something altogether different. Had something changed about her since her unfortunate incident in Vienna? Could complete strangers recognize her probable shift in society's acceptance? "Surely," she pressed, suspicion taking root, "there was something else."

He reflected a moment, then leaned closer. "Lady Trembel's scent wasn't that of the angel's share."

"Angel's share?" Her face must have betrayed her ignorance. Was this was more Irish flattery?

He glanced away and laughed softly before returning his gaze to her. "The angel's share is that portion of fine Irish whiskey that evaporates in the distillation." A decidedly seductive gleam simmered in his gaze. "It's been my experience that women who drink overly much find themselves in positions that—"

"You believe I'm a drunkard?" she sputtered in outrage. Her cheeks flamed anew.

He smiled. "Not all would find the scent of whiskey about a miss as appealing as I do, but—"

"I erred in my cologne water!" she insisted perhaps a bit too loudly. A few heads turned their way. She dropped her voice. "I thought a stronger base would carry the florals."

"And a very fine error it was."

The impudent, nonconforming misfit was laughing at her! She could see his amusement in the creasing about his eyes, hear the blitheness in the timbre of his voice. The cad!

"Now if you'll excuse me," he said. "I should try to find—"

"May I remind you, sir, that I am the sister of a duke." She pitched her voice low and cold so he would know her displeasure. "I'm not certain how a man as common as yourself gained entrance to this reception, but your accusations are not appreciated."

He stopped his determined egress. His shoulders shifted back, and if she wasn't mistaken, she heard a button bounce on the floor. He turned, then glared down his decidedly handsome nose at her.

"I believe I've already apologized for my misapprehensions. My only defense is that I had assumed your company would be highly desired by any man." His nostrils flared. "I trust you will forgive such a *common* and erroneous assumption." He lifted her fingers as if to kiss her hand, but she jerked them away, striking his injured lip in the process.

Fresh blood rose on the wound. More heads turned their way.

Guilt and shame filled her. She wouldn't have acted in such a lowbred manner if she hadn't been provoked. A truly noble lady would have risen above the taunt. "I have a handkerchief," she murmured, opening her reticule.

"No." He reached into a pocket of his ill-fitting jacket. "I wouldn't wish my common Irish blood to stain the linen of a sister of a duke."

He removed a white handkerchief, but the white linen pulled a red cloth, which was attached to a blue cloth, which pulled a yellow cloth in succession. Rafferty froze, the white handkerchief clenched in his hand while the colored cloths dangled in a nautical line to his pocket. He swore beneath his breath, something rather derogative coupled with the name "Phineas."

Abrupt barking laughter sounded from various directions. Arianne tried, unsuccessfully, to conceal her own amusement. Rafferty's glance of anger and embarrassment seared straight through her levity. She immediately regretted her unkind words, but he gave her no time for apologies.

"Good evening, madam," he said, stuffing the colorful assortment in his pocket. "I trust you will take pleasure in the likelihood that our paths shall never cross again." He turned on his heel. "I know I shall."

He strode from the salon without a backward glance.

"So . . ." Kitty appeared by her side. "What did you and the handsome Mr. Rafferty have to discuss for such an extended time? He certainly appeared to be taken with you."

She glanced at her friend's teasing face. At least Kitty's initial description of "handsome devil" had been accurate enough, though Arianne wasn't entirely convinced about the handsome part.

"It seems he's in the market for a wife and wished for my recommendations," she improvised. No need to confess that Mr. Rafferty had mistaken her for someone's paramour.

"Have you anyone in mind?" Kitty asked, scanning the crowd.

"I'm not certain we'll see Mr. Rafferty again," she replied.

"Pity," Kitty said. "He was the most interesting man here this evening."

"Do you think so?" Arianne glanced in the direction of his departure. She had to admit that the stranger had captured her attention like none other. "He was the only one brave enough to actually engage me in conversation," she said, adding a soft laugh for Kitty's sake.

"I wonder who we might ask that would know more about him?"

"It doesn't matter." Arianne gazed toward the doorway. "I think we've seen the last of the arrogant Mr. Rafferty."

RAFFERTY HAD BARELY LEFT THE TOWN HOUSE WHEN Phineas stepped from the shadows. "Did you find her? I didn't see anyone leave in a green gown."

Rafferty hesitated a moment, so absorbed in his thoughts that he had to stop and remember Phineas had been waiting to follow a woman en route to a tryst. A woman who most certainly would not be the interesting, the willful, the class-conscious Lady Arianne.

"The note wasn't for a rendezvous," he snapped, scanning the street for an available hack. The last carriage in the row held promise. While earlier he had been in no hurry to get to the reception, now he couldn't wait to put distance between him and the marrow-lacking upper crust.

"How do you know that?" Phineas studied him a moment. "You opened it! What did it say?"

"Something about dogs and Yanks and death." Rafferty reached in his pocket, removed the envelope, and slapped it into Phineas's hand, all without breaking his fast stride. "The wrong woman opened the note. After the seal was broken, it was pointless to question the others. They would deny any knowledge."

The last hansom was indeed available. Rafferty barked a destination to the driver and climbed inside.

"Dogs and Yanks. That's odd." Phineas joined him in the dim interior. "And we still don't know who his contact is? The mysterious woman in green?"

Rafferty glanced toward the town house. "At least we know one woman who she is not," he muttered. Even Barnell knew the wisdom of avoiding the likes of Lady Arianne Chambers.

· Two ·

NO FIRE CRACKLED IN THE BEDROOM GRATE, though the night had turned cool. Although she shivered in her thin night rail, Arianne refused to ask the servants to lay a fire and then clean the cinders and soot just for her comfort. She pulled a paisley shawl from the back of a chair and draped it over her wrapper, hoping the added warmth would spread to her fingers and toes.

The London town house belonged to her brother, William, the Duke of Bedford. While he anticipated the arrival of an heir at Deerfield Abbey, his ancestral estate and her childhood home, she thought to use its asylum while she contemplated the recent cruel turn of events and their effect upon her future.

So quiet, so empty in the large town house, she shivered as much from the sense of isolation and withdrawal as from the temperature. Such a change from her stay at the British ambassador's residence in Vienna. Between the ambassador's large family and the many people who called, she'd had little time to be alone. There, she imagined herself part of a large, happy family, so unlike her own childhood. In hindsight, perhaps the joy and freedom of her time in Vienna had contributed to her foolish infatuation with Baron Von Dieter. She'd forgotten happiness always came with a cost.

Sitting before the mirror at a japanned coiffeuse, she pulled the shawl tight like a lover's embrace. It was too quiet in this house. No distractions to pull her from melancholy thoughts, but then she supposed she needed to become accustomed to the silence. Her future held little hope of sharing with another. Not after Vienna.

Silly that she, the supposed matchmaker, had bungled her own opportunity for marriage. Her brothers seemed so content with their married lives, she had hoped a commitment to the Baron would afford her similar happiness. But that was not to be. Memories of the Baron she'd like to forget led to exasperating thoughts of her more recent encounter. That man . . . that Mr. Rafferty, with his arrogant look of disdain, had thought she was someone's mistress.

She glanced into the mirror before her, studying her reflection. Had he seen something lurid about her, something taboo? Granted, she wasn't the same innocent miss she had been before she went to Vienna. Baron Von Dieter had seen to that. She grimaced at the memory. She was wiser now. Wiser about the steps men took to get what they wanted without consideration for the women they hurt in the process. Did such knowledge leave a trail on one's face? Did her humiliation show?

"I thought I'd check on you before I retire," Mrs. Summers, Arianne's widowed teacher from the Institut Villa Mont Blanc and now her paid companion and chaperone, said from the doorway. "You were so quiet on the ride home."

"Do you think I look different?" Arianne pulled lightly on her brows to better examine her eyes.

"Different from what, dear?" Mrs. Summers moved deeper into the room to stand behind Arianne's chair.

"Different from how I appeared before I met the Baron," Arianne said, turning slightly to examine each cheek. "Does the shame show on my face? Perhaps in my eyes?"

Her teacher glanced down, averting her gaze from the mirror's reflection. "You know how sorry I am that I trusted the Baron to do right by you, Arianne. I wouldn't have let down my guard otherwise. We all expected that he would slide an engagement ring around your finger."

The regret evident in Mrs. Summers's reply tugged at Arianne. She too had been shocked when he announced his engagement to another, after the promises he had made to her. She glanced at her bare fingers. It wasn't the loss of a ring that concerned her; she'd enough jewels of her own. It wasn't even the loss of her maidenhood, though disgrace had repercussions beyond that single night. In a way, she found comfort that such an unpleasant experience would not be repeated. However, the uprooting of trust and faith in another, she couldn't forgive.

"The way he looked at you . . ." Mrs. Summers sighed, oblivious to the pain she resurrected in Arianne. "To this day I just don't know what made him change his mind."

But Arianne knew. At least she suspected. She had felt compelled to be honest with the man with whom she thought to spend the rest of her life. Thus she'd told him of her recent discovery that the man who sired her was not the old Duke but rather a tenant farmer. Later that night he'd come to her room and promised her "tainted" bloodline would not affect his feelings. That was his proof.

But before he left, he told her she wasn't all she should be. That a sullied bloodline could not promise quality. She should have known then, expected what he planned to do, though she thought they would talk. She'd been raised the daughter of a duke. No one could claim she was less. But he did. At the ball held to announce his engagement, her name had been replaced by that of Miss Sharpe. A woman Arianne herself had introduced to him. The memory brought a woeful smile that did nothing to lift her spirits. One could almost say Arianne had been the matchmaker that day. Even now the pain, the embarrassment, and the scorn of the Baron's rejection resonated deep within her. She'd left Vienna the next day without speaking to him and returned to England to hide in her brother's lonely, cold, empty town house.

"Please believe me." Mrs. Summers glanced up. "I never would have consented to you going on those long rides without a chaperone, nor would I have pretended not to hear footsteps in the corridor at night." The firelight caught the glisten in her eyes. "I thought he loved you."

"As did I," Arianne said softly. Her heart twisted. "But it is clear he did not."

"I'm surprised your brothers haven't rushed forward to defend your honor." Mrs. Summers swiped at the corners of her eyes before her hand came to rest on Arianne's shoulder. "They should have forced the blackguard to marry you."

Her former teacher's loyalty lifted her spirits a little. She patted the older woman's hand. "I wouldn't have wished for marriage to a man who didn't love me. I remember my mother's pain at the hand of my . . . the old Duke. I've resigned myself to living a quiet, independent life." She smiled at her teacher's reflection. "As for my brothers"—she glanced down—"I haven't told them."

"You haven't written!" Mrs. Summers exclaimed. "Why, I'm tempted to take my hand to pen. They should know what happened!"

"No," Arianne stated forcefully. "I forbid you to write them. It would come to no good. I would not wish for marriage to the Baron under those circumstances." Nor would she want William to feel guilty about sharing the recent discovery of their parentage with her. There was little William could do to change recent events, but Arianne would spare him the pain of trying.

"But the gossip!" Mrs. Summers exclaimed. "Don't you know what will happen to you when news of the Baron's insult reaches London? You were used, child. He should pay for that."

And marriage to her would be the punishment? No. She didn't want that. Fortunately she didn't need that.

"Even without a husband, I shall never be destitute," Arianne said. "My brother's allowance will keep food in the larder and coal in the grates." His money couldn't alleviate her loneliness or eliminate her shame. She would have to learn to live without the sort of company she'd enjoyed these many years. She'd have to learn to live without the sort of joy she saw on William's face when he married his heiress.

"The ambassador said he would do everything in his power to keep the news from leaking to London society," Arianne continued. "While I realize he can't stop it forever, we should have a little more time to enjoy London. Then I suppose we can retire to Sanctuary, my dower property in Worcester. A quiet life alone in the country." Arianne sighed. "It's not the end of the world."

"It is for someone like yourself who has spent most of her

life involved in embassy parties and politics around that very world," Mrs. Summers grumbled half under her breath.

Arianne chose to ignore her. "Still, the question remains," she said. "Do I look like someone's mistress?"

Mrs. Summers sighed. "No, child. You still look as fresh and beautiful as a new dawning day. If someone mistook you for a mistress, it was probably his own lustful yearnings speaking—nothing else. Now, best you get to sleep, or else someone will mistake you for a paid chaperone with packed luggage under her tired eyes."

Arianne hugged her former teacher. "I'm glad you agreed to be my chaperone. Your loyalty and friendship mean more to me than all the silly parties and receptions in London."

Mrs. Summers's cheeks flushed. "To bed with you now, else there won't be any silly parties or receptions to attend."

As soon as Mrs. Summers left, Arianne's shoulders heaved with an inner sigh. A few weeks ago, she thought she had the world figured out. She thought she'd found the key to a life with a safe companion by her side, someone who'd never raise a hand to her. In hindsight . . . well, what was done was done. No one would invite such disgrace into a marriage. She had mussed too many handkerchiefs over the incident. Yet her eyes moistened anew, and she knew she'd muss another.

THE NEXT MORNING, MRS. SUMMERS'S WORDS CAME BACK to haunt Arianne when she opened her morning paper to the society news column.

> *Mrs. Albert Sugden announced that she will have the honor to host the Baron Von Dieter, his sister, Miss Marianne, and his fiancée, Miss Sharpe, when they arrive from Vienna this week to enjoy the sights and amusements to be had during the London season. A ball has been planned in their honor. Mrs. Albert Sugden had the fortune to meet the Baron when she recently traveled to Vienna . . .*

"He's coming here!" Arianne exclaimed, clenching the ironed paper hard enough to wring the ink from the page.

"Who, dear?" Mrs. Summers asked from the opposite side of the table. "That young man from last night who set you into such a dither?"

Arianne grimaced. "I was not in a dither." Though in truth, thoughts of Mr. Rafferty had kept her restless most of the night. Not thoughts of him, she corrected herself. Thoughts of why he'd selected her as the suspect mistress. Yes, that was the gist of it. Certainly it wasn't his smoldering stare, or his devilish lips that she'd managed to set to bleeding, or that seductive rhythm in his speech. She shook her head. "No. Definitely not. I was referring to the news that the Baron is coming to London with his horrid sister and his new fiancée."

"I don't recall you calling Marianne 'horrid' before." Mrs. Summers calmly sipped from her teacup.

"That's because you didn't see her superior gloat when the Baron announced his future wife. I always suspected she was disappointed in her brother's choice of me. She managed to show her colors when I was most vulnerable."

"Perhaps the Baron is coming to London specifically to seek you out," Mrs. Summers said. "Perhaps he wants to apologize or offer an explanation for his actions."

A sharp pain knifed its way through Arianne at the thought of seeing the Baron again. Maintaining a calm façade while he waltzed with his newly announced fiancée in Vienna had been difficult. So difficult, she pleaded a headache and left before the dance was through. She had no intention of letting him see the blow he had dealt. "An apology will not change the damage he has done to my reputation," she said, willing her hands not to shake. "Besides, what he may seek to mend, I believe his sister intends to destroy."

"So what do you plan to do?" Mrs. Summers asked. It was clear she had no solutions to offer beyond seeking her brother William's assistance.

"I'm not certain." Arianne thought a bit. "I don't plan to see him." That much she knew without doubt. To look into his eyes and see pity reflected there would just be too painful. "A meeting like that would set tongues wagging, I'm afraid," she said with a nonchalance she didn't feel.

"If he still gazes at you as he once did, the ton would most certainly whisper," Mrs. Summers agreed. "But you can't stay here and hope to avoid him. Perhaps it's time to visit one of your brothers."

To appear suddenly at one of their country estates unannounced would surely elicit a number of questions on their part. Questions she'd be hesitant to answer.

William's ancient butler, Hastings, appeared in the breakfast room as silent as a vapor with a note upon a tray. He carried the silver platter to Arianne. "For you, my lady."

She stared at the cream envelope for a moment, hesitant to open it. What if it was an invitation to the Sugdens' ball? She coughed modestly, thinking to plant the seeds of an onset of illness, then removed a single sheet from the envelope. Once she recognized the embossed letterhead she managed a deep breath of relief, then quickly scanned the brief contents. "There is one place I intend to go," she said with a quick nod to Hastings. He retreated as silently as he arrived.

"Where would that be, dear?" Mrs. Summers inquired.

"Lord Henderson says that he is desirous of a meeting this afternoon." Hiding her concern from Mrs. Summers, she wondered why the head of the Home Office wished to speak to her. Had he learned of the incident in Vienna?

"Perhaps the diversion will present a solution to this problem." Mrs. Summers shook her head. "I just don't understand whatever made the Baron change his mind. I had honestly thought your matchmaking skills had played in your favor this time."

"Accidental," Arianne said as she picked up a mister to spray the fishbone fern sprouting on the corner plant stand. She'd have to speak with the housekeeper about a better regimen for these plants before she left on her next trip—wherever that may be. If news of her misadventure had reached Lord Henderson, it might be time to settle into Sanctuary. She hoped not. She wasn't ready to isolate herself from the world just yet.

"Did you say something?" Mrs. Summers asked.

"I said my supposed matchmaking skills are purely accidental," she said as she took her mister to spray the plants in the next room.

"Accidental or not," Mrs. Summers called after her, "it's time Cupid's Mistress fell under her own magic."

Magic? Arianne swallowed her laugh. If she truly possessed

magic, the Baron would be sitting on a lily pad luring innocent flies in his own stagnant frog pond and the arrogant Mr. Rafferty would be . . . Well, she mused, she wasn't quite sure what she'd make him. Though the vision of a four-footed animal with a loud bray crossed her mind.

· Three ·

"So, Rafferty..." Lord Henderson stood behind his desk in his London quarters. He gestured for
Rafferty to take one of two chairs opposite. "What were your
impressions of last night's reception?"

Rafferty pondered the selection of chairs, not entirely comfortable with his back toward the door, but stepped before a
high-back chair off to the side, thus minimizing unanticipated
threats. Surviving in the murky world of government secrets
made such ordinary decisions a complication of risks.

"You can let down your guard, Rafe," Lord Henderson said,
compassion warming his eyes. "You'll be quite safe here."

Rafferty nodded toward the window before accepting the
seat. "Nevertheless, I left Phineas watching your doorstep." He
retrieved the folded paper from his pocket. "These are dangerous times. We intercepted a note from Barnell last night suggesting something is afoot. If the Fenians are preparing for
another assault, the two of us together could make an appealing
target."

"A note?" Henderson took the paper and scanned the brief

contents. "How did you get this?" He raised an eyebrow at Rafferty. "Or perhaps I shouldn't inquire . . ."

Rafferty grinned. "A thief tried to rob Phineas and me while we walked to the reception. We lightened his pockets instead."

"Walked?" The second eyebrow rose to join the first. "Unlike your usual haunts, hansoms traverse Mayfair."

"I was in no hurry to arrive." Rafferty averted his gaze. Henderson could never understand his discomfort around the upper crust. While he may be as well educated as the gentry, the similarities ended there.

Henderson glanced at the note. "How do you know the 'B' is for Barnell?"

"The thief admitted as much. It was a slip of the tongue. One he instantly regretted."

Henderson lowered to his chair, dismay in his expression. "I was afraid of this. Lord Weston was concerned that recent events in America suggest the Fenians are exploiting the immigrants for money and arms to stage another attack on the Queen. While I don't understand the full measure of this message, I'm certain 'Yanks' refers to the Irish immigrants in America."

"What recent events?" Rafferty asked, suspicious. "If the Fenians have spread to America—"

"Basil Toomey has been spotted there."

Rafferty lurched from his seat. Toomey! He'd searched so long for the foul beast, he'd given up hope of finding him alive. He'd assumed the devil had claimed one of his own and the bastard's soul burned in eternal hellfire. Now, to discover that the villain still lived . . . his jaw tightened. "I'll sail immediately."

"Sit down, Rafe. I understand your urgency, but there's more you need to know."

"I'd prefer to stand," Rafferty insisted. "The more time spent here, the less opportunity I'll have for catching the bastard."

"Sit!" Henderson glared, pointing to the chair. "Toomey will still be there when you've heard all that I have to say." Reluctantly, Rafferty acquiesced, and Henderson continued. "I can't allow you to hunt Toomey in America as you might here.

There are matters of diplomacy involved . . . especially now. I sent you to that reception last night for a reason."

"You knew about Toomey earlier?" His eyes narrowed. Lord Henderson knew of his determination to find Toomey. Why had he kept this information secret?

The butler, a man old enough to be Henderson's grandfather, interrupted. "Excuse me, my lord, but Lady Arianne Chambers requests an audience."

"Excellent. Send her in." Henderson smiled, then glanced at Rafferty. "I invited Lady Arianne, as you may have need of her unique abilities. I had hoped you two would meet at the reception." His brows raised in question.

"Unique abilities?" Rafe was familiar with women who possessed unique abilities of a basic, more intimate nature, but Lady Arianne Chambers had already assured him that "a sister of a duke" would have no such inclinations. Pity that. His dreams had run rampant last night of that very same lady panting about her relationship to the Duke as he clasped her pert little bottom, while his common but straining—

"Lord Henderson." Green finery burst into the room, banishing his pleasant reverie. Both men immediately stood. Lady Arianne swept right by Rafferty in her headstrong march toward Henderson. A lavender scent trailed in the wake of her flounces and lace. Drat. She'd corrected her fragrance from last evening.

Not a shy, retiring miss, this Lady Arianne, he mused. His mother, may she rest in peace, may have likened her to a fairy merrow. What a shame that such energetic passion had been wasted on a woman determined not to use it in a way that mattered.

"Lady Arianne, how lovely to see you again." Henderson nodded. "Thank you for coming."

"I must admit I was surprised by your note. Especially as I had a disturbing encounter last evening and wished to consult you about—"

"Me?" Rafferty interrupted.

She quickly turned toward his voice, shock halting her tirade. Her widened eyes sampled the whole of him, before focusing on his injured lip. A soft pink rose from her neck, and for an instant, he imagined her upper-class brain could read his decidedly lower-class thoughts. He lowered his eyelids and offered his best provocative smile. Shocking the prim and proper Lady Arianne was proving most entertaining.

"You've met Mr. Rafferty?" Henderson nodded in his direction, a twinkle barely hidden in his eye. "He's one of my best investigators and well suited for the part he's to play. I had hoped you would have an opportunity to observe him."

She was certainly observing him now, he thought with an inner victorious gloat. The colleens at Brannigan's would have already removed his shirt if he were to offer them this same unspoken invitation. The flush rising from her neck turned a shade darker, yet otherwise she appeared unfazed. "We met yesterday evening," she said hesitantly, her gaze still latched onto him. "A pleasure to see you again, Mr. Rafferty."

She was a miserable liar. He'd wager she was just as uncomfortable as her perusal was making him. His earlier lurid imaginings had inspired certain areas of his body to action. Fortunately, she turned her attention away from him and toward Lord Henderson, allowing him opportunity to compose himself.

"I'm sorry, did you say you needed my help for a part in a play?" Lady Arianne's brows knitted in confusion. "I assure you I have no talents in theatrics. Perhaps—"

"Not a play, my lady." Henderson gestured toward the chair beside Rafferty. "Please take a seat. I have much to explain."

Lady Arianne sat, allowing the two men to reclaim their seats as well.

"I have already mentioned to Mr. Rafferty that recent events in America require his attention. We only have a small diplomatic presence in America. Too small to even warrant an embassy. Therefore, I propose to send Rafferty to Washington, D.C., as the British minister to head up the legation there."

"British minister?" Rafferty exclaimed. "That's preposterous!" He could hardly search for Toomey if he were entangled in diplomatic hogwash.

"Lord Weston is the British minister in Washington," Arianne protested. "Why would you replace him with Mr. Rafferty?"

Compassion replaced all vestiges of humor in Lord Henderson's face. Rafferty leaned forward, anticipating this might be "the event" spoken of earlier.

"It grieves me to tell you in this manner, Lady Arianne. Especially as I know you've a close relationship with Lord and Lady Weston and Kitty, their daughter, but . . . Lord Weston has been murdered."

"Murdered!" Her eyes widened while color drained from her face. Fearing she might faint, Rafferty stood, prepared to catch her should she slump in unconsciousness. He needn't have bothered. She snapped open a fan and directed a current of air toward her face, but she never lost awareness. Impressed, Rafferty reclaimed his seat. Lady Arianne was apparently made of sterner stuff than the gentry lassies he'd had occasion to meet.

"How is that possible?" she gasped, dabbing at the corners of her glistening eyes with the tip of her glove. Behind the flurry of her fan, hidden from Henderson's observation, her lips trembled. Only Rafferty, seated to her right, saw her silent fight for control. Damn. He remembered too well his own battle for control when as a young boy, the headmaster sternly informed him that a Fenian bomb had made him an orphan and that tears were not to be tolerated, especially not in public. Damn English with their stiff upper lip.

Rafferty retrieved his handkerchief from his inside pocket and extended it in offering. She raised her glance to his, her lips fighting for a semblance of a grateful smile before she reluctantly accepted the linen. In that moment, Rafferty wished he had met the man that elicited such an emotional reaction from this courageous young woman.

"Lord Weston was the kindest man I know." She delicately pressed his cloth to the sides of her nose. "Does Kitty know?"

"This is not the sort of information that is conveyed by a note," Lord Henderson said. "I'll call on her as soon as I finish here."

"She won't take the news well, I'm afraid." Lady Arianne bit her lip as if to hold in a sob. Rafferty almost reached to take her hand, offer her support, but he knew such gestures would not be appreciated, not from a man like him.

"Who . . . who would do such a thing?" she asked.

"That's precisely what I'm sending Mr. Rafferty to investigate," Henderson said. His lips tightened in his own acknowledgment of grief. "He's one of my best."

"Mr. Rafferty?" She sniffed, then cast him a dubious glance. "You are sending Mr. Rafferty as a British minister?"

Henderson's lips twisted in a sympathetic smile while his eyes remained fastened to Lady Arianne. "I believe you are beginning to understand why I sent for you."

"I do not," Rafferty interjected. "With all due condolences to Lady Arianne on the loss of her friend, I don't think—"

"Mr. Rafferty may be a wonderful investigator," Lady Arianne said, addressing Henderson as if Rafferty hadn't spoken at all, "but he won't suit. What does he know of diplomacy? He doesn't even know how to dress properly for an evening reception. How can he pass for a British minister at more demanding functions?"

Henderson glanced at him, his brows lowered. "You dressed inappropriately?"

"My jacket ripped in the earlier scuffle," Rafferty explained. "I exchanged jackets with Phineas. But that is not the point—"

"He will not be taken seriously," Lady Arianne continued as if he wasn't sitting right beside her. "Who will be his hostess?"

"I don't need a hostess," he grumbled. "I'm perfectly capable of—"

"If he doesn't have a hostess, no woman in society will attend a legation event. If the women won't attend, neither will the men." She abruptly turned toward Rafferty. "You must have a hostess. Is there a wife?"

He shook his head.

"A cousin? A niece?" she asked as he continued to indicate no.

"Lady Arianne, you have the experience to make the perfect hostess," Henderson said. "I thought you might—"

Her jaw dropped. "You cannot expect me to marry him!"

"Good Lord, man! She's the sister of a duke," Rafferty spoke over her protest.

An uncomfortable silence settled after their joint loud remonstrations. They glanced at each other for a moment as if suddenly realizing the other existed, then quickly averted their gazes. The expansive room felt much too constrictive. Rafferty rose and moved to the window, believing it would be easier to think if some distance existed between him and Lady Upper Crust.

Strange that she had leapt so quickly to thoughts of marriage, but then wasn't that the focus of all vacuous lassies of her sort? He frowned, recognizing that "vacuous" did not fit this particular lady. Thus it was all so predictable that she would protest such an arrangement. Miss Prim-and-Proper to be wed to Mr. Dark-and-Dangerous. He had to swallow the chuckle that the thought inspired.

Lord Henderson's calm voice sounded behind him. "I was going to ask if you could recommend someone to act as hostess? Your reputation as a matchmaker has given you knowledge of all the available women that might consider a match with Mr. Rafferty—"

"I'll not marry a stranger just so women can drag their husbands to social events," Rafferty grumbled. He glanced out the window, noting Phineas dressed in a multilayered cape, pretending to be a cabman at the station across the way. Phineas turned toward the window and scratched his nose, signaling that he was alert and watching but had noted nothing of interest.

"I cannot imagine a single woman who would consent to such a proposition." Lady Blue Blood huffed behind him. "He hasn't even a title to recommend him."

"Then what do you propose we do?" Lord Henderson sounded exasperated. "Rafferty must have a hostess as soon as possible so he can investigate Lord Weston's murder."

"And track Basil Toomey," Rafferty added. It was likely not a coincidence that Toomey appeared in America and a diplomat's death ensued.

Rafe watched Phineas tip his cap to a matron hurrying her young charge past the cab station. Given his remarkable theatrical abilities, Phineas could probably do a convincing masquerade of a hostess. The mental image caused him to shake his head in silent laughter, but the thought sparked an idea. He turned away from the window. "What about an actress? Surely Phineas knows of someone who could act the role for the right price."

"An actress!" Lady Arianne exclaimed, her face contorting in disgust. "An actress would never know the sort of deportment one needs to be the hostess of a diplomatic legation. If society were to know that an actress—"

"But they won't know," Rafferty interrupted. "Because you would teach her how to act, what to say." The idea gained substance in his mind. "Her ruse would allow me the time to unravel the murder and locate Toomey. I'm certain he has a hand in this."

"It might work," Henderson agreed. "As long as the masquerade doesn't extend for an overlong period of time. It might work."

"No," Lady Silk-Stocking protested. "Those women, they're little more than . . ." Her face began to color.

Lord help him but Rafferty enjoyed her discomfort. The aristocracy had no hesitation about proclaiming their superiority over individuals no more than two feet away—but at the first mention of something as basic and ancient as a tumble under the blankets, they fussed and blushed and pretended innocence.

"Yes, Lady Arianne?" Rafferty taunted. "What are they precisely?"

Her spine stiffened, and she refused to look at him. "They're . . . unsavory women."

"Then one should make a convincing wife"— he leered at Henderson—"at least behind closed doors."

She stood. "Really, Mr. Rafferty. I must leave if you gentlemen are going to discuss such coarse topics."

"My apologies, Lady Arianne." Rafferty bowed in her direction. "I forgot for a moment that you are not a farmer's daughter but a woman of higher station."

She glared at him, in no way amused by his levity.

"Arianne, please stay," Henderson interceded. "I'm sure Rafferty will mind his manners." His glower served as reprimand. Rafferty's smile faded. "Now, if we can find a suitable candidate to play the role of Mrs. Rafferty, do you think you could teach her what she'll need to know in a short time?"

Lady Arianne narrowed her eyes. "How short a time?"

"I'd like you to travel to America with the actress." Lord Henderson paused as if suddenly inspired. "Do I not recall that it was through your instigation that your brother met his American wife?"

Rafferty noted the resurgence of pink on Lady Arianne's

throat. While the poor woman did not wear her heart on her sleeve, her delectable throat was apparently another matter.

"I met Mrs. Winthrop in Switzerland and mentioned my brother's qualities to her," Arianne said. "However, I don't consider that an instigation. It was more of an accident, really."

"Yet they are now happily married." Henderson smiled. "As am I, I might add. Lady Henderson and I are in debt to your . . . accidents."

"This is all well and good," Rafe interrupted. "But I must sail immediately. Just send word when the woman is due to arrive and I'll—"

"Hold on, Rafferty. I'm not through with you yet," Henderson warned. He turned back to Lady Arianne. "I'll arrange passage for you and the actress on a steamer. You can use the pretense of visiting Mrs. Winthrop to justify the trip, but in reality you'll be teaching the actress how to play her role." He spun toward Rafferty. "And you will cross with them. You'll need time with the actress in order to portray a convincing husband."

Rafferty was about to protest, then decided instead to let the elegant Lady Arianne do it for him. After all, she'd made it perfectly clear that she found his company more trial than pleasure. The popular sister to a duke wouldn't want to forfeit the parties and receptions London offered. When she declined the offer to teach an actress to act like a lady, this tenuous house of cards would collapse. Henderson would allow him to sail to America and find Toomey on his own. Yes. No need to protest and further annoy his employer. Rafferty crossed his arms and waited.

Lady Arianne bit her lip and studied her gloves for a moment. She was most likely determining the most gracious way to turn down Henderson's suggestion. The aristocratic set probably maintained a whole list of rules about issuing a simple "no." Rafe turned his gaze to the back of the room, just so the satisfaction of her refusal wouldn't show on his face.

"I'll have to bring Mrs. Summers as my chaperone," she said cautiously. "And my maid. I couldn't legitimately travel without Kathleen."

What the . . . ! Rafferty jerked his gaze in disbelief back

toward Lady Arianne's stoic profile. Had he totally misread her? Was she as mad as a hatter?

"Of course." Lord Henderson smiled. "Accommodations will be arranged for the three of you."

"No!" Rafe protested. Within moments he stood directly in front of her chair. "There'll be no parties, no fancy dress balls, no social"—he waved his hands in the air while he searched for the right word—"falderal." The ribbons on her hat trembled with the currents of his tirade, yet she appeared unfazed. "This is not a pleasure cruise. You'll miss your life here, I promise you. I'm chasing a murderer, not some titled dandy."

"Lord Weston's murderer." She tilted her impassive face toward his. He searched her face for false expectations but found none. Moisture still glistened where she had dabbed at it earlier. Her voice sounded hard, cold, and dead serious. "Yes. I know."

Tension simmered in their locked gaze until Henderson tapped him lightly on the shoulder. Reluctantly, Rafferty broke the connection and turned toward him. "Until Phineas can acquire an actress for the role, Rafe, I'd like you to spend time with Lady Arianne so she can teach you the finer points of being a British minister."

Rafferty glared. "If this is punishment for wearing the wrong jacket, I'll remind you it was the result of a scuffle." Wasn't it bad enough he'd have to endure Lady Prim-and-Proper on the long passage to America?

"There's more to being a British minister than fashion," Henderson scolded. "If I didn't think you capable of this assignment, I would send someone else." His voice softened. "Perhaps after Lady Arianne knows your character, you too will be the happy recipient of one of her 'accidents.'"

Fine. Condemn him to hell. The response building in his gut would have deflated Henderson's buoyant mood and singed the ears off Lady Arianne. His hands fisted beneath the cover of his crossed arms while his lips tightened to keep the curses inside. The sting from his split lip reminded him that just a few moments in this woman's company last night had drawn blood. A week with her and he'd need a coffin. Never was a man in more need of a drink.

"Rafferty, will you escort Lady Arianne to her carriage?

And send in Phineas while you're about it. I'm sure he'll know where to start on our search for your wife."

The man laughed! Damn his eyeballs.

"You two, however, should start meeting immediately," Henderson continued. "Under the auspices of Mrs. Summers, of course." He smiled to Lady Arianne but wisely avoided Rafferty's glare.

"Good day, Lady Arianne." Henderson bowed over her hand. "Thank you for offering your services to the Crown. I'm sure you have much to do to prepare for the journey ahead."

ONE GLANCE AT MR. RAFFERTY CONFIRMED ARIANNE'S suspicion that he was not pleased with her participation in this diplomatic masquerade. She turned toward the door without waiting for his sullen self to join her. Would he be surprised to know she was not entirely enthusiastic about this venture herself?

"Why?" he asked, once they had left the room. "Why did you agree?"

"Sir! I am a patriotic British citizen," she responded. "Why wouldn't I agree to help where needed?"

She heard his soft laughter and scowled in his direction.

"I have no doubt of your patriotism, my lady, even if you seem overanxious to leave England. I think there is more to this than meets the eye." He accepted his hat and stick from the ancient butler.

Christopher! She had forgotten that Henderson said he was an investigator. She'd have to be more careful about masking her own secrets. In truth, leaving England offered an unanticipated carrot. No one could fault her avoidance of the Baron and his new fiancée if she were abroad. Besides, she didn't wish to be anywhere in the British Empire when news of the Vienna incident reached her brother's ears. She wasn't sure what William would do, but she was fairly certain he wouldn't cross the Atlantic to do it. He had sworn that his last trip, to claim his American wife, had rendered him so seasick, he wouldn't consider another ocean trip under any circumstance.

She turned to face the knavish Rafferty while Henderson's butler opened the front door for them. "Lord Weston was a dear friend. I will do everything in my power to aid the capture of the one responsible, even if that requires our continued association."

The sanctuary of her carriage waited a short distance away. She forged ahead without waiting for assistance from Mr. Rafferty. While she was vaguely aware of him scratching his nose, then jerking his arm thumb-up over his shoulder, she didn't see any gentlemen waiting for an audience with Lord Henderson. If it hadn't been for the jacket incident, she would have questioned this Phineas character's existence.

Mr. Rafferty stopped her just as she was about to step into the carriage. "Lord Henderson suggested we promptly begin meeting for instruction. Might I suggest you visit my humble abode tomorrow about two o'clock?" He hastily scribbled something on a card then held it between two fingers.

The rogue! As if she would fall prey to that rather obvious ploy. "Might I remind you, sir," she snapped, "that I'm to be the teacher and not the one receiving an education."

She climbed into the carriage, pulling her skirts in after her. The liveried footman closed the door with a thud. Rafferty's wolfish grin dimmed. Strange. At times the exasperating man charmed her into believing she was desirable. Then other times he seemed determined to prove her insignificant. Lord Henderson vouched for his intelligence and competence, but she had her doubts. He was just so unpolished . . . so physical . . . and yet . . . She remembered his face when he pulled those attached handkerchiefs from his pocket—his embarrassment and his vulnerability. Her heart twisted beneath her stays. Hadn't she recently been a public victim of those two emotions in a Vienna ballroom?

She glanced at him standing on the walk. He would need copious lessons to be a convincing British minister. Lord Henderson was right. They needed to start immediately. She leaned out the window.

"You may come to my brother's town house tomorrow afternoon. We can begin then."

His smile lit up his entire face and, to her dismay, had the same effect on her. Lord help her, she'd not have another man trample on her affections.

He squinted up at her. "Where would I find your brother's town house?"

"You're the investigator," she replied, one brow lifted. "Figure it out."

· Four ·

THE NEXT DAY, ARIANNE RAIDED THE SMALL CON-
servatory attached to the town house for ingredients in a
new fragrance recipe. Even the process of choosing fresh fragrant petals failed to divert her mind from the meeting in Lord
Henderson's office. In retrospect, she probably shouldn't have
baited Mr. Rafferty like that. Challenging him to find her brother's town house might encourage him to uncover yet more
information about her, information she'd prefer to keep private.
Quite honestly, she wasn't sure she had the mental resources
to stay one step ahead of him. Not now. Not with all that filled
her mind. She placed her basket filled with delicate violets on
the worktable she used to develop her concoctions. Mrs. Summers occupied a chair near a bright, sunny window where she
worked a needle and thread through a piece of linen.

Poor Kitty. Surely Lord Henderson had conveyed the news
by now. How had she taken the loss of her father? Although
Arianne had recently lost the man she called Father—the old
Duke—the two could not compare. Lord Weston had been more
a loving father than the Duke.

Would Mr. Rafferty be able to find the culprit? She reached

for her mortar and pestle, wondering at the probability. He seemed more concerned with that Toomey fellow than hunting a murderer.

Would that rapscallion be able to fool anyone into thinking he was a legitimate British minister? Arianne had her doubts. Though she had to admit, his appearance in Lord Henderson's study improved vastly over her initial impression at the reception. She almost hadn't recognized him, he looked so elegant and . . . competent. Her lips curved at the memory. Of course, the moment she had heard Mr. Rafferty's voice, that deep soft velvet voice that tingled along her spine like flower petals nodding in the wind, she recognized him, or rather her body did, even before she turned to face him. She couldn't deny the tingling sensations that raced down her spine whenever he spoke. God should never have blessed such a man with such a voice . . . or perhaps it wasn't God's handiwork . . . The peal of the pestle striking the mortar's side interrupted her reverie.

"Is something on your mind, Arianne? You appear to be woolgathering." Mrs. Summers glanced up from her needlework. "Are you still upset about that strange man at Countess D'Orange's reception?"

"No, I'm not upset . . . exactly," Arianne replied, choosing her words carefully. "Lord Henderson explained that Mr. Rafferty is reputable and not the gate-crasher I had assumed him to be." Though loathe to admit as much to Mrs. Summers, her impressions of Mr. Rafferty were far more complex than that. So complex that she hadn't been able to sort them out for herself as yet.

"Then perhaps you should explain why you are grinding the life out of those poor violets. I thought distillation was a gentle process."

"I wasn't planning to distill these. I was going to . . ." Arianne glanced at the slimy mush staining the bottom of the mortar bowl. "Never mind." Obviously, she hadn't been paying attention or she would have stopped before the flowers were totally eviscerated. She set the mortar and pestle aside, then wrung her hands on a towel, watching Mrs. Summers's calm, methodic progress on the linen.

"Mr. Rafferty may come here this afternoon," Arianne said,

then grimaced. "Lord Henderson asks that I teach him about proper demeanor in diplomatic situations, as well as that actress." Arianne had already told Mrs. Summers about the procurement of an actress as well as the timely trip to America.

"He *may* come? You're not certain?" Mrs. Summers pulled on her thread without an upward glance.

Arianne untied her apron, then hung it on a hook near the counter. Watching her staid teacher quietly working, she wished with envy that her own riotous thoughts and worries allowed such serenity. "Mr. Rafferty was so very free with his displeasure over the need for instruction, I believe he may possibly stay away."

"He'd defy Lord Henderson?" Mrs. Summers asked, seemingly unaware of Arianne's scrutiny.

"I think Mr. Rafferty is a libertine," Arianne pronounced. "I imagine he'd defy the Queen if she intruded on his plans." She really had no basis for her harsh declaration beyond his involvement with fisticuffs before the reception and that rebellious nature that set a part of her conventional self quivering whenever he was near. Yes, she supposed such a man would take matters in his own hands in spite of society's rules of conduct. Her spine tingled. That dangerous prospect made her both envious and fearful, an unsettling combination that set her on edge.

She glanced at Mrs. Summers, who showed none of Arianne's conflicting emotions. An idea began to take root. She approached Mrs. Summers's chair and crouched down beside the older woman. "I was wondering . . . perhaps you would be better suited to be his instructor."

"Me?" Mrs. Summers's eyes widened behind the magnifying lens of her glasses. "Oh no! It was difficult enough to teach you girls how to be proper ladies. I could never teach a grown man." She shook her head. "I think you're far better suited for this task than I. You've attended embassy receptions and parties and balls . . . while I sat with all the other widows watching the gaiety of you young folk. You'd be a better judge of what's acceptable in these modern times than I." She bent back to her needlework without further issue.

Arianne stood, her arms folded across her chest. There was

some truth to that, though perhaps not in the way Mrs. Summers implied.

Hastings interrupted. "Pardon me, miss, but there's a Mr. Rafferty to see you. He says he's expected."

Her breath caught. He'd found her! She shouldn't be surprised. She wasn't exactly hiding, but she wasn't sure he would actually appear at her doorstep. The longcase clock in the hallway sounded two bells, eliciting a quick frown. He was punctual . . . for a libertine. She glanced toward Hastings. "Could you show him to the blue salon? I shall be down immediately."

Hastings nodded. The door closed silently behind him. Arianne turned to Mrs. Summers.

"He's here!" Arianne paced in a tight circle before the chair. "I've been so preoccupied with thoughts of Kitty and the impending trip that I haven't given much thought to what I should teach him . . . if he were to really come." She stopped and turned pleading eyes toward her teacher. "What should I do?"

Mrs. Summers set her needlework aside, then stood. "I think you should go and greet the man." She placed a hand at the small of Arianne's back and walked with her toward the door. "I'm sure appropriate lessons will come as you assess his particular needs. What will be his first social obligation as head of the legation?"

"You mean after he expresses his condolences to Lady Weston?" A sob caught in her throat as she was reminded of Lord Weston's demise. Mrs. Summers nodded and waited until Arianne could continue. "Generally the first obligation is to meet the ruling entity of one's host country."

Mrs. Summers smiled, her eyes warm with encouragement. "That sounds like a good place to start."

ARIANNE APPROACHED THE SALON BUT PAUSED IN THE hallway to observe Mr. Rafferty studying one of her brother's paintings. Although most of the family portraits hung at the ancestral estate of Deerfield Abbey, the London town house had a fair allotment. Interesting that of all the paintings on the walls, Rafferty would choose that particular landscape, her favorite, to study.

He was a fine-looking man, from his powerful shoulders to his trim hips. She was to mold him into a gentleman, but there was nothing "gentle" about him, except perhaps his hair. The thought made her smile. His hat lay on the cushion of a nearby wing chair, allowing her a glimpse of his full, thick black hair. While the rest of him warned of contained savagery, his hair almost beckoned touch. A bit longer than current fashion, the ends curled much like that of a young boy. If she were to trim it, would he lose some of his threatening qualities, much like Samson of the biblical tales? Surely, it was that sense of danger surrounding him that set a low vibration in her bones whenever she saw him.

"This is one of your brother's early works," he said without glancing in her direction.

"I . . . I didn't know you realized I was here." Flustered, she soothed the front of her black skirts. "Are you familiar with my brother's work?"

He turned his gaze toward her. "I heard your footsteps and"—he sniffed—"jasmine today?" A slight smile lifted his lips. "Were you studying me, Lady Arianne?"

Caught in the act! Her faced warmed. "You are not an unattractive man, Mr. Rafferty. I apologize if I made you feel uncomfortable."

"On the contrary." He straightened. His gaze swept over her with a knowing smile. "Perhaps it would make you feel at ease if I admit that I find you attractive as well."

His comment had the reverse effect. The appreciation in his eyes nearly took her breath away. But she reminded herself that she had been in a similar situation before. Baron Von Dieter had blinded her with compliments, and she had foolishly believed them all. She was no longer a gullible little miss, but then what exactly was she? She took a deep breath, lowered her gaze, then strode into the salon. "I've been thinking about what we should discuss today, Mr. Rafferty. I've been reminded that your first order of business in Washington will be for you and your wife to call upon the president of the United States."

His eyes creased as his smile deepened.

"Did I say something amiss?" she asked, failing to see what caused his amusement.

"I find it difficult to reconcile the words 'my wife' with a nonexistent personage," he explained. "I'm sorry. You were speaking of President Garfield?"

"Yes, the very same." She smiled, pleased that Mr. Rafferty was finally taking his role as British minister seriously. She absently picked up the heavy white ivory queen from an unfinished game of chess that she and Mrs. Summers had begun last evening. Her brother had written that the set was once owned by Napoleon Bonaparte while in exile at Saint Helena. It was only one of the many extravagant purchases her brother William had made after he'd married his heiress. Arianne slid her fingers over the intricate carving, wishing she had some of William's sense of tactical maneuvering. She walked a very fine line with this man. "I see you've done some preparatory study."

His lips tightened. In less time than it took to advance a pawn a space on the chessboard, the temperament in the room shifted. "I assure you, my lady, I do read." His eyes narrowed in her direction. "The American president's recent election was reported by the *Times*."

Her cheeks heated. She hadn't meant to insult him, yet apparently she'd done just that. "I didn't mean to imply . . ." She set the chess piece back on its square, then clasped her hands in front of her, determined to clear some of the tension that crackled in the air. "I fear we may have begun on the wrong foot. I can see that you are a gentleman. Perhaps if we were—"

"But that's where you are wrong, miss." Rafferty fixed his gaze on her and moved closer, like a hunter stalking prey. "A learned man once defined a gentleman as one who never inflicts pain." The cut on Rafferty's lip reminded her that he was quite capable of that very thing. Goose bumps lifted on her arm.

Rafferty stepped close, too close. A tremor slipped down her spine. She tried to step back, but the chess table pressed her backside, blocking her retreat. He moved closer. A fragrance redolent of something earthy and familiar teased her senses, but she hadn't the leisure to dwell on that now. Not when this powerfully built man stood near enough to steal her breath.

"By that definition, I'm not a gentleman." His dark eyes bored into hers. "Do you understand?"

Her hand pushed the hard muscle of his chest to stop his further advance. At least, that was her intent. She glanced at her fingers that registered his heartbeat, the pulsing life of him, the vitality.

"There are all kinds of pain, Mr. Rafferty." She glanced up, capturing his arrogant gaze. "Not all of them leave marks like that on your lip. Some leave bruises on your heart, even on your soul," she said, remembering how her "gentleman" father had abused her mother and how the "gentleman" Baron had stolen her future. "Yet wounds are often inflicted by so-called gentlemen."

He glanced at her hand, still lightly pressing his chest, then caught her gaze. His eyes softened with a strange curiosity. "What do you know of pain, Lady Arianne?"

The tender concern in his voice ripped her from hurtful memories. She quickly snatched her hand from his chest and glanced away. Christopher! What was she doing revealing her scars to a stranger? Why had she lingered over the feel of him when she had only meant to stop his advance? She attempted a smile to gather her thoughts. "Forgive me," she said, flustered. "You were referring to that Toomey fellow, weren't you?"

His fingers, sheathed in buttery soft leather, touched the edge of her jaw, guiding her gaze back to his. She fought to maintain a calm façade, while a conspiratorial smile filled his eyes, then spread to his lips. He stepped to the side, letting her compose herself while he appeared to study the chessboard. "It is true that I'm determined to see Basil Toomey pay for what he did to my family."

Their connection severed, Arianne's traitorous hand stole to her throat. Drawing a deep breath to slow her racing heartbeat, she reminded herself of her earlier resolution to be immune to masculine attraction. Only heartache waited along that path. "What . . . what exactly did he do?"

"He placed the Fenian bomb that killed my parents and little brother." Rafferty's words fell hard and cold in the dispassionate way of tragedy worn smooth by time. She'd heard the same tone in her own voice on those rare occasions when she spoke of the old Duke's treatment of her mother. With two fingers, Rafferty pinched a black rook and let it hover over the board. "He confessed. He even took pride in the deed." He lifted a brow her way. "I'm surprised you aren't familiar with the name. It was in all the papers. You do read, Lady Arianne?"

She smiled, wise to his jest. She supposed she deserved that jibe for her own supposition. "Yes. I read. Frequently, in fact. However, I was too young at the time of that bombing to read the papers. I do remember mention of the incident in later years."

"Perhaps you remember that he managed to escape the hangman with the help of his Fenian friends?" Rafferty set the rook down, on a different square than it had been before, then turned back toward her. "Time is my enemy. I'd be on my way to America right now if not for this ridiculous notion of procuring a bride."

"It's not ridiculous. I assure you a wife is an absolute necessity." Arianne paused, uncertain if she should continue. She took a breath, deciding he deserved her honesty. "I'm not certain, however, that an actress will be able to convince anyone that she's married to a British minister. She won't have the background, the experience . . ."

"Then the actress and I should be perfectly matched, as you don't believe I can convince anyone that I'm a British minister," he challenged. Though he hadn't reacted at the time, her words to Lord Henderson had obviously left a wound.

She bit her lip, wishing she could take back those sentiments. That was the trouble with giving voice to one's thoughts. They always came back to haunt you. One would think she had learned that lesson with the Baron. She lowered her gaze. "I may have been hasty in my judgment."

"Oh . . . ? And to what do I owe this change in opinion?"

She wanted to say that she felt a certain kinship for him, as he'd grown up without a family, much as she had. Granted, she had lost her mother at a young age, but given that the old Duke could barely tolerate the sight of her, she'd been abandoned as if she had lost both of them. She understood the loneliness of living among strangers. Glancing at him now, she allowed that her first impression of unsuitability was likely misguided. But she didn't want to admit as much, not to him. "A hunch," she replied simply.

"A hunch?" He laughed, and the infectious sound forced a smile to her lips as well. His eyes creased with humor, filling her with a sort of giddiness. "Are you a gambling woman, Lady Arianne?"

"No . . ." She grinned up at him until she realized she had held the posture overlong. Embarrassment warmed her cheeks. He must believe she was little better than a chambermaid, all doe-eyed at his smile. The seductive rakehell!

Glancing away, she crossed to the fireplace, increasing the space between them. "No, Mr. Rafferty, I am not. But if we don't proceed with today's lesson, I fear I may have misplaced my faith." Taking a deep breath, she hoped to banish lingering traces of light-headedness. "Let's begin with introductions to the president, shall we? At least the American ceremony is less rigid than that of meeting the Queen."

Humor continued to light his face. He slowly crossed to her position, denying her the comfort of distance. "Presentation to the old girl is hardly as demanding for men as it is for women. We don't have to bother with the height of our white feathers or the length of our trains."

She gasped. "You know about the rules for a presentation to the Queen?"

He had a wicked smile. "Don't you?"

"Yes, of course I do . . ." It hadn't been so very long ago that she had to worry about those very things. She glanced at Mr. Rafferty, unsure if he was teasing her or if he truly knew the long list of rules for a proper presentation. The only thing she could discern from his expression was that he enjoyed her astonishment. She tapped her fingers on the fireplace mantel. "I'm beginning to believe you are full of surprises, Mr. Rafferty. I'm not certain what to make of you."

"If I understand Lord Henderson's charge, you're to make a very proper English gentleman out of me," he replied, a bit of laughter evident in his voice.

Suddenly her task didn't appear to be as difficult as she had initially imagined. "Yes," she agreed.

He leaned close and spoke in such intimate tones that she had to concentrate to understand his thick Irish brogue. "Then you're bound to fail, as I'm as Irish and as common as they come."

Before she could think of a response, he turned and collected his hat from the chair.

"You're leaving?" she asked. "We haven't finished!"

"I believe we have for today. I'm to meet Phineas and"—he

sighed, then brushed the nap of his hat—"God willing, meet my new wife."

His chin tilted in her direction. "Your mourning attire suggests that you intend to pay a call upon your friend, Lady Cardiff. The news struck her particularly hard. I'm sure she'll be grateful for your emotional support."

"You've seen her?" Based upon his narrow participation at the diplomatic reception, she had the impression that Mr. Rafferty tended to avoid women of high station.

"I accompanied Lord Henderson yesterday to assure Lady Cardiff that I would do everything possible to find Lord Weston's murderer."

"And Toomey," Arianne added quickly. "He's the real reason you're doing all this, isn't it?"

"And Toomey," he agreed slowly. He studied her for a moment. "I suspect his presence in America is connected to Lord Weston's murder. As to the other, I'm a patriotic British citizen; why wouldn't I agree to help where needed?" He plopped his hat on his head and bowed casually. "Good day, Lady Arianne."

Her very words from yesterday. The cad.

"Mr. Rafferty." He turned toward her. "I don't think you truly value my contribution to this endeavor. While you may not be concerned about the impression you make upon the Americans, I am. First impressions are the lasting ones. I fear you will come to regret not having invested sufficient time in matters of social responsibilities. I may not be a gambler, but I'd put money on that."

An eyebrow raised along with one corner of his lips. While he didn't laugh at her little speech, he certainly appeared to find humor in it. The scoundrel.

His gaze shifted from her face to the velvet draperies by the window, to the Millais painting over the fireplace, to the inlaid tripod table supporting the chess set, before returning to her. His lips tightened. "Maybe you should. I'd wager you'd find favorable odds."

RAFFERTY STEPPED OUTSIDE AND TOOK A DEEP BREATH. The air tasted sweet in this part of London, devoid of the sewage and coal dust that fouled many of the streets where his investigations led him. Still, there was an honesty in the poorer sections of town. A man with coin in his pocket had no need to prove himself. He was lord of his own circumstance.

Here one was judged not by his accomplishments but by his birth. Money was lavishly spent on the most ridiculous refinements, fine porcelain urns to support leafy ferns, ceilings with paintings of plump cavorting cherubs, lavish draperies that puddled on parquet floors. Thousands had starved in nearby Ireland while the British landlords collected rents to purchase carved ivory chess sets. He shook his head, wondering how the Duke managed to sleep at night when his money could buy comfort for so many.

There was much to do before they left for America and little time to accomplish it all. He had, indeed, arranged to meet with Phineas, but he also needed to confer with the many eyes watching Barnell. The identity of the lady in green was still a mystery. She might still play a part in unraveling the plot behind Lord Weston's murder.

He flagged down a two-wheeled hansom. Even finding transportation was easier in this end of town. After shouting directions to the driver, he climbed onto the worn leather bench.

Lady Arianne was a pleasant distraction, too pleasant by half. Given his current pressing commitments, he had thought to avoid any "gentleman" lessons, but curiosity had carried him to her doorstep. Her fiery spirit shone through, even while she wore that morbid mourning attire. Not a hair out of place, not a smudge on her face, not a distracting speck of white on her trim, curvy silhouette. Though she admitted she had been hasty in her judgment, she obviously still looked down her pert little upper-class nose at him. What was it she'd said? First impressions were the lasting ones? What she needed was one night in his bed, then those impressions would be altered. That brought a smile to his lips. The woman would benefit from having her corset loosened, and he was just the man to do it.

Of course, her straitlaced, prudish world would most likely be turned upside down once she stepped aboard that steamer. Lady Arianne probably anticipated sailing on one of those large luxury transatlantic steamers that were all the rage. He had tried to warn her in Lord Henderson's office, but she was determined to see this through. Yes, her extravagant, well-ordered world was about to spin on its head. And an amusing spin it promised to be, provided he stayed near to catch her should she fall.

· Five ·

BRANNIGAN'S HAD FEW AMENITIES. THE FURNISH-
ings were sparse, the chippies hard, and gin and beer
flowed easily. It was not the sort of place one would expect to
find a well-mannered gentleman, which was precisely why
Rafferty favored it.

He loosened the neck cloth he'd worn to please Lady Arianne's ladylike sensibilities and crammed it into his pocket.
Then he removed his jacket and hooked it over his back with
his thumb. Even the heavily besotted customers scrambled to
move out of his path as he made his way toward the back
wall.

A dirty wharf rat with a full set of whiskers slumped in a
shadowy corner amid the alcohol vapors. Rafferty narrowed
his glance, then noticed a bottle of Irish whiskey by the sailor's
elbow. He smiled. Phineas! No one else would dare occupy
Rafferty's table.

Rafferty approached, then poured a finger of whiskey into
a waiting empty glass. "Why the disguise?"

"Someone's been asking about me." Phineas glanced up at
him, his eyes stark against the dirt-smeared face. He kicked a

chair out from under the table. "Didn't want to be too easy to find."

"Any idea why?" Rafferty dropped his jacket on a dry stretch of wooden table before settling into the chair.

Phineas emptied his glass. "Could be any one of a hundred reasons."

The topic was now closed. Rafferty had always assumed Phineas had shady dealings in his past. His talent at disguise evolved from a need to escape, just at Rafferty's talent with his fists developed from too much practice. They both respected each other's secrets, so he let this one pass unchallenged.

"I found an actress." Phineas lifted fake gnarled eyebrows. "She's young and not well known. You'll meet her tonight after the curtain."

"You work quickly." Rafferty tried to mask his disappointment.

Phineas studied him in quiet assessment. "I thought you were in a hurry."

Damnation. Sometimes he wished Phineas didn't know him half as well. Rafferty tossed the alcohol to the back of his throat, letting the satisfying warmth spread outward from his gut. "I'm in a hurry to get to America. Not to be saddled with a pretend wife in the process." In spite of Lady Arianne's insistence, he wasn't convinced a wife was essential.

He poured another finger, letting the rattle of clinking glass fill the silence. Rafferty frowned at Phineas's scrutiny and swirled the light amber liquid in his glass. "She's willing to travel, then?"

"For the right price. She wants to meet you first."

"Reasonable," Rafferty agreed, then sipped the whiskey. The alcohol burned the split in his lip, reminding him of Lady Arianne and her references to past wounds. What could such a pampered, well-bred woman know of pain? He scowled thinking of the bastard who would—

"Any word from the net?" Phineas asked, referring to the street lads and cooperative coppers that Rafferty paid to be his eyes and ears about London. Lord Henderson, unaware of how Rafferty got his information, once claimed Rafferty landed leads to criminals like fish in a net. The name stuck.

Rafferty shook his head, as much to respond as to clear his recent conversation with Lady Arianne from his thoughts. "I made the rounds before coming here. Barnell has been staying close to home. A few members of parliament have paid him calls, but that's to be expected. No sign of the mystery woman."

One of Brannigan's resident sporting women approached their table with an eye on Rafferty, but Phineas chased her away with lewd shouts and a seaman's curse. Rafferty hid silent laughter behind a tight smile, then lifted his glass. "You didn't have to frighten the poor chit."

"You're married now," Phineas muttered with a twisted grin. He poured more whiskey into his own glass. "You would have turned her down anyway. Your cap is set for Lady Upper Crust."

Rafferty choked on his swallow of whiskey. Gasping for breath, he managed to inhale more fiery alcoholic fumes. Phineas jumped up and pounded his back with resounding whacks, which did not help at all.

"Wrong hatch," Phineas explained in a gruff tone to those who bothered to glance in their direction.

"Enough," Rafferty rasped, waving Phineas back to his seat. "Enough." A few deep, slow draughts of air into his lungs loosened the constriction in his throat. While frowning at Phineas, he managed in a breathy whisper, "Lady Upper . . ." He sucked in more air. "Why . . . say that?"

"You've never cared enough about a woman to complain before. You've done nothing but complain ever since you met this one."

"Never met . . . anyone . . . as irritating." His voice scraped like a man on his death bed. Surely someone who haunted his dreams and invaded his thoughts that much could be called an irritant. Besides, there was that one overriding concern. He jabbed a thumb at his own chest and rasped, "Not good enough."

"There is that," Phineas conceded in solemn agreement. Rafferty tilted his head to glare a response, but it was wasted. Phineas emptied his glass. "We should be on our way if we're going to catch Miss St. Claire."

"Who's Miss St. Claire?" Rafferty managed with a bit more strength.

Phineas pushed his chair back, then lowered his chin to bellow like an old sea crab. "Your wife, mate." He stood, then swung a battered cloth sack over his shoulder. He slapped Rafferty on the shoulder. "She awaits."

PHINEAS'S RAPID TRANSFORMATION NEVER FAILED TO amaze Rafferty. Once they climbed into a hackney, Phineas retrieved a bottle and a large cloth from the bag and in minutes had a clean face, devoid of a bushy beard and eyebrows. A tug on a seeming void of teeth produced a black cap. A clean shirt and his magician's jacket emerged from the sack to replace his seaman's togs. With a few twists, a truncheon of the sort carried by coppers became a stylish walking stick. While Rafferty was still fumbling with his neck cloth, Phineas popped a flat disk into a top hat.

Rafferty leaned forward to peek into the bag's opening. "Is there a rabbit in there as well?"

Phineas smiled. "Not today."

THE HACKNEY RATTLED TO A HALT AMID A SWARM OF people outside the Britannia Theatre.

Phineas looked out the window. "Our timing is perfect. The show just let out." He glanced back at Rafferty. "Wait here and I'll find her."

"And then what?" Rafferty grumbled before Phineas could close the hackney door. Waiting in a hackney felt akin to asking a clock to stop ticking.

Phineas glanced down the walk. "The Bard and Bull caters to the performers. We'll take her there to talk." He shifted his gaze back to Rafferty and grinned. "After that . . . it's up to you." The door closed. Phineas signaled to the cabbie, then disappeared into the crowd, once again blending into the surroundings.

"Up to me," Rafferty groused and glanced out the window. "If it was up to me, we'd be halfway across the Atlantic by now."

He watched the activity on the street awhile, then noted one of his lads waving his arms. "What the . . ."

Rafferty exited onto the street, gave the hackney driver some money, then crossed to see the boy.

"I saw 'im, sir. Mr. Barnell. 'E was with a lady."

"Where did you see him, Jamie?" Rafferty asked, scrutinizing the crowd.

"They went that way, sir." Jamie pointed down the street, in the opposite direction from Phineas's cafe. "Round that corner."

"Good job, lad!" Rafferty ruffled the boy's head, then tossed him a few coins. He heard the boy's jubilant cry behind him as he followed the path suggested by the sighting.

The corner represented the intersection of two streets: one well traveled and busy with the theater patrons and their noisy carriages, the other quiet, and dark. Rafferty scanned the gaslit sidewalks. Empty. Either the two had entered one of the many storefronts facing the road, or they were out of sight, around a curve in the road just a block or so away.

He proceeded cautiously to a stage door entrance to the theater. No one waited outside. He continued past darkened storefronts, but not so much as a candle glowed to indicate a presence behind the glass. The street noises gradually faded behind him. A smell of rotting garbage drifted on the same breeze that pushed an empty can along the cobblestones. A rat scurried down a gutter. Water dripped, the sound amplified in the vacant street.

Rafferty reached the curve and scanned the sidewalks. A movement farther down the street on one side caught his eye. Perhaps it was the closing of a door. Perhaps it was . . .

"Rafferty!" Even from this distance, he recognized the irritation in Phineas's voice. No point pursuing Barnell and his lady friend now that Phineas had announced his presence. He turned slowly.

Phineas stood at the opening of the road with a woman by his side. With a quick glance over his shoulder, Rafferty reluctantly made his way back to the busy street. The lad could have been mistaken, or Barnell could have slipped behind a door, but the woman who was to play his wife was a certainty and waited for him a mere block away.

Her blonde hair was bobbed, not like the rich chestnut of Lady Arianne's hair, coiled with the promise of a lush curtain when let down in the company of a lover. The actress held herself well, though she lacked that defiant chin that epitomized

Lady Arianne. This one was more diminutive, less of a challenge. From the low cut of her neckline, he guessed she wasn't about to defy anyone. He smiled. Yes. He would guess from that neckline that she had a far more giving nature than Lady Arianne. What did Phineas call her? St. Claire? He almost laughed out loud. As he neared the waiting couple, he could see there was very little saintliness about Miss St. Claire.

"Miss St. Claire." Phineas gestured toward Rafferty. "Allow me to present your husband, Mr. Michael Rafferty."

"Delighted to meet you, Miss St. Claire." Rafferty bowed over her extended hand.

"As am I, Mr. Rafferty." Her calculating gaze slipped around his features like that of an experienced Fleet Street dove. What she saw apparently pleased, as her lips turned in an amused smile. "However, I haven't accepted this role quite yet. I should like to get to know you better."

"That can be remedied," Rafferty said, offering his arm. Together the three of them walked back the way he had originally come.

"Were you in this evening's performance?" Phineas asked. "It's disappointing that *She Stoops to Conquer* has to close its run."

She shook her head. "Not tonight." She shifted her gaze to Rafferty. "I was the understudy for Miss Hardcastle, but I did manage three performances. Perhaps you had occasion to see me?"

She was an attractive miss with a sly charm that lacked Lady Arianne's reserved polish. Was that something an actress could learn in time? He recalled Lady Arianne's opinion that an actress would not suit. Could she be right? And what did that say about his abilities to pass as a proper British minister? Rafferty shook his head. "I'm afraid I haven't had that pleasure."

Phineas and she conversed about inconsequential topics, acting venues and playwrights, until they arrived at their destination. Rafferty waited until they were seated and the wine poured before he turned the conversation to more significant matters.

"Miss St. Claire. While I'm pleased my friend, Mr. Connor, was able to locate such a talented individual in a short time . . . you do understand that we will be traveling overseas?"

"Yes. In fact, I'm looking forward to it." Her face brightened. "I do hope our travels will take us to New York. I've heard that there's something afoot called 'vaudeville' and acts are auditioning—"

"If you accept this role," Rafferty interrupted with a stern glower, "no one is to know that you're an actress. There will be no auditions of any sort." He glared at Phineas, questioning if Miss St. Claire understood exactly what would be demanded of her. Was this the best he could find? When Phineas didn't meet his gaze, he turned toward Miss St. Claire. "You are aware of the role you'll be expected to play?"

"You require someone to act the role of the British minister's wife." She offered a coquettish smile. "Your wife." Beneath the table, Rafferty felt her hand slide down the length of his thigh. A smile spread across her face. "I can be very convincing as a wife."

"A pretend wife," Rafferty reminded her, gripping her exploring hand to halt its progress before she reached the inside of his thigh. "But there is more to this part than playing a wife."

She tugged her hand free. "I have a knack for quickly learning my lines."

"There'll be no lines to memorize," Phineas added with a quick apologetic glance toward Rafferty. "You will have to be . . . extemporaneous."

She raised her brow and sipped at her wine.

Phineas filled Rafferty's glass. "I think you'll be pleased with Miss St. Claire's stage presence once she understands her role. But she insisted on seeing you in person before she decided to accept."

"The role of a wife is a delicate affair," she explained with a practiced pout. "I wanted to be certain that the leading man was worthy of my best efforts."

Rafferty smiled tightly. "Do I pass inspection, Miss St. Claire?"

Her smile smoldered with seduction. Rafferty recognized her experience ran more along the lines of mistress than wife. Given the jewels on her fingers and the tiny butterfly tattoo above her right breast, he suspected she was not lacking for men willing to offer favors.

"Why are you doing this?" he asked. "You do not strike me as a woman without means."

She understood his implication. It appeared in her sly smile. "There is . . . an association that I would like to end. Distance would be advisable."

"You're afraid of him?" Rafferty's jaw set. He saw Phineas tense as well. Neither felt mercy for a man that would raise a fist to a woman.

Miss St. Claire lowered her gaze and raised her glass. The liquid vibrated with a tremor. "I suppose I'm curious as to how it feels to be viewed with respect by the ladies of society." She smiled tightly. "One could say this would be research for the stage."

"Or for another life," Rafferty said quietly.

"We've a tutor to help you learn the social responsibilities and mannerisms of the position," Phineas added. "She'll be traveling to America so as to offer instruction on the way."

"Instruction?" Miss St. Claire sipped her wine, and a mischievous gleam replaced her earlier apprehension. "There are certain aspects that will not require—"

"Of course, you'll be provided with a new wardrobe," Phineas continued. "And steady pay for the time we're away."

She smiled. "And a handsome, wealthy husband to boot."

"A pretend husband," Rafferty amended, lifting his glass for a toast. "We won't actually be married."

"But we'll have to be convincing, won't we?" Her tongue moistened her lips. "You should start by calling me Eva."

"Eva," Rafferty repeated, a grin upon his face. Well, why not? She was offering him the sort of intimate knowledge a man would naturally have of a wife. The sort of knowledge, he was quite certain, that would not be available from the high-and-mighty Lady Arianne. She probably stopped at a church just to pray away her earlier brazen act of touching his chest.

He knew Lady Arianne would balk when she saw their mode of transportation. She was liable to make his days a living hell. Why not allow Miss St. Claire to provide his nights with a bit of heavenly delight? The ring of their wineglasses meeting signaled agreement. "Most definitely." Rafferty caught her gaze. "Convincing we shall be."

• • •

THE NEXT DAY, RAFFERTY AND HIS "WIFE" CALLED UPON Lady Arianne at her London town house. Hastings ushered them into the same blue salon as before.

"Look at this room!" Eva gushed. "Will our residence in America be like this?"

Rafferty supposed that her patrons had been careful not to invite her into their homes. The life of a kept mistress tended to be one of isolation.

Eva danced from one overstuffed chair to the next. "It's Louis the Fifteenth!" She slid her hand over the blue silk fabric, then twirled about as if she were on a stage and not in a duke's sitting room. Her delight in the opulence of the surroundings, not to mention the sight of her shapely ankles, brought a smile to Rafferty's lips.

"I don't know what our quarters will be like in America, but I doubt Lady Arianne will approve of dancing on her fine Persian carpets." Rather than insist she stop, he leaned against the doorjamb and enjoyed more of Eva's private performance.

"Why? Is she a dried-up, old hoity-toity whose idea of fun is a juicy piece of gossip?" Eva's pose mimicked a dowager squinting through a quizzing glass.

He was contemplating an appropriate response when Lady Arianne spoke behind him. "I should like to hear the answer to that myself."

Rafferty straightened in a snap, embarrassed that he'd been caught off guard but determined not to show it. Eva dropped her pantomime and turned toward the doorway.

"Lady Arianne Chambers." Rafferty cleared his throat. "Allow me to present Miss St. Claire, the actress who will portray my wife."

Eva dipped in a curtsy. Arianne simply nodded, then shifted her gaze to him. Waiting, he supposed, for his answer to Eva's ill-framed question. He focused on Arianne. "As you can see, Eva, Lady Arianne is neither old nor is she dried-up."

Arianne held his gaze, waiting, he supposed, for a denial of Eva's "hoity-toity" charge. Well, she'd have to wait till her aristocratic blue blood turned decidedly red for that. He raised a brow, daring her to reply.

She shifted her attention to Eva. "You are quite the beauty," she said, though her gracious smile did not seem to reach to her eyes. "I'm certain all eyes will be upon you and Mr. Rafferty at the parties in Washington. Now, let me take a good look at you."

She walked around the girl, inspecting her the way Rafferty supposed her brother inspected a racehorse. "Good posture. We'll need to get you some appropriate clothing. My maid should be able to adjust some of my gowns." She glanced at Rafferty. "That should save us some time."

He smiled to himself, pleased that she had referred to them as "us." Perhaps she wasn't the adversary she pretended regarding this venture.

Arianne took Eva's hands in hers. "I'm certain Mr. Rafferty has impressed upon you that no one can know about this role." She searched the girl's face. "This is not a stage performance." She paused. "The consequences could be severe if anyone were to discover that you and Mr. Rafferty were not married. The worst sort of scandal would result."

Eva stiffened. "I'm well acquainted with both the precautions and the consequences of scandal."

Arianne's gaze softened. She nodded as if in reply to some silent communication between the two. She even smiled her acceptance. Bloody hell! Rafferty wished she'd smiled that way at him.

Eva turned toward Rafferty. "Perhaps I won't be playacting his wife. I've been told the captain has the right to marry passengers on these kind of trips."

"Not my captain," Rafferty grumbled beneath his breath, dusting imaginary lint off his hat.

"Did you say something, Mr. Rafferty?" Arianne inquired innocently.

He cleared his throat. "I was saying that I should leave you ladies to become better acquainted. Now that we have someone who can act as my hostess in Washington, I need to make a few arrangements so we can depart as soon as possible."

Arianne glanced at Eva. "We have a great deal to accomplish in a short time. Fittings for some"—her glance slipped to Eva's low-cut bodice before returning to her face—"appropriate attire, lessons on diplomatic responsibilities, lessons on diplomatic personnel . . ." She turned toward Rafferty. "A month would be preferred, but with hard work, we shall be ready in two weeks' time."

"We don't have two weeks." Rafferty popped his hat on his head. "There'll be time for lessons on the voyage, but it's important that we arrive in Washington as quickly as possible. I already regret the loss of this week." He glanced at Eva. "I'll return to retrieve you about—"

"No," Arianne interrupted. "If we have so little time, then I believe Miss St. Claire should stay here to make full use of the limited time available."

Astonished, he studied Arianne. "Are you certain? Actresses generally do not take residence in this part of town."

Eva smiled wickedly. "More actresses live here than you might suppose, Mr. Rafferty."

Arianne offered a condescending smile. "While I appreciate your concern, I think it best that Miss St. Claire remain here to acclimate herself to what will be expected of her."

It was a strong argument, just unexpected from one who continued to draw a clear and precise line between the privileged and the lesser born. As much as it aggravated him to agree, he nodded.

"Excellent," Arianne said, obviously pleased with her conquest. "I'll send a footman along with Miss St. Claire to collect her belongings. After she's settled in, we'll begin working."

"Very good." Rafferty started to leave.

"Mr. Rafferty?" Arianne called.

The tone of her voice made him wary. The last time he'd heard that tone, she was disapproving of his inappropriate attire. He stopped, then turned.

"Would you and Mr. . . . I'm sorry, I don't know his family name . . . Mr., uh, Phineas join us for dinner this evening?" Something about her gracious smile just didn't suit her tone. "I believe it's time we met."

He held her gaze a moment, suspecting he could almost see little diabolical wheels turning in her mind. Devil take him, she was up to something. Probably she planned a retaliation for that "hoity-toity" omission.

Reluctantly, he nodded. "It will be our pleasure."

Though from the glint in her eye, Rafferty wondered if Phineas might have to attend as his food taster.

· Six ·

THE RHYTHMIC PELTING OF RAINDROPS DIMINISHED the usual rattle of the hansom's interior. In the dark confined space that smelled of damp wool, Rafferty fidgeted. The invitation tonight was akin to inviting a lamb for sacrifice. He just wasn't certain of the manner of slaughter. He'd have to spend a portion of the evening avoiding the advances of an actress planning the next step in her climb toward respectability, and another portion catering to Lady Arianne, who constantly reminded him that she was above his reach. As if that were something he could ever forget. Either way, he was bound to be caught in the middle.

Phineas bumped his shoulder in the process of pinning a white flower to his own lapel.

"Look at you," Rafferty said with pretended disgust. His head rocked with the sway of the hansom as it rattled along the slick cobblestones. "You look like a popinjay."

"I happen to believe that one should look his best when invited to dinner, especially when the invitation comes from the sister of a duke."

"We were just invited this afternoon," Rafferty reminded

him. "The kitchen wouldn't have sufficient time to prepare a meal worthy of that sort of turnout." Phineas was overdressed in his estimation.

"Admit it, Rafe. You just haven't my sense of stage presence." Phineas twisted in the confined space to appraise Rafferty's attire. "You managed to dress like a banker . . . How very ordinary."

"That's true," Rafferty acknowledged, checking his pocket watch to measure their progress. "It's probably the reason Henderson assigned the role of British minister to me. I'm not sure anyone would take a diplomat wearing that embroidered green velvet waistcoat seriously."

Phineas grumbled, then pulled a mangled bunch of dainty blue blossoms from his pocket. "Here. These should spruce you up." He reached to pin the stems to Rafferty's lapel, ignoring his complaints. "Each flower has a meaning," Phineas explained as he secured the flowers. "I'm wearing a bellflower, which means gratitude. I wish our hostess to know that I'm grateful for being included in this evening's festivities." His voice dropped. "I'm not always, you know."

Rafferty glanced suspiciously at Phineas. "And what's the meaning of these little blue things?"

"Those are forget-me-nots." Phineas glanced out his side window. "I think the name is self-explanatory."

"What message is that supposed to convey?" Rafferty groused. "That I'm afraid she'll forget about me once this dinner is over?"

Phineas turned to face him. "I don't think that's possible. Lady Arianne will remember you long after this venture." He returned to his perusal of the passing street. "Of course, I'm not entirely convinced of the sentiment of those memories."

Rafferty scowled, then glanced askance at his partner. He hadn't thought about it before, but Phineas's ability to blend into the woodwork most likely caused him to be overlooked for society invitations. His theatrical friend didn't realize how lucky he was. "It's difficult to reconcile the old sea dog with an authority on flowers."

Phineas shrugged. "It's something the flower vendor said."

The cab rocked to a stop before the town house. Rafferty exited first to pay the cabman while Phineas proceeded toward the oak door. Rafferty joined him, but before he could rap the door with his silver-capped walking stick, the door opened and Hastings ushered them inside. They shed their outer garments and umbrellas in the grand entrance hall while Hastings hurried off to announce their arrival.

"Rafferty, will you look at this place?" Phineas's voice dropped in awe, his neck straining to see into the far corners. "It's a thief's paradise." He pointed to a walnut side table. "They put silver candlesticks out in the open, and look at that tray. I'll bet even the porcelain pot holding the flowers cost a pretty penny."

"They'll be counting the silver when we leave," Rafferty murmured. He glanced at the tray laden with small cards, some with folds in corners, most just a name in elaborate print. He didn't recall seeing such an accumulation when he first arrived for a lesson with Lady Arianne. He reached in his pocket for his card case and withdrew his own card.

"What are you doing?" Phineas asked. "We're being announced."

"She refused my card once before." Rafferty chuckled beneath his breath. He tossed his card on top of the assortment. "Let's see her refuse it now."

Approaching footsteps padded on the thick carpets. They both straightened in anticipation of Lady Arianne's arrival.

The moment he saw her, Rafferty knew he had again erred. Arianne was breathtakingly beautiful and dressed to the nines in a blue gown that made his fingers twitch to rest on those well-defined curves. He stood frozen, afraid to open his mouth for fear of the gibberish that might spill out.

Her glance slid over him, pausing at the incongruity of the blossoms on his lapel. She bit her lip. Was that amusement he saw in her eyes? His stomach clenched. Hell. Once again he was inappropriately attired. He should have just stayed at Brannigan's. Well, blast it all! Fashion should be of little consequence given the serious matters at hand.

Beside him, Phineas cleared his throat, dragging Rafferty back to the present. "Lady Arianne Chambers," Rafe said, "allow me to present Mr. Phineas Connor. You may recall meeting his coat on an earlier occasion."

"Yes. I remember." Lady Arianne extended her hand. Phineas

bent over her gloved fingers. "Have you any tricks in your pockets this evening, Mr. Connor?"

Phineas blushed. Rafferty thought he'd never seen the like before. She had a charm, Lady Arianne. Too bad she hadn't seen fit to use it on him.

Phineas smiled. "No, my lady. I do not."

"In that case, I wonder if you would do me a favor?" Her eyes sparkled, her smile sincere. Rafferty imagined Phineas would be powerless to resist her request. He was already in her spell.

"Just for this evening, could you pretend that you are the French ambassador?"

"Mais oui!" Phineas exclaimed. "I would be delighted."

"Excellent." She laughed, an infectious sound, a bewitching sound. Impatient, Rafferty waited for her to turn back to him. Instead she grasped Phineas's arm as if they were old friends. "Then I shall play the role of your wife."

"Even better," Phineas responded.

Rafferty felt a punch in his gut unlike anything he'd experienced in a fight. Phineas was to play Lady Arianne's husband? Clearly she didn't know the lengths Phineas would go to perfect a role. Rafferty's eyes narrowed.

Phineas responded with something that elicited shared laughter between them. Rafferty didn't hear the words, but he recognized the sentiment.

She swept her vast skirts aside and said, "Shall we join the others?"

That was it? After their exchange in the salon this afternoon, he was to receive a less warm welcome than Phineas, a complete stranger? And what about these "others"? As Phineas and Lady Arianne started forward, Rafferty had a sinking feeling about the evening.

"Wait!" he called. Lady Arianne stopped and glanced over her shoulder.

"Who am I to play this evening?" he asked.

"Why, yourself, Mr. Rafferty." He could see the spark of humor in her eyes. "After all, you *are* the British minister." She faced forward, and together she and Phineas continued down the hall. "This way, Mr. Rafferty. Your wife is waiting."

He followed Phineas and Lady Arianne into a rose room

with enough gilded furnishings to continue the pattern of riches evident in the blue salon. Two ladies engaged in conversation on plush sedans. He almost didn't recognize Miss St. Claire in her rust gown with lace that reached up her neck. The fringe that had vibrated with every movement of her body had disappeared, as had her bold, suggestive smile, leading him to surmise that the afternoon had not been a peaceful one. He felt certain he'd never met the older woman in the sedate brown.

Lady Arianne made the introductions, elevating Phineas to Lord Connor for purposes of his ambassadorship. Rafferty's jaw tightened. If a title was important for her make-believe dinner party, how much more important was it in real life? No matter how well he performed at this new assignment, he would never be good enough for—what did Phineas call her?—Lady Upper Crust. Never.

Sobered by this reality, he almost missed the rest of the introductions. He nodded to the woman in brown and recognized her name as the chaperone. She smiled and said the darndest thing. "So you're the one."

"I beg your pardon?" He must have misunderstood.

Arianne clapped her hands for attention. Rafferty shifted his gaze, noticing how Arianne's face glowed with enthusiasm, how her eyes sparkled in the gaslight, and how the cloth of her gown teased and titillated. It hugged her curves in all the places he wished his hands could explore—yet covered them from his eye, keeping her separate, out of reach. His gut clenched. Like all the exquisite furnishings in the Duke's residence, she was top-drawer, not for the likes of him.

Eva moved close to his side. "I'm to keep this gown for entertaining in Washington. Is it not hideous? All this lace." She slipped her fingers beneath the lace insert in such a manner that Rafferty suspected the purpose wasn't for comfort but to draw his eye to her chest. "She said my gowns were not appropriate."

"Every role has its costume," he said, looking back at Arianne. "You're here to learn from her."

Eva's eyes widened a moment before she purred low, running her hand down his lapel. "You should follow your own advice."

Capturing her hand, he moved it back to her side. "Careful." He tilted his head in reprimand.

She sighed longingly, then glanced about the room. "This place . . . can you imagine living here? I've never seen anything so lovely."

His gaze never left Arianne. "Neither have I."

"IN THEIR NEW POSITIONS," ARIANNE ANNOUNCED, "MR. and Mrs. Rafferty will be expected to host and attend formal dinners of state. I am pleased to report that the kitchen staff rose to the challenge of displaying their talents on short notice. While I'm not certain the Americans follow this exact protocol, tonight's dinner shall be presented as a formal dinner of state with eleven courses."

"Eleven courses!" Eva gasped. "How can a body eat that much food?"

"Small portions," Mrs. Summers replied, patting Eva's hand.

Arianne smiled to herself, both enjoying the rare opportunity to play hostess instead of guest at a grand dinner and pleased with her inspiration to use a formal dinner to prove her worth to Rafferty. Expecting him to be overwhelmed and humbled beyond his experience, she shifted her gaze to meet his.

Far from what she anticipated, she caught a glimpse of yearning before his expression changed to resignation. He turned and murmured something to Miss St. Claire, who wrapped her arm around his as if she were a delicate flower and he the supporting trellis. It could be that he yearned to be free of the clinging vine, but . . .

"Perhaps we should pair up to attend dinner, dear," Mrs. Summers prodded, reminding her that this was a teaching experience.

"Yes, of course," she replied with a mental shake. She raised her voice in imitation of Mrs. Summers's teaching tones. "Often envelopes are placed in the hallway to instruct the gentlemen who to accompany into dinner. However, with only two gentlemen present, I thought we could dispense with this formality. Remember that the lady you escort should be seated to your right." She glanced to Phineas. "Mr. Connor, you shall be my escort. Mr. Rafferty shall accompany his wife and Mrs. Summers."

As the person of highest social standing, Arianne was obliged to enter the dining room first, but in this instance she wished she was on Rafferty's arm. She'd have to wait for Mrs. Summers's report to hear if he stood and gawked at the dizzying display of her brother's silver and crystal. He would surely recognize that he was out of his depth and in need of her assistance when he sat down to a plate surrounded by four forks and knives. Perhaps then he would take her contribution to this venture seriously.

"Is it only the five of us?" Phineas asked, hesitating in view of the dining table. "Or are twenty more guests scheduled to arrive?"

"My brother tends to entertain large gatherings." She had requested only a portion of the table be set for their needs. Even so, the opulent sight carried an impressive impact. Phineas guided her to the head of the table, a position that allowed her to clearly observe her other guests.

A footman assisted in seating Miss St. Claire, who managed a dramatic flair even in that small exercise, while Rafferty escorted Mrs. Summers to Phineas's left. He showed none of the surprise or discomfort that she had envisioned. Blast!

"Is something not to your liking, Lady Arianne?" he asked, taking his seat to her right. "I detect a frown."

"Oh no," she brought herself back to her surroundings, ignoring the tingling down her spine at the lyrical sound of his voice. "I was just . . . woolgathering, I suppose."

While one footman served the hors d'oeuvres, another poured white wine into one of the three glasses by each plate setting.

"Oysters!" Miss St. Claire laughed. "And I was afraid I wouldn't recognize the food." She began to lift the half shell with her fingers.

"Mrs. Rafferty." Rafferty's velvety smooth murmur caught Arianne's ear. He discretely wiggled the trident-shaped oyster fork.

"Oh!" Eva replaced the shell on the plate, then looked about the table before selecting the correct utensil. She smiled her appreciation at Rafferty. "Pardon *moi*."

Phineas cringed.

"It's probably best to stick with English," Mrs. Summers

suggested with a sympathetic smile. "I don't think the Americans speak French."

Eva rolled her eyes before she sampled two of the mollusks. With a sly grin, she glanced toward Rafferty, her oyster fork dangling from her fingertips. "You know they call these Aphrodite's delight. It's said that eating oysters increases one's—"

"Eva!" Phineas scolded.

"We don't discuss such things at the table," Mrs. Summers counseled. "Remember, this is a state dinner. You'll be seated with strangers who will be forming an opinion about your character by your conversation."

Arianne recalled hearing that same advice while in school. In a fond sense of déjà vu, she could predict Miss St. Claire's complaint. Though the girl was too stubborn to realize it, Eva was fortunate to have Mrs. Summers's guidance about limited conversational topics. Arianne relaxed while Mr. Connor and Mrs. Summers launched into a litany of suitable topics that lasted through the soup course.

"Now that you've spent some time with Miss St. Claire, do you think the ruse will succeed?" Rafferty asked quietly, as the soup bowls were whisked away to be replaced with a serving of poached salmon.

Arianne contemplated the flamboyant actress, who seemed more enthralled with studying the table accessories than participating in the conversation. "Today she's been more interested in the props than learning the role, but with time, she may be passable."

"Passable?" Rafferty raised his brow. "She assumed the role of devoted wife readily enough."

Arianne hid a stab of resentment beneath a soft laugh. "I have no doubt that she will charm the men." She resisted the temptation to question the degree of the actress's devotion to any one man. However, a glance at Rafferty made her suspect he surmised the same. She shook her head. "It's the wives who worry me."

"The wives?" Rafferty sipped his wine, waiting for her to continue. She found a quiet comfort in the way he listened to her, took her opinions seriously.

"Miss St. Claire has a certain . . . defiance that I'm afraid may hinder your efforts." She raised her fork for a bite of salmon.

He considered her statement a moment. "Miss St. Claire's life, I'd warrant, has not been an easy one. We're asking her to change some basic instincts that have aided her survival. She may surprise you with her ability to adapt to new surroundings."

"I must say, you seem remarkably comfortable with all this," Arianne said, silently admitting defeat to her plans to intimidate him with etiquette. If anything, he encouraged her own breach of etiquette by tilting his head toward her. Her fingers ached to sooth the black strands from his brow.

Rafferty placed his fork on the plate a moment before it was whisked away. His wicked smile quickened her pulse.

"Along with reading, I've been known to eat upon occasion." He emptied his white wine glass, then waited while the footman poured the red for the joint course. He winked at Arianne before sampling some of her brother's excellent vintage. "And drink."

Phineas turned with a smile. "Aye, in this we have bountiful experience."

Recognizing the reprise of her earlier faux pas about reading, Arianne tightened her lips. Apparently, Rafferty didn't forgive easily. She selected a small serving of Chicken Lyonnaise from the server. "I've seen others puzzled by the varied tableware. Your wife, for instance, is having some difficulty appreciating the differences in the beverages for each course."

Rafferty followed her nod down the table to see his actress wife disagreeing with Mrs. Summers over the removal of the partially filled sherry glass that had been poured with the soup course. "She hasn't lived a life of excess," Rafferty observed.

"And you have?"

A slow smile slid across Rafferty's face, making her think of the cat that stole the cream. "I've had occasion to dine at a well-laid table. Even an oaf from the lower classes can learn manners on occasion."

"I don't believe you're an oaf from the lower classes," Arianne said. She watched him over the rim of her wineglass. "I'm not certain yet what you are, but you're decidedly not an oaf."

The servers cleared the joint dishes and brought the covered dishes of lamb and beef sirloin with vegetables. She reminded herself to eat sparingly, as they were only halfway through the meal. Rafferty, however, showed no restraint.

"Your brother employs an excellent cook," he said after sampling some of the chateau potatoes. "I appreciate that you've given Eva an opportunity to practice her table etiquette before we sail. I imagine we won't be having such elaborate meals once we board."

A cup of Roman Punch replaced Arianne's empty plate. The icy sweet slid down the back of her throat while she mulled over Rafferty's words. "Many of the transatlantic steamers serve dinners worthy of a state affair. The White Star Line most notably has excellent service." She scooped the small sherbet spoon around the inside of the cup to capture the last of the ice. "Miss St. Claire should have plenty of experience by the time we reach our destination. Do you have an idea as to our departure date?"

Phineas frowned at Rafferty amid the removal of the sherbet cups and placement of the game dish. "You haven't told her?"

The two exchanged a nervous glance that made Arianne decidedly uncomfortable. Narrowing her eyes at Rafferty, she waved off the server bearing a tray of roasted squab. "Told me what, exactly?"

Phineas took a peek at the tray. "That's not dove, is it?"

"I believe it's pigeon, sir," the footman said.

"Phineas won't eat doves or rabbits," Rafferty murmured to Arianne. "Something about professional courtesy."

Phineas also waved the server off. "I haven't ruled out working with pigeons, as yet."

"You were about to tell me when we are to depart for America," Arianne insisted. An uncomfortable foreboding settled in her throat. Rafferty's avoidance had not helped matters.

He reached for his burgundy. "You understand my need to arrive in America as soon as possible."

She nodded while he sipped his wine.

"Now that we have an actress who has agreed to play the role of my wife"—his lips lifted in a parody of a smile directed toward Miss St. Claire—"there's no reason for us to dally here any longer."

She was about to protest that they were working on important preparations for the task ahead, but Rafferty held up his hand.

"Accordingly, I've booked the first steamer that can accommodate our party. We leave on Friday."

"Friday! We can't possibly leave on such short notice," Arianne exclaimed. "We have gowns to purchase and gifts to select for presentation. We can't accomplish all that's required in just two days!"

"We need presents?" Eva interrupted.

"Then I suggest you concentrate on those things that can't be provided on the steamship." Rafferty smiled. "If it's beneficial, I shall gladly forfeit my etiquette lessons to allow you more time."

She frowned, feeling defeated by this turn. "Squeezing years of training into a few days certainly isn't ideal, Mr. Rafferty, but I suppose we'll be able to continue our lessons on the voyage."

"But we'll need to order gowns," Eva whined. "Appropriate gowns."

Arianne absently waved her hand. Her mind raced, prioritizing what needed to be done in the little time available. "I suppose my maid could alter more clothing to suit Miss St. Claire."

"I'm still proficient with a needle and thread, dear," Mrs. Summers interjected. "Perhaps I can be of assistance."

Arianne smiled her gratitude, while the dance of plate and crystal removal resumed once again. Salad plates and appropriate flatware appeared. A lovely asparagus salad was placed before her.

"We'll do our best to have everything ready," Arianne said. "I wouldn't want to hinder the discovery of Lord Weston's killer for the sake of a gown or two." From the corner of her eye, she noticed Miss St. Claire slump in her seat, then correctly predicted Mrs. Summers's reprimand to sit up straight.

Arianne pushed the asparagus aside, preferring to eat only the lettuce. "Which line will we be using?" she asked Rafferty. "I believe Inman is the swiftest."

"So I've been told, but the Inman ship won't be departing for America for another two weeks," Rafferty said. "It only takes about eleven days to cross the Atlantic. We've found another vessel that will arrive in America before the Inman vessel leaves port."

"Then it's White Star!" She smiled. The White Star Line

was known for its elegance. At least they wouldn't travel in discomfort.

"I do hope we'll travel first-class," Eva said to Mrs. Summers. "I've never traveled first-class."

"No, it's not the White Star Line." A slight twitch in Rafferty's jaw raised the small hairs on the back of Arianne's neck. She set her fork on her plate. Even lettuce wouldn't properly digest with the unease roiling in her stomach.

The servers appeared once again in their clean white gloves and silent service. Plates were removed from the left, and a small plate of pâté de foie gras was served on the right. Arianne was ready to dismiss all the service staff from the room. How was she to think with the constant changing of plates and glasses?

A sauterne was poured in her glass, and she sipped at it greedily, the sweet wine assuaging the acrid taste of foreboding. "You have me at a loss, sir."

He looked her straight in the eye. "We'll be sailing on a tramp steamer that hauls cargo across the Atlantic. She has berths for ten passengers beyond the crew. I've booked three cabins for our use."

"A . . . a tramp steamer? I'm not sure what that is?"

"It's a steamer that doesn't run on a set schedule. Instead, it travels from port to port as needed." Rafferty watched her carefully.

"I've not traveled on one of those," she said hesitantly. Nor had anyone she knew. "Where is its port?"

"London. The *Irish Rose* is currently docked at the Royal Victoria Dock. There's a rail spur if you'd prefer a railcar to a carriage," Rafferty replied.

"A train." Eva sighed dramatically. "I've traveled by train."

"It'll be a short ride," Mrs. Summers assured her.

The pâté plate disappeared somewhere in the midst of conversation; Arianne wasn't sure when. While she would normally lick her lips over the chocolate-painted éclair, she found she really had no appetite for dessert. She nibbled lightly in the hopes that the chocolate would lighten her sense of gloom. But even the rich, sweet treat had no effect. She waved her hand at the fruit and cheese plate that represented the eleventh and final course.

There would be no elegant dinners, she imagined, with so few passengers. No varied assortment of passengers with which to share acquaintance. "What does one do as a passenger on a tramp steamer?" She hadn't realized she'd spoken her thoughts until she heard Rafferty's response.

"We read."

· *Seven* ·

THE NEXT MORNING, ARIANNE SAT WITH HER TEA and newspaper, hoping for a few moments of contemplative silence before another trying day. The rain from last night had diminished, but the sky remained bleak, depressing. A heavy sigh pulled up from her chest as she considered all the work ahead to prepare the obstinate Miss St. Claire for the difficult task ahead.

"Good morning, Arianne." Mrs. Summers, already attired in her day dress, walked over to the sideboard to pour some tea. "Any interesting news in the paper today?"

Arianne glanced down at the political editorials, realizing that she couldn't remember a single word she'd read, if indeed she had read. She hadn't been able to concentrate for thoughts of Rafferty, Miss St. Claire, the work to be done, then Rafferty again. She refolded the newsprint and placed it aside.

Mrs. Summers looked askance. "Last night's dinner was a success, don't you think? If we could manage five or six more such dinners, I think Miss St. Claire will be stage ready."

"We don't have five or six more days to practice," Arianne groused. "Have you begun packing?"

Mrs. Summers smiled. "I never really unpacked from Vienna. I suspected this London visit would be of short duration."

"Why do you say that?" Arianne asked. She hadn't considered the length of this stay; her only thought had been to escape Vienna.

"Well, they always are." Mrs. Summers spread jam on a toast slice. "It's not as if you have a real home." Arianne began to protest, but Mrs. Summers waved it aside. "Oh, I know you have that tiny country estate, but it's really not your nature to be away from the city."

Arianne wanted to disagree, but she had to admit that her one stay with Nicholas and his wife at remote Black Oak had her yearning for the bustle and company of a large city's social strata.

"One can only make so many vials of fragrance before even that loses its attraction," Mrs. Summers added, pulling the society pages from the paper.

Again, Arianne bit back her protest. At one time, her scent concoctions had pleasant results, and she happily devoted time to them. Now, she was just too preoccupied with weightier issues to pay suitable attention to balancing florals.

"Arianne," Mrs. Summers said absently as she perused the paper. "Eva will be expected to make and receive calls once she is in Washington, will she not? Perhaps you should use this last day to let her accompany you as you return the calls you've been ignoring."

"But the packing—"

"Kathleen and I will finish packing for both you and Eva. You two need to leave the confined environment of this house."

Hastings, on her request, brought the silver tray from the hallway filled with the cards from refused callers. Mrs. Summers eyed the collection. "I imagine most are matrons with marriage-minded daughters. Those should provide adequate practice for Eva. Just close your eyes and pick one."

Arianne played along. Shielding her eyes, she selected a card, then peeked. With a laugh, she turned it so Mrs. Summers could see the name. Mr. Michael Rafferty.

Mrs. Summers almost snorted her tea.

"I can't very well pay a call to him, especially with Eva in tow. She would never leave." Arianne laughed, then caught a whiff of a faintly familiar fragrance. She sniffed Rafferty's card. Patchouli. How apropos that a plant known for its seductive qualities would lend its fragrance to Rafferty. She stirred her finger through the rest of the cards. "I'm afraid these matrons would be shocked to find Rafferty's card touching those of their lofty stature."

"Would they?" Mrs. Summers asked earnestly, then dabbed her lips and chin with the napkin. "He certainly behaves as a gentleman if one can judge from last night. Granted, he hasn't a title, but I wonder if those matrons wouldn't consider him husband-worthy."

True. Even Arianne was beginning to believe Lord Henderson's choice for a British minister may not have been as farfetched as she originally believed. The actress, on the other hand . . .

"Choose another card," Mrs. Summers urged.

She did. "Mrs. Edward Ledsmore. I believe she's shopping for a husband for her niece, Eugenia." She sighed. "It would be nice if just once someone were purely interested in me and not Cupid's Mistress."

Just saying the name reminded her of that misunderstanding the night she first met Rafferty. So much had happened, it seemed so long ago.

"Best pick a few more cards," Mrs. Summers advised. "It'll be some time before you see these people again. Might as well make a full day of it and give Miss St. Claire some well-needed practice."

AS THE BROUGHAM TURNED TOWARD HOME, ARIANNE glanced over at Eva. She was proving to be a marvelous mimic, even managing to adopt Arianne's dialect. Mrs. Summers had been correct; the more calls they made, the more the actress molded to the façade they'd created.

The carriage rolled down Bond Street, passing a doorway mantled in black. The Cardiff residence. Immediately Arianne pounded on the back wall of the brougham, then called out new instructions to the driver.

"We're going to make one more stop," Arianne explained.

"This time to a true diplomat's wife. Her father was the British minister murdered in Washington."

"Lady Weston?" Eva asked.

"Lady Cardiff," Arianne corrected. "Lord Weston was her father."

The carriage rattled to a halt. A footman quickly opened the door and assisted the two women to the pavement. The wide walkway bustled with nursemaids pushing prams, servants and footmen delivering messages, and the occasional young lady on the arm of a gentleman.

"If she is deep in mourning, she may not see us," Arianne cautioned before rapping upon the door. "I hope she does, though. I will miss her company the moment we leave England."

However, her concerns were needless, as the two were promptly welcomed inside. Lady Cardiff, subdued in her black garments and eyes still reddened by recent tears, greeted her with a quick hug. "Thank you," she murmured in Arianne's ear. "Lord Henderson told me of your plans to accompany Mr. Rafferty. I was afraid I wouldn't see you before you left." She turned toward Eva. "And who is this?"

"This will be Mr. Rafferty's hostess," Arianne said. "I was hoping you would be able to offer her some advice."

"Are you a relative of Mr. Rafferty?" Kitty squinted. "A distant cousin perhaps?"

"I'm to be his wife," Eva answered.

Kitty smiled at Arianne. "I see Cupid's Mistress has struck again."

Arianne almost bit her tongue to keep from admitting that it was playacting. The three women settled into the parlor for tea and a brief chat. Kitty offered suggestions to Eva that Arianne imagined were common sense. But then, all discussion of visits and protocol would be new to Eva. Arianne's lessons on etiquette supported Kitty's advice about expectations. After a short while, Eva's lip began to quiver from all she had to absorb. Afraid Eva might change her mind about accepting the role, Arianne suggested the time had come for them to return to the town house.

Glad they had stopped, Arianne led Eva toward the waiting

carriage, but before they'd crossed the pavement, Arianne heard a familiar voice call her name. She turned and froze.

The late afternoon sun glinted off Baron Von Dieter's blond hair. Lips that had kissed her in an intimate fashion lifted in greeting. Heat blossomed on her cheeks. She hadn't expected to see him or his fiancée here, or anywhere for that matter.

She wished she could sink into the pavement and let the earth swallow her so she could avoid this embarrassing meeting. She glanced to the Cardiff residence, but no sanctuary waited there. If only they had stayed just a few moments longer, she might have avoided the Baron altogether. She turned to Eva.

"Would you wait in the carriage?"

"You don't want to introduce me?" Eva said, her nose lifting a notch in the air.

"Please," Arianne insisted, her chest constricting by the minute. "It's a personal matter."

After one last look at the approaching couple, Eva turned and walked to the waiting carriage. Arianne took a deep breath and pasted a pleasant smile on her face.

Miss Sharpe tightened her grasp of the Baron's arm, as if she suspected Arianne would snatch him away. After her humiliation, that was unlikely. However, the possessive gesture made Arianne wonder just how much the woman knew.

"You left Vienna in such a hurry." Baron Von Dieter lifted her fingers to his lips. His gaze held hers and begged for attention. "Much was left unsaid."

She wanted to yank her hand back. No, that wasn't true. She wanted to slap his face. However, neither action would be proper, and both would lead to explanations. Perhaps he felt some shame for his actions and hadn't confided in Miss Sharpe.

Arianne forced a smile and addressed Miss Sharpe. "I apologize for not expressing my congratulations on your engagement earlier. A family emergency had called me away."

"That was not—" the Baron began.

"I hope all is now well with your family," Miss Sharpe interrupted, her gaze narrowed like a satisfied cat. She knew. Blast! There would be little hope of avoiding gossip now. "I do hope we shall see you at the Sugdens' next week."

"Yes." The Baron perused her from head to toe, a wide, salacious grin on his lips. "You must come. We might find a quiet corner to . . . reminisce?"

Arianne stiffened. "I'm afraid I shall be gone next week. I'm leaving for America shortly."

"But I must speak with you!" the Baron insisted. Then, apparently conscious of his fiancée's surprise, he lowered his tone. "If I may . . . before you depart on your journey."

"That will be impossible." All at once, Arianne was perversely pleased that they sailed so soon. "We leave in the morning."

He grasped her arm. "I need to explain. I'll come tonight."

His fiancée gasped.

"No, Karl," Arianne said quietly. "I will not see you."

"May I be of assistance?" Rafferty's familiar voice eased the tightness in Arianne's chest.

The Baron scowled over her shoulder and released her arm.

"Mr. Rafferty," Arianne exclaimed, almost giddy by his timely rescue. But as her gaze darted to Rafferty's face, she questioned if her exhilaration was premature. He looked as if he planned to skewer the Baron on the spot. Surely he couldn't know of the history between the Baron and herself. She tempered her enthusiasm. "I'm so . . . pleased to see you here."

The Baron frowned. "You know this man?"

"Mr. Rafferty is a newly appointed British minister," she said with a smile, "and a dear friend." Rafferty's threatening glare softened as he turned to her. She saw his wariness and . . . enjoyment. Though she wasn't certain if the enjoyment resulted from seeing her, or from challenging the Baron. Either way, she rejoiced to see Rafferty.

A moment passed and then another. Suddenly she realized she had neglected to make introductions.

"I was about to call upon Lord Cardiff," he said, ignoring the others. "We've been meeting for the last week. Would you care to accompany me to speak with Lady Cardiff?"

It was the escape she'd hoped for, but she couldn't return to see Kitty, especially with Eva waiting in the carriage. "I've just come from there myself," she said with a nervous glance to the Baron. "Perhaps you could escort me to my carriage, instead?"

He nodded, extending his arm toward the brougham.

"Good day." She nodded politely to the Baron and Miss Sharpe. As she moved away, Rafferty's hand settled at the small of her back. She stiffened a moment, then relaxed. A delicious warmth radiated up her spine, inspiring an unanticipated confidence. Rafferty winked at her in response, as if they were co-conspirators and he was not rescuing her from an awkward situation.

"A dear friend, indeed," Miss Sharpe snipped behind her. "It just goes to show you can't make a silk purse from a sow's ear."

"Arianne, it wasn't my decision," the Baron called after her.

Her step faltered, but with the subtle pressure of Rafferty's hand, she continued to the carriage without looking back. Miss Sharpe's anguished whispers faded behind her.

Once they reached the carriage, and the offensive couple had moved safely down the pavement, Rafferty dropped his hand from her back. Mourning the loss of that strangely intimate connection, she faced him, embarrassed that he had witnessed her in that predicament. "Thank you," she said, her eyes lowered. "I wasn't prepared to see him so soon."

"I take it he's the reason you are running away?"

She looked up sharply. "I'm not running away," she bristled. "Lord Henderson specifically asked that I assist you. You were there. You heard him."

Rafferty tilted his head in appraisal. "You could have said no."

She didn't respond. To do so would be to admit certain fears that she preferred to keep to herself. She shifted her gaze toward the carriage, then toward the ground behind Rafferty, then toward her hands—anywhere but toward Rafferty's face.

He tipped his hat. "Till tomorrow, then." Then he crossed the wide pavement to the Cardiffs' front door.

Arianne slipped onto the carriage bench, anxious to leave this embarrassing encounter. She hoped Kitty had not witnessed the confrontation and prayed Rafferty wouldn't mention it to Lord Cardiff. Somehow she knew, though, that he wouldn't.

"Who was that man?" Eva asked, once the carriage jolted forward.

"Someone I'd prefer not to remember," Arianne replied. She turned her face away from the window as they passed Baron Von Dieter and his fiancée. Whatever she had once felt for him was gone. "He was someone I thought I knew, but I was mistaken."

· *Eight* ·

ON ANY GIVEN DAY, THE VITAL ENGLISH PORTS bustled beneath the concerns of commerce and transportation, perhaps even more so at the Royal Victoria Dock, which had been constructed specifically for steamships. Hydraulics powered an elaborate system of winches and pulleys lifting massive weights of cargo and lowering them slowly into the deep, cavernous holds of the ocean-bound ships. Or, conversely, relieved the holds of inbound vessels of their precious agricultural goods so necessary for England's growing population. A railway spur added the hiss of steam and squeal of metal to the cacophony of industry. The scent of water, rot, and sweat weighed heavy in the air, reminding all in the vicinity that England was an island dependent on this very activity. Stevedores and dockmen scurried on the earthen banks like ants, servicing the patient metal giants secured to the docks with ropes the thickness of Arianne's arm.

No stranger to traveling by ship, Arianne scanned the hulls of the vessels attached to the dock, searching for one with the name *Irish Rose*. She found it, and her heart sank.

This was not a four-stack liner used to transport large quantities of wide-eyed dreamers in luxurious, and not so luxurious, accommodations. That much was obvious. The *Irish Rose* hadn't even the grace and elegance of the three-mast sailing vessels that still plied the trade to more local shores. The *Irish Rose* appeared more of a plodding draft horse in need of a bucket of oats and a good night's rest before hauling the next day's laden cart.

"Is she safe?" Arianne asked no one in particular. They had debarked from the carriage that carried them to the far east side of London, to the Royal Victoria Dock. While her brother's footmen and porters unloaded the sizeable quantity of luggage needed for a venture of this undertaking, she had wandered down the length of the railway spur in search of their ship.

"She'll get us to our destination in one piece," Rafferty answered. As he and Mr. Connor had not joined them on the trip across London, she wasn't aware they had already arrived. She spun around, surprised to discover he was a few steps behind her.

A proud glint graced his eye, perhaps because they were all about to embark on a mission to track his nemesis. He'd made no secret of his eagerness. His chin pointed to the waiting steamship. "No need to worry on that score."

But she was worried. Whenever she'd traveled over water before, the vessel at least looked seaworthy. This one-funnel monstrosity had passed its prime decades earlier. That is if it had a prime.

"What are those orange brown spots? It looks as if the rose is starting to decay."

He was not amused. "Rust. However, it's only cosmetic. All the important mechanisms function."

That was not especially reassuring. "Isn't there another more substantial vessel we can take?"

"Not that leaves in our time parameters."

She bit her lip. "I can't swim," she confessed.

"What?" he yelled as the train whistle signaled its intent to depart. He took her arm and guided her toward the metal bridge that connected the dock to the deck of their ship. "I can't hear you."

"I can't swim," she repeated, surprised that the admission was easier the second time around.

"That's the whole point of the boat, isn't it?" His eyes crinkled. "Lord Henderson did not ask you to swim across the ocean."

His levity didn't lighten her apprehension, nor did his mention of Lord Henderson. She was well aware that this was not another excursion to avoid going home.

"What if there's a problem and the boat sinks?" she asked, hurrying to keep up with Rafferty's stride. "It's been known to happen."

He laughed. Laughed! "At this latitude, the ocean is so cold that if you were tossed into the waves, it wouldn't matter if you could swim or not." Almost to support his words, a chill wind whipped at her face, tugging the straw brim of her hat. She clasped her shawl tighter with her free hand. They dodged a stack of laden crates. "Your breath would freeze and your arms would be numb before you could move them enough to churn water." He directed her up a flight of metal steps that led to the connecting bridge. Aware of his heavy step behind her, she hastened her climb. "All that fabric would tangle your legs and drag you down to the sandy bottom." She stepped aside at the top of the stairs, and he rose alongside her, a wide grin on his face. "So you see, it doesn't matter if you can swim or not."

The prospect of drowning froze her forward progress. Her feet refused to carry her even the short distance across the bridge.

Rafferty smiled down at her, then tugged her forward. "Don't worry. The *Rose* won't sink. If it will ease your anxieties, I swim like a selkie. I won't let you drown."

She reluctantly set a foot on the bridge. "What's a selkie?" she asked.

"A selkie?" He raised his brow and heightened that delightful brogue in his voice. "They're legendary creatures from Irish folktales. My mother once told me she thought I might be one. Selkies appear mortal on land but revert to seals in the ocean. They can be either a man or a woman, but a man selkie is said to be both very handsome and have great seductive powers over women."

Arianne laughed. "And you believe you might be one of these legendary characters?"

"I suppose that remains to be seen." He offered the support

of his arm while she stepped onto the ship's deck. "But I have managed to seduce you across that bridge and into the care of Captain Briggs."

She looked back, surprised that she had crossed the bridge without anxiety. Rafferty introduced her to a man with wide gray burnsides who waited near the bridge opening. "I'm sure the captain can direct you to your quarters. I want to check with Phineas to make sure all the luggage was loaded correctly and that the other members of our party know the way." He tipped his hat, then began to cross the planking.

"Mr. Rafferty?"

He turned toward her.

"Are we taking this vessel just because it's named the *Irish Rose*?" she teased.

"No, my lady, we are not," he replied, that proud glint returning. "We are taking this vessel because she belongs to me and sails upon my command." He raised his gaze to the captain. "And I command this steamer will get under way as soon as possible."

"As you wish, sir." The captain saluted him, and Rafferty headed back ashore.

Arianne turned to the captain. "Is that true?"

"Yes." The captain held out his arm, indicating their direction. "The Raffertys have been in the shipping business for many years. When his father died, Rafferty's uncle kept the business afloat until the lad could take over. Those were difficult years for all concerned, but we managed. The reputation of the Raffertys keeps us afloat. There's some that ask specifically for the *Irish Rose* to ship their goods." The captain beamed with pride. Arianne had her doubts. Only someone who had not seen the *Irish Rose* would trust their cargo to its keeping.

"Even though he owns the *Irish Rose*, we haven't seen much of Mr. Rafferty these past years. He must be in a hurry to arrive in America, as we'll be traveling light."

"Light?"

"Our cargo holds aren't filled to capacity. We've got some textiles from Ireland and India, some wine and whiskey from Spain and Ireland, and of course, English mercantile, but not as much as we can hold."

"I would think forgoing a full cargo would be expensive."

She glanced about as they progressed down a flight of steps and through narrow hallways. Though the *Irish Rose* was small by contemporary standards, with so few passengers, there should be adequate space and privacy to continue their lessons.

"It is." The captain inserted a key into the lock on the door and twisted. "He's in a hurry, that one."

And Rafferty owned this? She had suspected that he was not the commoner that he claimed, but she had no idea that he was involved in anything outside of the Home Office. She remembered Mrs. Summers's remark that several of the matrons would be interested in Mr. Rafferty for their young charges. At the time, Arianne had scoffed at the idea, but now she had to concede that Mrs. Summers was correct. Rafferty was proving to be a man of many surprises . . . pleasant surprises, she amended, remembering the spreading warmth of his touch on her back yesterday.

Opening the cabin door, she surveyed what would be her home for the next eleven days. She and Mrs. Summers would share what would be considered a second-class room on the big liners. At least the cabin's porthole presented a view of the docklands. Given the sinking feeling in her stomach, she needed that reminder that she wasn't beneath water.

The room was clearly meant for sleeping, as the space wasn't sufficient for more. With that in mind, she made her way back to the top deck for the open air. Spying Eva and Mrs. Summers intently watching the dock below, Arianne glanced over the rail to see what captured their interest.

Rafferty. She smiled. She should have known. Down on one knee, he was crowded on all sides by the filthiest ragtag group of children she'd ever seen. Keeping him in her sight, Arianne made her way to join the others at the rail.

"Where did they come from?" she asked Mrs. Summers.

"I'm not sure. They just appeared," she replied. "I don't think I noticed children on the docks when we arrived."

"He's paying them," Eva said, a combination of awe and annoyance tinging her voice. "See? He's pressing something into their palms." She opened her parasol to shade her face from the sun. "Word spreads quick when there's money to be had. If he's not careful, they'll trample him over to get to his pockets."

Rafferty didn't appear to be in danger, at least not of the sort suggested by Miss St. Claire. The boys looked at him with respect, not as a wealthy mark. And he . . . he regarded them with compassion as well, almost as a family. The thought gave her pause and a different perspective on the surprising Mr. Rafferty.

"HERE YOU GO, LAD. HERE YOU GO." RAFFERTY MADE his way around the group, placing a few coins in the middle of each extended hand. "Thanks for seeing me off, lads."

"Where're you going?"

Rafferty glanced to his right, smack into eyes too big and too worried for the tiny face surrounding them. His heart twisted. The hollows beneath the young one's eyes spoke of hunger, the sort that even the youngest of this wealthy nation shouldn't endure. Rafferty slipped some extra coins into the young boy's hand, then ruffled his head. "Do you remember Phineas? The one with the rabbit?"

The boy nodded. Most of them remembered the magic show Phineas had performed for them on occasion. "Well, Phineas and I are sailing across the ocean to America."

"Will you be coming back?" another asked.

"I always do." Rafferty smiled. He'd left on shorter trips before, but this was different. "I just can't tell you when that will be."

"What're your instructions while you're gone?" one of the older boys asked.

"Keep your eyes and ears open and sharp, especially as it concerns Mr. Barnell. Tell Pickins"—he pointed to an older boy—"if you see something." He turned his gaze to Pickins. "If you think it needs to go higher, tell Lord Henderson. You know where." The boy nodded solemnly.

Rafferty looked around the circle. He'd gotten down on one knee so he could see their faces. They were good boys, loyal and trustworthy, but they knew too much of the hard side of life for such young ages. The *Irish Rose* released a steam blast, an announcement of imminent departure.

"Where's Jamie?" Rafferty asked. The one boy who'd actually seen Barnell's mystery lady was missing from the gathering. "Anyone seen him?"

They each shook their heads, so Rafferty gave a little extra blunt to Pickins to pass along to the missing lad. The captain waved a signal to Rafferty. With the assistance of the boys, Rafferty released the ropes tethering the *Irish Rose* to the dock, then he quickly dashed across the plank bridge moments before it was hauled aboard.

As the boys waved from the shore, Rafferty saw Jamie running toward the group. Jamie waved to Rafferty, then the lad's face slackened a moment before he pointed toward the stern. "That's her, Mr. Rafferty. That's the one."

Rafferty followed the direction of the gesture. The complete roster of the ship's passengers lined the rail, but four women stood in the center, three known to him and the fourth a stranger. The steamer continued to put distance between the boat and the shore. Rafferty cupped his hands around his mouth and yelled, "Which one?" to no avail. The boy continued to point, but Rafferty could not discern a differentiation. One thing was clear, though. A traitor had boarded the *Irish Rose*.

RAFFERTY DID NOT ATTEND DINNER THAT EVENING. Arianne told herself her disappointment stemmed from her inability to see how he interacted with the new passengers. As a British minister, he'd be expected to make new acquaintances on an ongoing basis. If he approached all strangers the same as he had with Baron Von Dieter, this would be a problem. She told herself she needed to observe and critique his methods of initiating conversation, but even she couldn't convince herself that this was the true reason for her disappointment.

She missed him. Clean and simple. She had wanted to ask about the collection of street urchins that had surrounded him at the dock or the meaning of that one boy's pointing gesture. She had hoped to hear the voice whose rhythms played like music to her ear.

Instead, she met their fellow passengers: Mr. Barings, a charismatic London merchant, Mr. Skylar, a shy young man returning to his home in America, and the Shulmans, a German couple excited to travel abroad.

Everyone dressed for the meal, for what else was there to do? The food was adequate, though not to her brother's standards. She recalled Rafferty's warning that the meals would not provide occasion to practice table etiquette. He was correct as it pertained to state dinners. Excellent table etiquette, however, was never wasted, no matter the size of the gathering.

As decided earlier, Eva was to remain Miss St. Claire until the end of the voyage so as to explain their separate rooms. Upon Arianne's insistence, Eva's experience as an actress was not to be mentioned.

Eva's abilities to draw others into conversation impressed Arianne. Perhaps she would succeed as a hostess after all. While that thought should have been satisfying, it wasn't. Arianne couldn't explain why. Indeed the whole day and dinner had been unsettling.

"You look tired," Mrs. Summers said when they returned to their tiny cabin. "Perhaps you'd like to retire early this evening? It has been a tiring day."

Arianne noticed Mrs. Summers had left her knitting out. It would be difficult for her to pursue that activity with the lamps extinguished for sleep.

"I think I'd prefer to take a moonlight stroll," Arianne replied. "Walking might help settle my stomach and the fresh air clear my head."

"Would you like me to come with you?" Mrs. Summers had already swung a shawl over her shoulders.

"No. I should be fine," Arianne said, her hand on the door handle. "I won't be long."

RAFFERTY LEANED OVER THE RAIL, LETTING THE WIND cool his coal-streaked face and billow his unbuttoned shirt like a sail behind him. His collar, waistcoat, and jacket lay in a rumpled heap at his feet. The crescent moon, sometimes obscured by racing clouds, graced the swell of the black waves with a thin white crest, visible one moment, then gone the next.

Throughout the earlier daylight, they had traveled the channel between England and France. Once they had passed the long arm of Cornwall, Rafferty knew his beloved Ireland would lie directly north. Out of his line of sight, but there nonetheless. The *Irish Rose* would continue across the Atlantic to America's eastern shore, carrying him away from his home and all things familiar—except for the killer, the one he hunted. Thoughts of Toomey had plagued him every waking day for so many years, he'd become more familiar to Rafferty than his memories of Ireland. Soon Rafferty would put those tumultuous thoughts to rest.

He heard footsteps approaching and knew Phineas had joined him for the passing ritual.

"Did I miss it?"

"I think we're passing now," Rafferty replied. The captain had sent a message that the *Irish Rose* had moved sufficiently west to be as close as they would come to the green isle. The note had arrived just in time. After working away his frustrations heaving coal in the boiler room, Rafferty needed this quiet moment of self-reflection. Together, he and Phineas stood silent for a few moments at the rail.

"Have you considered the absurdity of it all, Rafe? That you, a son of Ireland, are traveling to America to impersonate a British minister in order to catch a fellow Irishman?"

Rafferty chuckled softly to himself. Phineas's summation was all the more preposterous given this particular would-be British minister was filthy with coal dust and stinking with the sweat of hard labor.

"Which is more ridiculous do you think?" Rafferty asked. "A filthy Irishman as a British minister? Or one Irishman seeking to arrest another when we're both seeking Irish independence?" He glanced at his friend. "Do you think we're doing the right thing?"

Phineas remained quiet a moment or two, all humor gone from his face. "Don't let his politics sway your course. The murder of innocents only serves to inflame the parliament against our cause. You're chasing a murderer who just happens to be Irish."

"I'm chasing my own arse, I think." Rafferty dropped his head between his hands. "Why me, do you think? The Home Office is bloody overrun with titles. Why choose someone like me to play the role of a fancy diplomat?"

"Is that what drove you to join the stokers?"

"I was spoiling for a fight and didn't think you'd be amenable." Rafferty raised a brow in Phineas's direction, but he failed to get a rise out of his friend. Or maybe Phineas just couldn't see his expression buried beneath the coal dust. Either way, Phineas waited patiently, so Rafferty explained about Jamie pointing to Barnell's associate.

Phineas whistled low under his breath. "At least we know it's not Lady Arianne."

"Do we?" Rafferty challenged. "She was at that reception. She was wearing that green dress, and she could very easily be traveling with us to make sure Toomey slips through my fingers once again."

Phineas narrowed his eyes. "You don't believe that."

In his heart, he didn't want to believe that Arianne would have anything to do with the Fenians, but logically he had to keep his heart out of the equation. Rafferty sighed. "At this point, I'm not sure what I believe."

They heard light footsteps and the feminine rustle of skirts before they heard her voice. Both men straightened, and while Phineas turned to greet the newcomer, Rafferty hastened to tuck his shirt into his trousers and pull up his braces.

"Mr. Connor. Mr. Rafferty."

"Lady Arianne." Phineas smiled. "This is a pleasant surprise, isn't it, Rafferty?" He poked Rafferty with his elbow. Frantically working on the uncooperative shirt buttons, Rafe turned his head to call over his shoulder. "Yes. Pleasant surprise."

"Is something wrong, Mr. Rafferty?" Arianne inquired. More curiosity than concern laced her voice.

His shirt was mostly buttoned, but soiled and blackened from the dust on his hands. He retrieved his waistcoat and slipped that over his shoulders, wishing all the while he had access to Phineas's unraveling string of handkerchiefs to wipe the soot from his face.

"Rafferty was building a head of steam," Phineas explained, a hint of humor in his voice. With his top three buttons still undone, Rafferty turned to face Lady Arianne.

"I suppose that's why you failed to join us for dinner," she said. The wind pulled at the wide flat collar on her pristine white dress. She shone in the moonlight like a beacon of purity and virtue. Saint Arianne. He bit back a scowl. Yes, that about explained the gulf between them, a saint and a well-experienced sinner.

"I . . . I was concerned," she said.

"There was no need." Rafferty swiped his hand over his cheeks in an attempt to remove some of the black dust.

"If you'll excuse me," Phineas interrupted, "I need to investigate those discrepancies of which we spoke. Good evening, Lady Arianne. Rafe."

Phineas left them alone in the moonlight on a deserted deck. Rafferty expected Lady Arianne to make some excuse to hurry back to her chaperone rather than share the moonlight with the likes of him.

Instead, she turned her back to the rail, reminding him of her fear of the ocean. Obviously the vast expanse of sea hadn't the calming effect for her as it did for him. "I must admit," she said, "I was hesitant to believe your story of being a selkie. But seeing you like this, I can well imagine you as a black seal darting toward home."

Her easy smile set him at ease.

"Home," he repeated with a glance across the unbroken field of dark water. It had been so long since he'd been back in Ireland. "In a way, I suppose this rusty bucket of a ship is my home. I've spent more time on this deck than on my home soil."

She nodded. "Captain Briggs mentioned that your uncle took you in after your parents died."

"Were murdered," he snapped.

Her smile lessened, and he instantly regretted his sharp rebuke. Just as that guarded expression had begun to fade from her face, he'd gone and snarled at her like a bulldog. He turned toward the water and silently cursed, running his hands through his hair. "It's habit," he explained with self-remorse. "Basil Toomey roams free while my family molders in the ground."

She touched his arm. The contact sizzled through his muscles as if he'd touched a white-hot poker and yet couldn't pull away. "You'll find him," she said, before withdrawing her hand.

He looked down at his arm, noting a clean imprint of three fingertips on his otherwise grimy shirt. "Your gloves," he said with a jut of his chin.

"Oh." She rubbed her filthy fingertips briefly together. "Nothing Kathleen can't clean." An awkward smile twisted her lips, then disappeared. She fidgeted for a moment.

"Tell me about your home," he said, hoping to recapture the easy banter they'd shared before his outburst.

Her face brightened. "It certainly wasn't a ship." She laughed briefly, earning his smile. "My childhood home is in Bedfordshire, but I didn't spend much time there. My father preferred that I stay in schools far away from London."

Her lips pressed tightly together. There was more to the story, he gathered from the pain in her eyes.

"I wanted to thank you for talking me over the bridge," she continued. "I imagine you think it's silly of me to be afraid of drowning. We live on an island, after all."

"I don't think it's silly. Many people have fears that—"

"I saw someone drown once," she interrupted. "One of the girls at school toppled a boat on a lake. She wasn't far from shore, but we couldn't reach her, and she drowned. I'll never forget it."

Her face assumed a ghostly melancholy pallor. He had no doubt that the childhood experience had left a mark. But still she remained at the rail, obviously wishing to talk. He relaxed a bit. "Lord Henderson said that you're well traveled. How did you manage to leave England if you feared the water?"

"I only took short trips to get from one land mass to another, never anything like this." She shivered. Rafferty picked his jacket from the deck and draped it around her shoulders. While he suspected her shake was motivated more by fear than chill, she smiled her gratitude at his gesture. "My brother survived a trip to America. I suppose I will too."

"Is that why you agreed to come?" he asked. Jamie's pointing finger still haunted his thoughts. He doubted she would admit if she were in league with Barnell, but it would comfort him to hear her give a valid reason.

She cocked her head. "It's important that you succeed in this endeavor. While I want to see Lord Weston's murderer brought to justice, I also believe the integrity and reputation of the British legation must maintain a high standard."

There it was. She couldn't have said it any plainer. "You still believe a common bloke like me has no place representing the British government. Just because I haven't some fancy title—"

"Not at all." She turned to him, her eyes searching his face. "I had my doubts in the beginning, but I think that might have been an overreaction on my part. When we first met, I was insulted that you considered me someone's mistress, and I may have inappropriately carried that resentment into that discussion with Lord Henderson."

"But I overhead some fool refer to you as—"

"Yes. I remember that silly nickname." Her sharp glance stopped him from repeating the name that vexed her so. Her smile quirked. "You've shown me both intelligence and knowledge of etiquette. I concede to Lord Henderson's judgment and have no doubt you'll represent England remarkably well." She bit her lower lip, her eyes wide and imploring. "You'll find Lord Weston's killer as well. I have no doubt."

She believed in him! He wanted to kiss her there in the moonlight and finally taste those luscious lips. He wanted to wrap his hands around her tiny waist and kiss her until all thoughts of manners and etiquette and diplomacy were chased from her head. He wanted to show her that her vote of confidence was not misplaced. In fact, in certain areas—such as kissing a fine lady senseless—he quite excelled. However, his hands and his face were covered in coal dust like a common laborer. An elegant, sophisticated woman such as Lady Arianne wouldn't appreciate having her fancy white dress ruined by the likes of him. He balled his hands into fists to keep from reaching for her.

"It's Miss St. Claire that concerns me," she said with a frown.

"Miss St. Claire?" My God, Arianne was radiant. Desire burned in his blood in places the cool night wind couldn't reach. She was fiery determination and dewy freshness and so . . . impeccably clean. His fingernails bit into his palm. She glowed like a goddess beyond his mortal grasp.

"She has an obsession for adulation as if her every appearance should result in applause. I don't believe she'll be able to maintain her façade for an extended period of time, and I don't believe she sincerely cares about the impression she makes." She gazed up at him, soft and yielding. "You deserve someone better than that."

Her words struck him in the gut. She thought *he* deserved better? He who knew the gutters of the docklands better than the wide streets of Mayfair? The one who sought release by pummeling flesh or hoisting a shovel of coal?

The clouds parted, letting moonlight wash over her upturned

face. Intuitively, his head lowered toward hers for just a moment, before he remembered just who it was he was wishing
to explore in the biblical sense. His entire body ached to pull
her tight, to let her feel the effect she had upon him, but he
couldn't. Sister of a duke aside, she deserved someone better
as well. She deserved someone she wouldn't be embarrassed
to introduce to her brothers, someone from her own class,
someone . . .

She lifted on her tiptoes and placed her lips to his. She kissed
him. Ever so gently, ever so innocent, except for a moment's
tug on his lower lip. He stood there, stunned. It wasn't his
imagination, was it? She had kissed him. Him . . . a no-count
common Irishman, covered in sweat and dirt as if he'd crawled
from the very bowels of hell.

But the kiss held no passion, none of the fire that burned in
her eyes when she spoke about diplomacy. She kissed him as
she might have kissed one of her brothers, except for that tug
at the end—*that* held promise.

She gazed sweetly into his eyes. "Good night, Mr. Rafferty."
She turned and began to walk away.

No. He frowned. This would not do at all. Christ almighty!
Not when she was leaving him as hard as the railing beneath
his hand. Not when she initiated the kiss. He clasped her thin
shoulder covered by his jacket. The moment she turned, he
used the empty arms of the jacket to tug her back to him.

His nose trailed the side of hers until his hungry lips found
their match. He felt her hesitation, the immobility of her pert
little mouth, but at the urging of his tongue along the crease of
her lips, she opened. He took full advantage, tasting the sweet
nectar of her mouth, longing to crush her against his chest so
she'd know the full extent of his desire.

Her hands on his chest proved his undoing. A roar sounded
in his ears like the life-giving pulse of the ocean. Keeping his
hands on his jacket, he pulled her closer, wanting to encompass
her, needing to pull her into the yawning emptiness inside.

She broke the contact of the kiss. No matter. His lips explored a path from her earlobe down the soft moonlit skin of
her neck.

"Mr. Rafferty." She pushed against his chest. "Mr. Rafferty,
please."

The moment he recognized her struggle, he froze, then slowly released her. Sweet Jesus! What was he doing? Forcing himself upon Lady Arianne, a saintly woman above his station, a sister of a duke!

She wavered in front of him as if the ship's motion affected her ability to stand. He resisted the urge to hold her steady. As the black smudges on his jacket and on her face showed, he'd done too much holding as it was.

"I must go," she said, though she stood in place. "Mrs. Summers will be expecting me." She started to turn away.

"Wait," he called, stopping her exit. "You best give me the jacket else she'll suspect . . ."

"Yes, of course." She slipped it from her shoulders and held it out to him. "Good night." She turned, then as pretty as you please, walked to the stairs that led below deck. Pausing at the top, she glanced back at him. He wasn't sure if she smiled before continuing down the stairs.

He stood and gazed at the empty stairway, wanting to follow and haul her back to the abandoned deck, yet knowing the impossibility of such an action. Damnation! He frowned. Now he had an entirely different kind of frustration to work off. He grabbed his collar from the deck and started the long descent to the boiler room. At this rate, they'd reach the American shoreline in record time. "Next time, my lady," he murmured to the empty deck. "Next time, I'll be the one doing the initiating. Then we'll see what kind of fire burns within Cupid's Mistress."

· *Nine* ·

SHE MUST BE OUT OF HER MIND, ARIANNE SCOLDED herself. What was it about Rafferty that made her want to ignore society's rules of behavior? The moment she had seen his open shirt flapping behind him like a sail in the wind, she was drawn to his side. He was so intensely male and . . . commanding . . . standing like the lord of the ocean at the rail. She wanted to see his broad chest. She knew it was wrong, but now that she was a ruined woman, there could be no further harm in an innocent peek. Blast that Mr. Connor for blocking her view.

She paused outside her door, fumbling in her reticule for her room key. The process would be easier if her mind wasn't constantly drawn back to Rafferty's bulging arm muscles caressed by the wind and linen. She sighed. How foolish to be jealous of the wind. That man would be best served if he never wore a jacket. How would it feel, she wondered while leaning against the hallway wall, to be held in those strong, taut arms? A sigh escaped her lips. Christopher! Anyone who came down this hallway would think she'd been drinking to excess. Maybe she had, she smiled, recalling the salty taste of Rafferty's lips.

She dug again for the key, but the door opened before her fingers could wrap around it.

Mrs. Summers stood in her nightgown, her eyes rounded like the bottom of two wine bottles. Then they narrowed. "Arianne. Where have you been? You look like you've been cavorting with the devil."

The door across the hall began to open. Mrs. Summers grabbed her arm and pulled her inside the tiny cabin. She smiled across the way. "Good night, Miss St. Claire."

After closing the cabin door, Mrs. Summers turned to Arianne. "Why do you have black soot on your cheek?"

"I do?" Arianne slipped to the washbasin to remove the evidence of her encounter with Rafferty, not that Mrs. Summers would suspect that he was the source of the smudge. It's not that she did anything terribly wrong . . . not like she had with the Baron. Still, she could feel the chaperone's scrutiny of the rest of her attire. Arianne presented her pristine front to Mrs. Summers. "How's that?"

The older woman's gaze slipped from Arianne's face, to her bodice, then her waist, before returning to her face. "You were gone a long time."

"It was a lovely night for a stroll," Arianne said, pretending nothing had occurred. Perhaps some of Eva's acting skills had rubbed off given the time spent in her company. Arianne turned so Mrs. Summers could help unfasten her gown. "My brother says that seasickness hits once the ship crosses into deep water. I don't know if I'll be afflicted like him, but I thought to enjoy a refreshing night stroll while I could take advantage."

Once freed from the back buttons and the flounce and trim of the overskirt, she could step out of her dinner gown. It was fortunate that only her lips touched Rafferty, as the limited storage space meant her gown would have to be worn for another meal aboard the steamer.

"Did you see Mr. Rafferty?" Mrs. Summers asked.

She made the question sound like an accusation. Arianne considered her reply carefully. "I saw Mr. Rafferty speaking with Mr. Connor." She twisted around to see Mrs. Summers. "Why do you ask?"

"I thought perhaps something other than the wind put that flush in your cheeks."

Arianne laughed, then unhooked her corset. "You needn't worry. Nothing happened."

"No?" Mrs. Summers took the discarded corset from Arianne and handed her a night shift. "I failed you once, Arianne. I don't intend to fail you again. From now on, I'll be accompanying you on your night strolls."

Arianne hid her scowl as she climbed into her berth in the tiny cabin. Mrs. Summers extinguished the lamps, thus plunging the room into semidarkness. Moonlight filtered through the porthole, the same moonlight that had shone on Rafferty, starkly highlighting his powerful frame and yet illuminating both conflict and desire in his eyes.

He'd kissed her with a passion that made her knees weaken and awareness sizzle up from her core. That she wanted more scared her enough to break off the kiss. She never wanted the Baron in such a shameful fashion. Was this earthy awakening the legacy of her natural father?

There was no confusing Rafferty's yearning, yet he held something back. At first, she had thought he was concerned about mussing her gown—and that might have been a part of his hesitation. Still, she wouldn't have thought he was a man that would have let a few smudges stand in his way of something he desired. No, there was something else . . .

She certainly hadn't been shy about making herself available for a kiss. A proper lady wouldn't have stood alone on a deserted deck with a man like Rafferty, but then she could hardly be considered "proper" anymore, could she? What harm could an innocent kiss do? She scowled in the darkness. Certainly none if Mrs. Summers held true to her decision to become Arianne's shadow.

She sighed. Tonight was probably the first and last opportunity she'd have to experience any kind of intimacy with Rafferty, or any other man for that matter. But it certainly wasn't the eyes of any other man that haunted her dreams or that currently made her toss and turn in the tiny berth. She reminded herself that she would see Rafferty tomorrow in hopes that knowledge would cure her restlessness. It only made it worse. Christopher! How was she going to survive eleven days?

• • •

THE NEXT MORNING, MRS. SUMMERS ROUSTED ARIANNE at what seemed a particularly cruel hour.

"We're not at your brother's house," she insisted, forbidding Arianne to drift back into slumber. "The captain said that breakfast is available for an hour only. There will be nothing until a light lunch if we miss this opportunity."

Arianne dragged herself to a sitting position. "I'm exhausted. I didn't sleep well."

"Too much fresh air last night," Mrs. Summers pronounced, helping Arianne to dress. "You'd sleep better if you didn't take those strolls after dinner."

Arianne supposed she was partially right, but her sleeplessness had nothing to do with fresh air and everything to do with the man she'd kissed. Now that the moonlight had given way to clear, bold sunlight, Arianne worried about her spontaneity. What did Rafferty think of her impulsive act? Had she been too confident? She was tempted to return to her bed to avoid facing him but then realized that on a ship this size that would be impossible. She might as well get the awkwardness out of the way. Besides, she needed to talk to Rafferty and Eva about a schedule of classes so they'd be properly prepared for their new roles.

She and Mrs. Summers made their way to the dining saloon. Most of the passengers had already helped themselves to the meager breakfast spread. Arianne quickly scanned the room, noting Rafferty's absence. Eva had engaged Mr. Barings in a lively conversation about the state of London theater. While Arianne was pleased to see that Eva could maintain the dialogue without assistance, she worried that Eva might let her theatrical background slip into the conversation.

"I hope she realizes that an actress is not a suitable past for the wife of a British minister," Arianne murmured to Mrs. Summers as she poured tea.

"Let's sit with her," Mrs. Summers said. "If the conversation turns to that territory, I'll steer it in a safe direction."

Arianne obliged, though the theater was not one of her interests. Perhaps that was the reason for her lack of enthusiasm for an actress in this role. That made her pause. Had she let her own preferences discriminate against the choice of Miss St. Claire? She glanced down the table, watching Eva's animated face glow in response to something Mr. Barings had said. No, she decided. More likely, it was a matter of trust. Even now she wasn't sure if Eva's reaction to the conversation was real or acting. And what of Eva's feigned attraction to Rafferty? Was that real?

Arianne set her spoon alongside the barely touched bowl of porridge, her appetite for the wholesome but unappealing dish gone. She was about to return to her cabin when her nose detected a new scent. Warm, exotic, seductive . . . The fine hairs lifted along her neck, and she knew, just knew, that Rafferty had entered the saloon.

A vibrant thrill raced from the tips of her breasts to her feminine core. Dear heaven, what was wrong with her? Even after the Baron had . . . Well, she'd never had this sort of reaction to a kiss. She noted Eva's gaze had lifted to the newcomer. Her lips curved with a knowing appreciation. Mrs. Summers's gaze lifted as well, but not with appreciation. If she hadn't realized it before, her chaperone's glance confirmed that she definitely harbored suspicions.

Rafferty approached the head of the table. "Good morning." The sounds of his voice prompted a delicious warmth to slip through her veins. "Ladies." He nodded a salutation. "I hope you enjoyed a good night's rest."

The dark circles under his eyes suggested he had not. Somehow she found comfort in that. Stubble graced his chin, a thin line beneath his nose, and another thicker patch beneath his lower lip. Lord help her, she couldn't tear her gaze from that patch, which only drew attention to his full lip. How had she managed to muster the courage to kiss that mouth? And how would it feel with that dark, scratchy stubble? Her breasts tingled beneath her confining corset.

"Did you forget to pack your razor, Mr. Rafferty?" Mrs. Summers challenged, an unusually sharp note of accusation in her voice.

Rafferty ran his hand over his chin and smiled. Arianne melted a little.

"My apologies, Mrs. Summers. I overslept this morning and didn't wish to prevail upon the kitchen staff to hold breakfast on my account." A soft curve touched his lips. "I believe Lady Arianne has plans for the use of this saloon this morning."

Their lesson! She'd forgotten that she'd requested the use of this room in between meals. She cleared her throat while her mind scrambled to choose a subject for their instructional setting.

"Yes. I propose we—"

"Lady Arianne?" Eva interrupted. "I'm afraid I'm not feeling well. I wonder if I may be excused this morning? I can rejoin your group in the afternoon, if that is agreeable."

She certainly didn't look unwell, especially for an actress. But as Arianne needed some time to plan how to use their time, she decided not to challenge her. "Of course." She smiled. "Perhaps we all need time to acclimate to our new surroundings. Shall we try again at two o'clock?"

Rafferty smiled at Mrs. Summers. "I'm certain to have located my razor by that hour."

"Lady Arianne and I would be most appreciative," Mrs. Summers replied, her glare as sharp as a dagger.

Oh dear. Arianne rose from her chair with the intent to return to her cabin, knowing Mrs. Summers would follow behind. She needed to have a talk with her chaperone or this journey would be intolerable. She needed to work out a plan for lessons. And she needed time alone to just think. So much had happened in the past week, she had lost her firm footing. When she agreed to this venture, she hadn't counted on an attraction to Rafferty. A ridiculous attraction, she reminded herself. At voyage end, they would part and go their separate ways. One rash decision on her part had already altered her life. She didn't need a repeat performance.

Just then the floor shifted beneath her, as the *Irish Rose* plowed through a swell. She swayed a moment before placing her hand on the wall to balance herself. If only she could balance her life as easily.

LATER THAT AFTERNOON, WHEN ARIANNE AND MRS. Summers returned to the dining saloon, Arianne had determined to approach their first lesson on board as if the events of the preceding evening had not occurred. While Rafferty arrived on time, Eva had still not joined their party, which limited the benefit of her teaching . . . unless . . . She critically studied

Rafferty a moment. "I believe we should make you resemble a diplomat."

"You don't like the way I look?" he asked, eyebrows raised.

That was difficult, because the truth was, she very much liked the way he looked, or more accurately, she liked the way she felt when she looked at him. "You don't look the part."

"For the love of God, woman," he muttered, his face darkening as if thunder could roll from his mouth and lightning shoot from his eyes. "Do we have to go through this again? I know how to dress appropriately. We are on a ship and I didn't think—"

"It's your hair. It's too long."

His jaw slackened. "My hair?" His ire faded by the second. "Now you dislike my hair?"

"I don't dislike it," she said, almost as an apology. "However . . . did you see any of the other men at Countess D'Orange's reception with hair as long as yours?"

"I don't know." He seemed perplexed. "I wasn't looking at the men. I was looking for a woman in a green gown." His eyes sparkled with that mischievous twinkle. "I was looking for you."

"Then trust me in this. None of the other men had hair below their earlobes."

He studied her face a moment. "All right. Then cut it."

"Me?"

"Yes, you. You're the authority on the appropriateness of . . . everything. I place my head in your hands."

Mrs. Summers froze in the act of hemming a skirt for Miss St. Claire. Arianne could feel her chaperone's interest in the discussion even though she hadn't said a word.

"I've never cut hair," Arianne said. "Why not Mr. Connor? Perhaps he can—"

"Phineas!" Rafferty barked a laugh. "Why, he'd chop it all to pieces just to render me a laughingstock. No, I think you should have the honor."

"Mrs. Summers?" Arianne swirled toward her in desperation. "Have you any experience in—"

"No, my dear, I do not. Though I agree with your assessment. His hair defies convention." She dug in her sewing bag. "I'm sure I have a pair of sharp scissors that you can use."

Rafferty shook his head like a wet dog, then threaded his fingers through the hair at his temples, pulling it away from his face. "I insist that no one else cuts my hair," he taunted.

Arianne narrowed her eyes. She'd been so critical of everything about his appearance that he was daring her to fail. "All right then." She rolled up her sleeves. "How difficult can cutting hair be?" She had experimented with cutting hair in finishing school; they all had. But that was only trimming the ends to give a smooth line across the back. Now that she was a mature woman, her hair was artfully piled on her head. A smooth line was no longer expected. "I suppose you should pull a chair over to that basin." She pointed to a basin used to gather soiled plates.

"You're going to cut it now?" His eyes widened.

Ah . . . she saw the chink in his armor. He had expected her to back down.

"Yes, I believe I will. That way if I do no better than Mr. Connor, your hair may recover by the time we arrive in Baltimore."

"Recover?"

"Precisely." She glanced about the room. "We'll need something to collect the hair as it falls. A bedsheet should do. Mrs. Summers, could you ask Kathleen if she could locate two extra bedsheets, shampoo and a comb?"

"Your maid . . . perhaps she has some experience . . . ?" Rafferty asked.

"But you insisted that I have the honor, Mr. Rafferty. That was the word you used," she said, picking up the scissors and snipping the air. "Wasn't it?"

"Next, you'll be telling me to grow a mustache like that Crenshaw fellow."

"Oh no." Her gaze drifted over his upper lip, and her voice dropped. "I would never do that."

Mrs. Summers returned with two neatly folded sheets. The first, they spread on the floor in front of the basin, then waited while Rafferty positioned a chair on top. The second, she tied to cover him. "So you won't get wet. It will be easier to cut if the hair is damp," she explained.

"Good." He smiled. "From the look of those scissors, I was afraid you intended this to be a burial shroud."

"Not yet." She grinned, enjoying the banter. "Just relax, Mr. Rafferty." She pressed his shoulders down so that he'd slide to the edge of the seat. "Lean back and let me pour water over your hair."

"Somehow this is not how I envisioned an etiquette lesson."

"Neither had I." She tested the temperature of the water. "But we do what we must."

LORD GOD IN HEAVEN! DID THE WOMAN NOT REALIZE what she was doing?

As she leaned over him to turn on the faucets, the sculpted mound of her breast hovered an inch from his lips. His eyes fixed on the fullness of her, watching the rise of her lacy blouse as it teased and taunted with its close proximity. He clenched his teeth, tempted as he was to catch the froth between them and pull her near. She was so close, he could almost see her lady corset beneath the blouse and the gentle swell above. Lean a little closer, he prayed, imagining his tongue coaxing her rosy nipples into unladylike nubs of arousal.

Suddenly, warm water, comforting as a leisurely bath, flowed over the top of his brow and around the sides of his face. Like a fine Irish whiskey, it warmed and soothed, before her hand, soft and gentle, followed the path of the water. His groin tightened. He firmly gripped the arms of the chair, attempting to cease the decadent thoughts the warmth, the water, and her teasing breast inspired.

"Is the water too cold?" she asked. "I thought you flinched."

Lord help him, he couldn't be held accountable for his lips if he unclenched his teeth to speak. Instead, he shook his head, the action liberating droplets of water like some shaggy beast. A few drops found their way to the linen covering her chest, and satisfied with the surroundings, the drops began to spread.

He should close his eyes. A gentleman would close his eyes. His lips curved. Fortunately, he never claimed to be a gentleman. He watched the moisture spread into a small circle of translucence. An obscured view of a blue ribbon threading through lace appeared beneath her blouse. His imagination filled in the rest.

Arianne gathered his dangling locks into a queue. With a firm hand she secured it to the back of his head, then slowly dragged the other hand down its length, presumably pushing the water before it. He closed his eyes, imagining her competent hands wrapped around another length doing much the same thing. Once. Twice. Without thinking, he issued a soft groan.

She stopped. "Am I hurting you? Did I pull too hard?"

Sweet Jesus, how was he to answer that? Beneath the sheet and his clothes, he could feel his cock fighting for similar ministrations.

"It's all right," she said, straightening. "I think we're ready to cut now."

He carefully pushed himself to a sitting position, letting the sheet hide his arousal. He grimaced, imagining her horror if she knew. As if her soft lady hands would ever touch anything so . . . so . . . much in need.

"You're awfully quiet, Mr. Rafferty." She pulled a comb through his wet locks. "Are you afraid of my talent with scissors?"

He rubbed his chin. Arianne's obvious talent was precisely what he did not wish to discuss. "No. I was just thinking I'm glad I shaved before I came here. Wouldn't want you taking a straight blade to my neck."

She laughed and parted his hair down the middle to his forehead. "That's unlikely. I've not—" He jerked upward, catching her by surprise. "What's wrong?"

"No, you don't." He racked his fingers through his wet hair, obliterating the center part. "You can cut my hair, but you won't turn me into one of your dandies."

"One of my what?" She frowned down at him, then shook her head. "The symmetrical look with a center part is all the rage in London."

"If you'll look out that porthole, you'll note we're not in London anymore."

"I hadn't realized you were so vain, Mr. Rafferty." A gleam shone in her eye.

"Not vain, just . . . just . . . I won't look like one of those," he grumbled, imagining the guffaws were he to appear at his old haunts all sissified.

"One of those what?" she asked, perplexed.

"A sod, woman." He could feel his face redden. Next she'd be complaining that he'd used such banal language in the presence of a lady, but what was he to do? She'd forced it out of him.

His hand pushed the wet hair to the right. "Just . . . just part it on the side."

The comb scraped a new path. He'd just begun to relax when a new horror struck him. "And no side curls. No matter what the fashion in London."

She laughed again, and his fears abated. "I promise."

So he relaxed, listening to the snip of the scissors and experiencing the pleasant sensation of her fingers threading through his hair. She moved about him, lifting sections, then snipping off the ends. Every now and then she would stare intently into his face, not really seeing him, but moving her gaze from side to side.

She was so above his station, did she ever really see him? Or had her attention always been of a cursory manner? She had flawless skin, he noted. And clear blue eyes that he knew from experience could shift in a moment from the color of a sun-filled sky to that of a thunderhead rolling swift over the water.

Every time she moved, the faint scent of roses stirred in her wake. She must have an entire floral shop at her disposal. He'd have a hard time seeing a nosegay in another woman's hand and not thinking of Arianne. Good Lord, was she ruining him for other women? He hoped not, for surely once the *Irish Rose* reached its destination, she'd be gone, and he'd be on his own.

"Mrs. Summers, can you look at this?" she asked, uncertainty in her voice. "His hair isn't lying as flat as it should."

Mrs. Summers crossed to stand behind him. "Oh dear."

The sympathetic tone of her voice caught his ear. "What?" he exclaimed. "I thought you knew—"

"I'm not a barber, Mr. Rafferty," Arianne said. "Your hair doesn't look bad; it's just not as I envisioned."

"Where's a mirror?" He stood, letting the sheet covering him fall to the floor. It wasn't that he was vain, he assured himself; he just didn't wish to look like a fool.

"Doesn't it feel more comfortable?" Arianne edged backward toward a china cabinet, her smile uncertain. Did she just hide a hand mirror behind her back? "Lighter perhaps? I removed a great deal from the back."

He ran his hands down the back as if they had eyes to see. The hair was indeed shorter, but if his fingers were an indication, disheveled. He pulled a knife from his boot and tilted the flat shaft in an effort to see his reflection. The front wasn't as bad as he expected.

"You must admit the shorter hair gives you a more dignified appearance," Arianne said.

"The dignity of a man comes from more than the cut of his hair," Mrs. Summers intoned.

"But it can be jeopardized if the man resembles a fool." Rafferty turned his head from side to side, but he still couldn't see the back.

"Sorry, I was detained," Eva said, walking into the saloon. "I'm afraid the motion of the boat—" Her eyes widened. "What happened here?"

Her tone confirmed his suspicions.

"I was trying to make him look more respectable," Arianne said, her voice apologetic. "But I've never cut a man's hair and now . . . well . . . He can't always wear a hat."

Eva strolled over and brusquely ruffled her fingers through Rafferty's hair. He fought to keep his annoyance from his face. "I can fix it," Eva said. "I've fixed worse."

"Thank you." Relieved, Arianne hugged her. "You've come to our aid again. Thank you so much."

Eva picked up the scissors and moved them deftly across the back of Rafferty's head. Eva shaped his hair on a diagonal, and while the end result was shorter than even Arianne intended, it didn't look bad.

"It's all a matter of following the shape of one's head." Eva stood back to observe her work. "There. Much better. Is there a hand mirror so he can see?"

Arianne shyly produced the one she'd hidden. She should be grateful for Eva's intervention. And she was . . . but once again she'd fallen short. Lord Henderson had recommended her as an expert, yet none of the lessons she'd prepared for Rafferty seemed to be working the way they should. Perhaps the Baron was right. She wasn't all she should be.

Rafferty employed the hand mirror and beamed his thanks to Eva while Arianne looked on.

Phineas interrupted. "I was wondering, Lady Arianne, if I might borrow the likes of Rafferty for a moment."

Rafferty stood. Phineas broke into a wide smile. "Well now, you look like a proper Englishman, and not the devil himself." He glanced at Arianne. "I do believe you may have created a silk purse from a sow's ear."

Rafferty grumbled something, but Arianne didn't really hear it. Instead she was remembering those same words from Miss Sharpe. *You can't make a silk purse from a sow's ear.*

"That would take more than a haircut," Rafferty grumbled.

"My thoughts exactly," Arianne said, thinking of the Baron. Perhaps he wasn't the catch she had imagined.

· Ten ·

THE *IRISH ROSE* HAD CROSSED INTO DEEP WATER. Arianne knew this, not by the change in the color of the sea or the shift in the taste of the air, though both of these things occurred, but by the increased roll and pitch of the vessel. Walking on deck was difficult, but staying in an enclosed room even more so. The fresh air helped keep one's stomach settled, but Arianne was troubled by the small explosions of spray that fell like rain on the deck when the bow sliced through a wave with a thud. The salty water splashed on board in its attempt to pull the vessel under, then scampered through the drainage holes with a hiss of failure to return to the sea. She reminded herself of Rafferty's assurances that the *Irish Rose* was seaworthy, but the hissing water whispered otherwise.

Eva, as well as several other passengers, stayed in their cabins, victims of mal de mer. However, after two days of such confinement, they ventured forth. Arianne renewed her efforts to teach Eva and Rafferty the proper rules of conduct. They discussed the fourteen different types of forks and the eleven types of spoons. Rafferty left before they covered the knives. She reviewed the responsibilities for maintaining the household, the responsibility and management of the servants, the rules on invitations and seating for dinner parties, and the rules for proper dress for various occasions. Arianne grew tired of hearing herself speak, and she imagined Eva and Rafferty felt much the same.

After dinner each night, the passengers tended to linger about the dining saloon, playing cards, watching Phineas practice his magic tricks, and often indulging in drink. Inevitably the group would erupt in song. One evening, Mr. Skylar brought a fiddle to the saloon and accompanied the boisterous group in their medley. The music inspired Arianne.

"We are going to have a dance," she announced.

"Dance?" Rafferty shook his head in disbelief. "You wish to stage a dance on the *Irish Rose*?"

"I love the idea!" Eva leapt up in pantomime of a waltz.

"There's not enough room," Rafferty scoffed. "This isn't the White Star Line."

"I'm well aware of that," Arianne murmured irritably, then forced a smile. "I've spoken with Mr. Skylar. He volunteered to play some melodies on his violin so that you and Eva might have the opportunity to dance together. You'll be expected to do as much in Washington."

"Just Eva and I?" His gaze held such intensity and promise that her mouth dried to the consistency of the calling cards about which she had earlier lectured. She had difficulty framing a reply when Eva came to her rescue.

"Mr. Barings will want to join us, and I'm sure that German couple will want to dance as well. Certainly one of the gentlemen will wish Lady Arianne as a partner." She twirled by on one of her rotations around the dining saloon.

"Yes. One of the men most certainly will," Rafferty replied. She noted his omission of "gentle." "However, I'm afraid I haven't the proper clothes available for a dance." His lips lifted in a smirk, a jest.

"As this will be a lesson and not a public soiree, the appropriateness of attire is not as important as it would be otherwise," Arianne counseled, wondering about his many excuses. "Mr. Rafferty, you do know how to dance, don't you?"

The smirk faded. "The dancing I've done would not be appropriate for your aristocratic parties. Just as the dancing you've done would not be appropriate for mine."

"Then I suppose that's all the more reason we should practice," she insisted, choosing to ignore his scowl. "Tonight after dinner we can meet near the stern where there's sufficient room for several couples."

Eva ended her dancing demonstration by hugging Rafferty's neck. She leaned close to his ear. "Tonight, we'll dance under the stars."

AS EVA HAD PREDICTED, THE NIGHT SKY GLITTERED with stars that sparkled like cut diamonds flung to the heavens. Kathleen helped Arianne into a walking suit of gray toile that was destined to be altered to suit Miss St. Claire. While it wasn't the most current of fashions, Arianne always liked the fuller skirt and the bold black trim. As she anticipated watching Eva and Rafferty dance, and not participating herself, she'd chosen a suit for the brisk night air. After witnessing Eva's earlier display of affection, Arianne wasn't quite as enthused about this evening's entertainment as she had been when she first conceived the idea. Eva arrived on the deck with one of Arianne's altered dinners gowns, a pale green satin and lace. She looked lovely, Arianne thought, and sure to catch Rafferty's attention.

For his part, Rafferty joined the party looking stunningly handsome in a chesterfield jacket and crisp white shirt. Arianne began to wonder if there ever was an occasion when his appearance didn't take her breath away. Phineas accompanied him to the deck, but with harmonica in hand, he joined Mr. Skylar on the metal housing that made a makeshift stage.

They began with a waltz. As Arianne had suspected, Rafferty pleaded ignorance of the steps. Once Arianne demonstrated, he led Eva about the stern, managing to trounce on her toes only two or three times. Eva refused to dance with him on the next song, complaining her toes needed to recover. She did, however, accept Mr. Barings's invitation to waltz. Arianne made a mental note to speak to Eva about the etiquette surrounding the acceptance and refusal of dance invitations.

"Would you honor me with a dance?" Rafferty asked her, hesitantly.

"The honor would be mine," she replied. She placed her hand lightly on his forearm, feeling the hard muscle there. He slid his hand up and down her side as if searching for just the right spot to hold her. His hand settled at the curve of her waist, but there was nothing settling about the awakening beneath his fingers. A comforting heat spread through her frame in all directions and ignited in the most private of areas. He stroked the inside of her arm from her forearm to her elbow before lifting her hand. Stimulation tingled up her arm even through the barrier afforded by her jacket.

"Shall we?" he said with a lopsided grin. The music began, and he guided her through the steps. He was stiff and uncertain, but he only stepped on her toes once. His concentration centered on the count and not her; still, she enjoyed the sway and swirl of the waltz held in his arms. The music came to an end.

"Again," Rafferty called to the musicians.

"Are you sure you don't want to try something else?" Arianne asked. "Perhaps a galop?" She saw Captain Briggs swirl by with Mrs. Summers on his arm. She smiled in amazement, not having actually seen Mrs. Summers dance before. "I believe we have enough to try a quadrille."

"No," he replied, narrowing his eyes. "I want to master this . . . with you."

That familiar look of determination, the one she remembered from the reception, settled in his gaze. If Rafferty approached everything with the same intense determination as he did the waltz, she could understand Lord Henderson's faith in the man.

"Very well," she said. "Then look at me, not your feet. Don't count; listen to the flow of the music. When you're ready . . ." She captured his gaze, hoping to distract him from that intense focus. She succeeded. She saw it in the softening of his jaw. "Then so am I."

They soared together across the stern of the *Irish Rose* beneath the approving stars. His initial apprehension faded, replaced by surprise and then desire as they swirled with the violin. When the last note was played, his hungry gaze slipped down to her lips. She thought he might kiss her, there in full view of the passengers. She dismissed the warnings and alarms sounding in her head. She wanted his kiss. She longed for his kiss. She parted her lips.

"Arianne." Mrs. Summers tapped her arm. "Miss St. Claire would benefit more from Mr. Rafferty's attention."

The spell was broken. "Yes," she said, gazing into Rafferty's eyes, watching regret replace desire. Or were those her own emotions reflected in his eyes? She stepped back. He hesitated a moment before he released her arm. "I suppose she would," she said, though not convincingly.

Arianne once again resumed the role of teacher as she watched her students practice the waltz without the passion she'd felt in Rafferty's arms. She noted that Rafferty kept his gaze on Eva, and she didn't offer any complaints of sore toes.

"This dance was a delightful idea," Mrs. Summers observed. "They make a wonderful couple, don't they?"

Arianne chose to keep her opinions to herself. "I saw you dancing with Captain Briggs," she said.

"He's a lovely man," Mrs. Summers replied, a bit flustered. "He has been explaining to me all about the navigation of the ship and the taking of soundings. He's really very brilliant."

"That's reassuring," Arianne said. At least one person on the boat was brilliant. It certainly wasn't her. Rafferty would waltz out of her life in just a few days. Knowing that, a brilliant person would put her emotions under lock and key.

"A wonderful couple," Mrs. Summers said again as Rafferty and Eva swirled past. "A perfect match."

THE NEXT DAY, ARIANNE DESPAIRED AT THE LIMITED confines of her cabin, the boat, and unfortunately, the company. Mrs. Summers seemed ever underfoot. Arianne was free of her only when she was teaching the etiquette class, and that aspect of the trip had become humdrum and monotonous.

She watered the plants she'd brought from England, then fussed with her vials of fragrance out of boredom. Kathleen had reported that Miss St. Claire would again not be present for a morning etiquette lesson. If today was similar to the previous week, Arianne suspected the actress would make a surprising recovery by afternoon.

"Is it seasickness?" she'd asked Kathleen.

"I wouldn't know, miss," the maid had replied, averting her gaze.

Once Kathleen had finished her duties and left, Arianne repeated her question to Mrs. Summers. "Do you think Miss

St. Claire is truly ill, or do you suppose there is another cause for her absence?"

Mrs. Summers looked over her glasses. "What are you suggesting?"

"I just wonder . . ." Arianne took a seat across from Mrs. Summers. "She's always ill in the mornings. My brother said that when he made the crossing he was ill at all times."

"Then perhaps it's not seasickness," Mrs. Summers replied dispassionately. "She's an actress eager to leave London. She could be with child, but that shouldn't matter, as she's playing the role of a contented wife."

"Contented wife. I believe my mother's experience shows that to be a contradiction in terms."

Mrs. Summers put down her pen. "Your mother was an exception, Arianne, not the rule. Many women find joy in marriage."

"Joy?" Arianne made a pretense of sniffing at an opened bottle of lavender water. She had thought there'd be joy in submitting to one's husband, or one's soon-to-be husband. However, her experience with the Baron had divested her of such foolishness. She recapped the bottle. "I don't see why. Anyway, as Eva is not married, this conversation is pointless."

Mrs. Summers cocked her head, then removed her glasses. "Is something wrong? You seem particularly snippy of late."

Arianne opened her mouth to protest but realized Mrs. Summers had a point. She shrugged and placed the lavender water back in her traveling case. "I suppose I'm bored. There's not much to do on this ship. I've already read the book I brought for this crossing. There are no newspapers to follow the events of the day." She stood and stretched her arms. "I'm weary of card games, I've seen all of Phineas's magic tricks, and there aren't many people to talk to." She decided not to mention her discomfort at the "contented wife" observation in regard to Miss St. Claire. She wasn't certain why the concept pricked her so.

Mrs. Summers sighed. "I don't know how you will ever survive living alone in that country house. You thrive on the excitement of city living."

"I won't be alone," Arianne said. "You'll stay there with me, won't you?"

Mrs. Summers glanced at her. "Perhaps you should go up to the top deck for some fresh air. Captain Briggs mentioned Mr. Rafferty maintains quite a selection of books in his quarters. If you speak to the captain, I'm certain he could arrange for you to borrow a few."

It was a good idea, and she could use something new to read. Smiling, she reached for her gloves and parasol. "Captain Briggs. Not Mr. Rafferty?"

Mrs. Summers placed her glasses back on her nose and picked up her pen. "I imagine Mr. Rafferty, like Miss St. Claire, is difficult to find in the mornings. It wouldn't surprise me if the two are taking their married roles seriously."

That made her pause. Arianne's smile faded. "I won't be long," she said as she left the cabin.

THE SEA BRINE GREETED HER BEFORE SHE OPENED THE door that separated the steps from the top deck. She hoped to see Rafferty, just to remove the sore taste left from Mrs. Summers's comment, but he was nowhere to be seen. She stayed as far from the rail as she could manage, though it was difficult not to catch the expanse of the ocean from the corner of her eye. Anxiety tumbled in her stomach, not unlike the powerful engine that drove the *Irish Rose* forward amid great rumbling and vibration. With one hand on the metal housing of the interior and the other clasping her parasol, she walked toward the bow and under the raised area the captain had called the bridge. The exercise felt invigorating, the day pleasant. She turned toward the stern, and about midship, she noticed a gathering of men and boys cheering and shouting. She could only see the backs of the crowd, but curiosity pulled her forward.

She meant to stay on the outskirts of the bawdy crowd, but a group of gawking young men joined in the fray behind her. Soon she was jostled into the midst of the gathering. She spied Phineas watching and cheering along the inner ring of the group. She worked her way to his side.

"Lady Arianne," he said. "What are you doing here?"

A dull thud rent the air followed by a loud cheer. She turned toward the middle of the circle to see Rafferty in fisticuffs with a swarthy, bare-chested bear of a man. Her jaw dropped in shock. Blood trickled from Rafferty's nose and spotted his shirt.

"Hit him again!" someone yelled.

The larger man pulled back his fist. Arianne was about to shout "No!" but before the words could leave her mouth, Rafferty adeptly shifted his weight, avoiding the punch. Her lips pressed in a line. This was ridiculous. Someone would get hurt with such nonsense. She lowered her parasol, thinking to use it as a weapon to knock sense into the two fighting men. Phineas's arm barred her way before she could step forward.

"Let them fight," he said. "Rafferty can hold his own."

Indeed, she saw Rafferty land a punch to the man's ribs. Before the larger man could recover, Rafferty followed with his left hand, catching the man on his chin. He staggered back from the blow, and the crowd cheered.

Her eyes slipped over Rafferty's muscular form, his broad back, the confidence of his movements. A delicious sort of appreciation washed over her and settled in her belly. A lady shouldn't enjoy such an exhibition of brute strength. But she couldn't deny that in this instance, she did. Unlike his opponent, Rafferty fought in his shirt and braces. She found herself wishing he weren't such a man of decorum.

"Why are they fighting?" she shouted to Phineas.

"Why else? Boredom and ignorance." He pointed to Rafferty's opponent. "The big bloke there is new to the *Rose*. He insinuated that Rafferty was a traitor, so Rafferty punched him."

Phineas's tone suggested Rafferty had no other choice. She watched the two of them grapple as if in some strange primitive dance. The oaf threw a punch that missed its intended target but caught Rafferty's shoulder. Rafferty landed a punch with much greater effect.

"Why would anyone call Rafferty a traitor?" she asked. Perhaps this was the ignorance to which Phineas had alluded.

Phineas glanced at her askance. "You really don't understand the emotional pull of home rule, do you?" he added as cheers accompanied another of Rafferty's punches.

"I know that home rule is the term some use for an independent Ireland."

Phineas nodded. "England hasn't granted that independence, so England is often viewed as the enemy by the Irish. Rafferty works for England. So the Irish—" His sentence was interrupted by more cheers.

"Call him a traitor," Arianne finished. How ridiculous. Anyone who knew Rafferty would know of his love of Ireland. "I suppose that's what you meant by ignorance," she yelled over the noise of the crowd.

Phineas shook his head. "I meant that anyone who challenges Rafferty to a fistfight is a bloody fool." Then he smiled. "But the other is true as well."

As if to punctuate that observation, Rafferty's fist connected to the larger man's jaw with a bone-to-bone crunch. The oaf staggered for a moment, then crumpled to the ground. The crowd swarmed into the center of the circle, reaching to pat Rafferty on the back. On the far side of the circle, Mr. Barings exchanged money with another man. They weren't the only ones.

Many of Rafferty's exuberant well-wishers, she noted, were gawky older boys and young men—reminding her of those boys on the dock. They surrounded him, reaching out to pat his back or shake his hand. As Rafferty moved, so did his followers.

Someone dumped a pail of water onto the "bloody fool." The man sat up and shook his head like a dog in the rain. Rafferty reached a hand down and helped him up. They shook hands, though she wondered if the oaf was fully aware of his actions. Then Rafferty turned toward Phineas and froze.

His gaze searched hers. He raised his arm to wipe the blood and sweat of battle on his sleeve, all the while jostled by his supporters.

She wasn't sure what she should do. She didn't truly condone fighting in such a brawlish manner. Certainly it wasn't the sort of thing in which a diplomat should indulge. But at the same time, she was proud of him, gladdened by his success. He'd stood up for himself and didn't allow the oaf to besmirch his name. In hindsight, she wished she would've done something similar for herself when the Baron made her out to be a fool. Her lips slipped into a smile. Good for Rafferty.

His lips hesitantly turned up as well. Soon she could see his dimple flash even as he was jostled by the well-wishers. Then, Eva stepped from the crowd. She rushed to Rafferty, brushing a moistened handkerchief against his injuries.

It wouldn't surprise me if the two are taking their married roles seriously. Mrs. Summers's words struck at Arianne's heart as she watched Eva's ministrations. The woman certainly didn't look ill as Kathleen had reported that morning. Eva hadn't dressed in a fashionable day dress. Her long hair lifted loose in the breeze, she didn't wear a hat, nor did she carry a parasol. She had none of the required accoutrements for the role she had deigned to play, yet she had Rafferty's full attention as she dabbed the cloth near the corner of his lip. Instantly, Arianne realized she didn't fit here, in this gathering. She had not been invited nor particularly wanted.

Being the outsider, the misfit, was not unfamiliar. She knew the tightening of the throat and heaviness in her stomach from the holidays she stayed at school because her father didn't want her home. That sense of dismissal was revisited when so many men avoided her simply on the basis of that ridiculous nick-name. She was the intruder, the one that didn't belong, just as she had been for most of her life. The one others carefully walked around, afraid to touch . . . afraid to love . . . afraid to marry.

Phineas turned to collect a wager and didn't notice as she joined the dissolving crowd. No one missed her as she walked away. No one noticed the straightened spine or her rapid blink-ing to keep tears at bay. Mrs. Summers was wrong. Arianne knew she'd be perfectly content in her country sanctuary away from the people who would hurt her by exclusion, gossip, and rejection. She didn't require their presence any more than they requested hers. Once she delivered Rafferty and his actress to their Washington destination, she'd book a ticket on the largest steamer she could find and retire to the country where she wasn't constantly confronted with all that she was not.

RAFFERTY TURNED HIS HEAD TO SEE ARIANNE, BUT SHE was gone. Part of his victory elation drained out of him. Where did she go? He had expected her to be disappointed that once again he hadn't lived up to her diplomatic standards. He had failed her. But then she smiled, almost as if she was proud of his victory. What a moment that had been . . . and now . . . was gone.

The crowd dispersed as the men returned to their stations. Rafferty thanked Eva for her attentiveness, then accepted the congratulations of Mr. Barings, who appeared by her side. That done, he made his way to where Phineas counted his winnings before anyone else could intervene.

"I'm pleased to see that you made a profit on my fists," Rafferty observed.

"I'm not a foolish man, Rafferty. I take advantage when I can." Phineas shook the hand of the man who had just paid him.

"Lady Arianne was here. Where did she go?"

"Go?" Phineas glanced around the deck. "She can't be far." He smiled at Rafferty. "It's a small ship."

Rafferty cursed beneath his breath. Phineas was of no help. "I can't go running after her. Not smelling and looking like this." Rafferty checked the starboard side for the seductive swish of skirts beneath a lacy parasol. Finding none, he turned back to Phineas. "Did Kelly have supporters?"

"Only the foolish ones that believe size is all that matters," Phineas said. "Every dog has supporters when money rides on the outcome."

Rafferty nodded, hesitant to ask the question for which he was afraid of the answer.

"She was worried about you," Phineas said, his voice lowered. "I could see it in her eyes . . . and indignant that someone would challenge your loyalty."

"Indignant?"

Phineas nodded. "If I hadn't stopped her, she would have taken Kelly on herself. She pointed that parasol like a military general."

The image of Arianne as a general made him smile. She would preside over the battle as she had over an eleven-course meal. That the very proper sister of a duke was willing to do battle to defend his name lessened the recurring sting of accusation. But that didn't explain why she left.

"What about Eva?" Rafferty asked.

"I didn't see her until the fight was over. Do you still think she's the lady in green?"

"It would make the most sense." Rafferty pushed his hair back. He had to admit, even if Arianne did butcher his hair, the cut was more comfortable on a warm day such as this. Glancing down the main deck again, he wondered why he felt the need to find her. He'd see her in an hour or so for another of those blasted lessons, when she would criticize something about his clothes, his manner. Perhaps this time she'd criticize the way he held his fists, his fighting stance. The thought brought a smile to his lips.

"Go," Phineas said. "Wash up for your diplomat lessons. I'll ask around to see if anyone wanted your blood for more than the shillings a wager would bring. Maybe that will lead to the lady in green."

So Rafferty returned to his cabin for a quick wash and a change of shirt. However, when he reported to the saloon, Mrs. Summers was there alone.

"Lady Arianne is not feeling well," she said, her eyes narrowed in accusation. "She asked that I take her place."

Eva arrived, dressed in one of Arianne's reworked day dresses.

"Now that you are both here, we'll start with a review of the salutations of the various foreign heads of state by country and hierarchy. We shall begin with the Russians . . ."

· *Eleven* ·

"A STORM IS BREWING," PHINEAS COMMENTED AS the lone server placed bowls of a thin soup before the diners. "It's building in the east. Looks like we'll be in for some rough weather."

"A storm?"

Rafferty glanced to Arianne. Those were the first words he'd heard from her lips today. Normally she was the perfect conversationalist, engaging those around her to exchange pleasantries. But she'd kept her gaze to her plate thus far this evening, avoiding conversation. Just as she had all day by hiding in her cabin. Just as she intended to continue hiding if those fear-rounded eyes were any indication.

Captain Briggs cleared his throat. "I'm trying to avoid it by running south. The worst of it should pass behind us, but I've instructed the cook to serve a light meal, just in case. It's going to be a horse race."

Mr. Barings groaned. "Don't speak to me of races. I've lost one purse already."

"With your experience behind the wheel, I'm sure we'll be in no danger." Mrs. Summers smiled at Captain Briggs. Rafferty could swear that the man's chest expanded with the compliment. Come to think of it, Briggs had been taking supper with the passengers more frequently this week.

"You shouldn't have bet against Mr. Rafferty," Arianne interjected, catching Rafferty's attention.

What's this? She was defending him? She raised her gaze to meet his.

"He was fighting for his honor," she said. "One should take extraordinary measures to protect their honor. Once lost, it is irretrievable."

There was such a haunted, almost desperate quality to her eyes that for a moment he thought she spoke from experience. That wouldn't be possible. Not for Lady Upper Crust. He captured her gaze, but after a pause she glanced aside.

"While I don't approve of the brutality of pugilism," Mrs. Summers said, "I'm not aware of this question of honor. What precipitated the disagreement?"

"A bloody brute of a man suggested Mr. Rafferty was not a true son of Ireland," Phineas said.

"There are those," Rafferty said, "that believe indiscriminate bombings are the only path to independence. I am not one of them."

"Yet you resorted to violence to protect your claim." Mr. Barings picked up his wineglass and leaned forward. "Interesting. Don't most disputes for independence result in a war?" Eva fidgeted beside him, a telling nervous gesture. "Perhaps your objection is not to violence but to independence itself," Barings concluded.

The sound of silver hitting china echoed round the table. Rafferty withdrew his bandaged knuckles to his lap. "What precisely are you suggesting, sir?" he challenged.

"I'm suggesting it was wise of Lord Barnell to have you sent to America so you wouldn't disrupt his important work back in England."

"Lord Barnell . . . ?" Rafferty repeated. Could it be true? Could Barnell be behind Rafferty's selection as British minister? He glanced to Arianne as if she held the truth.

"How soon will we reach America, Captain?" Eva asked with a tense smile.

"A lot depends on how much this storm blows us off course.

You never know about a good storm at sea. However, I'd guess we should pull into port within two days."

Rafferty narrowed his eyes in Barings's direction. "Remind me, sir, what is your business in America?"

"I've some family there that I've never met. I thought I'd take time to see a bit of the countryside, possibly expand my business overseas."

"I, for one, will be happy to have Mr. Rafferty in America," Mr. Skylar, the shy American, spoke, diffusing some of the tension at the table. He hadn't been to many of the dinners this week and avoided conversation when he did. "That's why I came to dinner this evening," Skylar said, as if reading Rafferty's thoughts. "I wanted to congratulate you. You really put on quite a show this morning."

"Are you a pugilist, Mr. Skylar?" Mrs. Summers asked.

Rafferty thought the question silly, as one could easily see that the man fought little more than the occasional book.

"Not really," Skylar said, with a wince. He turned his gaze to Rafferty. "But I'd like to learn if you could show me some of your punches."

"Of course," Rafferty replied. "The early morning is best. We can practice on the top deck."

Arianne wrinkled her brow as if confused. Surely, even she couldn't object to his teaching the young man a few punches? The moment passed, and she turned toward his new admirer.

"Mr. Skylar. As you're from America, perhaps you can tell us your impressions of the new president."

"I don't know much about him," Skylar replied. "He was the dark horse compromise when the Republicans couldn't get Grant nominated."

"But he is well accepted across the country?" Rafferty asked. Americans elected their leaders in a totally different fashion than England. He hadn't a complete understanding of it.

"I'm not sure politics is a fit conversation with ladies present," Mrs. Summers said with a thin smile.

"Why is that, Mrs. Summers?" Eva challenged. "Is it because women haven't the right to vote? Does that make politics an unfit topic?"

Rafferty had to hide his smile. Obviously, the etiquette lessons were wearing thin on Miss St. Claire as well as himself.

The lesson on salutations of foreign dignitaries had him threatening to turn the ship around. While the material might have been important, he preferred Arianne's instruction.

"It could have gone either way when the votes were counted," Mr. Skylar said, ignoring the women's conversation. "But the Republicans carried the electoral college." He grinned at Rafferty. "They said it was the Irish vote that got him New York."

"A large number of my countrymen have settled in New York," Rafferty said while he pondered the concept of an electoral college.

"Miss St. Claire and I were discussing that very subject," Mr. Barings said, with a glance toward Rafferty. "It's a sad state of affairs when a country's major export is its own people."

Rafferty thought perhaps he'd loosened his fists on the wrong person. Mr. Barings seemed anxious to engage in some verbal fisticuffs of his own.

"They say the Irish vote was one of the reasons Garfield chose an Irishman for his running mate," Skylar added.

"An Irishman?" Rafferty drew back surprised. He'd spent his research on the office of president, not the secondary positions. "An Irishman is the head of such a vast country as America?"

"Chester Arthur is the *vice* president. If something should happen to President Garfield, then he would become the president," Mr. Skylar explained. "Actually, it was his father who came from Ireland. Chester was born in America, otherwise he couldn't be on the ticket."

Eva leaned forward. "But if someone were to deny leadership to their own—"

"To Ireland," Phineas interrupted, lifting his wineglass. "May her sons"—he nodded toward Eva—"and daughters someday rule their own country and not that of everyone else."

The men laughed and joined in the toast. Rafferty caught Phineas's eye. It was the reaction they'd been waiting for.

A roll of thunder interrupted the joviality. Captain Briggs stood to excuse himself. "Enjoy the rest of your dinner. Sound carries a great distance over water. Still, I should return to the wheelhouse. Ladies." He nodded to each but lingered over his farewell to Mrs. Summers. Rafferty hid his smile. The old sea dog hadn't forgotten all his tricks.

Rafferty waited a bit longer, not wishing to alarm the others, especially Arianne, who had blanched upon hearing the thunder, before he excused himself to join the captain.

"It's a big one, Rafe, and heading straight for us." Briggs stood on the bridge peering east through a pair of binoculars. Rafferty didn't need the optical aid to see the sky flash with lightning. "The barometer is sinking fast."

"Will she hold?" Rafferty asked, referring to the *Rose*.

"Well enough," the captain replied. He handed the binoculars over to Rafferty, who peered at the growing swells. "She's been through worse in her time. I'll turn into the storm when it's time so the waves won't hit us broadside. But it's going to be rough."

"How long?" Rafferty asked. The wind had already picked up in force, slapping his face and neck with a warning of what was to come.

The captain shrugged and looked at his pocket watch. "It's moving fast. I'll guess we have about ninety minutes, maybe less. Where will you be?"

"You'll need pressure. I'll help the boys in the boiler room."

A CRACK OF THUNDER STARTLED ARIANNE AWAKE AND sent her bones resonating like a plucked string upon a fiddle. Light flashed through the small porthole, and another crack sounded as if to split the sky overhead. She thought to leap from the bed, but then she realized the bed, indeed the entire cabin, was in motion. The *Irish Rose* was battling a storm and being tossed mercilessly upon the waves. Could the nautical antique survive such brutal force? Could they?

Arianne struggled to remember what the captain had said about life jackets . . . They were in the lifeboats. But how were they to actually get to the lifeboats when the ship lurched right and left so unpredictably?

"Arianne," Mrs. Summers called. "Are you awake?"

"I wish I weren't," she replied, feeling her stomach protest the violent shifts in motion.

"I'm afraid we're going to perish at sea," Mrs. Summers said, pausing for another volley of thunder to fade. "I've lived a full life, but you . . ."

"We're not going to die," Arianne replied with a certainty that she didn't believe. *Stay calm. Stay aloof.*

"I'm going to be sick," Mrs. Summers moaned. "Please, a basin . . ."

Arianne pushed herself upright, ignoring her own complaining stomach. Using the walls and archways for support, she stumbled her way to the basin, lifting the bowl from the wooden base. Holding the basin with one hand, she fought her way back to the berths and Mrs. Summers. Her brother had mentioned various remedies for the vile mal de mer he'd suffered on the crossing. Of course, she couldn't remember a one of them now.

"Keep this." Arianne placed the basin near Mrs. Summers. "I'll find help."

Her thin wrapper had fallen to the floor by the foot of the bed. It took an effort to retrieve it with the movement of the ship, but she managed. Swallowing the bile that rose in her throat, she made her way to the door, then to the door opposite.

"Kathleen." She banged on the wood. "Are you and Miss Eva all right?"

She thought she heard a gurgled, "Yes, mum," but she wasn't certain. "Are you ill?"

This resulted in a definitive, "Yes."

"I'm getting help," Arianne called. "Stay calm."

But where was help to be found? She glanced down the corridor; the hanging oil lamps swayed violently with the ship's motion. *Rafferty.* He would know what to do. It was his ship after all. His room was removed from those of the ladies. She'd need to make her way to the stairs and down to the next level. Bracing both hands on the walls of the corridor, she inched down the passageway—until a wind gust extinguished the lamps. The corridor was plunged in darkness.

Lightning flashed, exposing the stairway at the end. She'd taken a step toward that goal when the ship heaved, knocking her to the canvas floor. The moans of the vessel fighting the elements could have been her own. Her teeth rattled from the vibrations of the powerful steam engine, but she crawled forward on hands and knees, finally reaching the circular metal stairs that wound through the many levels of the *Irish Rose.* With a particularly loud clap of thunder, the door at the top of the stairs blew open. Seawater rushed in claiming victory, splashing in every direction, and soaking her in the process.

Like a fragile shell tossed by the waves, the ship rose, then fell with a slap, before lurching sideways. They were all going to drown! Braced by the corner of the stairwell, Arianne cringed in terror, huddling in her sodden linen. If she stood, she would likely pitch headfirst down the stairway into the bowels of the ship. She could crawl back down the passageway, but for what purpose? To die in the tiny cabin when the ocean claimed the *Irish Rose*? Why did she ever agree to this perilous voyage? Was a watery grave better than the scorn of society? She sobbed, letting her tears mix with the cold rain driven by shrieking winds through the unlatched door.

Just as she thought she would die alone in a cold metal stairwell, footsteps thudded on the stair rungs, rising toward her. She curled tighter into her wet corner, pulling her saturated robe snug around her.

DAMN HIS EYES FOR INSISTING THEY TAKE THE *IRISH Rose*, Rafferty chastised himself. He'd kept the vessel in service out of respect for his father's legacy and to keep Captain Briggs and the crew employed and solvent in a cruel world. Briggs had assured him the *Rose* still had the wherewithal to make the Atlantic crossing, but Rafferty had his doubts. One of the pipes conducting steam sprung a leak in the boiler room, scalding the arm of a stoker. Rafferty had wound his shirt around the pipe to contain the pressure. Once they were out of the storm, a repair could be made, but for now the material offered sufficient blockage. He hadn't realized until he traveled the underbelly of the ship how much of the mechanics were held together by makeshift, hurried patches, piecemeal fixes that were never meant to be permanent. Damn Briggs's estimation. He must have let stubborn pride and nostalgia cloud his judgment.

Rafferty shook his head. Hadn't he done the same thing? Let pride and something else cloud his judgment? If he hadn't wanted to impress Lady Arianne with his father's legacy, perhaps he would have waited to make a safer crossing on one of the larger, swifter liners. While it was true that the *Irish Rose* would deliver them to their destination before the luxury liners, he hadn't intended to place anyone's life at risk in the process.

Phineas tended to Kelly, the wounded man, while Rafferty finished Kelly's shift. The captain sent a message that they were through the worst of the storm. The *Rose* still battled the swells, but the wind had decreased and the hard rain lessened. Rafferty thought to check on the passengers, doubting that they had managed to sleep through the turmoil. He bounded up the winding stairs; the higher he climbed, the more the pitch of the ship tried to shake him from the rails.

He saw her just as he rounded the turn for her floor. Huddled in the corner like a wet kitten, she was. His heart caught in his throat.

"Arianne!" He tried to stoop beside her, but the ship tossed him on his bum. "What're you doing out here?"

She just trembled. He wasn't sure she even heard his voice, enmeshed as she was in some personal hell. Water, he remembered. She had said she was afraid of drowning. Why then in blue blazes had she left her cabin?

Rafferty wrapped his arms around her, resettling her into his lap. Two circles of dusky rose pressed against her thin, damp chemise, drawing his gaze. He cursed softly. Now was not the time to be thinking about her soft woman flesh curled against his chest. But his John Henry took note, aroused by her scent and touch.

Tear tracks glistened on her fine porcelain skin. Her hair, loose and wet, covered his arm. Fear-filled eyes gazed up at him. Her lips quivered. "We're going to die, aren't we?"

"No, lass. No." He remembered her hesitancy to board the ship, her fear of the water. No wonder she was as pale as the foamy caps on the sea. "It would take more blusterin' than that to sink the *Rose*." But not much more, he thought, remembering how his shirt was responsible for holding the pressure until a patch could be applied. The ship was well past her prime. *Aren't we all?* Phineas's words echoed in his head. Time hadn't stopped when that Fenian bomb took his family. For the last ten years he had chased Toomey without thought of the passing years. Now with a fine, decent woman huddled next to him, he wondered if chasing Toomey had been the best way to honor his family. "Ssh, my darlin', I promised I'd keep you safe."

His earlier guilt at risking so much for a week's head start in chasing Toomey loomed large in his mind as he held the trembling woman in his arms. Her gown was thin, not meant for roaming the passageways of a ship manned predominately by men. He squeezed her tight. Though the danger had passed, he wasn't willing to let her go just yet.

He kissed the top of her head, though she didn't seem to notice. It was just as well. As soon as she'd dried out and realized the sun would shine again, she'd want no more of him, common oaf that he was.

Phineas bounded up the stairwell, stopping when he saw the two of them. "Is she all right?"

"Frightened out of her wits," Rafferty replied. He jutted his head toward the door to the top deck. "Can you close that tight? She's soaking wet. It must have opened in the storm."

Phineas continued up the steps. The click of the latch echoed down the stairway. When he came back down, he peeled off his oilcloth and handed it to Rafe. "You need this more than me."

Rafferty nodded toward the passageway. "Check on the others." His gaze slipped over the woman shivering in his arms. "I'll take care of her."

RAFFERTY WASN'T SURE IF IT WAS THE GENTLE ROCKING in his arms or the lulling sound of his voice, but Arianne eventually relaxed. The violent pitch of the ship evened out, and though rain still beat on the roof of the stairway, the roof no longer rattled with the rain's battering force.

"Why did you venture out here?" Rafferty asked. "I thought to find you in your room."

"Mrs. Summers . . . Kathleen," she tried to explain.

"I've sent Phineas to check on them," Rafferty said. "He'll know what to do."

"Stay with me, Rafferty." She clung to him as if he were the life jacket she needed to survive. "I don't want to be alone."

If this were any other woman, he'd take her back to his

room, strip off her wet clothes, and bundle her warm and dry in his bed. But this was Lady Arianne. He doubted she would appreciate the ruin to her reputation, and strangely, her opinion of him mattered. Her upturned face filled his vision. He knew what he had to do. "I won't leave."

And he didn't. He held her until she fell asleep. He thought to take her back to her room, but by then he was too exhausted himself to stand. So he held her.

Phineas came back to say Mrs. Summers and Kathleen were doing better, now that the sea had calmed. He moved them to the same room so neither would be alone.

"Wasn't Eva with Kathleen?" Rafferty asked in a whisper.

Phineas shrugged. "Not tonight." He nodded toward the woman in Rafferty's arms. "What are you going to do with her?"

"Hold her." He smiled down on her tousled head. Her ladyship had turned to him when she was scared. Him. A common Irish bloke with a bad haircut. Such an opportunity to hold her in his arms was unlikely to present itself again. So for now he'd take pleasure in this. "I'm going to just hold her. It's what she wants."

Phineas nodded and quietly disappeared down the stairway. Rafferty planted a soft kiss on Arianne's head, taking care not to wake her, then whispered into her dreams, "It's what I want too."

· Twelve ·

SORE AND DAMP, ARIANNE OPENED HER EYES IN the dim light of the stairwell. She wasn't dead. She took a tentative breath to test that theory. A soft snore accompanied by a warm, moist breath sailed by her ear. Rafferty. She smiled. Such a delicious feeling to be in his arms. Hearing the rhythm of his breath in sleep felt more intimate than anything she had shared with the Baron.

Thoughts of intimacy and the Baron reminded her that Mrs. Summers would be expecting her in the cabin. Arianne had best find her way back before the woman began to point fingers and make unjust accusations.

A soft light slipped through the window on the door above them. The powerful engine sent tremors through the walls, pushing the ship through the sea. The *Irish Rose* had survived the storm, just as Rafferty had said it would. Now it was time for her to survive as well.

She tried to slip unnoticed from Rafferty's arms, but the oilcloth covering them pulled on his skin. He woke and blinked like an owl before wincing painfully as he shifted his position. "Good morning." He yawned. "Is it morning?"

"It's early," Arianne murmured. "I should go back."

His arms tightened around her. "You don't like sleeping on the floor here with me?" he asked in jest, his lips slipping into a silly half smile she loved.

"I like it too much," she answered. "But Mrs. Summers will be worried about my welfare."

He loosened his arms, allowing her to stand. "Best keep the oilcloth, love. It's less revealing than the robe."

She stopped and looked at him. Did he say what she thought she heard?

"What?" His eyebrows raised in question.

She shook her head lightly, then pulled the cloth across her chest. Rafferty slowly gained his feet, his stiff motions suggesting his back was not appreciative of the time spent sitting in the corner. It was difficult not to stare at all that lovely male flesh unfolding for her benefit. Making a conscious effort to look him in the eye, she tried not to be distracted by his bare chest, or the number of scars that marked his skin, a vivid reminder that Rafferty was a most unusual diplomat. "Thank you," she said tenderly. "Thank you for keeping me safe."

"I preferred the way you thanked me before," he said, straightening to his full height. "On the top deck that first night."

The kiss! He remembered! She'd tentatively kissed him that night for helping her board the *Irish Rose*. She'd never forget that sense of being desired. There could be no harm in repeating that moment. She stepped close, demurely closed her eyes, and offered her lips to him.

RAFFERTY HAD BEEN CALLED MANY THINGS BUT NEVER a fool. He'd regretted not showing her the full depth of a real kiss that first night. He wasn't about to let this second opportunity pass, even if it meant he would pay for it with a slap across the face.

He slipped his hands beneath the oilcloth to find the natural curve of her waist. Then he pulled her against his chest, letting his hands roam up her back, keeping her tight. His lips claimed hers. As soon as she parted them with a soft gasp, his tongue took advantage and explored with abandon. He thought she might pull away. Much to his surprise, her hands slipped up behind his head, pulling him down for more.

Sweet Jesus! His hands slid up her sides until he could cup her unbound breasts in his hand. His thumbs found the rosy centers that he had glimpsed last night and quickly stimulated the nipples into two hard berries that he yearned to taste. They scraped across his chest as his arms lifted her, then set her down so that her back pressed the wall.

One of them broke the kiss; he wasn't sure who. Urgent need pulsated through him while his lips found her cheek, her neck. He heard her gasp, but she didn't push away or protest.

He could have her right there. His John Henry was fattened and ready. Want and need throbbed with such a passion that he could barely think straight.

A door latch clicked. Immediately, he put his hands on the wall by either side of her, shielding her with his body. She pressed her forehead into his chest. Tiny puffs of heated air slid over his stomach toward the waistband of his trousers. Sweet Jesus, this was agony.

Footsteps ambled down the steps.

"Rafferty? Good lord, man," Briggs said. "Where do you find the stamina?"

The captain continued down the winding steps. Once he had passed their floor, Arianne let out a long breath and straightened. He did so as well. Jesus! What the devil was he thinking? This wasn't some common strumpet.

"I . . . I have to go now," she said.

Rafferty just shook his head. She started to leave when he remembered. "Your maid is in the room with Mrs. Summers. Where will you go?"

"I can't stay here." She looked down her front. "Not like this. I need to change into something suitable. For that, I have to go to my room." She took two steps down the passageway, then stopped. "Thank you . . . for everything."

SHE SHOULD FEEL HUMILIATED FOR HER ACTIONS, BUT she didn't. She'd used up all her shame on the Baron. The sad truth was she hadn't felt a fraction of the fervor with the Baron that she had just now with Rafferty.

She'd been alone for so long, desperate to find the contentment her brothers had found with their spouses. The intense hunger and blazing desire that she'd just experienced in Rafferty's arms was so much more than the Baron's polite pressing of lips. She'd never wanted more of him, not the way she wanted with Rafferty. Perhaps Karl recognized that as well. He'd freed them both from a passionless marriage.

Looking back toward the stairwell from her cabin door, she saw he was still there, watching. His hands pressed on either side of the passageway as if he alone held the *Rose* together. From this distance, she could see that she'd failed in changing him into a nonthreatening, suitable negotiator. He looked predatory and male and ready to charge down the passageway and claim her once again. Christopher, she wished he would. A titillation lifted the tips of her breasts and raced to that center between her thighs. The feeling was so intense, her fingers almost slid to that very place to fill the void she felt there. She opened the cabin door and escaped inside before she did something she knew she would regret.

She could see now that the Baron had not desired her in the same way as Rafferty. Even so, the Baron had abandoned her once he had sampled her in that private way. Rafferty could do the same. Rafferty only wanted her because he believed she was a lady, she reminded herself. Once he learned the truth, he would feel betrayed and leave. Arianne leaned back against the cabin door, reliving her body's response to Rafferty's hands and lips. Would she forever live in this cruel hell where granting the one thing that her body craved would lead to another abandonment?

She couldn't risk that. This time, she reassured herself, she would keep her legs pressed tightly together. The voyage must soon come to a close, and Rafferty would bid her farewell. This time she would part with her head held high.

RAFFERTY WAITED UNTIL SHE ENTERED HER CABIN, AND then waited some more. She might come back. If he had his way, the door would open and she'd run back down the passageway and into his waiting arms. He didn't expect that to happen, of course. But then he hadn't expected her to return his kisses with such passion. Who would have suspected that beneath her cold and aloof exterior, and beneath those yards and yards of starched stiff linens and restrictive laces and Lord knew what else, a real woman smoldered? A real woman who if . . . if Captain Briggs hadn't interrupted, the men in the boiler room would have heard scream of pleasure.

The thought twisted his lips. Would she have let him go so far? Or more to the point, would he have been able to stop if she resisted? Lord, her skin was so soft and scented. She was quality goods, top-shelf. No question about it. But she didn't hold that over him. She'd been open . . . accepting.

Her cabin door hadn't opened. She was probably regretting turning to him for comfort when she was vulnerable. Chastising herself for coming on this trip to help improve the likes of him. And he repaid her efforts by taking advantage.

He shook his head. One thing was certain. He'd best find and deal with Toomey this time, because after Lady Arianne reported his abhorrent behavior to Lord Henderson, Rafferty would be tossed out of the Home Office on his arse.

He returned to his cabin, washed and changed, then stretched out on his mattress, but sleep wouldn't come. The room was too empty, too condemning. As much as he pounded the pillows, they couldn't duplicate the feel of Arianne in his arms, curled in slumber. In the end, he dressed and joined the ship's crew in the dining saloon as a hearty breakfast was set on the sideboard. Most of the men who had worked through the storm were sleeping after a long night of hard labor. The few who made it to the saloon were tired but pleased with their performance the night before. Captain Briggs took the empty seat next to Rafferty.

"I know I can't take the place of your father or your uncle, Rafe, but I feel I should offer some advice. I don't think Lady Arianne would take kindly to knowing you're pumping her maid." Though Rafferty tried to hide his surprise, a bit of it must have caught Briggs's eye. "I saw her legs between your own, and a bit of nightgown. I know you weren't just diddling in the corner."

Though tempted to reply to the "diddling" comment, Rafferty chose to let it pass. "You won't say anything?"

"To Lady Arianne? Of course not. But if you must varnish the cane, pardon my French, you should do it in your cabin."

Rafferty's lips twisted at the irony. "I assure you, that won't happen again."

Briggs started to leave, but Rafferty grabbed his arm. "There's something else for us to discuss." Briggs sat back down.

"You heard about the break in the boiler room?"

The captain averted his gaze. "Yes. Quick thinking on your part, using your shirt to bind the break."

"And Kelly?" Rafferty's voice was grim.

"He's got some blisters on that meaty arm of his, but he'll be all right. I've seen worse," Briggs replied.

"I don't want to see 'worse' coming from this ship," Rafferty argued. "I thought you said the *Rose* was seaworthy."

Briggs's chest puffed out. "We managed the storm last night. A pipe break like that could have happened anywhere." Rafferty caught the captain's gaze and held fast.

"All right," Briggs admitted. "We've got some rust where we shouldn't, and some belts are wearing thin. We've got some patches on pipes that need replacing. The sails need work, but we rarely use them. The *Rose* could use a good overhaul, if that's what you're thinking."

"I'm thinking it's time for the *Irish Rose* to retire," Rafferty said quietly.

"Retire?" Briggs's face twisted with indignity. "She's a good ship, lad. She's seen better days, true, and traveling the Atlantic is a challenge, but she's been a good, reliable vessel."

"She's a ship of the past, Briggs," Rafferty replied. "Her engine isn't as efficient or powerful as the new liners. Her cargo holds aren't large enough to make transatlantic trips profitable anymore." Rafferty's gaze bored into that of the captain. "The *Irish Rose* isn't worth risking your life or the lives of the crew."

"So what are you going to do?" Briggs studied his hands.

"I haven't decided yet," Rafferty admitted. "But whatever I do, I won't forget you, Briggs. You may not be my uncle, but you've been as close to one as a man can be. I won't forget you and the crew in my plans."

"That's all an old sea dog can hope for." He stood and shook Rafferty's hand. "Your uncle was a good man. He'd be proud of the man you've become."

Rafferty thanked him and watched him leave. Then he sat

back and watched the calm sea glide by the saloon's window while he pondered the ship's fate.

"I'm surprised to see you alone." Phineas slipped into the empty chair across from him. "After your late-night rescue, I thought you'd have company for breakfast."

Upon receipt of Rafferty's harsh glare, Phineas's smile faded.

"Nothing happened last night," Rafferty said. "Lady Arianne returned to her cabin intact and untouched."

"Of course, I wouldn't have assumed otherwise." Phineas averted his gaze.

"There's no need to assume. You didn't see anything, understood?"

"Understood," Phineas said, chastised.

They sat in silence with their coffee for a few moments. Around them tablecloths was changed and a finer set of china was placed on the sideboard for the use of the passengers. A wider selection of foods was added to the staples already present. Rafferty doubted many would venture from their beds to take advantage of the meal this morning.

Phineas slipped over to the sideboard and returned with toast points, jam, and butter for the both of them. He broke the silence with an angled smile. "I thought you should know that your wife did not pass the evening alone." He buttered a piece of the bread and tossed it into his mouth.

"My wife? You mean Eva?"

Phineas nodded, chewing contently. He followed with a sip of coffee before he continued. "When I checked on the other passengers last night, I heard a distinctly feminine voice in Mr. Barings's cabin. As I had verified the presence of the other women aboard, that left only Eva."

"If Eva is the lady in green, that would explain Mr. Barings's misplaced attitude," Rafferty mused. He reached for a piece of toast.

"It would explain a few other things as well, such as why she volunteered for this endeavor."

"She volunteered?" Rafferty paused in the process of buttering his toast.

Phineas cringed. "I'm sorry, Rafe. You were in such a hurry to chase Toomey that when Eva offered, I thought . . ."

"We'd only decided the day before to look for an actress. How did she even know of our need?"

"I had made some general inquiries at the Bard and Bull shortly after your meeting with Lord Henderson. I assumed word had spread that I was looking for a woman to travel abroad and that I would pay handsomely," Phineas said. "I never considered she received information from another direction. Was she at that diplomat's reception?"

Rafferty shook his head and consumed the buttered toast. "I don't know. I was so certain that note was intended for Lady Arianne that I could have missed Miss St. Claire." That reception seemed so long ago. So much had happened since. He looked at Phineas. "I do know this. It's time to stop playing at being a gentleman and learn the truth of what's going on. I believe it's time to talk to Eva."

"What about Barings?"

"If he's with her, we'll talk to him as well."

They rose in unison, but Phineas stopped to fill his pockets with apples and oranges.

"Is that for practice, later?" Rafferty asked. Phineas filled some of the breaks in his stage act with a little light juggling. It wasn't his forte yet, but Rafferty was certain that with time, it would be. Phineas was like that.

"No. I'm still hungry." Phineas tossed an apple to Rafferty.

Rafferty caught it in one hand and laughed. He turned to leave the saloon and stopped. Lady Arianne stood an arm's length away watching the boyish play with the apples. A flush rose on her cheeks when he faced her.

She recovered first and nodded her greeting. "Good morning, Mr. Rafferty. Phineas."

Strange that she always addressed him with the formal salutation. To his best friend, she offered the familiarity of his first name. Phineas made a pretense of returning to the sideboard. Rafferty sought out her gaze. "Did you sleep well?"

She shook her head. "Not much at all." She dropped her voice to an intimate tone that only he would hear. "But it was a pleasant evening, nonetheless." Her lips turned slightly at the corners like a secret smile.

A warmth spread through his veins that he couldn't attribute to the coffee. She was not furious with him over the liberties taken. He let his eyelids drop, so that only her beautiful face filled his view. "Yes." He nudged his bandaged knuckles against her soft, refined ones, wishing that his aim could be higher, to the beckoning swell of her blouse. "It was."

They stood that way for a minute, but a sound behind him broke the intimate moment. Her eyes widened. "You were just leaving. I shouldn't stop you."

Rafferty made a show of looking over her shoulder, though he knew her shadow hadn't accompanied her. "And you are alone." He stepped aside to usher her into the saloon. "Would you like us to stay to keep you company?"

She smiled, the warmth filling her eyes and him as well. "I came to collect some light dishes to take back to Mrs. Summers and my maid. They're much recovered this morning, but I hope something light in their stomachs will help even more."

"Do you need assistance with the dishes? Phineas and I would be happy—"

"I can manage." She glanced at Phineas but returned to him. "There is one thing that you can do for me."

Odd that being of service to her in some small fashion had precedence over unmasking a traitor or determining the livelihood for a full crew and the ship. Yet it did. He eagerly awaited her command.

"I understand you have a library of sorts?" She blushed anew, probably remembering that silly repartee they'd exchanged about reading. The memory widened his smile.

"Yes, I do. Though I'm sure it's not up to the standards to which you're accustomed." He thought he heard Phineas mutter something behind him.

"I wonder if you'll allow me to see it? I realize we've almost reached our destination, but I've exhausted the material that I brought for this journey. If I could borrow a volume . . . ?"

"Of course you may. Perhaps after this afternoon's lesson—"

"I don't believe we'll have an afternoon lesson," Arianne interrupted. "I imagine after the turbulent night we could all use the time to repose."

"Yes. That would be wise." He searched her face, noting the deep purple shadows beneath her eyes. He wanted to say something witty, something personal, something that would let her know what last night's experience meant to him. But they were not alone, not like last night. "My library will be at your disposal whenever you find the need."

"Good day, gentlemen." She nodded.

After they had left Lady Arianne and the dining saloon well behind, Phineas audibly sighed. "You must admit, your conversations with Lady Arianne were much more interesting before nothing happened last night."

Rafferty glanced askance at Phineas. "I won't even pretend to know what you mean."

· Thirteen ·

RAFFERTY POUNDED ON BARINGS'S CABIN DOOR. "Let me in, Barings. I need to talk to the both of you."

They could hear movement inside, but no reply. Rafferty glanced at the hinges . . . rusted. Just like everything else on the *Rose*. He called again. "Don't make me break the door down, Barings. I will if I have to."

After a minute, the door opened a crack. "I don't know what you mean. I'm the only one here."

"We know better," Rafferty said before applying a shoulder to the door. It swung open, banging on the inside wall. Behind Barings, Eva stood in a wrapper belted loosely at her waist, one wing of her tattoo clearly visible.

"How dare you!" Barings yelled, backing up to shield Eva.

"How dare you fraternize with an unmarried woman in your quarters?" Rafferty countered. "Especially one who is supposed to be my wife?"

Barings laughed, a cruel sound. "Don't confuse acting with reality, Rafferty. Eva would never marry you. The thought of pretending to be your wife turns her stomach."

He raised his brows in her direction. "Really? You certainly seemed enthused when you had your hand on my thigh."

Barings rushed forward, but Phineas stopped him. "Don't be a fool, Barings."

"I was acting," Eva spat. "I needed the money, and I did what I needed to get it."

Rafferty glanced back to see Barings struggling against Phineas. "Let him go. I don't mean either of them any harm. I came here to talk, nothing more."

Phineas released Barings, who retreated to stand by Eva. For all his defiance of Rafferty, he was protective of Eva. Even his expression softened when he looked at her. Rafferty imagined he would act similarly if the woman he cared for was threatened.

"I take it that Miss St. Claire means something special to you," Rafferty said with new insight.

Barings sighed. "I booked transit on this rust bucket solely because I learned my Eva was to be on it." He picked up her hand and held it tenderly in his own. "She's carrying my baby."

"You're pregnant?" Rafferty looked pointedly at her stomach.

"It's early," Eva said, defiantly. "I knew I had a limited period before it became obvious. As your wife, it wouldn't matter if I was in the family way. I could put the money aside to use for my child when my role was finished."

He couldn't argue with her logic. He glanced at Barings. "You'd allow her to pretend to be another's wife even though you cared for the woman?"

"I didn't know that she'd accepted your offer until it was too late." He averted his eyes. "Then when I heard of the money involved I thought, why not?"

Phineas looked to Eva. "You didn't simply accept our offer. You approached me about our need. How did you know I was searching for someone to play Rafferty's wife?"

"I was with a . . . benefactor at the Bard and Bull when May Tadworthy told me you were looking for an actress." She dropped her voice and patted her stomach. "May knew of my dilemma. I didn't want to take the position because it would mean that I'd have to leave London, but my benefactor . . . he told me to take the role and report back to him."

"I assume the benefactor was Mr. Barnell."

"He's a good man," Eva protested. "He's a parliamentarian. He told me that there's a plan afoot to gain the Americans' support of home rule and that you would stop it, if you could."

"A plan afoot for the Americans?" Rafferty felt his forehead furl. "I'm going to find a killer and bring him to justice. I don't know about some American plan." Although the comment made him reaffirm his belief that Lord Weston's death was tied to Fenian efforts. That was the only reason one could possibly believe he'd be thwarting some unknown scheme.

"What do we do now?" Phineas asked Rafferty. "You can't very well hunt a murderer if your movements are reported right back to the man responsible."

"Lord Barnell is not a murderer," Eva protested. "He's a kind man."

Rafferty ignored her. "We'll just have to proceed without a hostess. But that does not resolve the problem of what to do with these two."

"What to do with us? What do you mean?" Barings asked.

"I can't allow you to jeopardize my investigation. I'm sending Eva back to England. As you followed her this far, I presume you'll be inclined to follow her back again."

"You're not sending her back to England on this death trap," Barings insisted. "It's a miracle we survived last night. I won't chance her life on a return crossing."

Rafferty hated to appear influenced by Barings, but the man was correct. Rafferty had already come to a similar conclusion. "When the time comes, I'll send Eva back on the first large liner leaving for England, provided she stays in seclusion until then."

"What of Mr. Barings?" Eva asked. "Will he be in seclusion with me?"

"Only if he's your husband," Rafferty answered with a twisted smile. "We want to be proper about this."

"Lady Arianne has had quite an influence on you if you're concerned about what is proper," Phineas observed once they left the other two to discuss their future plans.

"That could be," Rafferty conceded. "Or it could be that I consider marriage to be the best revenge for those two." He smiled. "At least we no longer have to worry about a spy in our midst."

• • •

ARIANNE COULD BARELY STAND UPRIGHT BY THE TIME she returned with a light repast for Mrs. Summers and Kathleen. Yet there was no place to lie down, as both berths were occupied. Kathleen gave her the key to her cabin with the explanation that Eva would be absent. She couldn't provide other details. Arianne thought she'd pursue that topic later, when she could think straight. Not now. Not when she couldn't keep her eyes open.

A knock at the door awakened her from a wonderful dream. Rafferty was in it, holding a fistful of forget-me-nots. She left the berth to answer the door.

"Mr. Rafferty," she exclaimed, taking a quick peek at his hands. They were empty. "I . . . I can't ask you in. I'm here alone."

"Yes. Mrs. Summers indicated as much." His eyes slipped over her face while she noted his knuckles whitened on the doorframe. "I'm here to request your immediate presence to discuss an important development in our diplomat pretense."

It seemed a lot for her sleep-drenched mind to comprehend. "A development?" She blinked, hoping that action would chase the dream cobwebs from her mind. "Are we not still in the middle of the ocean?"

A self-satisfied sort of smile bloomed on his lips. "I'll tell you more when you come to my cabin." He must have seen her eyes widen with protest. "Phineas and Mrs. Summers will be in attendance as well. My cabin should provide the privacy and the additional room that we'll require."

"Mrs. Summers?"

His eyes crinkled. He glanced across the passageway as if he suspected the chaperone held a glass to the door. Arianne chuckled, knowing she probably did.

"It seems she's much improved," he said loudly.

Arianne said that she'd be there presently, closed the door, then rushed to freshen her face with a moist towel. Her skirt and blouse were hopelessly wrinkled as if she'd slept in them, which indeed she had. As Rafferty suggested the situation was urgent, she decided not to change. At least she could pat some lilac water on the worst wrinkles and thus freshen her appearance. Eva certainly wouldn't mind if she borrowed . . .

That's when she saw the letter.

She wouldn't have read it under usual circumstances, but the name *Barnell* at the top of the stationery caught her eye. She pulled the rest of the correspondence from the journal in which it was placed.

Dear Miss St. Claire:

May I extend sincere congratulations upon your securing the position of companion to Mr. Michael Rafferty. This shall require all of your extensive acting skills to maintain a façade of a seemingly loving wife while observing the traitor in his efforts to destroy our carefully laid plans. Should you encounter difficulty or need to convey secretive information to me, I've arranged for someone friendly to the cause to be placed within the legation. They will contact you to make their presence known. You may find assistance as well in an establishment called Finnegans on Hickory St. Someone will be watching for a woman of your complexion. Be assured that you have my gratitude for this endeavor and will be well compensated for your efforts upon your return.

B.

Eva!

Arianne felt the blood drain from her face. Eva had been a planted spy all along. A fury rose within her. All the time and effort Arianne had expended to train the perfidious wench, even to extend her own wardrobe to her . . . an actress, indeed! If anyone should be considered a traitor, it was Eva, not Rafferty.

Armed with the seditious letter, Arianne stormed down the passageway toward the men's section of the ship. Rafferty must see this. He should have trusted her instincts . . . or at least, she should have trusted her own instincts. Either way, the letter changed everything.

She had reached the men's corridor, then realized she wasn't exactly certain which of the doors represented Rafferty's. In hindsight, she should have waited for Mrs. Summers. At least there would be two of them in this predicament. She moved slowly down the passageway, hoping for some sign. She found it in a subtle trace of patchouli that lingered in the air. Rafferty had come this way recently. The scent intensified as she approached a door. Thus emboldened, she knocked.

Phineas greeted her. "Come in. We've been expecting you."

She entered in awe. Rafferty's cabin was easily three times the size of hers. A fine carpet covered the floor. Thick drapery hung near the head of a large mattress—one that appeared far more accommodating than the narrower one she had used the past week. The rich scent of patchouli permeated the air, explaining its presence in Rafferty's clothes. Did he know of its legendary powers of seduction? Somehow she suspected he did.

Rafferty stood before shelves of books, two leather-bound volumes in his hand. His eyes narrowed slightly. "You didn't wait for your shadow?"

"No . . . I know I should have, but I found this in Miss St. Claire's possessions." She held out Barnell's letter, straightening into her best aristocratic posture. "I don't think she will make a suitable wife."

He smiled. Smiled! The sort of smile that tingled her bones even from the opposite side of the room. "I tend to agree."

He glanced toward Phineas. "See if you can expedite Lady Arianne's chaperone." He winked at Arianne. "Tell her I'm plundering her charge's virtue. That should hurry her along. But leave the door open. We still have Lady Arianne's reputation to consider."

If he hadn't been focused on Phineas, he might have noticed her wince. There was no harm, she supposed, in allowing him to believe she had an unsullied reputation, but as she was condemning another woman for her deceit, her conscience made itself known.

"I've been selecting books for your perusal," Rafferty said to her. "Would you care to take a look?"

Was he mad? She had just uncovered a chicanery of prodigious proportions and he was selecting books? "Don't you wish to read this letter?" She waved it like a flag. "It suggests that Miss St. Claire has been in Barnell's employ all this time."

He examined the books in his hand while he meandered toward her. "Yes, I know," he said. "Phineas and I discovered that connection earlier this morning." A smile blossomed, even as he studied the titles. "It's no wonder the Home Office has its eye on you." His heated gaze took her breath away. "I know I would."

"Of course," she parroted, too flustered to really know what she was saying. She was agitated, not only because he was ignoring her discovery but because butterflies took up residence in her rib cage whenever he came near, and that . . . complication . . . she just shouldn't allow. Her breasts tightened at the sight of his hands holding the books and at the memory of how those very hands had held her body earlier. He slipped behind her, adding to her discomfort, but then moved to her side.

"I thought you might enjoy this book of Celtic folklore and all the stories of seductive mermaids and treacherous selkies." His intimate tones slipped in her ear, melting her insides to mush. "Or you might find the works of Jane Austen interesting. It is said that she loved an Irishman but rejected him due to his lack of property. She never married."

"That is unfortunate," she said, her senses reeling. "I know that I would consider—" Footsteps in the hallway interrupted her reply. Rafferty took a step away.

Mrs. Summers pushed the door wide. "Arianne, you should have called for me before you traipsed alone to this man's quarters. A den of iniquity, if I ever saw one."

Rafferty laughed. "These were my uncle's quarters when he plied the seas with Captain Briggs. He was not so much a man of iniquity as he was of comfort."

"My apologies, Mrs. Summers," Arianne said. "I found a letter in Eva's cabin that I felt needed to be seen by Mr. Rafferty immediately. Mr. Rafferty has been the perfect gentleman in your absence." She wasn't quite certain if that was true given the state of her racing pulse, but Mrs. Summers appeared to be comforted.

Rafferty took the letter from her hand and scanned it, his brow furled. "It appears we have more to concern ourselves beyond Eva's loyalties. Weston has spies in his employ as well."

"Spies . . . Eva? What is he talking about?" Mrs. Summers asked Arianne.

"I'm afraid the actress we hired to play the part of Rafferty's hostess is unsuitable due to her misguided loyalties," Phineas answered. "We no longer have a hostess for the legation."

Arianne passed the letter to Mrs. Summers while Rafferty poured an amber liquid into two crystal glasses. Over the patchouli notes, she distinctly could smell the fragrance of "the angel's share." He handed one of the glasses to Phineas.

"Didn't you say that Lord Henderson himself picked Mr. Rafferty to act as the British minister?" Mrs. Summers asked. "Why then is he referred to as a traitor in this letter?"

Arianne noted a muscle tighten in Rafferty's jaw. It wasn't fair that someone who strongly believed in truth and justice should be so branded by a falsehood. The accusation clearly hurt more than he allowed most people to see.

"Rafferty is not a traitor," she said. "The lie was used to turn Eva against him. Obviously, she can't be placed into such an influential position as the hostess to the British minister."

"Which just supports my original contention that a hostess is not needed." Rafferty poured wine into two glasses that he offered to Mrs. Summers and herself. "There's no time and no means to find a new candidate."

"No, Rafferty," Arianne insisted. "You will do a grave injustice to England if you follow that course." No one else had her experience to understand that a hostess was a vital, underestimated position in a small legation. She had to make them understand.

"I don't think we have much choice," Rafferty said. "I brought you both here to say"—he offered his glass up as a toast—"thank you on behalf of the Home Office for all that you've done. While appreciated, your combined services as teachers of diplomatic etiquette are no longer required."

"A bachelor minister will not be tolerated," Arianne said, ignoring the toast. "Lord Henderson acknowledged as much."

"Who made the mistake of hiring that woman?" Mrs. Summers asked.

"It's my fault," Phineas said. "Rafferty was in such a hurry to investigate the murder. I should have questioned Miss St. Claire more thoroughly."

"You're not completely to blame," Arianne said meekly. "I knew something was wrong, yet I didn't say anything. She wasn't as interested in the responsibilities of her position as she was her appearance. I admit I thought perhaps she was hired for other reasons."

"You thought she was interested in Mr. Rafferty," Mrs. Summers stated.

"You did?" Rafferty's eyebrows reached for his hairline.

"She was always so . . . enthusiastic when you walked in the room," Arianne admitted. She didn't add her jealous suspicions that Eva was sharing Rafferty's bed. In hindsight, she felt foolish for her suppositions.

"She did pretend to be pleased with the role, but I thought her admiration was over-practiced," Rafferty said. Then he smiled. "Actually, she was sincere in her attentions, but toward another passenger, not me."

"Who?" Arianne asked. She'd been so convinced Eva only had eyes for Rafferty, she hadn't noticed her interest in anyone else.

"She and Mr. Barings have approached Captain Briggs about a marriage at sea," Phineas advised.

"Cupid's Mistress strikes again," Mrs. Summers said with a tight smile. "Perhaps Lady Arianne could work her charms on a suitable stranger in Washington." Arianne just sighed.

"Mrs. Summers," Rafferty said, "I don't suppose you'd consider joining the Rafferty clan as my widowed aunt?"

"My dear boy, while I'm honored that you would consider me for such a position, I fear I must decline. A woman of my age and health would not be suitable for the hostess of a legation. Such a position requires youth and stamina. Two virtues that unfortunately I retain only as fond memories."

Even an aunt wouldn't negate the fact that Rafferty was a bachelor. That was the real fly in the ointment. Arianne shifted uncomfortably. If Rafferty didn't assume the role of British minister, the murder of Lord Weston would go unsolved while Rafferty chased Toomey. A competent, reliable wife had to be found and found quickly.

As she glanced around the silent faces at the table, a heavy weight settled in the pit of her stomach. The obvious solution would mean irrefutable public damage to her already privately damaged reputation, but to do otherwise meant a lifelong burden of guilt that she could have assisted in resolving the murder of a dear friend . . . and failed. It was a candle-snuffing moment.

• • •

RAFFERTY WATCHED ARIANNE. SHE BLAMED HERSELF for their current dilemma. He could see it in her unfocused stare and lightly trembling lower lip. The woman did not accept failure easily; it was a trait he admired. She'd been so confident that she could reshape both himself and Eva into respectable diplomatic representatives that to see it fail must be devastating. He wanted to hold her, support her, reassure her that she wasn't responsible for this debacle. But that was not possible given the other occupants in the room.

He sipped his whiskey. Of course, that was precisely the reason for the other occupants in the room. His desire to feel her in his arms again still smoldered in regions not discussed in polite circles—her circles.

"If the need for a hostess is that important, I can telegraph Lord Henderson and request that he send a more appropriate replacement," he said.

Arianne's gaze snapped to his. "But that will take weeks. Did you not say time was the enemy in investigating a murder? And what of the implied carefully laid plans to involve the Americans? Are you going to ignore that as well, all for your personal vendetta against Toomey?"

His eyes narrowed. "I'm not pleased with this solution, but I don't see that I have any other recourse. Unless you have a solution, I—"

"I do," Arianne said. "When we first met with Lord Henderson, I recall you suggested that I might be the perfect candidate for this role."

Mrs. Summers gasped. "Arianne, no!"

"That's true," Rafferty said, holding her gaze. She would be perfect, but the consequences would also be severe. It was not a course to be taken lightly. "If I recall correctly, you found the suggestion to be highly insulting. Which," he hurried to assure her, "was never my intention."

"Perhaps she could be introduced as your cousin," Phineas offered hopefully. "No one knows Rafe in America."

Arianne smiled at Phineas. "I'm afraid my relations are well documented."

"The illustrious daughter of a duke would have no Irish branches," Rafferty said, his brow raised. "Nor would they appreciate an Irish graft onto the family tree."

"Even a cousin would be considered inappropriate for a bachelor," Mrs. Summers said. She looked directly at Arianne. "It would have to be a wife . . . and a wife's country property would then belong to her husband."

A hard glance passed between the two women. Arianne bit her lip. After a moment she turned to Rafferty.

"When I first met you, I thought you lacked sincerity, sophistication, ability, and maintained no pride in your appearance," Arianne said.

Her criticism stung. He scowled. "Is that all?"

"I know now that you lack none of those things." She took a deep breath. "It's due in part to that knowledge that I shall rescind my objection and offer my services as a hostess."

He was stunned. To have such a competent partner by his side and a passionate lover in his bed . . . a man could not ask for more. That she would be the one to propose marriage was unusual, but he was discovering that much about his Arianne didn't fit the mold. He was flattered beyond belief. Her attention was directed elsewhere, but he murmured a soft prayer of gratitude nonetheless.

"Arianne! You can't!" Mrs. Summers said. "Your brother will not allow it."

"Should my brother hear of my actions, he will not be pleased," she conceded. "But as this posting is only a temporary one, there's a good chance he won't know of it. Only the Home Office has an interest in American society." She sipped her wine, but Rafferty noticed the liquid shook in her glass. She was more concerned about her brother's reaction than she pretended. That was all right; she'd have to trust his handling in this. He would explain to the Duke that she'd be well loved and well cared for. What man could find objection in that?

Rafferty beamed at his soon-to-be bride. She was everything a man could hope for. Now if everyone would vacate his room, he could show his appreciation in a more satisfying manner.

"Congratulations, Rafferty." Phineas slapped him on the back. "I'll notify Captain Briggs. You can be legally wed before we reach Washington."

"You misunderstand," Arianne protested. "It is not my intention to marry. I'm offering to step into the role that Eva vacated. Like her, I will only pretend to be his wife."

Rafferty's spirit plummeted. Perhaps Arianne was not so unusual after all. Foolish man. He should have known that the daughter of a duke would never consent to marriage to the likes of him.

"You should marry, Arianne," Mrs. Summers said. "Then, after this murder business is resolved, you can seek a divorce."

"A divorced woman is little better, socially, than a ruined one," Arianne said. "Worse, in fact, as she would have surrendered her property rights to her husband."

Rafferty buried the black fury that raged inside him. He kept his manner and voice deathly calm by fisting a hand behind his back. "You believe I'm interested in your property?"

"No, but it would be a consequence," she said, oblivious to his torment. He noticed Phineas had placed himself so as to shield Arianne if necessary. It wouldn't be, but he couldn't fault his reaction. Eva's betrayal hadn't cut nearly so deep as Arianne's refusal of him as a husband.

She turned toward him. "After you've found Lord Weston's murderer and your Mr. Toomey, you will regret being saddled with me," Arianne said. "I will retire to my dower estate and you can go forward with whatever it is you do when you're not chasing Toomey."

"Arianne—" he said.

She put her fingers on his lips. "Enough. This is the way it has to be."

"YOU SHOULD HAVE ACCEPTED HIS OFFER OF MARRIAGE," Mrs. Summers said as they stood in the passageway outside Rafferty's door. "No respectable man will offer for you after this masquerade."

"*He* didn't offer marriage," Arianne managed around the tight restriction in her throat. "Mr. Connor was the one who mentioned marriage, not Rafferty."

"You should have insisted upon it. I know you care for him."

Arianne thought of the sad bruised face of her mother, who was trapped in a marriage without love. Not that she thought Rafferty would ever hit her, but who knew? Without true affection, anything was possible. "No," she said. "I won't marry a man who doesn't love me. When this is over, I'll return to Sanctuary and live a quiet life alone."

Behind them she thought she heard the sound of glass shattering as if thrown at a wall. Or perhaps that was just the sound of her hopes of future happiness cracking into irretrievable fragments.

· *Fourteen* ·

"ANNIE!" LADY WESTON gasped. "IS THAT YOU? How you've grown, and so beautiful." She smiled with fondness. "Why, you could be one of those professional beauties I've read so much about."

"Lady Weston, I was so sorry to hear of your loss." Arianne grasped the woman's outstretched hands and kissed her cheek. "Lord Weston will be sorely missed."

"Thank you, dear." The older woman dabbed her eyes with a black-bordered handkerchief. "I miss him every day. I never fancied myself a widow, but I suppose I must adjust. We all must adjust." She turned toward Rafferty. "And who is this handsome fellow?"

"Allow me to introduce the new British minister," Arianne said. "Mr. Michael Rafferty will be taking command of the legation." Rafferty gave a curt bow to Lady Weston and raised a brow at Arianne, waiting.

"We've been expecting you, sir," Lady Weston said with a nod of her head.

Arianne's heart raced. The gold band on her finger felt awkward and tight. Now that she'd volunteered for this position, she was having difficulty sealing her fate. She motioned to the man behind them. "Mr. Connor"—Phineas stepped forward— "is an associate of Mr. Rafferty."

Lady Weston nodded in greeting, then looked perplexed. She stood on tiptoes to peer over Arianne's shoulder. "Is there anyone else?"

Rafferty reached behind Arianne and grasped her waist, tugging her closer to his side. "My wife failed to mention that we've recently married." He kissed her cheek like an overgrown schoolboy while Arianne managed to smile, all the while wanting to smack him away.

Lady Weston's jaw dropped. "Annie, you've married? Kitty didn't mention that in her letters. Oh dear, congratulations are in order. You shall make the perfect diplomatic wife."

"That's the general consensus," Phineas said a moment before Rafferty discretely jabbed him in the ribs.

"It was a quick and spontaneous ceremony," Rafferty said. "Not many know of it as yet." Arianne felt Rafferty's hand slide up and down the curve of her waist. The stays in her corset communicated the stimulation like a telegraph to more sensitive areas. She bit her lower lip in agitation.

"I shall write Kitty this evening," Lady Weston said. "She'll be so pleased at your good fortune. The legation is in need of levity and joyous news."

And then all of London would know of her marriage. It was a good thing William was at Deerfield Abbey.

"Allow me to express my condolences," Rafferty said, releasing Arianne and taking Lady Weston's hand. "While I hadn't the pleasure of knowing Lord Weston, I've heard nothing but wonderful things about him. He was a good man."

"Thank you," Lady Weston murmured. "Thank you for that. The newspapers weren't nearly so kind." She took his arm and led him deeper into the residence.

Arianne followed behind. "How could that be?"

"He was found in the company of another woman," Lady Weston said. "In a hotel, and not a particularly good one." She resumed her progress down the passageway. "The papers said he murdered the poor girl and then took his own life, but I know better." She ushered them into a salon. "Someone murdered my husband"—her voice broke—"and then tried to sully his good name."

"Michael will find the one responsible. Have no fear on that score," Arianne said.

Lady Weston motioned for them to sit.

"Have you decided to return to London?" Arianne asked, glancing about the room. Though adequately furnished, the small details that made a residence a home had been removed. No framed photographs graced the piano. None of Lady Weston's renowned china collection cluttered the walls.

"I'm taking Lord Weston back with me so he might be laid to eternal rest with his family. The SS *Oceanic* departs from New York in three days. I've already booked passage for the both of us."

"I apologize for my indelicacy, Lady Weston," Rafferty said, "but was your husband cremated?"

Lady Weston gasped. "We are not pagans, sir!"

"I had not thought you were, madam." Arianne observed Rafferty's attempted recovery. Blast! They should have spent more time on personal diplomacy. "May I inquire where your husband's body currently resides?"

"In a coffin, naturally." Lady Weston frowned as if he were deranged, then turned to Arianne. "I was afraid I would not be able to find something suitable here, but you'd be surprised at the local craftsmanship. We will have the full funeral service at home, of course, where Lord Weston is best remembered."

"My husband and I had hoped to pay our respects to Lord Weston before you take him home," Arianne said with a quick look toward Rafferty.

Lady Weston smiled and patted her hand. "I've placed him in the front salon for just that purpose. The newspapers couldn't stop those who truly admired him from paying their respects."

"Would you still have those newspapers?" Rafferty asked.

"I've instructed Evans to place them in my husband's office," she said. "Liars, all of them. I've banned those rumormongers from the legation." She turned toward Arianne. "The girl was as common as they come. Mary O'Shay was her name. My husband had higher standards. It is preposterous to think that someone of his station would have the slightest interest in a woman of that sort." She pulled at the black lace of her sleeve. "He was meeting her for some matter of state."

"I'm certain that he was," Arianne assured her, though she thought it unlikely. If indeed the woman was as common as Lady Weston represented, she surely wouldn't have knowledge of affairs of state . . . or would she? Arianne thought of Rafferty and his elevated position within the diplomatic community.

Tears glittered in the widow's eyes. "Why would someone want to harm my husband?"

"I don't have the answer to that now, madam. But rest assured I will presently." Rafferty stood. "If you'll pardon us, Phineas and I will begin upon that very investigation immediately." They stood to leave the room.

"Time is the enemy in an investigation such as this," Arianne reassured the widow, darting a glare at Rafferty. "Their abrupt departure is not a reflection on your gracious welcome."

RAFFERTY TURNED TO PHINEAS OUTSIDE THE DOOR. "There must be a policing force. Can you find out who they are and where I need to go to speak with them? I also need to know when the next ship is heading back to England. I intend Barings and Eva to be on it." Hopefully, he could dispense with that little annoyance fairly quickly. Briggs was confining them to the *Irish Rose* for the time being. Still, he'd feel more secure if they were on the way back and not free to meddle with his plans.

"I'm going to search Weston's office here. I'm going to need to see the room where the shooting occurred, and I'm going to have you see what you can find on this Mary O'Shay. Hopefully, I can find something in the office that will explain the purpose of their meeting."

"Are you certain you want to do that now?" Phineas asked. "Look at this place. It's as grand a house as I've ever seen. Don't you want to settle in first?"

"The trail gets colder with each passing day. I was sent here to find a murderer. That's what I intend to do," Rafferty said. He glanced across the passageway to the banquet room, with a table large enough for fifty. A twinge of anxiety slid down his spine. A murder investigation he could handle, but hosting some elaborate affair for a bunch of bloody aristocrats? He'd rather spend the evening with the stiff in the front salon. He'd never really trusted those people, the ones that felt they were somehow better than the rest of the population. He'd made an exception for Arianne, and look where that got him. What had Lord Henderson been thinking to put him in this position? He glanced back at Phineas. "Investigating a murder is all I know how to do."

"LET ME SHOW YOU THE HOUSE." LADY WESTON STOOD. "I've moved my few necessities to a smaller bedroom in anticipation of my return home. I imagine you're anxious to get settled."

"Yes," Arianne said. "It's wonderful to stand on a floor that isn't constantly shifting beneath one's feet. Now that we've reached firm ground, I'd like to stay awhile."

Lady Weston guided her through the massive house and sadly neglected gardens that served as both household and consulate. Introduced to the servants, Arianne smiled at each one, all the while wondering which was to be Eva's contact. While Rafferty was off trying to track a murderer, she would look into the characters of the servants a bit more closely.

Lady Weston led her up a wide staircase. "While there are no guests currently, we often have visitors staying at the legation. I believe this residence was chosen to house the British minister not only for its location but for its many bedrooms. I suppose your husband's associate will be staying here."

"For the time being."

"I'll instruct Evans to have his luggage placed in the blue room. It's the better of the lot." Lady Weston turned to the left at the top of the stairs. "This will be your room."

While any moderate room would appear large after spending the past week in a steamer cabin, this room appeared needlessly huge. A writing desk sat along one wall. Two comfortable chairs were placed in front of a brick fireplace. Why, the bed itself, dressed in inviting satin and velvet, was large enough for several people.

"Your closets and private water closet are down that hallway." Lady Weston pointed toward a passageway off the back corner. "And a tub is behind the screen. It drains, but the servants have to fill it. This way, it's removed from the vapors of the water closet."

"This is so lovely and grand," Arianne said. "Much larger than I anticipated." She peeked down the private passageway and was surprised to see it didn't connect to another bedroom as would be the custom in England. A small worry prickled at the base of her neck. "Lady Weston, where will Mr. Rafferty sleep?"

"Why, in this room, Annie." The older woman smiled indulgently. "The Americans design their houses differently than what we're used to." She glanced at the big bed. "I must admit, this was one of those adjustments we're so often asked to make in the diplomatic services. I hadn't shared a bed with my Lord Weston since my babies were born, but . . . I found it comforting." Tears glistened in her eyes again. She pulled out her handkerchief. "Oh, don't listen to me. As newlyweds, you'd spend more time together than apart at night anyway." She patted Arianne's hand. "I'm so glad you found someone, Annie. He seems like a fine young man. A little brash, perhaps, but that's to be expected with the young. I shall be anxiously anticipating the day you write to say you're with child." She cast an eye at Arianne's belly. "Unless, you're in the family way as we speak." Her eyes sparkled, and for a moment Arianne was gazing into Kitty's eyes. But the moment passed.

The possibility that she was pregnant was unlikely, but Arianne smiled for the sake of Lady Weston. She'd have to work out a different sleeping arrangement once she had the opportunity to talk to Rafferty alone. That is, if he'd speak with her. He'd stopped taking his meals with the other passengers after she assumed the role Eva had vacated, and he avoided her at every turn. She'd almost tripped over the book of Celtic legends that he'd left outside her cabin. The Austen, she noted, was absent. Even Mrs. Summers, who had been her companion for years, abandoned her, insisting Arianne had no need for a chaperone if she was going to pretend to be a wife. She said her good-byes when the ship docked, then, for all intents and purposes, disappeared. Arianne hadn't seen her since.

And she missed her. She missed having someone in whom to confide. She supposed she could talk to Phineas, but she knew whatever she said would find its way back to Rafferty. Bereft and alone, she reminded herself that Sanctuary would be like this. That thought was not encouraging.

"Is everything all right, dear?" Lady Weston asked. "I believe I lost you for a moment."

"I'm sorry." Arianne blushed. "What were you saying? My mind was just occupied with all that needs to be done."

"I was saying that I've arranged for the two of you to be introduced to the president at the Executive Mansion tomorrow. It was the least I could do before I depart."

"You will come, of course," Arianne said.

"A grieving widow doesn't make calls, Arianne. You know that. Besides, you won't need me. It's a simple matter of presentation." She smiled. "In Washington, you can't officially call on anyone until you've met the president. Calls are very important here, for both the minister and for you."

She led Arianne around the upstairs, opening doors for a peek inside the guest rooms, then moving on. "It's a shame that you arrived in June. The most important families will be moving to the countryside to escape Washington's humidity." She paused as if having sudden inspiration. "I'll introduce you to Mrs. James Blaine. That's what I'll do. She's the wife of the secretary of state and is still in town. She'll take you under her wing. You know, Mrs. James Blaine has a daughter about seventeen. I wonder . . . Kitty mentioned something about a nickname . . . Do they still call you Cupid's Mistress?"

RAFFERTY WORKED HIS WAY DOWN THE CORRIDOR, stealing a look inside rooms, until he found the one that appeared to be a combination library and office. Already he'd noticed one thing he found to be a definite improvement in America. The place wasn't crawling with servants in the way of the aristocratic residences back home. He hadn't seen a one of them in his search for the study.

Even though the sun burned brightly outside, the study was dark and stale. "The place could use some of Arianne's concoctions," he murmured, feeling his way to the window. He pulled and secured the long, heavy drapes, then opened the window to admit some fresh air. Then, he turned to see the task before him.

He wasn't the first to search the minister's office, that much was clear. Desk drawers hung open; papers were scattered. Any clues he might have found were most likely gone. A stack of newsprint had been placed on a large upholstered chair. The newspapers, most likely, that Lady Weston insisted contained lies and slander. It was as good a spot as any to begin.

He moved the papers to the floor near the large comfortable chair behind the desk, removed the insufferably hot jacket Arianne had insisted he wear, and tugged the uncomfortable neck cloth free from his collar. The recently admitted light found its way to a crystal decanter that painted a rainbow on a paneled wall. The late Lord Weston must have been an agreeable fellow, he decided, as he poured some of the decanter's liquid into a waiting glass. Thus fortified, Rafferty settled to work his way through the daily editions of something called the *Washington Post*.

Eventually, the light from the window dimmed, but Rafferty still had a few more papers to check. He spotted an oil lamp near the desk and deduced safety matches must be nearby. He pulled out the middle desk drawer and guessed by the scant contents that the drawer, like the rest of the office, had been searched and documents perhaps removed. Rafferty found calling cards, bottles of ink, a bottle of glue, stationery, envelopes, a gold fountain pen, a key, some strange coins—American currency he guessed—but no matches. On a hunch, he slipped the key into the lock above the drawers. It fit perfectly. Not that he was surprised. If anything of value had been in those drawers, it would have been removed by this time.

None of which helped him in his quest for more light. Rafferty slipped his hand into the drawer to explore the very back. His fingertips touched a metallic box. With a bit of prodding, he wiggled the box forward, but in the process he felt a paper skim the top of his knuckles. Something had been glued to the bottom of the desktop. The matches forgotten, Rafferty negotiated the drawer from its mounting mechanism and placed the drawer with contents on the desk so he could see the paper, but it was too dark to peer under the desktop.

The small metallic box, gold from the looks of it, that had

initiated his search was now readily available in the removed drawer and indeed full of thick safety matches. After lighting the lamp, he got down on his hands and knees to further scrutinize the paper. He discovered it to be of little consequence; something merely applied by the desk manufacturer. The paper had small rips missing, as if someone had tried to remove it, but it was glued tight.

Glue . . . He picked up the bottle of viscous fish glue from the drawer. The cheap glue didn't fit with the fancy embossed cards and stationery, the gold fountain pen, and small bottles of ink with self-droppers. Even the matches were stored in a gold container.

If Lord Weston was smart, and there was every reason to think he was, given Arianne's admiration, he may have assumed secrets hidden in conventional fashion would not remain secret for long. Rafferty flipped the drawer over, letting the contents scatter across the top of the desk. A small envelope had been glued to the bottom of the drawer, in the far back. Now this was something worth inspection. He opened the envelope and found another key, one different than the key for the desk. He turned it slowly in the light of the lamp. This one, he suspected, went to a safe. Footsteps thudded in the hall. He quickly pocketed the key and flipped the drawer so it was once again upright.

A knock sounded on the door. Rafferty called out permission to enter.

"Sir, it's time to change for dinner." It was the butler who had admitted them earlier.

"Thank you . . ." Rafferty struggled to remember if he had heard the man's name.

"Evans, sir."

"Yes. Thank you, Evans. I wonder if you can direct me to where my room might be?"

The butler smiled. It was a bit hard to distinguish, but Rafferty believed it was a smile. "The master's chambers are at the top of the stairs to the left, sir."

Master's chambers. He liked the sound of that. He collected his discarded jacket and neck cloth and proceeded to make his way upstairs, pleased with the progress for this first day.

• • •

ARIANNE INHALED DEEPLY. HER ROSE-INFUSED BATH-water filled the room with a lovely garden scent. Closing her eyes, she could imagine herself in simpler times, before the Baron, before learning that her father was not the Duke. She slipped lower in the tub, letting the warm, scented water barely cover her breasts. After a week and a half of sponge baths, the real thing felt luxurious, indulgent, and relaxing . . . until the bedroom door opened.

Arianne glanced in the door's direction, but the hinged screen around the tub blocked her view. It was most likely Kathleen returning, though it seemed she was hardly gone long enough. She smiled. Something about the warm water made minutes stand still, when of course they didn't. "Is it time to dress already?" she called to Kathleen.

Rafferty stepped around the screened enclosure, a wicked smile surrounded by the start of a raspy stubble. "Don't feel you need to dress on my account."

Panicked, she scrambled to cover herself with her hands, splashing water on the metal pad beneath the tub in the process.

"Your Ladyship," he scolded, shaking his head. "Have you forgotten that we are only temporary residents?" He reached for one of the towels left behind by Kathleen. "We wouldn't want to ruin the floors during our brief stay." He stooped so as to mop the water; however, that placed his head on a level with her own. She was so exposed and vulnerable. His gaze heated a path along her body like a living flame, scorching her from her neck to her toes.

Her eyes narrowed. "I had hoped our lessons would have turned you into a gentleman. I can see that they haven't."

He settled himself more comfortably on the floor and rolled the sleeve of his shirt, the fine dark hairs on his arm a sharp contrast with the crisp white linen. "I told you when we first met that I was no gentleman." His fingers dangled over the edge, drawing tiny circles in the water near the spot where her hand covered her breast. On occasion they touched her knuckle, trying to nudge it away, but she held firm. His mouth drew nearer. "You do realize that I've seen you before much like this."

"Never!" she challenged.

He ran his fingernails down the inside of her arm that covered the juncture of her legs. Even the Baron had not seen her thusly, preferring to do the deed in the dark and while she wore her nightgown. Her breath caught when his slow dragging finger touched the inside of her elbow.

"The night of the storm." His eyelids lowered as he stroked the curve of her hip. "You wore a thin nightgown that was drenched with seawater. I could see right through it."

She couldn't slap his hand away without exposing herself, so she closed her eyes and suffered in silence.

"Eva would have given me full access," he said.

"Eva would have given you a knife in your back as well," she replied.

His fingers paused in their sensual exploration of her side. "That's correct. While her ladyship prefers to aim straight for the heart." He pulled his hand from the water and shook it dry, then placed her dressing gown within reach. "Get dressed," he said. "Let's see how well you negotiate."

Her heart racing, Arianne patted herself dry as best she could, then slipped her arms into her thin dressing gown. Whatever had made her think he was anything more than a rogue?

She'd thought she'd have time to take a bath before he'd halt his work in the study. She wasn't even certain he'd remember the need to dress for dinner. Her cheeks must glow with embarrassment. Even as she tied the sash and clasped the lapels under her chin, she could feel the silk sticking to missed moisture, molding the gown to her contours. Christopher! How was she to negotiate anything from this damp, unsupported, downright humiliating position? For that matter, what sort of negotiations was he referring to?

She tentatively poked her head around the screen. From the sound, she suspected he was using the water closet, which meant she hadn't much time. Her dinner ensemble lay sprawled on the bed, right next to what appeared to be his discarded jacket. While she was tempted to grab her chemise, she would have to remove the dressing gown to put it on. Instead she tiptoed on the lush Persian carpet to the bed where she grabbed her drawers with the layered lace at the leg holes.

She hiked the dressing gown to her thigh, preparing to slip

her foot in one leg, when his footsteps sounded in the closet hallway. She pushed down the gown and hid the drawers behind her.

Taking a deep breath, she lifted her chin defiantly. "What exactly did you wish to negotiate?"

· Fifteen ·

RAFFERTY PAUSED NEAR THE BED, HIS GAZE FLIT-
ting over her form, lingering in the spots where the silk
molded to her breasts, her hips. Lord, he wanted her. As much
as he reminded himself that Lady Arianne was a thoroughbred
while he was a draft horse strapped to the plow, he wanted her.
Even though she'd rejected him—Christ, maybe because she
rejected him—he wanted her. His hands slipped to unfasten the
button at the top of his shirt. "There's only one bed."

Her gaze was locked on his fingers. He liked that. He unfastened the next two buttons. "There's only one room." He
unfastened the next two buttons, then slipped off his braces.
"We both need to change clothes, sleep . . . bathe." Did her
cheeks darken? Good. If he intimidated her enough, she would
move into one of the other bedrooms, making his life less com-
plicated. He pulled his shirt from his trousers and unbuttoned
the final button, letting the shirt hang open. "How does her
ladyship propose to do that?"

"I assumed that you, being a gentleman, would move to one
of the smaller guest rooms."

He laughed, slipped the shirt off his shoulders, and tossed

it to land on his jacket. "We've already established that her ladyship's presumptions are misplaced." He crossed his arms in front of him and pulled off his cotton undervest. Her eyes widened. She hadn't seen him like this before. He thought he should see some signs of alarm, but instead, all he saw was . . . appreciation? What was wrong with her? The door was right there.

He sat in a chair and worked on his boot. "Now the way I see it, Lord Henderson sent me to accomplish a mission and, by the grace of God, I plan to do just that." The boot hit the floor with a thud. He crossed the other to his knee. "Your Ladyship decided to come along on this journey," he said, raising an eyebrow at her, "for the thrill?" The second boot hit the floor. He stood and unfastened the button at his waistline. "By rights, I should have complete rights to the room, the bed, and the bath. But if her ladyship wants to exchange something—"

"Stop that," she said, or was it commanded? Well, it was about time. He was running out of buttons.

"Her ladyship speaks. What—"

"Stop calling me that."

He hadn't expected that. "Isn't that what you want, Miss Lady-of-the-Manor, Lady Aristocrat, Lady Uppity?"

"I'd prefer it if you called me Anne, or Ari, or Arianne." She pulled her fancy lacy drawers from behind her back, then rolled one leg into a fabric circle. Standing on one foot, she stepped through the hole.

"But aren't you the daughter of a duke?" he asked. He'd seen women get dressed before, but not with this sort of graceful dance.

"Not really." She stepped into the second leg, then bending forward, she pulled the material up behind her. "I am the sister of a duke, though."

If any of those flies they'd seen on their way to the legation were buzzing in this room, his gaping jaw would have swallowed them for dinner. She turned her back to him and pulled the fancy things up in front. He fell into the chair he'd just vacated. "How can that be, woman? Is this a riddle? You are either . . . wait! . . . wait one minute." He slapped his hand to his head. "You must be illegitimate! Don't tell me you're baseborn."

She picked up a frilly slip of linen from the bed. "I spent my entire life believing my father was the old Duke of Bedford. I only learned recently that he could not sire children. He arranged for another to take his place." She turned her back to him once again.

In short order, she removed the dressing gown. Her bare elegant back rose above her linen-encased buttocks. Desire slammed hard in his gut. She lifted her arms, offering the briefest glimpse of the sides of her breasts before white linen drifted down her back. She spun around to face him. Though her charms were hidden beneath the cloth, knowing there was just one layer between them had a tantalizing effect. They were the equals they'd been on the night of the storm.

"So you can see, I haven't aristocratic blood flowing through my veins. I'm not some highly sought prize. So if we could just treat each other with respect, I think we can survive this forced intimacy."

Rafferty stood. "You're wrong." He picked up the clothes she'd selected for him for the evening and tucked them under his arm. He headed for the door, but turned, his face as sober as a minister on Sunday. "You're still a prize," he said, "and a highly sought one at that."

RAFFERTY STOOD IN THE PASSAGEWAY AND LOOKED AT the closed door. That hadn't turned out quite the way he'd anticipated. Not that he hadn't supposed he'd be the one sneaking down the hall late at night, but he thought he'd at least manage another of those passionate kisses for his sacrifice, especially after he'd glimpsed her in her bath. He'd hoped to reestablish that sense of intimacy they'd experienced the night of the storm. He hadn't counted on gaining a piece of her soul.

Nor had he counted on her feelings of guilt when addressed as a lady. All this time he had felt less than her equal due to her aristocratic title, while she had felt less than an aristocrat because of her status.

One thing was certain; aristocrat or not, she would not approve of him standing bare-chested in the upstairs passageway. He looked down the hall. Now what? Phineas was behind one of these doors, Lady Weston behind another, both probably in some state of undress, much like himself. There were other doors as well, but who knew what awaited him there?

He heard women's laughter and footsteps on the wide staircase. Lady's maids, given the proximity of the dinner hour, most likely. He couldn't be caught like this, even by the servants. He opened the first door on the left and prayed the shock wouldn't jolt Lady Weston into an early reunion with her poor departed husband.

"Rafferty?" Phineas glanced to the door. "Even you know that a shirt is required at the dinner table. What are you doing?"

Rafferty explained that to maintain peace between he and Arianne, he'd agreed to dress in a room apart from her preparations.

"What about the sleeping arrangements?" Phineas asked. "Have you reached an agreement on that as well?"

Though he hadn't actually discussed it with Arianne, Rafferty already knew the outcome. While buttoning his dinner shirt, Rafferty glanced over his shoulder at the double bed in this guest room, obviously designed for a married couple. He looked back at Phineas, eyebrow raised.

"I was afraid of that." Phineas sighed.

"I can't very well go someplace else," Rafferty said. "The servants would know. The essence of a secret is that as few people are aware of the situation as possible." He replaced his trousers with a black pair and pulled the braces over his shoulders.

"It's a good thing I know you well, my friend." Phineas slapped him on the shoulder. "Just make certain to leave the room in the morning before the servants arrive, old chap. There are other sorts of rumors I'd like to avoid."

Rafferty smiled. "Agreed." He worked the silk neck cloth around the collar. "Did you discover anything today?"

"I found the shipping office," Phineas replied. "I don't think you want to put Barings and Eva on the same liner as Lady Weston. That one is sailing out of New York in a few days. The SS *Germanic* is due in Baltimore Harbor in two days. It'll stay in port for another three to unload the cargo, restock, and prepare for the trip back. That one might be the best bet for dispensing with Miss St. Claire."

"I knew the *Irish Rose* could beat the *Germanic* given our head start," Rafferty crowed.

"Maybe it would be best to keep Miss St. Claire here for a while," Phineas said. "Without someone to watch over her, she could bugger the works if she tells anyone what we're about."

"That's true," Rafferty said, considering. The two hadn't married yet, though they'd announced that was their intention. "Let's leave her on the *Irish Rose* for the time being. Briggs is taking the *Rose* up the coast for some repairs. Barings can stay on board with her if he likes." He checked the fit of his jacket in the mahogany-framed mirror. "So, what do you think? Will I meet Lady Arianne's lofty standards?"

"If those standards only concern appearance, I imagine you'll do." Phineas smiled. "Don't bungle the silverware, though."

Rafferty overlooked the implication that he failed in other areas. A wry smile twisted his lips. Arianne herself had made that quite clear. Rafferty glanced at Phineas. "Did I ever thank you for that quick course on silverware you gave me before Lady Arianne's eleven-course feast? I seem to recall I was in a foul mood that evening."

"That you were." Phineas's tone softened, perhaps to match Rafferty's own contemplative one. "But you've returned the favor on numerous occasions. Shall we join the ladies downstairs? I hope the legation has a superior cook. I could manage one of Lady Arianne's eleven-course meals."

Rafferty paused. "You go ahead. There's something I should do first."

"Don't take long, or I'll be testing Lady Arianne's theory on edible flowers." As if to confirm his appetite, Phineas's stomach growled. He was just about to leave the room when he turned. "I should have asked. Did you learn anything in the examination of the office?"

"I did," Rafferty said. "We'll discuss that later."

ARIANNE GRIPPED THE TALL BEDPOST WHILE HER MAID fastened the back of the rose pink satin bodice. "How are you getting on with the other servants?" she asked Kathleen.

"Just fine, ma'am." Kathleen tightened the fabric lacing so

that the long cuirasse bodice would mold seamlessly to her mistress's corseted silhouette. "So many of the girls are from Ireland, it's like being back home."

Arianne remembered Mr. Barings's observation on the *Irish Rose* about Ireland's chief export. Whole families of immigrants had traveled the Atlantic in worse conditions than they had experienced on the *Rose*. The thought made her shudder.

"I've been assigned a room upstairs with another girl from Limerick. Mrs. Watson, the housekeeper, seems fair enough—a bit gruff, but I've heard of worse."

Lady Weston had introduced Mrs. Watson when they made their house tour. The woman hadn't seemed gruff then, but the iron fist of most housekeepers was sheathed in a velvet glove when the mistress of the residence appeared.

"There aren't as many on the service staff as at the Duke's residence." Kathleen tied the lacing and hid the ends, then checked the drape of the satin flounce over the bustle. "They were anxious about you, ma'am. I told them you were as kind an employer as they'd ever have."

"Thank you, Kathleen." Arianne stepped from the bedpost to the front of the tilted mirror. She hesitated, soothing her hand over the brocaded silk panel that fell in the front of the dress. "Did they ask about Mr. Rafferty?"

"Aye." Kathleen moved to Arianne's side and patted a lock of hair in place. She smiled. "I told them that you'd just married and I hadn't had a chance to work under him yet." She hesitated a moment, then glanced at Arianne's reflection in the mirror. "I meant to wish you well, Your Ladyship. I wish I would have known about the wedding. I would have fixed your hair extra special or made a little tussie-mussie out of some of your flowers, if you would've let me."

"Thank you, Kathleen. Had it not been of such a sudden nature, I would have appreciated those efforts." She and Rafferty had decided not to tell Kathleen about the ruse. Only Phineas and Mrs. Summers were aware of the deception afoot, and Mrs. Summers had chosen to remain on the *Irish Rose*. She said Arianne didn't need her anymore. She was wrong. Arianne wished there was someone she could confide in about her attraction to Rafferty and the consequences to Sanctuary if she followed her heart.

"You look lovely, Your Ladyship," Kathleen said.

Arianne smiled in response and picked up her fan. "Then I suppose it's time to join the others." Evening had little effect on the heavy heated air of Washington. She could understand why so many traveled away from the city in the summer. Arianne had no wish to see the misery that July temperatures would bring.

Before she could reach the door, the knob turned and Rafferty entered.

Her breath caught. He looked magnificent. The perfect image of a confident, competent diplomat. She remembered Mrs. Summers's observation several weeks ago that debutants would be eager to be considered for Rafferty's hand, and gazing at the man before her, she'd have to agree. But it was the rougher, less refined Rafferty that stirred her senses. She had seen the powerful play of muscles across his chest and felt the rasp of his unshaven chin against her sensitive skin, and she knew those things lay beneath the tailored clothes. The memory made her body spring alive beneath her stays.

"You look lovely this evening," he said, crossing the room toward her. His eyes warmed. "I thought I should escort my beautiful wife for our first dinner at the legation." His gaze shifted to where Kathleen gathered Arianne's spent clothing.

Ah yes, it was part of the ruse. She smiled, accepting his kiss on her cheek.

He placed his hands on her constricted waist and pulled her against his chest. Her own hands lifted to his biceps. A wife would not push her new husband away, she reasoned. His lips traced a path from her cheek to her ear. "Are you ready?" he whispered.

In the back of her mind, another whispered, *Are you ready for me?* Arianne's body stiffened, fully engrossed in the humiliating memory of her willing submission to the Baron. A shiver raced down her spine.

Rafferty stepped back, his hands still on her waist. His brow furled. "Is something wrong?"

Arianne shook her head, even though the remnants of that shameful memory still tingled along her neck. "I'm fine," she insisted, snapping open the fan. "It must be the heat." She forced a bright smile on her face. "Shall we go down?"

• • •

THEY FOUND PHINEAS AND LADY WESTON WAITING IN the breakfast room, a smaller, more intimate dining area than the impressive banquet hall. A large floral arrangement graced the dining table set for four. Rafferty imagined Arianne's fingers twitched to remove the blossoms to subjugate to her various tortures. His lips tugged back in a smile as he perused his "wife." She had an analytical mind in the way she studied flowers, a quality he had foolishly overlooked when confronted with her diversion. He had thought she was simply a fashionable aristocrat with an overabundance of time and a lacking of practical application for it.

"Rafferty, you're smiling," Phineas announced. "You must tell us what has caught your fancy."

Rafferty sent an ineffective glare toward Phineas. "I was observing that my wife's beauty surpasses that of the floral arrangement." He shifted his gaze to Arianne, whose wide eyes reflected her surprise. "Such captivating charm should be immortalized in a flower of her own." He lifted his glass of wine. "May I propose a toast to the lovely, enchanting Lady Arianne Rafferty."

"Here, here," Phineas echoed and lifted his glass. Rafferty watched a lovely flush rise to her cheeks.

Lady Weston sipped her wine, along with the others. "You two remind me of myself and my Lord Weston, may he rest in peace, when we were young. I must say that it does my weary heart good to meet the man so obviously in love with my Annie." She pulled a handkerchief from her sleeve and dabbed it at her nose. "Her father was such a curmudgeon, I'm sorry to say. He never appreciated what a gift he had in Annie. I'm so pleased she found someone who values her the way we do."

Given his recent understanding of her true parentage, facts and clues were falling into place as if he'd been doing his own investigation. He glanced at Arianne, but she concentrated on her soup.

"Tell me, Lady Weston, does La . . . Arianne favor her mother?"

"She's the spitting image of that fair lady," she replied. "I've often thought that was the reason her father kept her in distant finishing schools all those years. The sight of his daughter reminded him overly much of his dearly departed wife, the Duchess of Bedford."

Or the sight of her reminded him of his unfaithful wife, Rafferty mused. Either way, Arianne suffered.

"It was kind of you to take her in," Rafferty said.

"We did what we could, but Annie was the daughter of a duke. We couldn't call her one of our own." She smiled at Arianne, who averted her gaze, biting her lip in the process. "But she was as close and dear to us as our Kitty."

Rafferty supposed he and Arianne had more in common than he'd anticipated. The Fenians killed his family while her father merely abandoned her. In both cases, they matured without a place to call home. He could see as well why Lord and Lady Weston were so important to her. Important enough to risk everything to restore a dead man's reputation? He frowned. Perhaps not. But Lady Weston's information did add to his greater understanding of the woman he would abandon later tonight.

"I wish I could stay longer to help you two adapt to Washington society, but it's time that I take Lord Weston home," Lady Weston said, slicing into her roasted veal. "I assume Annie has mentioned that I've arranged for you and she to meet the president tomorrow. I shan't be able to accompany you, but—"

"Tomorrow?" He looked at Arianne. "Phineas and I have already made plans for tomorrow."

"One does not refuse a meeting with the president," she said with a tight smile.

"Oh dear heavens, no." Lady Weston shook her head. "To refuse a meeting with the head of the host country would be a stain on the entire legation."

Rafferty grumbled beneath his breath. The president's meeting would push his own investigations back a day. Christ. They could have taken the SS *Germanic* for all the good the extra days did for him. He stabbed his veal with perhaps more force than needed. However, as he chewed, he remembered that if they'd taken the SS *Germanic*, he'd have missed Arianne's passionate kiss and the sight of her in that wet nightgown.

"I shall assume that one-sided smile means you appreciate the veal, Mr. Rafferty." Lady Weston sliced a small piece for herself. "The legation has an excellent cook."

"How did you know that we'd arrive in time to meet with

the president?" Rafferty asked. "The SS *Germanic* doesn't dock for two days."

"Lord Henderson sent a telegram that you had just left London by steamer. When I asked for the appointment, I thought you would have arrived several days ago." Lady Weston considered Rafferty. "You must have had a stormy crossing."

Rafferty and Arianne exchanged glances. He wondered if she remembered that uncomfortable stairwell with the same fondness as he.

"We encountered one storm at sea," Phineas said. "We survived it well enough."

Lady Weston shuddered. "I'm not looking forward to that aspect of returning home. But you've had the worst behind you. It should be smooth sailing for the both of you from here on."

Rafferty somehow doubted that. There was Arianne: calm, elegant, and stubborn as an ox in a peat bog when it came to him. There was a corpse in the front salon whose honor he was expected to vindicate, a spy in the household in league with the murderer who destroyed his family, and an introduction tomorrow to a man who probably expected a refined diplomat—not a charlatan like him. With all due respects to Lady Weston, she hadn't a clue what she was talking about.

· Sixteen ·

"A KEY," PHINEAS OBSERVED, HIS VOICE BARELY above a whisper. "What is it for?"

They had adjourned to Lord Weston's study, presumably for whiskey and conversation. Lady Weston had excused herself soon after the almond pudding. Arianne made her excuses as well, thus the men were free to quietly discuss Rafferty's discovery, ever mindful that a Fenian sympathizer in servant's attire still roamed the halls if Barnell's letter to Eva was correct.

"I suspect a safe," Rafferty said. "The question is where? I didn't notice a floor safe when I was here earlier."

They both turned toward a large painting of the moonlit Houses of Parliament and Westminster Abbey on the Thames. They carefully lifted the painting from the wall but found no safe hidden there. They checked behind the harsh photographic rendering of Queen Victoria, to no avail. For the next two hours, they quietly and carefully checked the wall behind each book in the study, but they discovered only painted wall, and in one section, a box of hidden cigars. Rafferty imagined Lady Weston disapproved.

"There's no safe in this room, Rafferty. Are you certain it goes to a safe?"

Rafferty squeezed the metal in his palm. "It's too small for a door. Based on the lengths he used to hide it, it's a safe key. But the safe could be elsewhere in the house. That way if one or the other were found, it would be more difficult to put the two together. Ingenious, actually."

"We need to search the entire residence?" Phineas asked, his displeasure evident. A floorboard creaked overhead, reminding them both that the hour had grown late, but it put something else in Rafferty's mind.

"Perhaps not," he said. "I would think Lord Weston, and all the ministers before him, would want to keep secret information private with access limited to those trusted most in the household."

Phineas furled his brow and shrugged.

"The master's chambers," Rafferty explained. "If we can't find the safe there, then we'll search the legation room by room."

ARIANNE SAT AT THE WRITING DESK IN THE BEDROOM composing a list of all she needed to do as the new mistress of the legation. The merchants opened their doors early in the morning, and she planned to be there. While she had ordered cards in London with Rafferty's name and Washington address, she needed to order new cards for herself. Fortunately, current etiquette stipulated that a woman's card should not include an address. The stationer should be able to process the order in a timely fashion.

She needed to speak with the cook about her expectations for meals and with the housekeeper regarding servants. Her pen paused. Eva's letter had mentioned someone in the employ of the house was sympathetic to Mr. Barnell's cause. She'd need to be observant. Perhaps this was something she could ferret out for Rafferty. He had so much on his plate, and yet . . . he took it all in stride. Even the unwelcome news that a presidential invitation took precedence over his investigation was met with little more than low-pitched grousing. She'd known other men who would have aggressively expressed their displeasure over something less significant.

A soft knock at the door interrupted her thoughts. Rafferty entered as if conjured from her musings. She pulled the lapels of her dressing gown together over her nightgown. An impulsive action on her part—silly, really, as the man had seen her in much less. The movement drew his gaze to her chest, making her feel as a mouse caught in the sights of a very hungry cat. She swallowed.

"I thought we had reached an agreement over possession of this room," she said, knowing there was little she could do to buttress her claim. Bravado remained her sole weapon.

"Have you forgotten that for the purposes of our subterfuge, my wardrobe and personal effects are here?" he asked, his eyes crinkled. "After all the effort you've expended to have me dress in this fashion, do you wish me to sleep in these clothes?"

"No, not at all." She relaxed and shook her head. "My apologies. I shouldn't have presumed . . ."

He eased closer to her, untying the knot of his neck cloth. "What exactly did you presume, Arianne?" His eyebrow raised. "Did you assume that I'd revert to the morally depraved scoundrel you first met in Lord Henderson's office?"

"I assumed you'd collect your clothes and change elsewhere," she said, holding her ground.

He laughed. "Indeed I shall, in deference to your innocence. But for the sake of any watchful eyes in the household, allow me to linger a bit longer in my own quarters." He removed his jacket, then disappeared into their shared closet.

He assumed she was still innocent. In many ways she still was. Her experience had not been expansive, nor particularly pleasant, but in all the ways that truly mattered, she could no longer claim that description. However, he had no need to know that.

She returned to her list. The timing of their arrival in Washington was awkward. According to Lady Weston, so many of those who mattered had already left the city for the summer. Given the restricted hours allowed for calls and the return of same, she'd have to race about the unfamiliar city like a street peddler hawking rotting fruit. They needed a social function that would draw those remaining in Washington to the legation.

A light repetitive thump from the tiny closet room caught

her ear along with the realization that Rafferty was taking extraordinary time gathering bits of his wardrobe. "Rafferty?" she called lightly.

No response. She didn't wish to raise her voice in case "the watcher" had ears as well. She decided to investigate.

The drawers in a small chest were extended while Rafferty judiciously slid his hand behind her gowns and foundation pieces that hung on hooks on the closet's walls. He rapped his knuckle lightly, listened, then moved on.

"What are you doing?" she whispered.

"Looking for a safe, or a hidden compartment behind these walls," he explained tersely.

She frowned. "Why would you believe there's a safe in the closet?"

"I found a key carefully hidden in Lord Weston's study. It has to fit somewhere." He rapped on another section before moving on again. "I've already searched the study."

A key! Now that was promising. No wonder Lord Henderson said Rafferty was competent. "What can I do?"

"Search the bedroom for a safe or a locked box." His knuckles tapped on a new section of the wall, then he stepped around a hanging gown to start the process once more. "I'm almost finished here."

Together they looked under tablecloths, tugged on the bricks on the fireplace looking for loose mortar, tapped on the walls, and checked drawers. Nothing.

A trickle of perspiration ran down her back. She grasped her fan off the desk and sat on the bed while stirring a breeze in the humid air. Rafferty's shirt was molding to his chest in a most flattering fashion. "Where do we look next?" she asked.

Wiping his brow with his shirtsleeve, he sat heavily beside her. "I suppose the key could be for a safety-deposit box in a bank or at a hotel. However, I would have thought he'd like to keep his secrets close. I know I would."

"We've looked everywhere in this room," she said. Strange. She should be frustrated by their failure, yet she felt exhilarated by the search. They were working together, not as instructor and pupil, nor aristocrat and . . . not. They worked as equals, and it was refreshing. She hadn't felt so free, unfettered by society's restrictions, since she was a child.

"You're smiling." He glowered, then his lips twisted to a smile. "Why are we smiling?"

"I was thinking this was fun, working together like this."

"It would be more fun if we found the safe." His eyes narrowed. "I thought Lady Weston packed all the family's possessions in anticipation of her trip." He pointed to a framed picture hanging on the wall near the water closet. "Why did she leave that?"

Heat rose to Arianne's cheeks. "I think she left it for me. Her daughter Kitty painted that portrait of me when we were both very young." She laughed. "I'm surprised she's kept it all these years."

Rafferty raised a brow and walked to the portrait. He pulled it from the wall with barely a glance at the girl in a freshly starched pinafore. "Eureka." He grinned. "Here's the safe."

While he reached in his trouser pocket for the key, she came to investigate. The key fit, and soon Rafferty extracted several documents, a letter, and a Webley RIC revolver. Rafferty looked at the gun and replaced it in the safe, but he carried the papers to the writing desk where the light was better. Arianne slipped onto the desk chair. Rafferty hovered over her shoulder.

Arianne held the letter so they both could read it, that is if the jasmine scent on her neck didn't distract him. She read the letter out loud, something about the assassination of Tsar Alexander II earlier in the year and the resulting influx of Russian immigrants.

Rafferty had no interest or concern about Russian immigrants. It wasn't part of his assignment from Lord Henderson. Instead, he listened to the lovely lilting sound of her voice and gazed at the wide expanse of skin from her earlobe, around her jaw, to her neck. If he leaned a little closer, he could nuzzle that neck with his chin, an enticing temptation.

She picked up another document. "Looks like shipping schedules," she said, oblivious to the true nature of his focus. "Look, here's the *Irish Rose*." She tapped the paper. "And here . . . and here . . ."

Rafferty's attention snapped to the paper. He pulled the sheet from her fingers to study it closely. The ships listed all traveled between Ireland and America with a stop in London along the way. While several ships were listed, the *Irish Rose* was listed more than most. "I'll have to take this up with Captain Briggs," he said. "Maybe he can make sense of it."

Arianne pulled the other letter from the envelope. Unlike the previous letter, this one was not written to Lord Weston. Arianne read:

> *Dear Rosie:*
>
> *I need your aid most urgently. I fear for my life. I have knowledge of a plan so foul I cannot write of it for fear this letter will be found. May I approach your employer? I cannot go to the police. Toomey will kill me. Please help.*
>
> *Your cousin,*
> *Mary O'Shay*

"O'Shay," Arianne repeated. "Isn't that the name of the woman found murdered with Lord Weston?"

"I knew it!" Rafferty straightened, slamming a fist into his open palm. "I knew Toomey was behind this."

"You believe it to be the same Toomey?" Arianne asked, incredulous.

"One and the same, but he won't get away with it," he said with grim determination. "Not this time."

Arianne pushed the papers aside to uncover the list she'd begun earlier. She wrote the name *Rosie* beside her note to talk to the housekeeper about the servants. Already they were making progress. She glanced up at Rafferty with awe, grateful that Lord Henderson had the foresight to choose Rafferty to solve the murder of her friend. He was going to make a fine British minister.

BY NOON THE NEXT DAY, ARIANNE PACED IN THE SALON. What was Lord Henderson thinking to assign Rafferty as British minister? He obviously had no regard for the significance of meeting President Garfield.

Lady Weston glanced at her with concern. "You're expected at the Executive Mansion at three o'clock. Did your husband say where he was going?"

Arianne chafed with the reference to her husband. While it

was highly doubtful that she would ever have the legitimate right to refer to another man as "husband," if she did, it would be someone who could be counted upon to be where he should, when he should. Her question was all the more awkward, as Rafferty had left before she rose for breakfast. She hadn't a clue where or when he had disappeared with his friend Phineas. To acknowledge that might cast aspersion on their separate sleeping arrangements.

Fortunately, Rafferty walked into the legation before she was forced to add another layer of falsehoods. Before he dashed upstairs to change, he kissed her on the cheek.

Lady Weston grinned. "I do believe that man takes every opportunity to kiss you. You are ever so fortunate to find a devoted husband, Annie."

Arianne smiled but decided this need to constantly embarrass her would be grounds for another negotiation.

The appointment with the president was a diplomatic necessity, as it opened the door for introductions to other diplomatic and political personages. Once the legation driver delivered them to the Executive Mansion, they waited in a small antechamber until called by the president's secretary.

"Mr. Rafferty, is it?" The bearded president walked around his desk and extended his hand. "It's about time they sent someone without some fancy title. Welcome to the United States of America, Ambassador Rafferty."

Arianne bristled at the incorrect use of title—Rafferty was not an ambassador—but knew enough not to comment. The ends of Garfield's full mustache lifted, the only indication of a smile.

"Mr. Rafferty is just fine, Mr. President." Holding his hat in one hand, Rafferty shook hands with the other. "And may I congratulate you on your successful campaign."

Garfield nodded his head. "Much to be done, much to be done." He turned to Arianne. "And this must be your wife, Mrs. Rafferty." Arianne dipped in a partial curtsy.

"Lady Arianne Rafferty," her husband corrected.

The president's tired eyes widened a moment. "I didn't know that could happen."

"My wife obliged me by marrying beneath her," Rafferty explained with that half smile.

"Don't they all," Garfield exclaimed with a hearty laugh. "I know my Lucretia did."

Arianne fought to keep her smile in place. Levity had no place in diplomacy.

"I wish you could meet Mrs. Garfield, but she's recuperating from malaria," the president said to Arianne. "Blasted mosquitoes."

"Please convey our best wishes for her full recovery," she said.

"She's convalescing along the New Jersey shore. I will pass along your wishes when I see her in a few weeks," he promised. "Mr. Rafferty, thank you and the missus for advising me of your arrival. I hope I can call upon your expertise should there be occasion."

"Most assuredly, Mr. President." They exchanged handshakes once again.

After they had left the strange oval room, another man with a drooping mustache and bushy sideburns approached from the far end of the hallway. Christopher, these Americans loved their furry lips! Even the Baron had confined his mustache to his upper lip and didn't allow it to droop down his face. At least Rafferty demonstrated a competent hand with a razor.

The man approached on their left. Rafferty's brow furled a moment. "Mr. Vice President? Mr. Chester Arthur?"

The man stopped cautiously.

"I recognize you from the illustrations in the *Washington Post*." Rafferty extended his hand and grinned. "I'm Michael Rafferty, the new British minister and a County Cork man, myself."

Wariness faded from the vice president's eyes, and he accepted the offered handshake. "It's a pleasure to meet you, sir. British minister, you say? Isn't that unusual given Ireland's political climate?"

Rafferty's eyes crinkled. "May I assume you have an interest in the parliamentary discussions on home rule?"

Arthur smiled cautiously. "My opinions on home rule are well known but are of little consequence. My loyalties are to my country and my constituents." He paused, his brow knitted. "Your name sounds familiar, but I can't place where I heard it." He studied Rafferty a moment and laughed. "I'm certain it will come to me after you're gone."

Rafferty introduced Arianne, and the vice president acknowledged her with a nod.

While they spoke, Arianne noted the scrutiny of a newcomer to the waiting area. She supposed the man was as shocked as she at Rafferty's aggressive behavior, introducing himself to a stranger without the recommendation of another, especially when the stranger was the second most powerful man in the American government.

As soon as they had left the Executive Mansion and were situated in the legation carriage, she let him know her mind.

"Did not Lord Henderson instruct me to assist you in areas of deportment? Why then do you not listen and ignore the very advice I have striven to teach you?"

"Christ. Not another lecture on attire. Arianne, I've cut my hair for your satisfaction. I've shaved. I'm wearing gray trousers, white shirt, swallowtail black jacket." He held up his hand. "Gray gloves." Then he thumped his finger on the top of his gray top hat. "Gray as well. I am the epitome of a proper British minister."

"You forgot to use your calling cards." She hated the whiney tone in her voice, but it just slipped out of her mouth.

He sighed. "Arianne, the people I'm accustomed to working with don't carry calling cards. They know who I am and why I'm there. I need time to adjust to this card business."

"We were late because of you," she complained as if he'd never spoken.

"We weren't late." He looked at the passing scenery. "We just didn't arrive as early as you wished."

That was true. She had hoped that by arriving early she would meet the president's wife, but then, that was not possible.

"I didn't know where you were."

"I left a note. I needed to speak with Captain Briggs."

"A note?"

"I slipped it under your door this morning before I left." He smiled. "I hope you thrashed around enough for two people in that big bed. We wouldn't want the servants to get suspicious."

She frowned. "I didn't see a note."

"Perhaps one of the maids moved it when they were cleaning your room."

"I requested that no one enter my room until I went downstairs for breakfast." She glanced at him. "I didn't want anyone to see I was the only one in the bed."

"Wise of you. Of course, we could remedy the subterfuge if we just shared the same bed. Eva would have done as much."

She swatted his knee with her fan. "It was considerate of you to leave a note behind. I suppose I could have overlooked it in my hurry to prepare for the introduction to the president. When we left England, I hadn't planned my wardrobe for such an occasion."

"You had no reason for concern. You had the eye of every man present."

A glow warmed inside her at his compliment. "Why did you need to speak with Captain Briggs?"

"The *Irish Rose* appeared several times on Weston's list. I wanted to see if the captain recognized a pattern to it."

"Did he?"

"No. Phineas is going to see if he can uncover its purpose."

While he tried to mask his concern, Arianne could tell that the list troubled him deeply. He slipped into his thoughts. She slipped into hers. Despite her earlier words, she was fairly certain Rafferty's note had disappeared before she had a chance to discover it. Which reminded her of her own list that she had begun last evening. One item in particular was in need of attention. It was time to learn more about the servants.

· *Seventeen* ·

RAFFERTY TAGGED THE STRANGER OUTSIDE THE legation as a policeman before the carriage settled to a rest. The man kept his back to the brick wall and watched the street as if to memorize the faces of the people passing by. That stance was the same on both sides of the Atlantic, as was the realization that an enforcer of the law outside one's door was never good news. Rafferty felt his muscles tense, preparing for a footrace. Too often his assignments in London had placed him, for all appearances, on the wrong side of the "Blue Devils." He forced his expression to remain calm and aloof as he opened the door and assisted Arianne out of the carriage.

"Would you be the British minister, sir?" the man asked with a respectful but dubious air.

"Yes," Rafferty replied, still wary about the man's intentions.

"My sergeant said you had questions about the murder at the Lincoln hotel. I was told to report over here directly." And he was none too pleased about it, if Rafferty read the tone correctly. Rafferty relaxed, suddenly appreciating the power inherent with his new title. He never imagined the police would make a special trip to be at his beck and call—to investigate some form of wrongdoing, perhaps, but not to answer questions. It was a bit of a heady realization.

Arianne had already entered the legation, anxious to share the experience of the presidential appointment with Lady Weston. Wishing to spare the women the details of murder, Rafferty invited the officer to join him in the study.

"Officer . . ."

"Simmons, sir."

"Officer Simmons, I read the account in the *Washington Post*," Rafferty said. "They described it as a murder and a suicide."

"That would be correct, sir." The man shifted uncomfortably. Rafferty indicated that he should sit. The policeman complied.

"Tell me how you reached that conclusion." Rafferty held up the crystal decanter in offer of a drink, but the policeman shook his head.

"Wasn't hard. She was lying on the bed. Stabbed in the chest, she was. He dropped the knife on the floor, then shot himself in the head. He couldn't have lived long."

"And the gun?"

"It was on the floor near his hand. He must have dropped it after the shot." Apparently he sensed Rafferty's unspoken criticism. "Lady Weston said her husband owned a revolver."

Rafferty didn't share that the gun her husband owned was still in the safe in the bedroom. "Did you ask Lady Weston what kind of gun Lord Weston owned?"

"No, sir. I didn't, sir."

"What kind of gun was used in the shooting?"

The officer made a great show of removing a notepad. "An English Bulldog revolver. One of those little ones that fit in a pocket."

"What do you know about the girl?"

"She came here by train from New York the day before her murder. She paid for the room. We found a note from Lord Weston, a stub from the train, and some coins."

"It was an amorous note?"

"It was a note with money so she could come and see him. She had that look about her, you know? Her clothes weren't fancy, but she was pretty. If you had seen her, you would understand why a man would send money to bring her from New York."

Rafferty thought of how Arianne always insisted that appearance said a lot about a person. Though he was quite sure this wasn't what she had in mind. From what he was hearing, he was beginning to believe that Arianne and Lady Weston had the right of it.

"Did you question anyone? Did they hear a gunshot?"

"There was a dox . . . a woman of the evening next door." He glanced up. "The Hotel Lincoln is the sort that keeps late hours if you know what I mean, sir." He looked back down at his notebook. "She ran out into the hallway but says she didn't see anyone. She knocked on the door a couple of times, but when no one answered, she notified the front desk."

"You wouldn't know this woman's name, would you?" Rafferty thought he might be able to learn more from talking to her directly.

"She called herself Dolly Madison, but that's not her real name. I don't think she wants to be known, sir."

Rafferty sighed, his frustration evident. "Did anyone try to find her real name?" The officer shook his head. "One last question. Was Lord Weston right-handed or left-handed?"

The policeman thought about this for a moment. "He must have been right-handed. He would have held the gun up like this." The man demonstrated. "Then pulled the trigger and fell, right there at the foot of the bed. There was blood everywhere. Why do you ask?"

"Thank you for making the trip out here." Rafferty extended his hand. "You've given me much to consider."

But the policeman didn't move. "You some sort of Pinkerton? What do they call them over there . . . a bobby or something?"

Rafferty smiled. "They call them police, and no, I'm not one of those."

"You're not like the usual sort on this row. They don't question our investigations."

"No. I suppose not." Rafferty considered a moment. "I'll say this, though. I don't believe Lord Weston stabbed Miss O'Shay. I believe another killed them both."

"Do you have any proof of that?" Officer Simmons asked, a bit more respect in his eyes than before.

"Not yet." Rafferty sipped from his glass. "But I will."

He walked the policeman to the front door. After Simmons had left, Rafferty strode into the front salon where Lord Weston rested in his coffin. Not wishing to be disturbed, Rafferty closed and locked the door. The oak coffin with gilt fittings rested on two small tables. It was a deep coffin, and the embalmed Lord Weston appeared comfortably ensconced in it. Significant damage had been done to the man's entire skull, but, true to the policeman's report, the bullet had entered from the right. However, if the shot had occurred as the policeman had indicated, Rafferty would have thought the thrust of the damage would be angled. Then again, perhaps it was all a matter of how he held the gun . . . if he held a gun. A bullet fired at close range by someone else would obliterate the skull just as effectively. Rafferty looked at the man who commanded such respect from Arianne, dressed as if to meet the president, down to the gray gloves on his cold dead hands. For what purpose? It was a sad way to come to one's end.

Rafferty replaced the lid, unlocked the salon door, and headed for the front door in sudden need of a breath of clean fresh air.

THERE WAS NO NOTE. ARIANNE CHECKED THE FLOOR near the door and the writing desk in case a maid had retrieved a paper from the floor. Nothing. Rafferty might not have spoken the truth about leaving a note, but she had her doubts. She was about to ring for the housekeeper when Evans, the butler, appeared at the door.

"I beg your pardon, ma'am, but a Mrs. James G. Blaine has come to call." He hesitated, as if he could see the uncertainties in her mind. "She asked specifically for you."

"Is Lady Weston about?" Arianne asked, surprised the woman hadn't greeted her at the door with questions about their executive appointment.

"She has taken to her bed, Your Ladyship. I'm afraid the thought of escorting her husband home tomorrow has upset her spirits."

Yes, Arianne supposed that would be a possible consequence. "Place Mrs. Blaine in the blue salon. I shall be there presently. Can you ask Mrs. Trembull to send up some tea?"

He nodded and left. Christopher! She wasn't even sure if women in America drank tea as they did in England. What did one offer during a social visit? Her discussion with the house-keeper would have to wait. While Arianne anticipated an in-troduction into Washington society, she hadn't predicted it would occur this quickly. Did everything in America occur at this breakneck speed?

Arianne entered the blue salon to find a handsome woman approximately twenty-five years her senior. "I am Lady Arianne Rafferty, Mrs. Blaine. I understand you wished to see me?" She extended her arm as an invitation to sit.

The woman smiled as she settled into a chair. "I realize you don't know me. Under ordinary circumstances I would wait for your call, but these are not ordinary circumstances. My husband is the secretary of state, which is the chief cabinet position under the president," the woman explained. "With the absence of the First Lady for guidance, I thought I should offer my assistance, especially as the numbers of political wives in Washington are dwindling due to the onslaught of summer. I've come with a proposition that you might find intriguing."

"A proposition?" Jupiter, she'd only arrived the day before. Should she be entertaining propositions—especially from strangers?

"You could bide your time here in this humid swamp waiting for the fall to arrive and with it returning diplomats. Or you could host an affair here at the legation and invite the wives remaining in the city. Many will even postpone their departure if a social event is on the horizon, especially if they're curious about a newcomer."

One of the maids arrived with a silver tea set on a tray. She set it down on a low table before Arianne. The arrival with accompanying clatter gave her a few moments to think.

"You wish us to host a reception?" Arianne passed a teacup to Mrs. Blaine. She could host a reception with her eyes closed; she'd been to enough of them.

Mrs. Blaine shook her head. "Receptions are too common an occurrence. No one will delay a vacation to the country for another reception. I believe a tea or perhaps a house party, something different. Of more importance, it must be immediate." She set down her teacup and cocked her head. "My dear, at the rate they are leaving, you simply can't meet the women you must know fast enough, nor, I suppose, can your husband. Thus you must devise a way to bring them to your door."

The idea held a certain appeal, as it was precisely what she had decided the evening before. Still, it seemed impossible given the rest of their agenda. "I wouldn't even know who to invite."

"That is precisely why you need my assistance. I'll provide a guest list as well as information on reputable merchants, and you do the rest."

While she thought it might be wise to consult with Rafferty, she decided a wife should be able to make such decisions on her own. After all, Lord Henderson had instructed Rafferty to trust her on social matters . . . or something to that effect. At least, he would have said it if he'd known she'd be the one playing hostess instead of Eva. Hostess. Didn't the title imply a social gathering? She sipped from her cup. It was already midweek, and she'd need time to order invitations, have them delivered, clean up the gardens . . . The gardens! "Would a garden party suffice?"

Mrs. Blaine paused to consider. "Many of the women are avid gardeners. I'm sure they would enjoy a tour of the legation's garden, but it must be before the weather becomes unbearable. Nothing wilts faster than a matron in the sun."

Arianne smiled; it was better than cringing at all the work this party would require. "I'll be sure to provide canopies for shade. Shall we say two weeks hence?"

"One week would be even better." The older woman sipped her tea. "I'll have the guest list delivered this afternoon."

"SEVEN DAYS!" MRS. WATSON, THE HOUSEKEEPER, GASPED, then thought better of her response. She hastily composed herself. "If Your Ladyship wishes to host a garden party, we will, of course, have all ready. It may require the hiring of some additional help. We haven't had a gardener since Mr. Wilkins passed on, God bless his soul. Will any of the guests be spending the night, Your Ladyship?"

"No, I don't believe so," Arianne replied, her mind preoccupied by other matters.

"That should make it easier, then. We'll need the extra girls for the serving, of course, plus we'll want to make certain—"

"Is there someone in the employ of the legation named Rosie?" Arianne interrupted.

"Not at present, Your Ladyship," Mrs. Watson said, surprised by the question. "We had a Rosalie Murray, but she left the legation about three weeks ago."

Three weeks. That would be about the time of Lord Weston's murder. Surely, this could not be a coincidence. "Why did she leave?"

"She disappeared. It was the day after Lord Weston's death. The girl simply left without giving notice. A most inconvenient time to take one's leave, I might add. Particularly with Mr. Jones's passing a week later. God bless his soul. Is that all?"

"Mr. Jones?" It certainly seemed a lot of the help had passed on recently.

"He was the old butler. It was a good thing Evans came to us when he did. A proper butler is necessary for a proper residence, especially with all the happenings of late."

"Hmmm . . ." Arianne thought she should mention this to Rafferty later. "I have one more question."

"Yes, ma'am?"

"Who has been in my room?" Arianne asked, watching the housekeeper carefully. No one was above suspect at this point.

"I beg your pardon, ma'am. Is something not to your satisfaction?"

"My husband left an envelope for me this morning. It seems to have disappeared."

"An envelope." Mrs. Watson's shoulders relaxed. Arianne supposed she had been concerned that jewelry had gone missing. "I will make inquiries among the chambermaids. One has surely seen the envelope in question."

"SEVEN DAYS?" RAFFERTY REPEATED AS THEY WERE SITting down to dinner. "Didn't you think to check with me before committing to such a project? Lord Henderson did not send me here to make the British legation a laughingstock in front of the Americans and foreign ambassadors. In fact, I believe you were engaged to prevent just such an occurrence."

She hadn't suspected Rafferty would have such a reaction to a simple garden party. "Mrs. Blaine thought it was wise. I'm hardly in a position to disagree with an authority." She wasn't gaining ground with him through this argument, so she tried a different strategy. "You won't have to do anything. I've ample experience to do this on my own."

"Woman, I'm investigating a murder," he hissed. "You have no idea of all that I have to do."

The serving staff's door opened, and a footman entered with servings of chicken breasts with vegetables. Lady Weston had declined dinner with them that evening, preferring a dinner tray earlier. She wished to have an extended night's rest in anticipation of her journey to New York the following day. Phineas had been gone since early that morning, leaving the two of them quite alone.

"I promise this won't interfere with your investigation. I'm going to need to hire some help to get the gardens ready, of course. That will mean a number of strangers with shovels and wheelbarrows and such. I can transplant the lavender and roses that I brought from England. Mrs. Blaine thought I may find some assistance and interesting plants at the United States Botanic Garden on the Mall." She noticed he seemed to be concentrating overly much on his plate. "I will expect you to make an appearance, of course, but otherwise . . ."

He glanced up with a resigned expression. "This is something you really want to do?"

She bit her lip. "I know we won't be here very long. Maybe it's foolish to attempt to meet the ladies of Washington's society. We most likely won't be here when they return in the fall." A weight settled in her stomach. Come fall, she'd be alone once more in remote Sanctuary. "All my life I've always been the guest at social affairs, never the hostess. I do. I do want to do this."

He smiled and lifted his wineglass as for a toast. "Then, my dear Arianne, let us negotiate."

· Eighteen ·

H̲A̲M̲M̲E̲R̲S̲ D̲R̲O̲V̲E̲ N̲A̲I̲L̲S̲ I̲N̲T̲O̲ T̲H̲E̲ L̲I̲D̲ O̲F̲ L̲O̲R̲D̲
Weston's coffin. The sound rattled the teacups used at
breakfast and pounded the reminder of mortality into the temples of all the legation residents. The men, mindful of low
rumbles of distant thunder, loaded the coffin into a waiting
hearse for transport to the Baltimore and Potomac rail station
as the legation carriage, adorned with black plumes as a mark
of mourning, followed close behind. Lord and Lady Weston
were bound on the first leg of their journey home.

While Arianne and Lady Weston waited in the noisy passenger terminal, Rafferty left to ensure the coffin was loaded
onto the freight car with care and respect. Arianne watched him
walk away and felt guilty about the lie they had perpetuated to
the woman she had once wished had been her own mother.
Once their charade was over, what would become of Rafferty?
Would he suffer repercussions from his involvement in this
pretend marriage? "He's a good man," she said, as much to
herself as to Lady Weston.

"Annie, I believe you've chosen wisely with Mr. Rafferty.
There is much that is solid and good about him. Trust him with

your heart, my girl. You don't always need to be the mature woman afraid to be less than perfect. There is no such thing as perfection."

Startled, she looked into the older woman's eyes. "How . . . ?"

"Here he comes." Lady Weston nodded down the platform toward Rafferty striding by a line of passenger cars. Arianne turned to see his determined strides and felt that same primitive resonance that vibrated within her from that first meeting.

"He'll protect you if you let him, Annie."

Arianne realized that Lady Weston was far more perceptive than she sometimes pretended to be. Perhaps the lady was as clever at duplicity as Arianne herself. How much did she know?

Lady Weston leaned forward and kissed Arianne's cheek. Then she kissed Rafferty's cheek once he rejoined their group. She whispered something in his ear and stepped back. "He would have approved of you."

Rafferty's twisted smile tugged at Arianne's heart. Lady Weston's endorsement affected him greatly.

"Lady Weston," he said. "I neglected to ask earlier, was Lord Weston right- or left-handed?"

"Why, left, of course."

The stationmaster called for the final boarding. Lady Weston glanced quickly at the both of them. "May you have many happy years together."

She accepted a porter's strong arm, and she climbed up the steps to the passenger car.

Saying good-bye distressed Arianne more than she anticipated. A heaviness collected in her chest while a sob gathered in her throat. With Lady Weston's departure and Mrs. Summers's absence, Arianne was truly alone.

The train strained forward, issuing a cloud of steam. The railcars jerked and slowly followed. Just as she was feeling forlorn and friendless, Rafferty's hand pressed lightly against the small of her back. That simple gesture lifted her spirits. She wasn't alone. She had Rafferty.

She shifted her gaze, admiring the sharp line of his cheekbone, the strong plane of his jaw, even the proud tilt of his tall hat. Perhaps Lady Weston was correct. Perhaps she could trust

him to know her secrets. Rafferty would surely do a better job
of protecting them than the Baron.

Together, they watched the car carrying Lady Weston until
it rolled from the station and out of sight. They reentered the
noisy terminal to return to their waiting carriage.

"What did she whisper to you?" Arianne asked, curiosity
getting the better of her.

Rafferty smiled warmly and was about to respond when the
shout of her name caught their attention.

The voice, instantly familiar, filled her with dread. She
turned to see her brother, William, striding toward her in an
imperial fashion, his face as ominous as the gathering storm
outside. She took a step backward, but Rafferty's strong hand
stopped her retreat. Rafferty was tense, ready for battle, his
eyes narrowed on William.

"It's my brother," she said, afraid Rafferty might greet him
with a punch to the jaw. "I didn't think he'd come after me."

Rafferty barely had time to glance at her when William was
upon them.

"William," she said, schooling her lips into a broad smile,
while her heart raced beneath her corset. She loved her brother,
she truly did. But his appearance meant one thing. He was furious and she was in trouble. "What a surprise to see you here . . .
in America."

"It is not a pleasant surprise, I assure you." He glared at
Rafferty. "Who is this?"

"William, allow me to present Mr. Michael Rafferty, the
British minister," Arianne quickly intervened. "Michael, this
is my brother, the Duke of Bedford."

Rafferty extended his right arm to shake William's hand,
while his left continued to brace her back. "It is a pleasure to
meet you, sir. Arianne has spoken often of you."

For a moment, she thought William was not going to accept
Rafferty's hand, but Rafferty continued to hold it out in defiance
of William's implied snub. William took Rafferty's hand and
held tight. "Who are you to my sister?"

Rafferty hesitated. She could tell he didn't want to lie, but
he couldn't very well tell the truth either.

"He's my husband, William." She straightened her spine.
"We were married by the captain of the *Irish Rose* on the cross-

ing." Both men turned to stare at her. William's jaw dropped a moment before he searched her ring finger. Rafferty's eyes crinkled with approval. "Now perhaps we can continue this conversation in a less public venue?" she bristled. "Our carriage is just outside. You'll know it by the funeral plumes."

Arianne turned smartly to lead the way, but deep inside she wanted to scream. This wasn't how everything was to work. William wasn't to know about this Washington experience. No one in England beyond Lady Weston was to know about it. Now, once their work was complete here in America, she would return to England in total disgrace. Even her own family would have little to do with her, once they learned the truth. With her handkerchief in hand, she brushed the corners of her eyes. The people she passed nodded their heads in sympathy to the woman in black. They assumed she'd lost a family member. Perhaps she had. She'd lost herself, her honor and dignity.

Suddenly Rafferty was there, striding beside her, his reassuring hand gently on her back. "Thank you," he said, so low that only she could hear. Those two words lightened the heavy weight in her stomach. *Trust him*, Lady Weston had said, and Arianne had. There was no going back now.

William's considerable luggage was loaded onto the coach. Rafferty helped Arianne into the carriage, then waited for the Duke to enter before he followed. William's valet climbed alongside the legation driver with an umbrella at the ready.

"How is my sister-in-law, William? Am I an aunt yet again?" Arianne asked once all were settled.

"Franny sends her love, and yes, I have a healthy son." He beamed, his pride cutting through the gloom in the carriage. However, as quickly as it arrived, the lightness faded. "Which is why I was not pleased to leave my wife and child behind to chase my little sister across the Atlantic. And you," he said to Rafferty. "British minister or not, you should have sought my permission and married my sister properly before God and family in a church."

"I agree." A twinkle crept into Rafferty's eye, and Arianne had a premonition that he was up to no good. "I fell in love with Arianne the first moment I saw her. I begged her to take me as her husband, but she'd have none of it." He reached for her hand and interlocked her fingers with his. "It wasn't until we sailed on the *Irish Rose* that we knew our love could no longer be denied. She honored me with her vow."

Arianne noted that he hadn't mentioned that the vow was to assist him to catch a murderer and certainly not to marry him. Her brother simply stared at Rafferty, unconvinced.

"Why are you here, William?" she asked, trying to ignore Rafferty's thumb as it played along the sensitive skin of her palm. "I'm surprised you knew how to find me."

"I received a letter from Mrs. Summers. She was concerned about some baron who may have taken advantage of you."

Rafferty's thumb stilled. She tried to free her hand, but at the slightest retreat, he tightened his hold.

"Just as I was packing my pistols," the Duke continued, "I received another letter from Mrs. Summers that expressed concern about a trip to America with some Irish ruffian." He glowered again at Rafferty. "She wouldn't have been referring to you, would she?"

"No, Your Grace," Rafferty replied. "I'm quite certain she was referring to my associate, Mr. Phineas Connor." Arianne again tried to tug her hand away, but Rafferty wouldn't let go. "However, Lady Arianne was not swayed by Phineas's considerable charms. Her eyes were for me alone, isn't that right, darlin'?"

She smiled tightly, fuming.

"You see, your sister would never give her heart to a ruffian, or even an honest man of the streets, or a man of little or no property." His voice strained, he let go of her hand. "Your sister was more interested in someone in dandified clothes who knows their way around an oyster fork and a bouillon spoon, and who has a suitable title." He glanced at her, his eyes hardened and cold. "Isn't that right, Lady Arianne?"

A lump sat in her throat. Was she that shallow? Was her head turned more by genteel trappings than the man himself?

The silence in the carriage was worthy of the funeral plumes that decorated it. Sad, mournful, something lost. The Duke watched the both of them but kept his opinions to himself.

Arianne cleared her throat. "How was the crossing, William?"

"Miserable, but at least this time I knew what to expect. I brought a ginger remedy for mal de mer, but without Franny, I couldn't get the dosage right." A strange smile twisted his lips. "Now that I'm here, I'd like to look around. Any society that produces a woman like my wife is one worth further study, I say."

The brougham slowed to a stop in front of the legation. Rafferty exited first, then assisted Arianne. The Duke followed. Rafferty signaled Evans to send footmen for the luggage. Arianne hurried inside to alert Mrs. Watson to a new guest and to find some lavender to lessen the pounding in her head.

ARIANNE WAS BARELY OUT OF EARSHOT BEFORE THE Duke pulled Rafferty aside. "I'm not certain what is transpiring here, but if I discover you are playing my sister foul, you will never see the verdant isles of Ireland again."

Rafferty cocked his head. He couldn't very well tell him that his sister had volunteered to be his hostess without the benefit of vows. "Arianne once told me that you and your wife had two weddings, one in America and a second in England."

The Duke smiled. "That's correct. I wanted to prove to those who were unable to attend the American ceremony that we were indeed man and wife."

"I would be amenable to a wedding with your sister that you could attend if that would satisfy your curiosity," Rafferty said. "You'd just have to convince your sister of the need."

The Duke seemed to consider this. "I still suspect you're the one Mrs. Summers warned me about. Be aware that I'm keeping my eyes on you."

Rafferty tossed his hands in the air and headed inside. For a man who could once blend into the shadows of a dark London alley and operate unseen by the aristocracy, he had so many eyes on his backside, he thought he might resemble a potato. What was another pair, more or less?

THAT AFTERNOON, RAFFERTY RECEIVED HIS FIRST OF-ficial call as a British minister. Mr. Blaine, President Garfield's secretary of state, braved the rain to appear at the legation. While primarily a welcoming gesture, Mr. Blaine did have a concern he wished to discuss.

"It's a matter of coffins," the long-bewhiskered Mr. Blaine said. "Irish coffins."

Rafferty's lips twisted. How ironic that he'd just super-vised the loading of Lord Weston's coffin onto a railcar that very morning and his first official call regarded more of the same.

"Lord Weston was looking into the problem at the time of his demise," Blaine continued. "As you know, Irish immigrants are coming to our shores in ever-increasing numbers."

Rafferty thought of the conversation on the *Irish Rose* on the way over. The potato famine began the emigration when his people couldn't find food. Now the land couldn't support the families trying to live off of it, so whole families filled the steerage section of the big liners trying to make a new life in America.

"Unfortunately, malnutrition for so many years and disease are taking their toll and many of the immigrants are dying," Blaine added.

"I don't believe that's a condition unique to the Irish," Raf-ferty said.

Blaine laughed. "No, indeed, it is not. What is unique, though, is their insistence on being returned to their native soil to be buried. The pine boxes are stacking up at all our eastern ports, New York and Baltimore in particular."

Rafferty recalled the wall of boxes he'd observed under a tarp at the Baltimore port when they'd docked. At the time he hadn't realized that they were coffins. His face must have be-trayed his distaste at the image.

"There's no problem with the odors. The corpses have been embalmed. It's just unseemly. The loading of so many coffins onto steamships is not the image we want for visitors to our shores."

"Lord Weston was involved in this in what manner?" Raf-ferty asked. He rubbed the back of his neck, the whole topic making him uncomfortable.

"He'd charted the destinations and the steamships used for transporting. He thought there was something unusual about the whole cycle, but he hadn't found the answer before . . . well, before he left us. The president doesn't wish to offend anyone, but he'd like the unsightly stacks of coffins to disap-pear. He thought your legation might have some suggestions on promoting cremation and returning the ashes to the old country, or burying the dead here, or . . . something that would alleviate the problem."

Rafferty remembered the list in the safe of shipping lines and the frequent mention of the *Irish Rose*. He suspected this was the purpose of Weston's list, but why did he lock it away in the safe? Such information could have been left on his desk. There was something more, but he'd have to speak with Phineas before he could be sure.

"I will see what I can do, and again, thank you for bringing this to my attention." He stood and escorted Mr. Blaine out of the study. They encountered the Duke in the foyer as he was preparing to see something of the city.

"Mr. Blaine, allow me to introduce my brother-in-law, the Duke of Bedford." Rafferty took particular delight in the Duke's odd expression at the mention of brother-in-law. "Mr. Blaine is the secretary of state of the president of the United States." *And he's come for my assistance*, he wanted to add for the Duke's benefit.

Although why the Duke's opinion of him mattered was beyond him. He never really cared before what the other titled gentry thought of him. Lord Henderson was the only aristocrat that had previously earned his respect.

"Mrs. Blaine and I are hosting a ball in honor of the Fourth of July. I'm certain the British minister and his wife are on the guest list. I assume you'll be on hand as well? I imagine the prospect of meeting a duke will bring the womenfolk back from their summer homes."

"I'm sure I can adjust my schedule to be present for the dance," the Duke said. "I have fond memories of a fancy dress ball I attended in Newport last year, just about this time of year, I believe."

Wondering if Arianne would appreciate his diplomacy, he smiled. "I'm sure Arianne will be delighted." Because Rafferty was absolutely certain that he was not.

THAT EVENING THE THREE OF THEM MET FOR DINNER in the breakfast room.

"Whatever happened to Mrs. Summers?" William asked, relaxing with a glass of wine.

"She's getting married," Rafferty said.

"She's getting married!" Arianne exclaimed. "To whom? When?"

"She's marrying Captain Briggs," Rafferty replied. "She apologized that she wouldn't be able to live at Sanctuary and said you'd understand that she was happy to no longer be alone." Rafferty sipped his whiskey.

"Why didn't you tell me?" She wanted to tap him with her fan to show her displeasure, but he sat too far away. "Where is she? I'd like to see her."

"She's living on the *Irish Rose* for the time being," Rafferty said. "I can take a letter to her if you like. I should see her tomorrow."

"Tomorrow? But the *Rose* is docked in Baltimore."

"Yes, but I need to speak with Phineas, and he's at the harbor. I have no way of contacting him unless I go and find him myself."

"Phineas Connor?" William's brows lowered.

"The same." Rafferty leaned toward Arianne. "Mrs. Summers had another message for you. She said to express her sincere gratitude to Cupid's Mistress."

"Mistress?" William growled. "You've been associating with a mistress?" He shook his head. "Ruffians and mistresses . . . Arianne, have you forgotten you're the daughter of a duke?"

Rafferty smiled in her direction, as if to say her brother's question vindicated his own mistaken supposition at their first meeting.

"But I'm not, am I?" she stated, her headache building at her temples. "I'm not the daughter of a duke."

"You were raised as one; that's what is important," William said. "You've the respect and decorum to be Lady Arianne. One's bloodline is just blood. It's the shaping that matters."

"The shaping?" She stood abruptly, and the two men leapt to their feet as well, which, even if it was the proper thing to do, just irritated her even more. A mocking laugh issued from her lips. "Then I was shaped to strive for perfection, because if I failed to hold my cup just so"—she held an imaginary teacup in the air—"if I failed in my order of introductions, or if my conversation was not sufficiently witty, my father would hate me and send me away again. I was shaped to be unwanted, to not have a home, to drift from embassy to embassy, smiling at my school friends' happiness and knowing none of my own. I was shaped to be afraid that should I find someone to love, he would beat me and desert me and desert me . . . without sanctuary." She glanced to Rafferty, hoping he'd understand.

A quiet descended over the room.

William broke the silence. "Arianne, you've always had a home with Franny and I." He frowned at Rafferty as if he were the root of her insecurities and not the old Duke. "And you'll always have sanctuary with us at Deerfield Abbey."

She smiled. It was the only thing that kept tears at bay. She sadly shook her head. "I don't want your home, William. I don't want to always be the sister of a duke. I want . . ." She looked at Rafferty, unsure what words to say, unsure what would satisfy the yearnings of her heart. "I want . . ."

She couldn't do it. She couldn't give voice to the emptiness inside her. So she did what she always did. She ran.

RAFFERTY WATCHED ARIANNE FLEE THE ROOM IN TINY quick steps. That confining dress wouldn't allow much more, which was good because that meant he'd always be able to catch her when she tried to run.

The Duke fell back into his chair, dazed.

"It's a good thing that your sister is the witty conversationalist," Rafferty said. "I'd hate to share your dinner table otherwise."

"I only asked about that bloody Cupid's Mistress. Who is that?"

"Your sister, you dolt." Was it possible that the brother hadn't a clue about his own sister? "It's a silly nickname someone assigned to her. It seems wherever she goes, love and happiness abound and people rush off to get married." He lowered his voice. "Except for her. I understand you were one of her victims."

"Me? Arianne had nothing to do with my wedding. It was arranged by solicitors and my mother-in-law."

Rafferty moved toward the door.

"Wait!" the Duke called. "Where are you going?"

"To my wife," Rafferty replied. "She needs me."

"Rafferty," the Duke warned flatly, "if you're not truly married to my sister . . . I will kill you."

"Right sentiment," Rafferty muttered under his breath. "Wrong man."

· Nineteen ·

ARIANNE STUMBLED INTO HER BEDROOM. WHAT had she done? She collapsed onto the bed. Mrs. Summers would have been abhorred by her display at the dinner table. In front of her brother, no less. What had come over her?

A tear dropped on the gold ruched silk of her dinner gown. She should call Kathleen and remove the dress before it was ruined. Another tear plopped on the bodice and spread in a moist circle, and still she didn't move. She was tired of moving, tired of packing and going to another proper place to be a proper guest for the proper length of time. Tired of smiling when she wanted to cry, tired of taking small bites when she wanted it all, tired of keeping secrets, tired of maintaining this farce, and tired of knowing what waited when it was all over . . . a lonely existence in an isolated country village.

How had it come to this? Hadn't she tried to be appealing to the Baron . . . the Baron with the wonderful sprawling family that was ever underfoot? Hadn't she let him do those things to her that would ensure his affection, even though it hurt like the devil and ruined her for other serious proposals? Hadn't she tried to be perfect? And yet the one thing that wasn't perfect, the one thing she thought necessary to share with her future husband, the one thing William said didn't matter—her bloodline—had cost her the future.

There is no such thing as perfection. Lady Weston's words echoed in her brain. The Baron would likely dispute that, she thought with a hiccup. Lady Weston had said something about Rafferty too, but Arianne couldn't recall it now. Something about protection, she thought, surprised at how just thinking about Rafferty made her feel better. He would protect her. That's what Lady Weston had said. Too bad she didn't say that he would love her as well.

The door opened to the bedroom, and he was there. She expected to see his lips twist into that half-smirk smile, like he had when he caught her in the bath, but this time he didn't smile at all. He turned and quietly closed the door, then crossed the room to her. He took her soggy tear-soaked hands in his and lifted her to her feet.

"I'm sorry," she said. "I shouldn't have said those things. A proper diplomat's—"

He kissed her. A soft kiss, a sweet kiss, a kiss that took the words right out of her mouth, an accepting kiss.

Then he wrapped his arms around her and pulled her tight, letting her tears soak his jacket. Her arms slipped around his waist beneath his jacket, then slid up his broad sheltering back. *He'll protect you.* Indeed, she felt safe here as she had never felt before.

"This is your home, Arianne." His breath warmed her ear, sending delicious currents to the rest of her body. "This is your sanctuary."

He was wrong, of course. This legation served only as a temporary home, like so many of her visits and stays. Once their mission was complete, he would leave her and move on. But she didn't give voice to her thoughts. They would ruin this wondrous, rare moment. His lips trailed down her neck, stirring a titillating awareness with each touch. The hollow core that she'd filled with self-pity started to give way to something else entirely. She moved her hands to his waist and gently pushed back.

"I . . . I need to remove this gown before it's ruined." She sniffed and managed a weak smile. She thought the hint that he should leave to allow her privacy would be adequate, but he stayed. His finger slipped beneath the blond bobbin lace that trimmed the square neckline and slowly traced the long path from her neck to the turn right above the line of her corset. Sensation sparked as if he had harnessed the lightning outside. She stepped back. "I'm fine now. You shouldn't leave my brother alone. I'll just call Kathleen for assistance."

"No need," he said. "I'll play your lady's maid." He stepped behind her and ran his hand down the back of the blue woven silk, the motion pleasantly reverberating down her spine. "Your brother has access to cigars and whiskey." He hesitated. "How is this thing fastened? No buttons, no laces . . ."

"The bodice fastens in front." She'd forgotten. Had she been in her right mind, she could have removed much of the outer dress on her own.

"The front?" He stepped back to the front and stared at her chest. "There are no buttons here either."

She laughed, more of a chuckle really. He did manage to lift her spirits. She pinched the gold piping that separated the ruched silk from the heavier bodice, releasing the first of a long line of concealed hook-and-eye closures.

His eyes widened. "Arianne, had I known, you would have been out of that dress much sooner."

She laughed outright and lightly pushed him back. "As you can see I don't need your assistance after all."

His face grew serious, his gaze capturing hers. "Yes," he said. "You do."

His fingers reached for the piping. Slowly, and with great concentration, he unfastened each succeeding hook and eye. While his fingers worked the tight clasps, his knuckles slid over the thin protection afforded by her corset. Her breath caught, sensing the contraction of the tips of her breasts. She bit her lower lip, enjoying the delicious sensations his ministrations caused, while agonizing over the confrontation that was bound to come.

She'd been here before. When another man's hands revealed and admired her skin. She'd enjoyed it then as well, basked in the attention, which was why she was having difficulty telling Rafferty to stop.

With the bodice unfastened, he slipped it off her shoulders, kissing the newly exposed skin. He caught the bodice with the attached back waterfall of silk and tossed it to the bed. Still standing before her, he reached around her waist to find the tie that released her skirts to puddle on the floor. The tie to release her tournure sat low in front of her corset. Just the thought of his fingers in that forbidden vicinity sent tingling throughout her entire body. She should stop him, send him downstairs, but her lips refused to work other than to gasp when her petticoat joined the rest of the silk on the floor.

He removed his jacket and tossed it in the vicinity of her bodice. His waistcoat soon followed. She wanted to smooth her hands over his chest, feel the powerful muscles she knew to be there, but instead she remained still, like a wooden doll . . . yearning for him to set her skin afire with his touch, while guarding her heart for the moment when he left her in disgust.

RAFFERTY GAZED AT HER THROUGH A VEIL OF LUST. HE wanted to taste her, he wanted her to cry out in decidedly un-ladylike moans of passion, he wanted her to experience the full extent of his desire. But she stood so calm, so aloof, as if the intimacy between a man and a woman were beneath her. Yet, she didn't protest. As he suspected from the time he intruded on her bath, she wasn't a shy, shrieking aristocratic innocent. She didn't ask him to stop, and dear God in heaven, he wasn't certain he could if she had.

He slipped his fingers under the lace of her pristine white satin corset. Then he unfastened the tiny hook between the swell of her breasts. He cupped the satin covering her breast and heard her first jagged intake of breath, but still she didn't assist or deny him.

He wanted her, but he wanted her to want him as well. Remembering her interest in his undressing that first night, he felt inspired.

"Unfasten my shirt," he said.

She did so with mechanical efficiency.

"Slide it off of my shoulders." He hurriedly removed his cuff links. He had to admit, she was a much better student than he had been at her lessons. "Touch me, Arianne."

Her hands moved to his chest.

"That's good." He returned to the fastenings on her corset. "It doesn't matter where, but I want to feel your hands on me whenever we're together. No matter what we do. Do you understand?"

She nodded. He unhooked the fastenings down the front of her corset, then added it to the collection on the mattress. Kneeling before her, he felt her fingers on his shoulders. He slid his hand down the length of her stocking on one leg and lifted her foot to remove her dainty blue shoe. Sliding his hands beneath her drawers, he unfastened her garter and removed the stocking before repeating for the other leg.

Standing before her, he gazed at her clad in her chemise and drawers. Still she neither encouraged nor resisted him. What had that bastard baron done to her? He swept his arm beneath her legs, lifted her into his arms, and carried her to the bed.

"I can't leave you tonight," he said, laying her on the mattress. Then he paused to unbutton his trousers and pull off his boots and socks. "Your brother suspects we're not truly married. If he hears me leave the room, I'm not sure he'll let me live till morning." He smiled, but Arianne did not. She had fear in her eyes, and he hesitated, wondering if he was adding to whatever she had suffered.

He lay down beside her and pulled her into his arms. Surely, she had seen the bulge in his drawers, evidence of his desire, but he wouldn't force himself on her. Her head resting on his chest, he rubbed the top of her head with his chin. "Now tell me what he did to you."

She stiffened. "What do you mean?"

"Mrs. Summers wrote your brother that she was concerned a baron had taken advantage. I saw how you reacted when you saw him in London. You were obviously running away from something to agree to this adventure." He trailed his fingertips along her upper arm. "But I want you to tell me. If that bastard baron hurt you, I need to understand how."

"Why?"

"I don't wish to repeat his mistakes," Rafferty said. "Arianne, your brother knows that we are presenting ourselves as married. Lady Weston believes we've shared this room. Eva and Mrs. Summers both know of your intentions. The Baron knows what he did. Your hope that no one in England will know of our actions in America grows distant with each passing day." He shifted, lifting her chin so she couldn't turn away. "Now, I know you refused my offer of marriage. I know I haven't a title or great sums of money or elegant manners . . ." She tried to interrupt him, but he continued on. "But I have a great desire for you. If we're to share this room and purport to be man and wife, then I need to know what that bastard did to you."

"He didn't force himself on me." He felt her swallow. "I allowed him to do what he wished. I thought it was proof of my affection."

"Has he seen you much as you are now?" He tried to keep his jealous anger from his voice.

"Yes," she answered. "But it was dark, and there were . . . blankets."

So he came to her room in the middle of the night, sneaking about like a thieving cutpurse in a dark alley. "Then what happened? Did he kiss you?"

"Yes," she admitted. "But his kisses . . ."

"Yes?" he encouraged.

"They weren't like yours. I like your kisses, Rafferty."

"Ah, darlin', thank you for that." He kissed the top of her head and felt her relax against him.

"I let him put his hands on my breasts. I liked that as well."

"I suppose he did too," Rafferty said, feeling jealousy flare up again.

"Then he crawled on top of me. He asked if I was ready for him. I wasn't certain what he meant, but he thrust into me."

Rafferty felt his teeth on edge. The filthy blackguard was fortunate an ocean existed between them. "Did he hurt you, darlin'?"

She didn't answer at first, telling him all he needed to know. "I think it was my fault," she said in a tiny voice. "I didn't do it right. The next day he announced his engagement to another."

He squeezed her shoulder. "When did you tell that miserable scoundrel that you weren't descended from a duke?"

"Earlier that day," Arianne said. "Why?"

Either the bastard was punishing her for something that wasn't her fault or he knew that would be his only opportunity to sample Lady Arianne. But she didn't need to hear that. "You must have believed he loved you," he said instead.

She nodded. The movement registered on his shoulder. "I trusted him. I wanted him to know about the bloodline before we were committed to each other."

"And yet he still came to your bed that night, the son of a cur."

"I thought it was proof that he loved me in spite of the broken bloodline."

"Arianne . . . the man misused you." He rolled on his side so he could see into her eyes. "There is nothing wrong with you. What happens between a man and a woman doesn't have to be painful. It's like kisses." He grinned. "Some men know how to kiss a woman; others don't." She smiled, which encouraged him. "Let me show you."

Arianne welcomed his kiss, gentle, healing. She returned the pressure and then slid her hand to the base of his neck, then to his shoulder. There was something thrilling about the touch of bare skin to bare skin. Something that sparked like the tip of a match. She wanted more of that sensation and pressed her chest to his. His hands slipped beneath her chemise and up her back. Soon he massaged her breasts, driving excitement lower. An ache throbbed from her core. She wanted more. She wanted to test Rafferty's suggestion that intimacy didn't need to hurt, but what if the problem had been her and not the Baron? What if Rafferty wanted her for this night only and then would abandon her just as the Baron had?

She pushed on his chest, until he stilled. "I can't do this," she gasped. "You said my brother suspects we're not married."

Rafferty's eyes were open but unfocused. It took several moments for him to speak. "He suspects, but he doesn't know. He's watching for signs, but Arianne, if he discovers that we haven't exchanged vows, he'll just make that happen. We'll be married either way."

He tugged on her waist, but she shook her head. She wasn't sure how to explain her confused emotions. She wasn't married to the Baron and he abandoned her. She wasn't married to Rafferty. Would he leave her in disgust as well? "This is too similar to before. I'm not ready, Rafferty. If you care for me, you won't make me do this."

• • •

HE HAD MEANT TO BE GENTLE, TO ALLEVIATE HER FEARS, but she had answered with an intensity that made him forget his original intentions. His hand slipped beneath her chemise to find her breasts. The fullness in his hand, enhanced by the tight nub, shot straight to his groin. Dear God, he wanted her, and he could show her what intimacy truly felt like. Not the painful education the Baron managed.

His hand slipped lower to the soft curve of her waist, then beneath the cotton of her drawers to her hip. She stilled, complaisant, guarded, just as she had been earlier. Damn it, he wasn't the Baron, using her body with the full knowledge that he would abandon her to the vicious wolves of society. Or was he? After this was over, how could he repair her reputation?

He had to convince her to marry him, common dog that he was. For that, she needed to trust him.

Rafferty withdrew his hand from her drawers and soothed her chemise to cover the skin to her hip. "I want you, Arianne. Make no mistake. But I want you to desire me as well. Until then we'll just share the bed, but not each other."

He thought he saw her lips twist in a slight smile before he turned her so her back pressed against his chest. She burrowed against him while he pulled her tight and linked his hand with hers. He kissed the side of her head before he rested his head on the pillow with thoughts of how he was going to survive this outer ring of hell.

· *Twenty* ·

🌱 SHE COULDN'T STOP SMILING. FEELING RENEWED, lightened of a heavy burden, Arianne lay in bed remembering how Rafferty had held her all night, planting soft kisses on her shoulder, tucking her tight against the wall of his chest. Such an intimate feeling to wake in the middle of the night, in the dark, in a borrowed space, and find another protecting you, even in his sleep. The Baron had not stayed with her, even after he had finished his prodding. Poor Miss Sharpe, to be stuck with a man like the Baron when there were men like Rafferty about. Even when he left in the morning to meet Phineas, he assured her he'd be back. In hindsight, perhaps ruining her reputation was the best thing that could have happened to her. Otherwise she would never have rushed to escape London, she most likely would have never met Rafferty, she certainly wouldn't have agreed to a pretend marriage, and . . . her brother wouldn't be watching her like a hawk. Christopher!

She hopped out of bed and rang for Kathleen. There was much to be done, invitations to send, workers to hire, canopies to order, weeding to begin. Perhaps it was a blessing her brother was here. She could put him to work as well. Then

Rafferty would return. Something bloomed inside of her at the thought. *You can trust him with your heart.* She was beginning to suspect that was true. He hadn't abandoned her when he learned she was used goods, and he hadn't tried to take advantage of her admission. She had thought he was only interested in her due to her relationship to the Duke. But now that William was here, she could see that Rafferty didn't cater to him in the manner that others did. Which meant Rafferty cared for her . . . for her. A ridiculous grin refused to leave her face.

"ARIANNE. MIGHT I REMIND YOU THAT I'M NOT ANOTHER household servant; I'm a duke," William boomed. He sat at Rafferty's desk in the study, a stack of stationery to his left and a listing of names to the right.

"Well, I have no need for a duke at the moment, but another servant would be deeply appreciated." After having waited at the printers for a rush order of invitations to be printed, her patience was wearing thin—especially for helpless dukes with a sense of entitlement. She decided to take a different approach and softened her tone. "William, you have the loveliest handwriting. This is little different from addressing letters." He appeared unmoved. "Would you prefer I arm you with a shovel to join me in the garden?" He scowled, indicating his displeasure with that assignment as well. Frustration kicked in. She put her hands on her hips. "Is there something more important to occupy your time?"

He pulled an envelope in front of him and picked up a pen. "I should have gone to Baltimore with Rafferty. At least then I'd be able to confront this Phineas Connor fellow," he grumbled.

She stopped at the door, then turned. "Phineas? Why ever would you wish to confront Phineas?"

"If he's the ruffian that Mrs. Summers wrote of, then I've a mind to accost him about putting your safety at risk."

She laughed. "Phineas is not to blame. You can rest easy on that score."

"So it was Rafferty . . . I suspected as much," he mused. Arianne felt her cheeks warm. She had blundered into that one. "Anne, tell me the truth. Are you and Rafferty truly married?"

Her fingers found the gold wedding band. "Why do you ask?"

"You never wrote to me about him. I received all manner of letters about things you were doing with some baron, and then nothing. I've come all this way only to discover you've married a complete stranger at sea?" His eyes widened a moment, then narrowed. "Are you pregnant? It's that baron's by-blow, isn't it? I bet Rafferty married you for your allowance. You *are* the sister of a duke."

Her face heated. "No, William. I'm not with child, and I don't believe Rafferty even knows that you send money every month. I don't believe he was at all impressed that I am your sister. At the moment, he's probably regretting it." She knew she was. "So if you'll excuse me, I have other responsibilities. Please let me know when the invitations are complete. I'd like to have them delivered today."

She leaned against the wall in the passageway for a breath. Thank heavens she wasn't as stubborn and obstinate as her brother. Acting as if he were too high and mighty to be addressing envelopes, please. "I'm a duke," she repeated in a mock singsong voice. Then it occurred to her that she'd been the very same way at times when dealing with Rafferty. The poor man. She owed him an apology. A smile bubbled to her face. This time she might concede the negotiations.

A murmur of voices and the stomp of feet reached her ear from the back of the legation. She walked outside. Six young boys moved about the garden. They looked like a passel of thieves in their shabby attire, except these thieves were vaguely familiar.

"Your Grace," one boy exclaimed, pulling a cap from his head. "It's me, Your Ladyship, Ben."

As he approached, she recognized Ben from the *Irish Rose*. She glanced about the others, realizing they too must have come from the *Rose*. Rafferty's boys.

"Mr. Rafferty sent us. He said you could use help and that we could use a good meal." His lips turned in a crooked smile. "I'd never been on a train before. The engine was smaller than the one on the *Rose*, but the cars moved so fast, I didn't think I could breathe."

Rafferty. She should have guessed. Thinking of her and sending the boys in the midst of everything else.

"How did you arrive from the station?" she asked. That was an uphill climb.

"We walked. It felt good after being on the *Irish Rose* for so long. Mrs. Trembull fed us. Now we're ready to work." He beamed. "It's been an adventure." She was about to direct them on the finer points of weeding when Ben remembered something else. "Mr. Rafferty told me to give you this." He pulled a folded paper from his grubby shirt. "And that." He pointed to a box on a garden bench.

While he fetched the box, she read the note. Rafferty said he wouldn't be home tonight after all. He and Phineas needed to check on something after dark. Disappointment dimmed her earlier enthusiasm. She hadn't realized how much she missed Rafferty until she knew he wouldn't be home. Ben returned with the box. Inside she found one of her missing pots of lavender and a wrapped flower bouquet, slightly wilted. Another note from Rafferty was tucked in the flowers. *I don't know what these mean, but they made me think of you.* Her heart sighed.

"Let me put these in water," she said. "I'll talk to Mrs. Watson about finding you boys some new clothes and a place to sleep. There's plenty of work for you to do out here."

She sniffed her bouquet, wishing Rafferty were here so she could thank him properly. She and her brother would have a quiet dinner this evening. Maybe he could help her with designs for some new gardens. She and Rafferty wouldn't be here long enough to merit changes to the household structure, but leaving a nice garden behind would be a gift to the new British minister. Leaving the legation in an improved state from its condition when assumed would be the proper thing to do.

"MY LADY, I'M SORRY. YOU NEED TO WAKE UP!"

"Kathleen?" Arianne fought to get her eyes open. She'd had entirely too much wine at dinner last night. "What is it?"

"The coppers have Mr. Rafferty. They've got him in jail."

"What?" She sat up in bed. "What are you talking about?"

"The police downstairs want to talk to you."

Arianne slipped on a concealing robe and tied it securely

around her. Her hair was loose, but it would have to do. She hurried down the stairs to where a policeman waited in the front salon.

He introduced himself as a sergeant with the Washington Metropolitan Police.

"Yes, Sergeant. What can I do for you?"

"We received a telegram from the Baltimore Police Department. They have a Mr. Michael Rafferty and a Mr. Phineas Connor in custody. Mr. Rafferty claims to be a diplomat residing at this residence?"

"Yes. He's the British minister in charge of this legation."

The policeman raised a brow. Clearly that wasn't the answer he anticipated. "If that's the case, the Baltimore Police can't keep him. He'll have diplomatic immunity. Someone will need to identify him. I believe he asked for you."

"Identify him?"

"Yes, ma'am. I'll telegraph that you're coming. An officer will meet you at the harbor station for escort. The Baltimore and Potomac runs a ten o'clock train."

"Thank you, Sergeant." He turned to go, but Arianne stopped him with another question. "Could you tell me, sir, what my husband was doing to cause his arrest?"

The officer flipped open his pad. "This could be wrong. Sometimes the operators get a code wrong," he said with a wry smile. "But it looks like public intoxication and disturbing coffins."

ACCOMPANIED BY HER QUARRELSOME BROTHER, ARIanne managed the ten o'clock train and, as promised, was met at the harbor train station. They were escorted to the police station, an awful place populated by scowling men in uniforms and others of questionable character and hygiene. Her appearance caused a stir before the sergeant on duty led them back to the jail cells. One would think they'd not met a proper lady and duke before.

Rafferty was lying on a metal bench, his eyes closed. He wore a pair of old trousers, a collarless shirt with rolled sleeves, and an old tatty waistcoat. It was little wonder the police didn't believe he was a diplomat. Phineas was barely recognizable in stained clothes, long sideburns, and bushy eyebrows. A large battered sack lay by his feet. His nimble fingers worked a coin, making it visible one moment and gone the next.

"He says he's the British minister," the sergeant said, nodding toward Rafferty, clearly skeptical.

"Yes. That's my husband." Arianne sighed. It was clear that all those lessons on attire were for naught. "The other is Phineas Connor, his associate."

"You're absolutely certain?" The sergeant waited a moment, then shrugged. "They don't look like any ministers I've ever seen, in church or out."

He slipped a key into the cell door. "The captain says there'll be no charges." He ran his truncheon across the bars, making a loud clatter. Arianne jumped inside her skin. Never had she envisioned being in such an environment.

"You're free to go, thanks to the lovely lady." The sergeant pulled open the door, then glanced at Arianne. "You might want to keep them in Washington. Less trouble that way." The officer left.

Rafferty's eyes remained closed, but his lips slid into a smile. "Morning, darlin'. Did you miss me?"

"Rafferty," she scolded. "What is the meaning of this? Look at you. You look . . ." He opened his eyes and sat up. Stubble covered his jaw. His unkempt hair fell forward on his brow. He hadn't slept well, she could see that. Something stirred deep inside. She was tempted to say he looked delicious, like warm chocolate on a cold morning, but that would hardly be appropriate.

"You look like a dissolute loafer," her brother said. "I can see why Mrs. Summers was concerned enough to write."

Rafferty squinted, then grinned. "I thought a dissolute loafer would be less suspect checking coffins. But it appears the harbor police disagreed."

"Coffins?" William looked as dumbfounded as Arianne felt. Coffins?

Rafferty stood, then stretched. He walked over to Arianne and kissed her cheek. She had to admit, he did make the extra effort to make their marriage appear convincing. She would miss this aspect when it was over. Her nose wrinkled. But she wouldn't miss the smell of this unkempt man.

"You brought *him*?" he said close to her ear. Unfortunately, it was close to William's ear as well. "Ben would have been more useful."

"Ben?" William asked. "Who's Ben?"

"Your Grace." Rafferty stretched his arm toward his cell mate, who had peeled one eyebrow from his face and was working on the other. "This is Phineas Connor, my illustrious associate." Rafferty swung his arm to indicate William. "Phineas, it is my pleasure to introduce the Duke of Bedford, Arianne's brother. I don't think he appreciates that we involved his sister in our nefarious schemes."

Phineas bowed, then extended his hand. "It's an honor to meet you, Your Grace. You have a lovely sister in Lady Arianne." He bowed to her as well.

Arianne glanced at the neighboring cells, at the men who studied her with interest. If possible, they appeared even more dissolute than Rafferty. The entire place made her yearn for a bath. "Whatever did you do to land in such a place?" she murmured.

"This cell isn't so bad," Rafferty said. "We've been in much worse. Haven't we, Phineas?"

"Indeed we have." Phineas grinned.

William mumbled something inaudible.

Arianne turned to Rafferty, confused. "What is all this business about coffins? I thought you came to Baltimore to speak with Captain Briggs. And what about the public intoxication? That's hardly proper behavior for a British minister."

"We weren't really," he said, crooking a finger beneath the sensitive underside of her chin. His eyes swept her face. She had the impression he was searching for her approval, or perhaps forgiveness. She melted a bit. Rafferty soothed an errant strand of hair back beneath her straw chapeau with a gentle touch that lingered. "The night guard wouldn't believe anyone would inspect coffins without first being intoxicated."

William huffed. "Well, that certainly explains it."

Her jaw softened and her cheeks lifted. Rafferty. He always managed to make her smile in the most dire of circumstances.

He turned to Phineas. "Are you joining us in Washington?"

"I've got another idea that I want to try." Phineas peeled off a sideburn, then wiped the remaining residue with a cloth from his sack. "I think I'll stay awhile longer."

"Be careful," Rafferty said, his voice stern. Phineas just nodded.

THEY TOOK A HACKNEY TO THE TRAIN STATION AND settled into one of the parlor cars, but as the route was a popular one, the explanation of coffins had to wait. They found three padded chairs in a line by the windows. Arianne sat between the two men. Immediately, Rafferty reached across the arm of the chair to lace his bare hand with her gloved one. From the glances of the other passengers, she could tell they thought she and Rafferty were an odd match. She with her fashionable traveling dress of patterned satinet, him with a drab waistcoat that would have been suitable for a chimney sweep. She with the posture trained by years in the best finishing schools, him slumped in the parlor chair in the relaxed manner of a man who hadn't slept. She could even sense William's disapproval, though he tried to hide it behind a copy of a discarded newspaper.

What the passengers couldn't see were all the things she and Rafferty had in common. The lack of a stable home, a devout loyalty to country and family, a determination to do whatever was necessary to solve a murder and capture a killer. A soft snore issued from his lips. William glanced over in disgust and rattled his papers some more before folding them and tossing them aside.

"Anne, I have to say something. I try not to be judgmental, but I think you could have found someone far more appropriate than this man. If indeed you are married, why him?"

She looked at Rafferty, seeing all his wonderful qualities. "Because he needed me."

William just shook his head. "That's not enough for a marriage."

Perhaps, but it was a start. Even Lord Henderson had recognized that Rafferty would need her assistance. He slept peacefully while holding her hand. *Touch me*, he had said. It almost seemed that it was her touch right now that enabled him to sleep in a moving railcar full of people. She thought of how he had comforted her two nights ago, how he had held her while she slept. How he had coaxed out her shame about the Baron and dismissed it as unnecessary for further anguish. Her affection for him was based upon more than the fact that he needed her. She needed him as well.

BY THE TIME THEY ARRIVED BACK AT THE LEGATION, THEY needed to change for dinner. Arianne noted that she had missed some calls, which she would have to return in the days ahead, and some acceptances had already arrived for the garden party. If only their progress on the murder was moving as quickly.

Rafferty explained at dinner that Mr. Blaine had expressed concern over the abundance of coffins bound for Ireland accumulating in the ports. He had gone to investigate and was surprised himself at the volume.

"I don't think one needs to actually open a coffin to count their number," William grumbled.

"I was more concerned that they might not be what they seemed. We managed to check three before the guard found us."

"And?" William asked.

"And they contained what you might expect. But we weren't able to do a thorough search."

"I believe Mrs. Summers would remind us that this is not a fit conversation for a dinner table," Arianne said. "I propose we discuss something else. Have I told you about my plans for the garden?"

Her diversion carried them through dessert. Believing Rafferty was still in need of a decent night's rest, she excused herself early from the dinner table, certain he would follow. She went upstairs and with Kathleen's assistance, stepped out of the numerous layers of clothing and slipped into her plain linen nightgown. She wished she had something nicer, but she hadn't anticipated anyone seeing her in such dishabille when she packed in London.

Kathleen removed Arianne's hairpins and pulled a boar's bristle brush through her tresses.

"Lady Arianne, may I ask you a question?" Kathleen asked.

Arianne nodded absently. Her mind was more interested in the sort of negotiation she might arrange with Rafferty that evening. She was determined to move beyond the kisses and hugs he freely shared.

"I share a room upstairs with two of the Irish maids. One of them is a friend of a maid who used to be employed here. She's heard me talk about how kind you are and how smart. The friend left the legation several weeks ago, but she has a problem. She needs to talk to someone, and I was wondering if you could help."

The story sounded familiar, but maids tended to come and go from one household to the next. Most likely the girl was needing a reference. "What's the friend's name?" she asked.

"It's Rosie," Kathleen answered. "Rosalie Murray."

· Twenty-One ·

RAFFERTY COULDN'T KEEP A SMILE FROM CREEPING
across his face. He poured whiskey into two glasses and
handed one to William. He never thought he'd be keeping company with aristocrats, much less a duke.

"You're grinning like a Cheshire cat," William harrumphed,
accepting the glass. "You remind me of my brother."

"The artist? I should like to meet him someday," Rafferty
replied. Which was rather unlikely, as Arianne had made it clear
that this marriage was a sham and held no promise of a lasting
commitment.

"So now that my sister has gone, what exactly were you
looking for in those coffins?"

They had moved to the study, which was more private than
the breakfast room. Still, Rafferty looked to the door. They
hadn't determined who in the household was to be Eva's contact. In fact, it was one of the reasons he'd asked Ben to exchange his seaman's rags for those of a footman. The boy had
a talent for ferreting out information, a result from his years in
the net.

Rafferty selected a chair in close proximity to the Duke so

as to keep his voice low. "As I mentioned before, I was alerted to the increase in the shipment of coffins. All the coffins are bound for Irish ports, and all are shipping from New York and Baltimore."

"Even in England we're aware of the high Irish immigration to those cities. Why the concern about a desire to return to one's native soil as a final resting place?"

"It wouldn't be a concern if the numbers weren't disproportionately high and consistent in quantity. I think something else is hidden in the boxes marked as coffins and smuggled back to Ireland."

William narrowed his gaze, studying Rafferty a moment. "I think I might have misjudged you, sir. Perhaps Lord Henderson hasn't completely lost his mind after all." He leaned forward. "So what do you believe is being smuggled, currency?"

"It's a possibility. I think the size of the boxes works well for guns, rifles, gunpowder . . ."

"Bloody hell, you say." William's jaw hung open. It must be a family trait, Rafferty thought, remembering Arianne's reaction to him the first night they met. "Is it the Fenians? Are they gearing up for an out-and-out war?"

"I have my suspicions as to the man responsible," Rafferty said, a cold determination settling into his gut. "He won't escape me this time, but there's something else afoot. If I'm correct, the smuggling has been going on for some time; it's only increased in volume these last months. Lord Weston had stumbled upon something that is being planned in this country, and it cost him his life."

"Here? What purpose could the Fenians have in staging something in America?" He laughed and sipped his drink. "It's the guns, I'll warrant. Weston learned about the guns."

Rafferty wasn't about to argue. It would serve no purpose. Lord Henderson had sent him, not the Duke, to America to unravel the mystery. No, the Duke had come to America to hunt down the ruffian who stole his deflowered sister from the safety of the Duke's London town house. He squinted at William. Did he know about the Baron's cruel punishment of Arianne? Taking her innocence because she hadn't the bloodline he'd imagined? He doubted Arianne had said anything to her brothers. She'd been too mired in humiliation for that.

Rafferty finished his drink and set the crystal on the table. "Well, Your Grace . . ." Interesting that Arianne despised the use of "Lady," while her brother by his very manner demanded the proper salutation for his title, yet his bloodline was as "tainted" as hers. "It has been a tiring day." He stood. "You're welcome to stay and enjoy the whiskey, of course, but I fear I must retire."

"Rafferty." The Duke tilted his head up toward him. "I believe you're a man of honor." He swirled the liquid in his glass as if he were stirring a pot. "I'll admit I wasn't convinced at first. But as a man of honor, I presume you will do the proper thing by my sister, if you haven't already. Still, I'd like to hear it from your lips. The two of you are married, correct?"

Rafferty twisted the ring on his finger. "I don't know why you'd believe otherwise."

"I asked my sister earlier why she married you. She said you needed her. Now, I'm not certain that is true, but I'm going to ask you the same question. What made you choose my sister?"

The answer was easy. "Because she needs me."

SHE WAS SITTING IN THE BED WITH ALL THE GAS LAMPS lit. He could only conclude she wanted to talk. If it had been any other night, he wouldn't mind, but tonight he was exhausted. He hadn't slept well two nights ago, as his mind had been too full planning a suitable revenge for the Baron. Last night, Phineas and he had waited till after midnight to commence their harbor expedition. The little sleep he'd found in the jail cell and on the train had not met his body's needs. His eyelids were fighting to stay open, and Arianne wanted to talk.

He doused the nearest lamp. "I'm so exhausted, darlin'. I'm anxious to hear of all the things that happened while I was away." He turned down another. "Can you tell me about it in the morning?" He shrugged out of his jacket and walked into the closet to put it on a peg.

"Did you see the flowers in the vase?" she asked. "It's the bouquet you sent me."

Oh yes. He remembered seeing the flower vendor at the harbor, selling bouquets to arriving and departing passengers alike. After their long ocean voyage, he thought her little trunk of fragrance concoctions must be running low. She'd appreciate the colors and the fragrances of the blossoms more than most. He slipped off his shoes and placed them together in the closet.

"The flowers each have a message. Do you know what they say?"

He was afraid of this. Phineas hadn't been around to instruct him on the flowers' meanings. He'd selected based purely on what seemed to suit his Arianne. He removed the cuff links from his shirt and remained in the small closet to avoid proving his ignorance.

"The calla lilies are lovely," she said. "They stand for feminine beauty."

He smiled. He'd picked correctly on that one, then. He started to unbutton his shirt.

"The tall spiked flowers mean ready armed." She laughed at that. "I suppose that's another way of saying you'll protect me."

"That I will," he said, too quietly for her ears.

"This little purple flower is a way of asking if I will go with you." She paused. "I think we both know the answer to that."

He frowned, not sure at all if he knew the answer, but then he hadn't realized he was asking the question.

"The white tuberose means dangerous beauty. It's a funeral flower. I suppose you were influenced by that nasty coffin business."

"It has an exotic sweet scent that reminded me of you," he called out to her. Although he had to admit, given that her brother had already sworn to kill him, they were both involved in a dangerous game. The flower was more applicable than he had imagined.

"This light green flower is interesting. It—"

"—is the color of your dress that drew me to your side the night we met," he loudly replied. Enough of this flower-meaning nonsense.

"They're beautiful, Rafferty. I want to thank you for your thoughtfulness." He put his shirt on a peg and began to remove his trousers. "I thought perhaps . . . you might like to negotiate."

Negotiate? He tossed his trousers in a heap on the floor and stepped into the bedroom in his drawers. "Negotiate what?"

"You have something that I want, and you need me to express my gratitude." Her eyes smoldered in the dimmed light. Her gaze slipped down the length of him like one of the evening delights working the harbor. "Compromise and negotiation," she said. "They're the keystones of diplomatic communication."

Whatever fatigue had plagued his body when he entered the room burned away in a bright flame of lust. But given her stillness two nights ago, he was hesitant to take advantage of her invitation. "If we were married, truly married," he said, "I would tell you that whatever I have is already yours."

He walked around the bed to dim the lamp on her side. When he reached for the knob on the gas jet, her hand slipped down the inside of his leg.

"Don't turn it off," she said.

Jesus, Mary, and Joseph! His eyes closed, and his groin tightened. Granted, it was his suggestion that she touch him. He told himself the experience would allow her to feel less alone, or maybe make him feel less alo—God almighty—this was killing him.

"We're not married, Rafferty. I feel it is only proper that I ask permission."

"Proper is not the word I'd use," he managed with difficulty. He abandoned the lamp to sit on the edge of the mattress. "What is it you wish, darlin'?"

"I want to see you, Rafferty," she said. "All of you."

Lord, his John Henry must have stretched another two inches at her request.

"It was dark that night with the Baron. I never saw what he was doing to me. I just felt . . ." She closed her eyes for a moment. "I want to see what a man looks like."

Rafferty stood, then tugged at the string at his waist that held the linen garment on his hips. Due to the effect of her appreciative gaze, the material didn't fall directly to the floor but rather snagged about his straining cock. He slipped his hand over himself to free the garment that slipped to the floor.

She gasped. Her eyes widened. "No wonder it hurt so," she whispered.

"No," he reassured her, while resuming his seat on the bed.

"I promise you. It doesn't always hurt. A woman's body has a way to ease a man." There was nothing easing about this conversation. He was as hard as the bedpost and afraid that would frighten her all the more. "Do you remember when he asked if you were ready?"

She nodded her head.

As much as he hated the Baron for what he did, he had to concede this one point. Rafferty brushed some strands of hair away from her pale face. "I think the Baron was asking if you were slick with moisture."

She looked at him as if he were mad. "Moisture?"

"Do this for me, darlin'. Reach between your legs and feel inside the crevice that shields your . . . virtue." Good Lord, what did women call these things? The terms he knew were sure to prove offensive to his elegant and proper . . . wife.

She blanched.

"Now, now," he soothed. "You didn't hesitate to cover yourself with your hand when I caught you in the tub." He smiled. It was a memory he would always cherish. "Do the same, but this time, let your finger slip inside." She didn't move. "You can do it beneath the blanket. I don't need to see."

But he could imagine. He saw the hesitant movement in the rise and fall of the bed linens as her hand inched toward the very region he'd suggested.

"Can you feel that it's moist?"

She closed her eyes and pressed her lips tightly together but nodded again.

"Now," he said. "I'm going to make it more so."

IF HER EARLIER ENCOUNTER WITH THE BARON HADN'T already condemned her to hell, this certainly would. She could feel Rafferty's gaze on her as her fingers slipped into the feminine cleft that was never named in all her years at school. It was taboo, dirty, unspoken of for fear of retribution, yet here she was exploring that very area while a man watched. Heat didn't confine itself to her cheeks; her whole body burned. With the palm of her hand on the fluff of hair that grew in that forbidden spot, she stretched her fingers past the folds that guarded her entrance. Yes, it was moist there, but that did not explain how her body could ever accommodate something the size of Rafferty.

The shame of her exploration eased when nothing untoward occurred. She had just begun to relax, when Rafferty's hand pressed her own exploring one. Before she could protest, she felt his hand mold her breast, and his mouth . . . Sweet Jesus! . . . moistened the thin night rail that covered her crest. He suckled her right through the material. Her body arched. Instantly, moisture flooded her fingers. Indeed, the entire area tingled with a sort of primitive yearning. He rocked her captured hand, forcing it to press parts of her she'd not touched before. Sensation flashed in lightning streaks of carnal anticipation.

"What is happening?" she gasped.

"Did you feel like this before the Baron took your maidenhood?" Rafferty asked, pausing in his titillating feast of her breast.

"No," she admitted. It had happened so quickly, she hadn't felt anything except a dry, painful scraping. But she didn't want to think about that now. She wanted Rafferty back at her breast. She wanted Rafferty exploring the depths of her cleft instead of herself. She wanted to feel how it should have felt had she been "ready." A drop of moisture pressed by velvety-soft skin nudged her hip.

Rafferty suddenly released her hand and sat up on the mattress. He turned away from her, mumbling something low and barely audible. She pulled her fingers away from her entrance, the tips wet and slick, and moved them to his thigh.

"Did I do something wrong?" she asked. Why else would he turn away? She was a failure as a proper society innocent and apparently as a wanton as well. Her body still vibrated with a needy tension.

"You did everything right," he said after a moment. "It's me who's fouling the works."

"You?" she exclaimed, incredulous that he thought he had somehow failed. "You've done nothing but what I asked."

He looked at her over his shoulder. "Darlin', it's a terrible thing that the bastard baron did to you. He took something that by rights didn't belong to him, and you're the one who's paying the price." He stood; his hand raked through his hair, and his cock bobbed as if it had a mind of its own. "Yet here I am wanting you, just like he did. I want to thrust inside you and show you the pleasure you were denied. But I've no more right to you than that bastard did. So what does that make me?"

Wanted. Desired. Needed. She wanted to scream but instead said nothing. She wasn't supposed to want him like this. It was to be a pretend marriage.

He reclaimed his drawers from the floor and pulled them over his extended cock.

"Your brother called me a man of honor tonight." He turned off the gas jet, plunging the room into darkness. "What honor is there in taking his sister without commitment or consequence?"

She heard his heavy steps round the bed. The mattress dipped to accommodate his weight.

Abandoned again. Deserted as before, only this time without the benefit of sexual congress. Tentatively, she reached her hand in the dark to touch his back. "You said to always touch you when we were together," she whispered.

"Not tonight, Arianne," he said. "It's probably best to leave me alone."

· Twenty-Two ·

HE'D BEEN AVOIDING HER FOR A COUPLE OF DAYS, being careful to only go to bed when he knew she was asleep, slipping out of bed before she was awake. One night he thought to just rest his eyes in his office before climbing the stairs to check if Arianne was asleep. Evans woke him the next morning slumped in one of the upholstered chairs in the office.

She'd been busy during the day making calls, receiving calls, scurrying about preparing for her garden party. He'd had some calls from some of the president's cabinet members, but those were made out of curiosity and boredom. There was not much to recommend politics in Washington in June.

The Duke was suspicious once again. He hadn't directly confronted Rafferty with accusations this time, but Rafferty felt he was constantly watched.

So he was surprised when Arianne knocked on the office door. The moment he saw her, something twisted in his gut, much as it had every night that she sat across from him at the dinner table, speaking to her brother, speaking to the footman, speaking to Ben, avoiding him. He could see her loneliness but felt powerless to help her, knowing exactly what would happen if he did. He stood the moment he saw her in the doorway and hoped perhaps she'd come to talk, much as they used to.

"I've brought someone to speak with you," she said, calm and reserved. Then she stepped aside and ushered in a frightened woman about a year or so younger than Arianne. "This is Rosie Murray, who used to be in the legation's employ. She needs your assistance."

How had she found her? The inquiries he had made through Evans had led nowhere. "Come in, Miss Murray. Have a seat."

As Arianne turned to go, Rosie looked back at her. Rafferty recognized her fear. "Arianne, please stay," he implored. "I believe Miss Murray will be more comfortable if you are present."

Arianne hesitated, then selected a chair near Rosie. He had a hard time taking his gaze off his beautiful, elegant pretend wife to focus on the fidgety Miss Murray.

"Miss Murray, what can I do for you?"

"I had a cousin named Mary O'Shay, but she's dead now," Rosie's thin voice said. "I'd like to send her home to her family in Ireland. There's a funeral home that will do it for nothing, but I can't get her body."

"Wasn't Mary O'Shay the woman who was found with Lord Weston?" he asked, to see her reaction.

"That was her." She raised her voice. "But she wasn't like they say she was."

"What was she like?" Arianne asked. It wasn't a question Rafferty would have asked, but it was the perfect question for Miss Murray. Rafferty could tell the woman relaxed just by describing her older cousin. Mary had a beautiful singing voice, she said, and was trying to find work as an actress in New York. She'd write Rosalie exciting letters about life in the big city and her new beau, but then the letters became more distant. The man acquaintance was something of a rebel, she said, and involved in a movement determined to free Ireland. Rafferty glanced over at Arianne, but she was intently listening to Rosalie's tale.

Mary had heard something, some dangerous plan that had scared her, Rosalie said. Her man friend had taken to beating her when he drank too much, and according to Rosalie, that was a lot. Mary said she needed to talk to someone in the government, so she turned to Rosalie. She had said she couldn't go to the police, and she was afraid her gentleman friend would kill her if she talked to anyone in New York.

Rosalie had approached Lord Weston about meeting her cousin, and he agreed, but then they both were killed.

"Do you think her man friend found them?" Rafferty asked.

She nodded her head. Arianne handed her a handkerchief, which she used to dab her eyes.

"Did she talk to you about the plan?"

Rosalie shook her head. "She was too scared."

Well, there was little more to pursue from that quarter. "Did she ever mention the name of this gentleman friend?"

"She never said his name. In her letters, she called him T. That was how she wrote his name, just a capital 'T.'"

Toomey! He knew it! The woman had every right to be scared if that was her man acquaintance. "Did you keep any of her letters?" he asked. Maybe he could find something Rosalie forgot.

"Lord Weston kept the one I showed him, but the rest are gone."

Another lead that led nowhere.

"Tell me what I can do to help you?" Rafferty asked again.

"The police buried my cousin in a potter's field when no one came to claim her. Money's been scarce since I left here."

"And you left because . . ." Arianne prodded.

"I was afraid he'd come after me. He might have known that I worked at the legation. So I left and stayed with a friend. If it hadn't been for Mary's burial . . ."

"Have you found other employment, Rosalie?" Arianne asked. "It mustn't have been easy without a letter of reference."

"I'm with a small family now, Your Ladyship. It doesn't pay the same, but I'm not liable to wake up with my throat slit."

Rafferty chose not to point out that one does not wake up under those circumstances.

"So what can I do to help you?" he repeated.

"The good people at the Irish Trust and Funeral Fund said they would make sure Mary was sent home good and proper. They said they would pay for the whole thing 'cause they're a charity for the common good and all. I've got two gravediggers that will dig up Mary from the potter's field, but they want to be paid cash money. I thought maybe as they say Lord Weston killed my cousin . . ."

"But you said you didn't believe that," Arianne protested. "You said she wasn't that kind of girl."

Rosalie lowered her gaze, suitably chastised. "But she wouldn't have been killed if she hadn't agreed to meet Lord Weston, and he arranged the meeting and all. So you see—"

"Lord Weston set up the meeting?" Rafferty asked. "He picked the hotel?"

Rosalie blinked. "He sent her the money for the train and told her to go to the Lincoln hotel."

"And how much do you need for these grave robbers?" He unlocked the desk drawers so he could retrieve the book of withdrawals on the legation account.

"They're gravediggers, sir. They said they needed two dollars."

At that price, he thought grave *robbers* would be more realistic. "One more thing, Rosalie," Rafferty said. "How did you find out about the Friends of the Irish Trust?"

"I found this notice, sir." Her face brightened. "I brought it with me. Would you like to see it?"

She pulled a paper folded over many times. He straightened it out and pressed it down on the desk before him. As Rosalie had indicated, this group was offering to arrange for shipment of her cousin's corpse and coffin back to Ireland, at no charge whatsoever. Strange arrangement, that. He knew well that the shipment of coffins was a costly affair, to say nothing of the steep expense to embalm the bodies. Only the wealthy could afford such services, which was one of the reasons the sheer numbers on the dock were confounding.

He withdrew a pen from its holder and a sheet of paper from the desk and wrote down the name and the New York address of the Irish Trust and Funeral Fund. Phineas was due back for a report. This sounded like something he could investigate. He set that aside to dry while he scribbled out a draft to the bank authorizing Rosalie double the sum she'd requested. While he didn't feel the legation was obligated to pay Mary's funeral expenses, Rosalie had provided some valuable information, even without realizing it, and for that she should be well compensated.

ARIANNE WALKED ROSALIE INTO THE HALLWAY. Spotting Ben, she instructed him to see Miss Murray home using the legation carriage. Then she returned to Rafferty's office, closing the door behind her. Immediately, he rose to his feet. He was so handsome, it twisted her heart that they had managed so successfully to avoid having a meaningful conversation in the past several days.

"Rafferty," she said. "I want to negotiate."

He paused on his way around the desk. "I see." He stroked his lip with his knuckle, reminding her of the kisses they once shared. "I take it there is something you desire?"

You, she thought but, of course, couldn't say. She clasped her hands behind her back and stepped toward him. He moved closer as well, with that half smile she loved and his gaze fixed firmly on her lips. "The garden party will take place in just a few days. I'd like you to attend and welcome the ladies."

"An appearance?" His eyebrow raised. He stood but an arm's reach away until he slipped his arms over hers, clasped her fingers above her bustle, and tugged her closer. "And what am I to receive for this sacrifice?"

She arched her back and lifted her chin. "What would you like?"

He took the bait and trailed kisses up her neck. Christopher, his lips made her weak in the knees. He dragged his nose to her cheekbone. "Is that a new scent concoction, darlin'?"

Heavens above, she'd forgotten how much she missed his sweet brogue until he murmured in her ear. "I'm experimenting with patchouli oils. I mixed it with—"

He captured her lips, or she captured his—she wasn't sure which, nor did she care. He backed her to a wall—the one with the stern photograph of Queen Victoria, if she remembered correctly. He braced his arms on either side of her shoulders and traced her cheekbones with his fingertips.

"You should marry me, darlin', so we can stop this pretending."

"I'm willing to be your wife in all the ways that matter, Rafferty." She wrapped her arms around his waist. "You could show me what the Baron couldn't. Then, when this is over, I'll have memories."

She felt the shift in him, saw the lust in his eyes cool.

"Memories? You could end up with a lot more than memories." His words whipped at her like cold driving rain. "You could end up with babies. Did you think of that? Would her ladyship even bother to tell the Irish cur of a father that she was carrying his whelp? We Irish breed like rabbits; isn't that what the English aristocracy say?"

He pushed away from her and walked back to his desk. He studied some papers, moving them from one side of the desk to the other. "This party seems more appropriate for your brother. I would think the ladies would have more interest in a duke than just another Irishman," he said without once looking up. "I assume garden parties, like knowing the proper uses for fifty different types of spoons, are essential for proper diplomatic appearances."

Tears stung her eyes; a lump lodged in her throat. "You don't understand." Her voice shook. "Marriage—a real marriage—is not a game for me."

He looked up. "And sharing your bed—sharing your body—is? Sweet Jesus, woman. I thought you had more pride than that."

She couldn't breathe. His words slapped across her face like an open hand. She turned on her heel and ran from his office, passing Evans and William in the hall. She stumbled up the steps and slammed the door to the bedroom.

Falling across the bed, she let the tears flow. It all came back. The resounding slap. Her father, the old Duke, screaming at her mother who lay crying at his feet, *I thought you had more pride than that.* She remembered that same look of disgust on her father's face whenever Arianne came home on holiday. "You look just like your mother," he'd say, then close himself away in his room.

William thought understanding the real reason her father acted that way would somehow make her feel better, but he was wrong. Knowing that the old Duke was not her true sire somehow justified his aversion. Arianne was disgusting to him. Living proof of the Duchess's perfidy. Just as the old Duke's violence toward her mother justified Arianne's need to keep Sanctuary for her own.

This is your sanctuary, Rafferty had said, but he didn't understand.

She knew one day he would turn to her with disgust. She should be surprised he'd waited this long. She'd committed the unforgivable. She'd given her virtue to someone who didn't deserve it. Then she'd given her heart to another who expected more.

DOWN IN HIS OFFICE, RAFFERTY SUNK HIS HEAD IN HIS hands, devastated. He'd never thought he'd ever ask a woman to marry him, and certainly when he did, he hadn't thought it would be an insult. But apparently to Lady Upper Crust it was. Damn it, he loved her. Why couldn't she see that? He hadn't meant to hurt her. Heaven knew he wasn't averse to bedding a willing lass a time or two, but Arianne was no laced mutton looking for a quick ride. She was the elegant, passionate, vulnerable Lady Arianne, who right now was deep in tears because he refused to take advantage of her.

"What did you do to my sister?"

He didn't need to look up to know who had entered his office. "Leave it alone, Bedford."

"I saw her run up the stairs in tears. She only cares about one person enough to let him hurt her like that." The Duke dropped into a chair in front of his desk. "Go apologize to her."

Rafferty pulled his head out of the nest of his hands just enough to see Bedford. "You don't know what you're talking about."

"I know you probably think you're right about whatever you're arguing about, but take it from me—a happily married man—the woman is always right. Give her what she wants. It'll make the both of you happy."

This was bloody ridiculous. He'd asked Arianne to marry him. She'd refused, and now her brother was telling him to just go have his jolly way with his sister without the benefit of marriage! How was he supposed to respond to that . . . diplomatically?

"Don't you have a wife and new baby in England?" Rafferty asked, sitting back in his seat. "Isn't it time to go see them?"

"My mother-in-law is there with Franny and the baby." William shook his head. "Deerfield Abbey is large enough for two hundred monks but not nearly sufficient for my mother-in-law and I to exist under the same roof."

Rafferty knew the feeling. "Tell me, Bedford, do you ever fight, engage in a little fisticuffs strictly for sport, of course?"

"Me? No, I'm more of a horseman."

"Pity that," Rafferty said, feeling the need to hit something.

"Go and talk to her," William continued. "You said yourself, she needs you. There's no pending confrontation between Queen Victoria and President Garfield that requires your immediate intervention . . . Go on and tend to your wife."

"I think you'd be wise to counsel her to concede to my wishes," Rafferty said, then rose from behind the desk. "Let me consider your advice, then I'll see what can be done."

But rather than follow his wife's path up the steps, Rafferty chose to put some distance between himself and the legation, between himself and Arianne and her brother, between himself and the entitled aristocracy. Arianne had sent Rosalie Murray home in the legation carriage, so Rafferty thought he'd flag down a hansom. The cabbie might know a thing or two about a drinking establishment where a man didn't have to think about diplomacy, compromise, or negotiation. Of course, he had to admit, when it came to Arianne, it was hard to think of anything but negotiation.

He stormed out the front door and saw Evans standing a short way down the street, talking to a stranger in a top hat. The man glanced at him, then commented something to Evans, who also turned in his direction. Another word or two was shared, then the two parted ways, Evans returning to the legation.

"Are you going out, sir? Should I call for the carriage?"

Rafferty stared at the departing man. Something about him seemed out of place; he just couldn't identify what that something was.

Evans followed the direction of Rafferty's gaze. "He was asking for directions, sir. Easy to get lost in this end of the city."

Unfortunately, Bedford wasn't having that difficulty, Rafferty thought. He managed to find his way back to the legation every bloody day.

"Would you like me to call the carriage, sir?" Evans asked again.

"No. I thought I'd walk a bit. Need to stretch my legs." With that he set off down to the first cross street and followed that till he saw some idle cabs.

FINNEGANS. IT WAS LOCATED IN THE SORT OF AREA that most reasonable men with coin in their pockets would avoid, which meant Rafferty felt right at home. The smell of rot and refuse mingled with the thick, humid air. The front windows to the establishment had been backed with a dark paper, thus allowing the patrons to drink without knowledge of the time or people passing. Paint peeled off the wooden exterior like bark from a tree. Rafferty smiled. With luck he would satisfy not only his curiosity but also his desire to feel his knuckles connect with flesh. He paid the driver, then went in.

The interior met the promise of the exterior. Enough young lassies worked the crowd that he imagined he might fill another need here as well. His determination to not take what Arianne offered was taking a toll. He ordered a whiskey at the bar and leaned his back upon it to study the patrons. Which one of these men would have come to Eva's assistance in her betrayal of Rafferty?

"You must be lost, love." A buxom brunette with a neckline low enough to distract sidled up to his side. He felt her quick check for his billfold and knew she came up empty. She was good, but not good enough.

He looked at her askance. "What makes you say that?" The woman laughed in response.

"Look at you." She spread her arm toward the jumbled occupied tables. "Look at them." She turned back toward him. "Either you're lost or you're looking for something, or someone. Which is it?" Her eyelids lowered in an attempt at seduction. "I can be a help, I can, with the proper incentive."

He didn't fit in? He glanced down at the tailored clothes

Arianne had insisted he procure. Good Lord, he was wearing gloves—so fine and light, he'd forgotten about them. His hair dangled only occasionally in his eyes these days. He supposed he must look the part of a rich dandy to the inside patrons— especially to the man in the corner who was watching him intently. "Who is that man?" Rafferty asked the woman. "The one in the corner."

His otherwise talkative companion suddenly turned mute. Rafferty reached into his inside jacket and withdrew his purse. Careful to conceal the contents, he withdrew some coins and handed them to her. Her greedy eyes watched as he replaced it in his jacket. "His name is Charles Guiteau. He's not a regular, but he comes in every so often. He has a soft spot for Sarah." She nodded with her chin to another woman working the tables. She turned toward him, placing one hand on his chest, while the other fingered his cheekbone. "My name is Constance. Do you have a soft spot for me?"

He captured the hand that was inching toward his billfold. He may no longer appear to be the ruffian he was once assumed to be, but that didn't mean he'd lost his wits. He imagined he could easily strike a price with Constance, and she would do the sort of things that Arianne couldn't even imagine, but he discovered he wasn't interested. She wasn't the woman he longed to sink into. This one wouldn't satisfy his body, much less his mind. "I think you're correct, Constance. I think I made a wrong turn when I came in here today." Holding her hand in place, he finished his drink in one long burning swallow. "So if you'll excuse me, I believe I'll be on my way."

It would do no good to make inquiries; not when he looked like a bloody government official. He'd have to leave the inter-rogation of Finnegans' patrons to Phineas. He hadn't really believed that Arianne could transform his sow's ear into a silk purse, yet he was faced with the proof. Rafferty pulled the woman's hand off his chest, then headed for the door. Before he could leave, a big brute—larger than the size of the door— blocked his path.

"There's a toll for leaving Finnegans," the bruiser said. Rafferty heard the scraping of chairs on either side of him. A smile crept to his face. At least he'd have the opportunity to accomplish one of his goals.

"And what might that toll be?" he asked.

"Whatever you have in that billfold will satisfy it," the brute said. "Hand it over."

Rafferty pretended to comply. He stepped to the side as if trying to hide the location of the billfold while he set his feet. Just as the clod was anticipating a fat purse, Rafferty threw a quick punch with his left that knocked the wind out of the brute's chest. As he tried to suck air, Rafe delivered a brutal punch with his right to the clod's jaw. Blood splattered, and he went down like a felled tree to the hushed audience in the bar. Rafe turned and checked behind him, but no one attempted to take the bruiser's place. Pity that. He stepped over him to leave the establishment. To his surprise, the hansom that had delivered him still waited outside.

"I didn't think you'd stay long," the driver said with a cackle, "but I'm surprised to see you walk out."

Rafferty directed the driver to the legation and climbed into the relative safety of the cab. He couldn't deny it. He'd changed from the man he was in London, and he could name the pert, elegant lady responsible. Now the question presented itself—was it for the better or for the worse?

· Twenty-Three ·

"WELCOME BACK, SIR."

Evans didn't comment on the bloodstains on Rafferty's gloves or the unwashed scent of Finnegans that seemed to saturate his clothes even in the brief time he was there, though Rafferty suspected he'd noticed. "Your wife and brother are currently dining in the breakfast room."

He hadn't time to change, and frankly, he didn't care to. He still mourned the loss of the person he used to be and wasn't ready to wash it away just yet.

"Rafferty!" Arianne rushed toward him the moment he appeared in the doorway. She was a vision, so elegant, so clean, and so very different from the women of his former existence. His groin tightened. He anticipated her revulsion when she got close enough to smell the remnants of Finnegans. Perhaps then she'd change her mind about "negotiating."

"I was worried when—" She picked up his hand. "What is this?" Wide eyes searched his. "Is this blood?"

"Relax, darlin'. It's nothing to worry about." He pulled off the gloves, tossed them on the sideboard, and leaned in to kiss her on the cheek. In case she hadn't gotten a good enough whiff, he walked her back to the table. "There was a small altercation at the establishment I visited." He grinned as he sat. "They were so enthralled with my diplomatic skills they were hesitant to let me go."

"Bloody hell, Rafferty," William said. "You were serious about fighting. I'm glad I didn't take you up on it."

Ben set a plate before him and winked, while another server poured the wine. Rafferty supposed it was Ben's way of congratulating him on the fight while conforming to Arianne's instructions on proper server etiquette. Smart boy to learn the art of compromise at such an early age.

Arianne signaled to Ben, then motioned him to bend low enough that she could whisper in his ear. Once that was accomplished, Ben left the room.

"We were just discussing Arianne's skill on the piano," Bedford said.

Rafferty gazed at her. "I didn't realize you could play." He sipped his wine. "What a lovely surprise."

"I'm not very good. I've been so busy getting the gardens ready, I've been too preoccupied to practice."

"You should play for us after dinner," William said. "I'm sure Rafferty would enjoy that."

"No," she said, emphatically. "I believe Rafferty has other plans."

"I do?"

"Yes, but we'll discuss it later . . . privately."

Her tone suggested there would be no further discussion about those plans at the dinner table, which suited him just fine. They hadn't resolved their disagreement from this afternoon, and he certainly didn't want any more of Bedford's advice on the matter. This was something he and Arianne would have to resolve in private.

"Did you see Phineas at this establishment?" Arianne asked.

"Not that I noticed, but Phineas has a way of being unseen," Rafe replied, spearing a piece of meat. "I do expect he'll be here tomorrow. I thought I'd have him investigate that funeral trust that Rosalie mentioned."

"You know, Rafferty." William's voice took a serious tone. "I'd be happy to assist you in this investigation in some capacity. Just because I have a title doesn't preclude me from having a brain."

Rafe glanced at his supposed brother-in-law. Had he under-estimated the man's usefulness because of his title? He had to admit he'd been prejudiced against Arianne when they first met because of hers. She'd proven that his assumptions about her were unfounded. Hadn't she found Rosalie in the midst of all her legation duties? She'd taken in Ben and the boys without complaint and worked with them so they might find useful employment. She'd handled many of the diplomatic responsi-bilities so he'd have time to do his investigations. Quite frankly she'd surprised him, and maybe her brother would do the same.

"I think I might have something you could do," Rafferty said. Bedford set his fork down and leaned forward. "My tal-ented wife made an observation today." He smiled over at Ari-anne, who looked wary. "She asked Rosalie about references. Don't you see? Everyone who works at the legation must have had references. Arianne and I have reason to believe that there is a spy in our midst. I would like you to secure the letters of reference for the staff and look at them for some sort of dis-crepancy. You and Arianne would have a much better apprecia-tion of what it takes to obtain such positions. Arianne has her hands full with other responsibilities at the moment, so I'm going to leave it to you, Bedford, to ferret out the spy. Whoever it is, they won't see it coming from you."

William nodded. "I can do this. I will do this. I won't let you down."

"I'm counting on you," Rafferty said. "I can vouch for Ben-jamin. If you need someone to work from the inside, Ben is your man."

William settled back, looking quite pleased with himself. "It's good to have a challenge. Something to occupy one's mind beyond reading the morning papers. Franny will be impressed with all I know now about American politics. Did you know that the major political parties have divisions within them? They have some colorful names. There's a group called the Half-Breeds. I thought it was a reference to some mingling with American Indians, but it's not. It's about reform to stop giving political jobs to political supporters. I suppose politics are the same the world over. We have the similar arguments in England."

"You met one of the Half-Breeds, William," Arianne said.

"Do you recall Mr. Blaine? I understand he originally planned to run in the Republican Party for the position of presidency against a supporter of another faction called the Stalwarts. It was all explained to us on the ship coming over. Neither of the two men could earn enough support to represent the Republican Party, so Mr. Garfield was brought into the fray as a compromise."

"Compromise," Bedford said. "It's the backbone of politics. So was this Garfield a man of the Half-Breeds or Stalwarts?"

"Neither, but he did put Mr. Blaine, a Half-Breed, in his cabinet, and selected a Stalwart, Mr. Arthur, as his vice president. We met Mr. Arthur at the Executive Mansion. He seemed a nice enough gentleman," Arianne said.

"He's Irish," Rafferty added. "Or rather his father is." There was something else mentioned in that discussion on the ship about Arthur that intrigued him at the time. What was it?

"Well, gentlemen." Arianne stood, causing Rafferty and William to rise as well. "The evening grows late. If you will excuse me." She crossed to Rafferty and accepted his kiss on her cheek.

Rafferty watched her skirts sway as she exited the room. He wondered at her serenity, given their earlier argument. Perhaps she'd seen his point.

"Even though I was initially frustrated that Arianne's actions were forcing me to leave my wife and son for an interval," Bedford said, "I must admit I'm glad to have spent the time getting to know her better, and you, of course. You surprised me, Rafferty. You're not at all the man I thought you would be."

Rafferty's expression must have warned he was on thin ice. William hastened to continue. "I was afraid Arianne would follow her inclination toward weak men. You see, she witnessed the old Duke's brutality toward our mother more than the rest of us. I believe to avoid placing herself in our mother's position, she chose unworthy candidates for her affection."

Having seen the Baron, Rafferty could attest to Bedford's observation.

"When she saw the blood on your hands just now," Bedford said, "I was afraid she would remember some of the violence she'd witnessed as a child. She handled it well, I thought." He startled, as if wakened from a reverie, and smiled. "So you see, you were a complete surprise to me. She chose well. Perhaps better than I could have for her." Bedford stood. "I believe I'll forgo the cigars tonight. Good night, Rafferty."

Rafferty sat back in his chair, listening to the world settle around him. Could Arianne have refused his proposal because she was afraid of his temper? He'd never hit a woman; the thought was repugnant to him. But it did explain her choice of that milksop baron.

Accusing her of licentious behavior was most likely not the best way to handle the situation. Bedford had been correct inasmuch as he should have gone to her to explain his concerns in a less accusatory fashion. He needed to show her that he was not volatile, that he could control his temper and, hopefully, his lust as well. For that, he might as well start tonight.

HAD HE NOT BEEN CONCENTRATING SO HEAVILY ON how to explain his concerns to Arianne in a controlled manner— and praying at the same time that she'd be asleep and thus spare him from a difficult conversation—he might have noticed that the light beneath the bedroom door shifted in a manner not conducive to gas lamps and the air had become infused with exotic floral notes. He opened the door to a room illuminated by flickering candles, on the mantel, on the writing desk, even on the floor by the paneled screen. Everything wavered in a soft, sensuous dance of light and shadow, including Arianne, who rose when he entered the room. She wore a fine lawn night rail, so sparse in decoration as to be common, but so thin as to render suggestions of the riches beneath, even in the candlelight.

"I had a warm bath drawn for you," she said. "Let me help you undress."

"Arianne—" he started to protest, but she silenced him with a finger on his lips.

"I want to do this," she said.

She stood before him, unfastening the buttons on his vest.

"About this afternoon . . ."

"Let's not argue tonight, Rafferty." She stepped closer, then slid her arms up his shirt to his shoulders, pushing the fabric of both jacket and vest with the back of her hands to let them fall on the floor behind him. He pressed his cheek briefly against her scented hair, inhaling the rich, sensuous notes of patchouli and luscious florals.

"Oh darlin', I'm sorry." He wasn't certain what he was sorry for, but he had a compelling need to apologize. His John Henry expressed its desire to make an appearance and make amends as well, based on the urgency in his groin.

Her talented fingers made quick work of his shirt buttons while he removed his cuff fasteners behind her back. His shirt soon joined the growing collection on the floor. He started to unfasten the buttons on his trousers, but she pushed his hands aside.

"Let me," she murmured. She finished the buttons and untied the string of his drawers.

"Touch me, Rafferty. I want to know it's you beside me in the dark." Her hands slipped inside his drawers at the hip, leaving him little option but to grasp her upper arms. Suddenly, she sank to one knee, tugging his clothes with her.

Sweet Jesus! His bobbing cock strained at the same level as her sweet lips. His fingers had progressed up her body as she slid down, and they now lingered on her head. He fought the urge to pull her face toward his cock, knowing that might scare her.

She removed his shoes and socks, just as he had done for her before, then kissed his upper thigh. His cock jumped, begging for attention most likely. So she gave him some. She ran the pads of her fingertips up his shaft. Then rising from her knee, she cupped him in her hand. Lord, if she was planning to lead him around by the cock, he'd happily follow. But she released him to tug at his hand. She led him to the tub and watched him step in.

He sank into the warm, scented water, feeling it rise and surround him. She knelt beside him and, soap in hand, smoothed it over his chest, across his shoulders, along his arms . . .

"Why are you doing this, love?" he asked, somewhat uncomfortable in their reversed roles.

She soaked a sponge in the water, following the same path as before. Droplets of the water splashed on her night rail, rendering visible what was before suggested. "I think you were right, Rafferty. I understand if I've been a disappointment to you."

"Not a disappointment," he protested.

She bade him to sit up so she could wash his back. Thus he couldn't see her face. He could just listen to her voice. "I know you're not like the Baron. You're a better man than him, more kind, more honest. I'm . . . used goods, but I love you, Rafferty. I can understand if you don't want—"

He stood up in the bath, not allowing her to finish. One of the candles sputtered out from the droplets raining from his body. He pulled her up to stand before him and pressed her close. Her thin nightgown acted as a towel, soaking the moisture between them.

"Say that again," he commanded, his heart racing in his chest.

"I love you, Rafferty. I—"

He kissed her like he'd never kissed a woman before, giving her every bit of his aching heart. He stepped out of the tub and lifted her into his arms. She laughed lightly, but he doubted she could see the wide grin on his face. She loved him, and that could only mean that she'd marry him and be his own.

He carried her to the bed, then laid her on the counterpane.

"Say you'll be mine, Arianne. That we'll always be together."

"That sounds like a negotiation . . ." she said.

"Say it."

"I've always been and will always be yours, Rafferty."

IT WAS HEAVEN, SHEER HEAVEN, THE THINGS HE MADE her feel. He followed her down to the bed, kissing her lips, her breasts. He tugged on her nipples, and she felt the flooding down below. She wanted him so desperately. She yearned to have him fill her inside, satisfy the craving that throbbed in her womb. He pulled the damp night rail from her body and just stood studying her in the flickering candlelight.

"I'm ready," she whispered.

"Not yet," he replied, sliding the length of his body between her parted legs. Dear Saint Christopher, she was near flooding with "readiness." Why was he making her wait?

He slid down the length of her, parting her legs even farther for his inspection. Her cheeks heated. It was one thing to be observed examining herself beneath the cover of a blanket and another for a man to actually inspect her there. She didn't have much time to think about it though, as a finger, his finger, slipped inside her. Such an odd feeling to have someone else lodged inside her, and it hadn't hurt. She was about to tell him exactly that when his tongue swept the cleft of her, ending at a spot of extreme sensation. She wiggled her body, trying to break free, but he continued his tender assault. A second finger joined the first, sliding up and down inside her. Her breasts lifted; her body arched. He used one of his talented fingers to massage the area where his tongue had laved, faster and faster. Suddenly a soothing calm, tingling in its intensity, silently exploded inside her. She thought she might have yelled, but she wasn't sure.

Rafferty worked his way back up her body. "Now, you're ready," he said.

He filled her with a gentle thrust, then waited while her body accommodated him. His arms stiff by her shoulders, he searched her face. "Does that hurt?"

She felt pressure and strain, but nothing like the scraping pain she'd remembered. She placed her fingertips on each side of his rib cage, feeling the power of him. This was Rafferty, her Rafferty, her protector and lover. She shook her head and smiled. "Not at all."

He started a slow pattern of thrusts before lowering to his elbows to quicken the pace. The tip of him reached deep inside her, pushing, stretching. She followed his rhythm with a thrust of her hips, helping him to reach some sought-after goal deep within her. Then he made a mighty thrust and held, his face twisted as if in agony. He laid his weight upon her, surrounding her with his body. It was a glorious sensation, touching so much of his skin with hers, hearing the sound of his heartbeat, and feeling the pulse of her own. Two people could not be closer, more intimate.

Rolling to his side, he gathered her up in his arms as if to never let her go. He kissed her forehead. "Thank you," he said.

Her head rested on his chest, listening to his heartbeat, feeling the surge of his breath in and out of his lungs, feeling the throb of her cleft from her initiation into true intimacy between a man and a woman. Having experienced Rafferty, she knew that her experience with the Baron was similar to sticking one's toe in the water and calling it a bath. She was Rafferty's, for as long as he wanted her, for as long as he needed.

"I love you," she whispered, but she wasn't certain that he heard. From the sound of his breathing, he was asleep. Sleeping with his arms around her and his lips to her forehead.

Her brother was right. A little seduction could yield enormous benefits.

· Twenty-Four ·

"PHINEAS. COME IN," RAFFERTY GREETED WITH A wide smile. "I was expecting you."

Phineas paused in the doorway. "I don't need to ask how you are. I haven't seen you in such good humor in . . . a long time. I take it life with Lady Upper Crust is agreeable."

Rafferty's brows lowered in a mild scold. "If you refer to my wife, Lady Arianne, life is more than agreeable."

Phineas grinned and extended his arm. "Congratulations, my friend." They shook hands. "I take it Cupid's Mistress made herself a match, and may I say she couldn't have selected a better man on which to work her magic."

"Thank you." Rafferty felt as if he were grinning like a schoolboy. He couldn't help it. Every time he thought of Arianne, and he thought of Arianne often, his lips raised of their own accord. This morning, she proclaimed herself "ready," but he could tell her nether lips were still swollen from last night. She should be much improved by tonight. "I believe I've convinced her that we suit so well in this pretend marriage that we should make it real."

"I thought when I saw you fell that addle-pate last night,

I'd find you in an improved mood, but this far surpasses my expectations," Phineas said.

"You were in Finnegans last night?"

He nodded. "I wasn't alone. I was with some professionals in the funeral industry."

Gravediggers, Rafferty translated. That made sense. They knew more about what occurred in the darkest of shadows than most. "Did you happen to notice a man sitting in some pleasant finery with a cocky stare?"

"Saw him straight off, though his finery was no finer than yours," Phineas teased. "His name is Charles Guiteau, according to one of the girls. He's not one of the Irish but likes the camaraderie. Anyone who stands a round in Finnegans finds he has friends."

"I thought I saw him here last night," Rafferty said. "Not here in the legation, but just up the street. Evans said he was asking directions."

"He was a long way from Finnegans, then."

"Did you discover who was to be Eva's contact there?" Rafferty asked.

"Likely the entire place would assist Eva if she walked in. The desire for home rule runs strong there. But I'd bet money it was one of the ladies. I'm guessing Constance, the one who tried to fleece your pocket."

Rafferty nodded. He pulled a scrap of paper from the desk blotter. "I have a company for you to investigate. They purport to pay for the transport of coffins back to Ireland."

"The Irish Trust and Funeral Fund?"

"How did you know?" Sometimes Phineas's ability to ferret out information amazed Rafferty, and he was somewhat used to it.

"I followed the money from the harbor. All those coffins have a stamp from the Irish Trust and Funeral Fund. The fund started in New York, but there's an office in Baltimore and another here. They aren't the sort of places with large sums of money to pay shipping rates, at least not from the looks of them. I think the one here in Washington does most of its business from a table in the back of Finnegans."

"Good work! Have you managed to look inside any of the coffins?"

"Not yet, but the *Irish Rose* is scheduled to take that load on the harbor to Ireland. I thought once they were loaded on board, we could have a look-see without interference from the guards."

"Briggs sent me a telegram that they'll be loading cargo for the trip home next Tuesday. The repairs were done earlier, but I think he decided to use a week for a honeymoon," Rafferty said. "Seems the magic of Cupid's Mistress has sprinkled on everyone but you, Phineas. I bet Arianne can rectify that."

"No, thank you," Phineas said with a laugh.

Arianne interrupted with a knock on the door. One glance to her red-rimmed eyes had him by her side in a heartbeat. "What's happened? What's wrong?"

"It's Rosalie. She was found dead this morning. Her throat slit. I think it might be my fault."

Rafferty pulled her into his arms. "It's no one's fault but the one with the knife. She came to you for money and she received it. You're not to blame." But his mind was already making connections. Rosalie wasn't attacked until after she had visited the legation. That would imply someone here was responsible. "Didn't Ben take her home yesterday? We need to know who else knew of her address. Has your brother gathered the recommendations?" He hugged her close once more and soothed a tear from her delicate cheek. "We'll find the one who did this, I promise you."

She smiled weakly at Phineas. "I only met her once, yet I feel responsible."

"Don't," Phineas advised. "Most likely her fate was sealed the day she sought an audience with Lord Weston to give him Mary's letter. You bear no portion of the blame."

She sighed and swiped her cheeks. "I'll go find William, but then I'll need to prepare for tonight."

Rafferty kissed her cheek before she left the room.

"This legation is a dangerous place," Phineas observed. "Hearts and bodies alike dropping left and right. Perhaps I'll pass the night elsewhere this evening."

Rafferty nodded. "It's a good thing this dance tonight is elsewhere. Had Washington's elite come here, we might have endangered America's entire political structure."

Phineas laughed. Rafferty, however, wondered if that could

be the motive. Toppling the political structure would certainly merit a few dead bodies, but how could the Fenians do anything in America that would impact England's structure? It just didn't make sense.

"Mary told Rosalie some foul deed was to occur in Washington," Rafferty mused. "Mary was desperate, as if the timing were close at hand, according to Rosalie."

"It's been several weeks since Lord Weston was murdered. Nothing of a foul nature has transpired yet . . . unless you consider that pile of coffins in the Baltimore Harbor."

"No. There's something else afoot." Rafferty suspected the murders dealt with more than a potential smuggling operation. From the sound of it, that operation had been going for some time but had increased volume recently. That would indicate preparation for another event, an event he suspected was to take place in Washington. He just didn't know the why, the who, or the when of the thing. "I feel as if I'm overlooking some critical clue. It's hovering just out of sight."

It was so frustrating. If he were back on the London streets where he knew the layout, the people to touch, the people to avoid, he imagined he would have this solved by now. So much had changed, though. He wasn't certain he'd be as effective in the streets and alleys as he had been before. His experience at Finnegans had shown him that.

"Tomorrow," Rafferty said, rising from behind his desk. "We'll sort through everything we have tomorrow. At the moment, I need to prepare for a ball." His lips pulled in a lopsided grin. "Had you ever imagined such a thing? Michael Rafferty at some fancy ball . . . invited no less."

Phineas just smiled. "I suspected it was only a matter of time."

NEWS OF ROSALIE'S MURDER DID NOT PROVIDE THE best base from which to prepare for a ball. Even the soothing lavender scents Arianne had added to the bathwater failed to ease her spirits.

"These cucumber slices should help relax you," Kathleen said, placing wet rounds on Arianne's closed eyelids.

"Perhaps you should try some too," Arianne said. "I know you were affected by the news."

"No one wants to hear of someone dying that way," Kathleen said solemnly. "I heard her family found enough money in her pockets to give her a decent burial. That was good fortune." More likely it was what caused her death, Arianne thought beneath the slices.

"Your gown is all pressed and ready. It's so beautiful; you'll look like a bride in all that white."

It would be her only opportunity to look like a bride, Arianne mused. No one would ever see her promenade down a church aisle draped in the white veiling of innocence. "The Americans celebrate the Fourth of July in grandiose fashion. As that is only three days away, the hostess decreed everyone should wear red, white, or blue, the colors of the American flag, tonight."

"You'll look lovely," Kathleen said.

"Even with swollen red eyes?"

Kathleen laughed. "When you stand next to Mr. Rafferty, your face lights up like a candle. No one will notice any different."

She should be surprised, but she wasn't. Just thinking about what she and Rafferty did last night certainly made her face heat like a flame. How naïve to think that what the Baron did to her was a statement of love. She knew now what passion entailed. What it meant to give and receive. And if this meant she was ruined, at least now she'd been ruined well. There was no reason not to continue this pretend marriage. She loved Rafferty with all her heart, even though he hadn't repeated those words back to her. Should he grow tired of her, she'd still have her Sanctuary, but she dearly hoped Rafferty wouldn't tire of her for a long, long, long time.

KATHLEEN PINNED TINY BOUQUETS OF BLUE HYACINTHS to the pouf of embroidered gauze that swept about Arianne's hips before gathering in a delicate cascade down her backside. Arianne added a bouquet of blue to the lowest point of the neckline, hoping to draw Rafferty's interest there. Just the thought of him caused her breasts to push against the top of her constricting corset, while a familiar tingling began at the bottom. Not now! she scolded herself. Ever since Rafferty had taught her the value of "readiness," she discovered her body was prepared at the most inconvenient moments.

Tiers of white lace defined her skirt, much like a wedding cake. She was the bride Rafferty never got to see but still taught to love. Kathleen added bits of lace and hyacinth bouquets to her hair while Arianne pulled on her long white gloves. Selecting a blue fan for contrast, she was ready to go.

Rafferty waited at the bottom of the stairs. Her breath caught. She'd never see him so handsome in his black tails with a blue cummerbund, a fashion she'd observed in India on a brief stay there. Christopher! There went the tingling again.

Her brother joined Rafferty at the base of the stairs, also in tails but with a red diagonal sash. Accompanied by these two, she imagined she'd be the envy of all the women at the ball.

"This is for you, Rafferty." She pinned a small bouquet that matched those on her dress to his lapel.

His gaze, warm and appreciative, skimmed her from head to toe. "Do they have a meaning?"

"Constancy," she replied with a soft smile.

"That will not be a problem," he murmured, a promise smoldering in his eyes.

She turned to her brother. "I have a rose for you as well, William." She pinned it to his lapel. "It's called an American Beauty."

"You'll have to find a bush for me to take home to my Francesca." He winked at Rafferty. "She's an American beauty herself."

THERE COULD BE NO DOUBT OF THEIR DESTINATION. Red, white, and blue bunting hung from every horizontal surface around the stately exterior of the house. Their carriage jostled with others for a point close enough to release the passengers. For a nearly deserted city, a sizeable crowd swarmed the wide veranda and first-floor rooms.

Shortly after they had arrived, Mrs. Blaine introduced them to all manner of people, some Arianne had already met through her social calls and through her garden activities. Rafferty shook hands and smiled at the right moments, but for the most part, he preferred to observe while Arianne engaged the people they met in conversation. Like a fish in water, she was in her element. She had to admit, she'd missed this aspect of city life.

The musicians took to their instruments, and the dancing began. Rafferty asked for the first dance, a waltz. With his hand on her waist and hers on his strong arm, he guided her around the ballroom. Though she missed the charm of twirling in his arms under the stars on a lonesome deck, the dance was magical nonetheless. William took her for a turn about the floor, but she preferred standing next to Rafferty to dancing with anyone else.

Rafferty engaged the affable Vice President Arthur in discussion. They discussed home rule, the vice president voicing a vote in favor of independence for Ireland, but as he quickly remarked, his opinion held no sway in another countries' politics. President Garfield, who was leaving the next day to visit his convalescing wife on the New Jersey shore, joined their discussion. When he mentioned his disappointment that he failed to gather some books to take to his wife, who loved to read, Arianne mentioned a wonderful book of Celtic myths and legends. With Rafferty's permission, she agreed to lend it to Mrs. Garfield. The president was delighted. Rafferty promised to bring the book to the train station before his trip.

Arianne hated to see the evening end. She would have loved to dance more with Rafferty, but she comforted herself knowing they'd have more such dances to share in the future. The future . . . It had never looked so bright. In London, she thought she was running away from the Baron when she was actually running toward Rafferty. The rhythmic jostling in the carriage combined with the late hour and Rafferty's comfortable shoulder lulled her to sleep.

"She's worn out," Rafferty said, shifting her a bit so she'd be more comfortable.

William looked out the window. "She didn't get much sleep last night." He smiled at Rafferty. "I take it you two resolved your differences."

"Arianne is the true diplomat between us." Rafferty's lips slid into a soft smile. "My wife knows how to negotiate."

"Take care of her. She's not as tough as she thinks," Bedford said. "Now that I've met America's gentry and I know Arianne is happy, I suppose I should plan my return to Bedfordshire. I'll finish the scrutiny of the servants, of course. But I can see you're capable to handle the rest without my . . . assistance."

Rafferty carried Arianne upstairs and managed the buttons, ties, hooks, and combs to get her undressed. He pulled the bed linens over her and took a few moments to study Arianne's face in the moonlight streaming through the window. Smoothing the hair from her face, he made a vow. "Bedford will have no cause for worry. I will always take care of you. Sleep well, my love. Have pleasant dreams. Tomorrow, I'll be here." He kissed her forehead, then climbed into bed himself for a few hours' sleep before he had to take the book to the train station.

It was a perfect evening in a perfect world, which, by the next day, shattered like the crushing of a fragile American Beauty rose.

· *Twenty-Five* ·

"RAFFERTY?"

Arianne wasn't fully awake, and he didn't wish to disturb her. She had a full day ahead playing hostess at her garden party. He just couldn't leave without a kiss to her forehead.

"Hush now, darlin'. I'll be back before you wake." At least, that was the plan. Deliver the book to Garfield, then rush to quietly slip back by her side.

"Don't forget the party," she mumbled.

"I won't. I promise." It tore him apart to leave. Only the comforting expectation of a swift return got him out the bedroom door.

THE BALTIMORE AND POTOMAC RAIL PASSENGER TERMINAL stood a block wide, all vibrant and new, like most of the capital city. Located on what was called the Mall, Rafferty could turn in any direction and see the political edifices, some still under construction. The city already bustled at this early hour on a Saturday morning. It was easy to understand the attraction this land held to his people. The honesty, the freedom . . . He could envision himself here in a more permanent capacity. The thought made him wonder how Arianne would feel living so far away from her brothers. Perhaps he and Briggs could establish a run in the shallow waters up the seaboard. It was worth consideration.

Even through the crowds of people, Rafferty spotted the president easily enough. A large man, Garfield talked with two of his cabinet members—men Rafferty knew through the legation—and two younger men, his sons perhaps. Rafferty approached the group, anxious to deliver the book and return to his sweet Arianne.

Suddenly, a man dashed before him, pulled a revolver from his pocket, and shot. Twice. The first bullet brushed Garfield's arm, spinning him in the direction of the second.

President Garfield gazed at his chest. "My God, what is this?" Then he collapsed to the station floor.

Rafferty lunged at the gunman, catching him from behind, and crashed to the ground. With little effort, Rafferty pinned him to the dirty floor, holding him until a policeman could cuff the bloody bastard and haul him to his feet. The gunman turned and grinned. The hair on the back of Rafferty's neck tingled. It was the man from Finnegans, Charles Guiteau.

"I am a Stalwart of the Stalwarts!" the madman exclaimed. "I did it and I want to be arrested. Arthur is president now!"

Rafferty understood instantly. It all became clear. This was the foul plan overheard by Mary O'Shay. The plan that ultimately cost her life. The Fenians planned to promote Arthur to president to use his influence with the Queen to support home rule. A group that would bomb innocents wouldn't hesitate to assassinate another, just to advance a favorite in political positioning.

With his hands cuffed behind him, Guiteau refused to budge even as the police tried to pull him toward the exit. He stared at Rafferty and yelled, "He's part of it! Arrest the Irishman! Arthur is president."

Immediately, bystanders fell about him, grasping at his arms and legs, punching his head, his shoulders, his stomach. He hadn't a chance with so many assailants. Just as he feared he might be pummeled to death, a policeman sorted through the angry mob. In spite of his claims of innocence, Rafferty was handcuffed and led out of the station like a common criminal.

ONCE AGAIN ARIANNE WAS SUMMONED TO A POLICE station, although this time it was in Washington. The news of the attempted assassination had reached the legation, though how Rafferty could be held as responsible defied logic. Both Phineas and her brother accompanied her, but crowds surrounding the police station wouldn't allow the carriage to get close. They left the brougham a block away and fought through the angry mob.

"String them up!"

"Shoot them like they shot the president!"

"No mercy for murderers!"

Shouts from the crowd assaulted her from every direction. Her heart hammered as she pushed past two men shouting out their favored form of execution. Rafferty had nothing to do with this. Why would the police be holding him?

A line of uniformed policemen stood in front of the station, forbidding entry to the crowd. Once she identified herself as Rafferty's wife, they let her and William pass but denied entrance to Phineas. The crowd booed and shoved, but she was granted access to the station, which resembled the only other police station she had visited. She approached the sergeant's desk. "What is the meaning of this? My husband had nothing to do with shooting President Garfield."

"The shooter said he's part of the plot, ma'am. That's enough to hold him."

"Plot? What plot?" Then it hit her. This was the "foul deed" that was mentioned in Mary O'Shay's letter! The plot that had already cost the lives of Lord Weston, Mary, and Rosalie. The evil people who would kill them wouldn't hesitate to hurt Rafferty. "Where is my husband!" she demanded. "I want to see him . . . now!"

The sergeant pointed to another uniformed policeman. Like those miserable mosquitoes, the uniforms were everywhere. "Take her back. Not him, though." He pointed to William. "He stays here."

She followed the policeman even while hearing William's

loud protests behind her. The sergeant apparently was not impressed with William's credentials as the Duke of Bedford.

Her escort pointed to a cell near the end of the hall. She traveled the length, ignoring the jeers and calls from others behind bars, until she was able to see Rafferty.

He was scraped and bruised. The skin around one eye was swollen. A hard lump formed in her throat. He lifted slowly from the bench, one hand on his side, to limp toward the bars where she waited. Dear God! What had they done to him?

"Morning, darlin'."

"Rafferty." She put her hand through the bars to slide down his face. "What happened to you?"

"I'll be all right, love, but listen to me. They won't give us much time. Tell your brother that Evans is the spy. He's probably the one who told Guiteau to implicate me."

"But why?" Arianne asked. "Why would they want to do that?"

"Because I know their plan. I didn't until Guiteau shot Garfield, but now I understand what they are up to."

"It's time, miss," the policeman at the end of the hall called.

"I'll get you out, Rafferty. They can't keep you here. You've got diplomatic immunity," she said.

"For the moment, I'm safer in here than outside." Rafferty attempted to smile, but the swelling made it more of a grimace.

"Then I'll get you a doctor."

"Time," the policeman repeated, then walked toward her.

"Get me Phineas," he murmured.

AN HOUR LATER SHE WAS BACK AT THE SERGEANT'S DESK. "My husband needs a doctor."

He didn't bother to look up. "All the doctors are attending President Garfield. Your husband didn't do an effective job."

"My husband had nothing to do with the assault on President Garfield," she huffed.

"Doesn't change the fact that no doctors are available." He kept writing in some sort of logbook.

"That's why I brought one with me." She placed a calling card on the logbook where it could not be missed.

" 'Dr. Phineas Connor,' " the sergeant read. He squinted up at Phineas. "I don't recall seeing you before."

"I'm not accustomed to making house calls in jail cells," Phineas replied. "But when the wife of a British minister calls, I listen."

The sergeant shifted his gaze to Arianne. "You're that duke's sister, aren't you?" She nodded. "Don't bring him back again." The sergeant went back to his log.

"Sergeant . . ." She spotted a certificate framed on the wall behind him. "Sergeant Morrison, you have no basis for holding my husband. Even if he did have a role in this foul circumstance—which he did not—you can't hold him as he's a foreign delegate. He has diplomatic immunity against arrest." The sergeant put his pen down as if he were preparing to listen, which was good, as she had plenty to say. "I'm sure President Garfield's secretary of state, Mr. Blaine, would tell you the same if he were here, but he's rightfully at the president's side and thus unavailable. However, I'm not asking for my husband's release. Given the crowd outside, he's safer in your custody, but he does need a doctor's attention."

Sergeant Morrison looked dubious.

"You can have a guard watch him," Arianne insisted. "He's a doctor, not a magician."

The sergeant considered, then pointed to the same officer as before. "Show him back." He turned to Arianne. "But you stay here. Only one visitor at a time."

THE POLICEMAN RATTLED HIS TRUNCHEON ACROSS THE bars. "Doctor here to see you. Stand back."

The cell door was opened, and Phineas, in the guise of a concerned physician with a black bag, gained admittance.

Rafferty glanced at the policeman who stood near the bars, watching them. "Dr. Connor. Did my wife call you? How is she?"

"She's concerned about you and said there'll be no garden parties until the president recovers." Phineas wriggled an eyebrow at him. "Now then, where do you hurt?"

Rafferty grinned. "Everywhere."

The guard softly snorted. Phineas pretended to peer into Rafferty's eyes.

"I think the lock is the same," Rafferty murmured, knowing Phineas would know he was referring to Baltimore.

"Um-hm," Phineas agreed. "Take off your shirt. Your wife said something about ribs."

Rafferty moved cautiously, because it did indeed hurt, though he suspected he'd only bruised his ribs. "I need tools," he murmured. Phineas moved across his chest, pushing in various key spots, pretending to look for tenderness.

The guard squinted. "He sure does have a lot of scars on him for a diplomat."

"Difficult negotiations," Rafferty answered with a raised voice. "The scars were the easy ones."

Phineas pulled a roll of some sort of bandage from his bag and started to wrap it around Rafferty's ribs. "There was a time when you'd already have the tools," Phineas said, keeping his voice low.

"Different tailor now," Rafferty answered.

Phineas wrapped the bandage over Rafferty's shoulder and secured it. "That should help," he said. He made a grand show of putting his supplies away and rummaging in his bag. "You should be okay in a couple of days. You won't look too pretty, but I imagine that wife of yours won't mind."

Rafferty started to reach for his shirt. Phineas picked it up instead. "Let me help you with that." Phineas held out the shirt while Rafferty backed into it. "Evans is gone," Phineas mumbled.

"Not surprised," Rafferty replied. "Check New York."

While Rafferty buttoned the front of his shirt, Phineas picked up Rafferty's jacket and brushed it off. "You certainly have a nice tailor, Mr. Rafferty. I'll hang up your jacket." He looked around the cell. "Or I'll just lay it here." He put it back where it originally was.

"Thank you, Dr. Connor," Rafferty said.

"I'd like to leave you with something for the pain." He tapped out a pill from a box and turned to the guard. "Can we get some water here?"

"Not while you're in the cell."

Phineas handed the pills to Rafferty, grabbed his bag, and waited on the other side of the bars while the guard went to retrieve a dipper of water.

"I'm not planning on breaking out if I can avoid it. They

don't have a reason to hold me, and I don't want to give them one," Rafferty said. "But it's good to know I can if I have to. Keep Arianne safe. With Evans on the loose, he might try to do more harm. Tell Bedford to keep checking; I want to know who he really is. The answer may be with Mary O'Shay."

The guard came back with a dipper of water to pass between the bars.

Rafferty looked at the tablet in his hand. "What is this?"

"Salicin," Phineas said. "From willow bark. It works. I've taken it. It does reduce the pain of sore muscles, but it's hard on the stomach."

Rafferty grimaced. He drank the water but palmed the pill. He handed the dipper back. "Tell Arianne I love her," he called.

"Tell her yourself," Phineas said. "They can't hold you very long."

"I DIDN'T EXPECT TO SEE YOU HERE."

Rafferty glanced up to see Officer Simmons, the policeman who'd worked the murder of Lord Weston. Rafferty grimaced. "I won't be here long. I had no part in that attack."

Simmons twisted his lips and leaned casually on the bars. "I'm tempted to reply that they all say that, but in this case I believe you." He narrowed his eyes at Rafferty. "Why you? Why did he point to you as part of his plot?"

"I've been wondering that myself. I have a theory. I think this attempted assassination is linked to the murders of Lord Weston, Mary O'Shay, and another, Rosalie Murray."

The policeman whistled low. "People die around you, Mr. Rafferty."

"I've noticed. I'm in the center of this. I'm the one to put the pieces together, but I can't do it here, and the person responsible knows that."

Simmons nodded. "So you're saying Guiteau is responsible for all those deaths?"

"No," Rafferty responded. "The man behind Guiteau is. The one who pulls his strings." He had no doubt that Toomey would be that master manipulator.

"Interesting theory. Can I help?" Simmons asked in acknowledgment.

"Get me cleared from these false allegations and let me do my job."

ARIANNE HAD COME BACK TO THE STATION THAT NIGHT with a pillow and the several special editions of the newspaper. They told her it was too late to see him, and they wouldn't allow the pillow, but the papers were approved. Rafferty suspected the sergeant read them before they were brought back to his cell, but it did give him something to do while he was waiting for release.

President Garfield still lived, but the doctors were having difficulty finding the bullet, believing it to be lodged near the spine. Rafferty felt truly sorry for the man who had only been in office for four months. He'd impressed Rafferty as dedicated and appreciative of the responsibilities entrusted to him. After several hours on the railroad station floor, he'd been moved to the Executive Mansion, together with a whole host of doctors.

In another article, Vice President Arthur was accused of being party to Guiteau's scheme. It apparently hadn't helped that Guiteau had proclaimed him president after shooting Garfield. That argument lacked substance. As did the accusations that Arthur conferred with a foreign diplomat who could do the deed without consequence because of diplomatic immunity. The foreign diplomat was being held for questioning. "I wish they'd get around to actually asking me something," Rafferty muttered. All interrogations were focused on Guiteau.

By Sunday, a few protesters remained outside of the police station. He overheard some of the policemen say that Guiteau was talking, wouldn't stop talking, in fact. He admitted he was angry that he was passed over as a French ambassador and so shot Garfield. It didn't seem to matter that Guiteau couldn't speak French and had no diplomatic experience. Rafferty wondered why the man would want such a position. Being a diplomat had brought nothing but trouble to him so far, except for Arianne. He would be eternally grateful for that introduction.

The police released Rafferty. While some grumbled that he was still a suspect, the captain had to bow to the principles of diplomatic immunity and the support of Officer Simmons, who argued there was no hard evidence against the British minister. For his own safety, he was led out a back door and placed with Simmons in a police transport to take him back to the legation.

They arrived at the legation the same time as a messenger with a telegram. Rafferty ripped the envelope open in anticipation that Phineas had urgent news regarding Evans.

RETURN HOME STOP TO BE CHARGED WITH TREASON STOP LORD HENDERSON

· Twenty-Six ·

"TREASON!" ARIANNE READ AND REREAD THE TELE-
gram. "Is this some cruel jest? There's no logic. Even the
Americans couldn't press a charge of conspiracy to murder."

"His diplomatic immunity will only go so far," Bedford said.
"The Americans could still deport him if they found sufficient
evidence that he was a party to that crime." He tapped the
telegram. "This is coming from England."

"Someone in England knew I would be indicted in some
sort of conspiracy regarding the attempted assassination," Rafferty said, deceptively calm. "Their argument would be that
I've helped to topple a political structure for one more favorable
to an Irish uprising."

"That's ridiculous." Bedford shook his head. "The American
government is unchanged, is it not? Garfield still breathes and
might survive that onerous attempt to take his life. There's been
no new Irish uprising. It's been years since the last Fenian
bombing."

"Precisely. My opponent has played his hand prematurely
in hopes of stopping my investigation. I must be close." Rafferty

shuffled papers on his desk just to keep his hands occupied, otherwise the walls might suffer the consequences.

"So this is a good thing?" Bedford asked, confounded.

"No. It's not a good thing." Rafferty gritted his teeth. His stomach soured. "But it is an indication of the treacherous lengths they will go to stop me." Of all the methods Barnell could have employed against him, this was the most low, the most foul. Treason! To question his loyalty, to brand him as a traitor for his dedication in finding the murderous bastards who killed innocent English citizens must be an act of desperation. Yet the consequences to his reputation could be long-lived. And Arianne didn't deserve to suffer those consequences.

"You do realize you will be dragged through the mud over this," Bedford said. "Most likely your name has already been sullied in the press. Your name and that of my sister by implication."

"It doesn't have to be that way," Rafferty said quietly.

Arianne quickly glanced up, her eyes wide. "No, Rafferty."

"What?" Bedford asked, wary. "Why doesn't it have to be that way?"

"Lady Arianne can always return to London after an extended holiday abroad in America," he said, focusing on Arianne. "Her reputation would be untainted by association to me, and she still has Sanctuary."

"Good Lord, man. What are you saying?" Bedford retorted, aghast. "She's your wife!"

"No." He wished he could say otherwise. "She isn't."

He supposed had he not been watching Arianne so intently, he would have seen Bedford lunge for his throat. The two wrestled on the floor, Bedford attempting to pummel him, Rafferty trying to stop him. Finally, Rafferty trapped Bedford facedown on the floor. The struggle hurt his recently bruised ribs like the devil. Thus Rafferty was content to just hold him still awhile.

"Get off of me, you lying son of a whore!" Bedford yelled.

"William, leave him alone!" Arianne cried. "It's not his fault."

"Not his fault!" Bedford shouted. "He's slept with you. I've seen him go to your room every night." He struggled unsuccessfully to shake Rafferty off. "Good Lord, I even heard you three nights ago. How can you say it's not his fault? He took advantage of you."

"I was ruined before, William." She stooped down close to him. "Ruined before I ever boarded the ship to come here, and not by Rafferty. I was running away from London, but Rafferty gave me something to run toward."

"You *will* marry my sister, you Irish bastard. Then she'll be a respectable widow once I'm through with you." His face turned red from his exertions.

"I've asked her twice," Rafferty said. "She keeps refusing me. The last time I asked for her hand was three days ago when you told me to have my way with her without benefit of marriage."

"I did no such thing," Bedford protested.

"Ah, but you did. I wanted marriage first, but you said to apologize and give your sister what she wanted." He smiled over at Arianne. "And I did."

His lack of attention gave Bedford an opportunity. He managed to shake Rafferty off his back and go for his throat. They rolled on the floor again until Rafferty gained his feet and allowed Bedford to find his.

"William, stop this!" Arianne yelled. "This isn't helping."

"It's making me feel a lot better." Bedford threw a punch that just missed.

"Bedford, I love your sister. I truly do. I'll marry her whenever you like, wherever you like." Rafferty put a hand to his bandaged ribs, breathing hard. "But she'll be marrying a traitor if I don't solve this puzzle."

That seemed to penetrate Bedford's thick skull. He lowered his fists, and Rafferty followed. He kept his focus on Bedford. "Or you can take her back to London and pretend none of this happened."

"No!" Arianne gasped.

Rafferty refused to look at her. If he did, he couldn't say what needed to be said to free her from a life tied to a no-account Irishman. He swallowed past the lump in his throat. "No one would need to know what transpired here. I'm certain her charms would appeal to someone more worthy than me."

Bedford straightened, considering. "Until this is resolved, she sleeps alone."

"Agreed." He nodded. "I'll take Phineas's room."

"No," Bedford said. "You'll share mine. There're two beds. I won't trust you otherwise."

"Fine. I'll only stay tonight. Tomorrow I'll be gone," Rafferty said, determined.

"Then you're returning to London." Bedford nodded. "I'll engage an excellent solicitor for you. It's the least we can do."

"I'm not going back to London until I've found the one responsible for all this," Rafferty said.

"But Lord Henderson—"

"Lord Henderson's cable was a warning to find the guilty party and unravel the mystery. He knows I won't go back to England until I find the one responsible. That's why he chose me for this position."

He couldn't avoid her any longer. He steeled himself and turned to Arianne. Tears glistened in her eyes. He fought the urge to pull her into his arms and reassure her that everything would be all right. Because it wouldn't, not for him. Nothing would ever be right again, now that he'd known the love of his life and had to watch her go.

"You're free now, darlin'. Now that your brother knows the truth, he can help find you someone more suitable." He tried to smile for her benefit. "Someone fancy and fine. Someone who knows all the right dances and the proper names of all those forks." He ran this thumb tenderly along her jawline, over her lower lip. "Someone worthy of Lady Arianne."

"What if I don't want to be free?" she asked, her voice thin and wispy. She must suffer the same constriction in her throat as he.

"You don't want to be tied to someone who's been branded a traitor." He kissed her on the forehead. "Consider your options."

He left the study to drag himself upstairs and find a place to rest his aching ribs. Bedford's voice stopped him. "What are you going to do?"

Rafferty braced his hands on the banisters that ran on either side of the staircase. His head hung from the sheer weariness of it all. "Whatever is necessary to clear my name."

"Where will Phineas find you?" Arianne asked.

He glanced over his shoulder to find her face. Clever girl.

His lips lifted, but he knew it couldn't have reached his eyes. Those days of unrestrained joy and contentment, of light and warmth—those days spent with Arianne—had all passed behind him. "I'll be at the harbor. He'll know how to find me."

WILLIAM WAITED TILL RAFFERTY HAD CLIMBED THE stairs. "There's no reason for us to stay in Washington." He guided his sister back to the study. "Rafferty said it himself. You're free, Arianne. No one really knows what happened here."

"I'm not leaving," Arianne said defiantly. "In deference to you, William, I'll abide by your decision regarding sleeping arrangements, but I'm not leaving Washington. Not while Rafferty is still here."

William poured himself a drink from the decanter. "Who was it?" When she didn't answer immediately, he elaborated. "You said Rafferty didn't ruin you. Who did?"

"Baron Von Dieter," she replied. "I met him when I stayed at the embassy in Vienna."

"This is the Baron about whom Mrs. Summers wrote?"

"Yes." She averted her gaze.

His eyes narrowed. "Did he force himself on you?"

"No."

"Then why did you give yourself away like that?" William asked, perplexed.

"I thought I loved him, and I thought he loved me." Strange that she could now discuss this topic as if from a distance. Rafferty had done that for her. He made her face what happened and understand in a way she couldn't before. "Karl said this would prove my devotion to him. I thought that by granting him liberties, he would be tied to me. That we would become officially engaged." She smiled at her naïveté. She could see now that she was desperate not to be alone. "I was wrong about all of it."

"I'd say you were wrong." William's face began to flush once more. "Once we're back in England, I'll pay a visit to this baron. He'll propose to you or I'll—"

"I don't wish to marry him, William," Arianne said quickly. "He's engaged to someone else, and I'm glad of it. Looking back, I think he was only interested in me because he felt I had a superior bloodline, like the horses you breed in your stables. When I thought we were to be engaged, I told him the truth about our father, our real father. I believe he came that night to punish me, to make me unsuitable for the gentry." It was so clear now.

"I'll still pay a visit to him," William grumbled. "Then we'll see what value he places on bloodline once he's been gelded."

She smiled. "You sound like Rafferty, William. You know, in some ways you two are very much alike. It's true what he said about marriage. He has asked me and I've refused. He did insist on marriage first, but I followed your advice and seduced him." Warm heat at the memory of Rafferty in the tub flushed her cheeks. She snapped open a fan. "This weather is merciless."

William studied her quietly for a few minutes. "I think you were right to refuse Mr. Rafferty."

"You do?" Her jaw dropped.

"A sister to a duke should be able to do much better than an Irish traitor for a husband," William said calmly.

"He's not a traitor." Anger seized her. "How can you say that? Do you not know him at all?"

"He hasn't a title."

"A title does not make a man. Look at the Baron; he had a title. He didn't have character, but he had a title."

"Rafferty hasn't any property, no skills to speak of . . ." He ticked off his arguments on his fingers.

"He has the *Irish Rose*. He has skills. How could you think otherwise?" She was flabbergasted. Were they talking of the same man? "Why, Lord Henderson wouldn't have sent him if he didn't trust Rafferty's skills."

"Yes," William mused as if her words were insignificant. "I can think of several men with nice estates who are looking for a wife to raise their brats and perhaps give them more. They'll overlook your altered state because you come with property. You won't mind if they're considerably older than you, will you, Anne? Those are the least finicky of the bunch when it comes to virginal wives. It's not as if you're interested in love."

"Stop it! I know what you're doing," Arianne warned. "I'm not interested in marrying for titles or property or money."

"You weren't interested in marrying for love or you would have accepted Rafferty's proposal, but you didn't," William said, jabbing a finger in her direction. "In hindsight, I believe that was smart. I'll have to deal with this baron, of course. Offer an incentive to keep quiet until we have you properly married. We should move quickly in case you're carrying Rafferty's child."

Rafferty's child! She hadn't considered that. She pressed her hands to her corset in wonder. Was that possible?

"I failed you, Anne," William said. "I see that now. I should have made arrangements for your marriage to someone worthy of a duke's sister long before you met the Baron. Look at my marriage. It was an arranged affair and turned out wonderfully. But then you know that as you had a part in the arranging, didn't you?" He smiled. "It's ironic that you did such an excellent job at picking out the perfect spouse for me, and yet the absolute worst for yourself. Fortunately, I can fix all that. This time we'll find someone suitable."

· *Twenty-Seven* ·

THE FACT THAT HE WOKE WITHOUT HIS THROAT slit was a good sign, Rafferty thought, remembering poor Rosalie. Bedford had been ready to tear him apart last night, and with good reason. Arianne deserved better; now she could have it. At least he'd taught her not to fear intimacy. Given the damage the Baron had done, that was an important lesson. She'd make a fine wife for some fortunate aristocrat. Unfortunately, it wouldn't be him.

But enough of maudlin sentimentalities; he needed to focus on the task ahead. He would have to take comfort in the fact that Arianne was safe and pack all those other memories away for a small whisper of warmth in a cold, lonely future.

It was Monday, July fourth. Independence Day, they called it here. Independence from England battled for and won a little over one hundred years ago. Someday he hoped Ireland would have a similar celebration, but he hoped it would be one gained through diplomacy and not blood.

Commerce came to a halt on this holiday. No cargo was lowered into the holds of the waiting steamers moored along the harbor. There was nothing he could do for the moment. He couldn't talk to Briggs, as he needed to know beforehand if Briggs was involved with the smuggling operation. Best to check out the cargo first and talk to him later.

Meanwhile he found a cheap hotel room to stay in. Give his ribs another day to heal. He spent the day thinking of Arianne, reliving her passion, remembering her face when he said good-bye. He hadn't even had the luxury of a good-bye kiss; not with her brother standing there.

The papers reported that President Garfield was still alive, though suffering a great deal of pain as a team of sixteen doctors poked and prodded for the bullet. In deference to his suffering, many of the planned holiday celebrations had been canceled, except for a fireworks display at the harbor. Rafferty didn't even bother looking out the window for a glimpse of the fireworks. It wasn't his country, it wasn't his holiday, and it wasn't a time for celebration. He pulled the blanket over his ears to muffle the sound and went to sleep.

The next morning, Baltimore Harbor was bustling, loading ships, unloading others. He walked the wharf, dodging the men, ropes, and crates, searching for the *Irish Rose*. She was tucked in between two larger, more impressive tramp steamers. It was easy to see Captain Briggs would've had to fight for cargo given the *Rose*'s smaller holds. Much of the goods on the docks would be unsuitable for the *Rose*. Just as the railroads had pushed the mail coaches into obsolescence, so the larger liners were pushing the *Irish Rose*.

Rafe dressed for the role of a stevedore, complete with a low cap to shade his brow. His black eye wouldn't be out of place in this company. He pushed his shoulders forward to look like he carried the world on his back and joined the line of working stiffs shouldering the coffins slated for the *Irish Rose*.

"Give me a hand here, mate," one of the hands called to him. Rafferty complied.

"You take the back corner; I've got the front. Ready?" On a signal, they both lifted the box onto their shoulders. "Heavy, ain't it? Just my luck, I get all the fat Irish." They carried the box to an area near the ship and placed it on top of a short stack. The stacks were tied together with a stout rope then attached to the hook of the ship's winch to raise from the dock and lower into the hold.

They went back for the next box marked for the *Irish Rose*. "Are all these going to the same place?" Rafferty asked.

"They're all headed for Ireland. That's all I know. Why the Irish come all the way over here to die, just to go back to Ireland, is beyond me." With a grunt, they hoisted another and moved it to the ship.

Rafferty helped load the coffins for the next two hours. By the end of that time, his bruised ribs hurt enough to make his slouch one of necessity rather than disguise. They took a break. Rafferty spotted Liam, his workmate, a pint.

"I haven't seen you here before," Liam said, licking the foam from his lips.

"I was working at the Washington docks but had some trouble." He pointed to his eye. "Heard Baltimore paid better. It's a bigger harbor, to be sure."

Liam proceeded to tell him the ins and outs of the loading operations, warning him to check carefully to see that he got paid the right wages for the right hours. Rafferty nodded at the appropriate intervals, pretending to listen carefully.

They had worked about an hour more when the foreman announced it was quitting time. Rafferty hid his cap in a niche on the harbor, then headed for the ramp to the *Irish Rose*.

"You there! Where do you think you're going?" the winch operator called.

"I left my cap on the last load. Can't afford to lose another. Let me check the hold and I'll be back."

"Well, hurry up with you, or you'll be spending the night with those stinking corpses."

Which was precisely what he intended to do. Knowing the ship as he did, it was easy to hide until the hatch was replaced, plunging the cargo hold into blackness. Anticipating such an event, Rafferty had slipped a small candle and matches in his pocket. The flickering light enabled him to locate the crowbar Briggs kept on the wall for emergencies. Securing the candle with a bit of wax, Rafferty pried the top loose on the first pine box.

Inside he discovered another pine box, though this one had none of the open slats of its protecting crate. With difficulty, he managed to pry the top off that one as well. This all would be much easier if Phineas were about. Rafferty lifted the lid in the dark recesses of the hold.

Sometimes it was helpful that the lighting was poor. A woman's body, just as one might anticipate for a coffin, slipped into view. She was a woman in her forties, he guessed, her hair streaked with gray, lying so close to the top of the box that her nose would eternally press the wood. A white sheet lined the box beneath her. After offering a silent prayer for her deceased soul, Rafferty pushed down on the sheeting. He felt a hard metallic rod. Sliding the metal to the side of the box, and careful to disturb the corpse as little as possible, he pulled a Springfield rifle from the pine box. It had a wooden stock with a long metal barrel weighing about three quarter stone. No wonder the box was heavy. By sliding his fingers along the bottom of the coffin, he counted four more rifles and ammunition.

Were they all like this? He'd have to open more crates and coffins. For that he'd need more light, as his small candle was quickly reducing to a tiny pool of wax. He had oil lamps and candles in his cabin. He'd just have to get there without being seen.

It wasn't difficult. A merchant ship in port didn't require a large crew. He made his way to his cabin but then heard voices behind the door. From the sound, he guessed Eva and Barings had taken over his quarters. He couldn't blame them, as his cabin was considerably larger than theirs, and for the time spent on the ship, there wasn't a good reason for them not to enjoy the space. The captain's cabin was of a similar size, but that one would be in use as well. Rafferty raided some vacant passenger cabins—there weren't many on the *Irish Rose*—and took two oil lamps. Thus equipped, he headed back into the hold.

Several hours later, he'd found more caches of rifles, revolvers, and gunpowder. Not all the coffins contained bodies, but all had weapons of some sort. The bodies must have been used to discourage the curious inspector. One would have to be fairly determined to find the weapons cache in some of the boxes.

One thing was certain. This shipment was never going to reach its destination. His stomach turned remembering how frequently the *Irish Rose* had appeared on Weston's list. How long had the *Rose* been involved in smuggling?

Treason. The word floated through Rafferty's conscious. Someone planned to make a case that he knew about the guns and the smuggling runs. This was the second part of the plot. The Fenians must be planning a huge uprising using the smuggled guns. Whether they were successful or not, the English parliament was bound to ask how the rebels got so many weapons, and the trail would inevitably come back to him. As owner of the *Irish Rose*, he would appear to have been aiding the enemy all along. No wonder they tried to dissuade him from investigating.

"I guess this puts me right in the shit house," he said, needing to hear something other than his own thoughts.

"Rafferty? Is that you?"

Rafferty turned around to see Captain Briggs with a pistol trained right at his back. Perhaps he'd been naïve in assuming his captain was unaware of the true nature of the cargo. Rafferty slowly raised his arms.

"It is you!" Briggs lowered the gun. "I heard noises and came to investigate." Rafferty lowered his arms as Briggs rushed forward to shake his hand. "So good to see you. After all that nonsense in the paper—" His eyes widened at the sight of the rifles leaning against the crates, and bags of gunpowder, stacked on the floor. "What the fu . . . festering inferno is all this?"

Rafferty had to grin. Obviously Mrs. Summers was still teaching etiquette . . . Or was it Mrs. Briggs now?

"You didn't know?" Rafferty asked. "The *Irish Rose* has been smuggling guns to Ireland."

"Smuggling guns? I was delivering coffins, not guns!" Not even Eva would have been able to sound so convincing. Rafferty relaxed, thankful that his trust hadn't been misplaced.

"It appears you were doing both." Rafferty stepped back so Briggs could see the efforts of Rafferty's foraging. "I haven't opened all the cases. This is just from about eight crates."

"Rafferty, my boy, I'm so sorry. I didn't know. I honestly had no idea," Briggs said. "Granted, I did think there were a lot of Irish wanting to be buried on the home soil. Made me sort of wonder where they were all going, but the freight came at a good time for us, with competition and all."

"Let's go up topside and talk about what happens next." Rafferty swiped his brow. "It's bloody hot down here."

They went up to the dining saloon where Mrs. Summers sat writing a letter.

"Jane, come see who washed in with the tide," Briggs said.

"Rafferty, how wonderful to see you." Her lips curved in a wide grin. She walked over and gave him a hug. He had to admit it felt good to be among people who actually liked him for a change. "Did Arianne come with you?" She looked behind him and down the hall. Her face didn't mask her disappointment.

"I believe she's packing to return to London with her brother," Rafferty said.

"Her brother!" Her eyes softened. "I suppose that's my fault. When I wrote him I had no idea that the two of you planned to fabricate a marriage. I suppose that did not go over well."

"The pretend marriage? Or her brother's surprise appearance?" He was tempted to add the charge of treason but declined. He shook his head. "It's a long tale, I'm afraid."

"We have all night," Briggs added. "Jane, can you rustle up some food for the boy? He's been working up an appetite. He and I have some serious business to discuss before we swap tales of matrimony, pretend and otherwise."

The food was good and the whiskey better. They moved to the wheelhouse to talk in private. Rafferty told him of the murders, of the false accusations and the treason charge. "So you see, this smuggling operation is the linchpin in the treason charge."

"What do you propose to do?"

Rafferty glanced out the window. The sky was dark; gas lamps cast circles of a yellow light on patches of the deserted harbor. The harbor police were down there. He knew that from experience. "I'm going to turn this over to the police so they can pursue the Irish Trust and Funeral Fund. I need to send a cablegram to Lord Henderson so that I'm removed from suspicion. We'll need to advise him as well of Lord Weston's list of ships and sail dates. If they were carrying coffins, they were also carrying guns."

"This will create more fireworks than that display over the harbor last night. They do put on quite a celebration to honor their separation from England here," Briggs observed. "I guess we won't be leaving tomorrow as planned."

"Most likely the police will want to confiscate the cargo. That's going to take a day to unload."

"What will they do with the bodies?"

"The freight's been paid," Rafferty said. "I suppose if the police seize the weapons and leave us the coffins, we can still take them home as their loved ones intended."

"The *Rose* isn't going anywhere tonight. The cargo holds are locked. Tomorrow, then. We'll advise the police in the morning," Briggs said. "What will you do? Will you be sailing with us back to England?"

"I haven't found Toomey yet. He's the one who killed Lord Weston and Mary, I'm sure of it. Phineas is in New York to see if he can gather more information. I suppose I'll join him there to hunt the bastard down. He's unfinished business." And the very business that drove him across the Atlantic in the first place.

Mrs. Summers . . . er . . . Briggs interrupted, saying she'd waited long enough to hear the details of Rafferty's experience as a British minister. Rafferty told her of their meeting with the president, Arianne's gardening activities and her plan for a garden party, and of course, the ball. Remembering Arianne in that white dress squeezed his heart at all he'd lost.

In return, she advised that she was indeed Mrs. Briggs, but Eva and Mr. Barings hadn't exchanged vows as yet. She suspected they were suffering from too much confinement with each other. "Sometimes, a little distance puts the value of a relationship in perspective."

Unfortunately, the issue of "value" was exactly what he feared. Once Arianne had returned to England with her brother and had spent sufficient time in his company with his privileged, upper-crust friends, she was bound to regret time spent with an Irish rogue pretending to be something he was not.

· Twenty-Eight ·

AS HAD BEEN PREARRANGED, BEN AND THE OTHER
boys arrived at the *Irish Rose* in anticipation of assuming
their seaman duties to cross the Atlantic one final time. A few
of the boys had decided to stay in America to take advantage
of the opportunities they'd discovered there. After welcoming
them on board, Rafferty accompanied Ben back to the crew's
quarters to learn if Arianne and the Duke had travel plans and
the vessel they were planning to take. Ben didn't know her
specific plans, but he did say that Arianne had not been her
usual cheerful self since the night of the ball. That made two
of them, Rafferty thought.

Rafferty had just returned to the top deck in search of Briggs
when he saw a stranger speaking to the captain. The *Irish Rose*'s
departure and destination had been posted in the transportation
offices. Based on Briggs's frown and shaking head, Rafferty
assumed the stranger was looking for cheap passage. Due to
the hazardous nature of the last crossing, Briggs had agreed to
make this return trip with the crew only, and Eva and Mr. Barings, of course. Rafferty, as the owner, thought to add his voice
to the captain's denial when the stranger pulled an English

Bulldog revolver from his pocket, the same gun used to shoot President Garfield.

Rafferty stepped behind cover. His own revolver would be useless at this distance, and he didn't want to start a gun battle with so many of the crew on board. The man indicated that Briggs was to climb to the wheelhouse. As the stranger turned to follow behind him, Rafferty saw his face. Evans.

Evans was tied to the Fenians and Guiteau, thus a killer and not to be underestimated. Rafferty needed appropriate weapons, and he knew just the place to find them. He slipped down the crew's stairway to make his way to the cargo hold. After lighting one of the oil lamps, Rafferty loaded ammunition into one of the rifles, stuck an unloaded revolver in the waistband of his trousers, and grabbed a box of ammunition for each. A sequence of bells signaled preparations for departure.

Shovels scraped in the coal bins as the trimmers filled their wheelbarrows and the stokers fired up the boilers. Rapid taps of feet rang on the steps as the boys assigned to cast the mooring ropes traveled topside. Evans was stealing the boat, or more likely—Rafferty gazed at the grand cache of weapons at his disposal—stealing the cargo.

If the cargo reached its destination, Rafferty was quite certain he would be found guilty of treason, to say nothing of being partially responsible for the deaths to come in a violent uprising staged in the name of Irish independence. If it came down to it, he would rather see the cache of guns rust away on the ocean floor than surrender them to the Fenians. Of course, if the cargo was to land on the ocean floor, the *Irish Rose* would have to go with it.

The ship groaned with the effort of turning the propeller through resistant water. The resulting vibrations shook the rifles leaning against the crates to the floor. The ship was leaving its berth, but not without audible complaint. She was an old girl, well past her prime, but if she had to be sacrificed, well . . . Rafferty hoped he'd survive to remember her fondly.

He picked up a keg of gunpowder and popped the lid. He laid a trail of black powder from the wooden crates to the door of the cargo hold and beyond to the bottom of the steps that led to the higher levels of the ship. Using the oil from the two lamps he'd left in the hold, he liberally soaked the wood of the crate at one end of the powder path and the canvas floor covering at the other. It was a deadly combination, especially given the proximity of the boiler room.

If he could subdue Evans and manage to get the ship back to port, he could forgo setting her ablaze, but if not—this was an option. Either way, he needed to get everyone off the *Irish Rose* before they left the Chesapeake Bay and entered the Atlantic. After that, odds of surviving even in a lifeboat would drop drastically.

With rifle in hand, he headed toward the wheelhouse. Ben spotted him, his eyes wide at the sight of the rifle. "Get everyone in a lifeboat," Rafferty snarled.

Ben began to ask a question. Rafferty cut him off. "Don't ask questions. Just do as I say. Use the stern lifeboats." Ben took off down the passageway. "And don't forget the two in my cabin," Rafferty called after him.

There'd be little protection in the wheelhouse. Windows wrapped around the upper portion of the walls so the captain could have a clear view of the surrounding waters. One gained access through use of either an outside flight of steps, or one on the interior that connected to a passageway outside of the captain's quarters. Mrs. Briggs would be there, which meant Mrs. Briggs was in harm's way.

Rafferty left the deck and headed for the captain's quarters. He opened the cabin door to a large, comfortable sitting room.

"Rafferty!" Mrs. Briggs dropped her sewing in her lap. "What are you—?"

Rafferty put his finger to his lips, urging her to be quiet. He drew close to her. "Find a life jacket and go to the stern," he murmured.

"But what of Charles?"

"I'll send him in a moment, now go!"

Mrs. Briggs disappeared down the passageway. The door that separated this section from the more public rooms clicked behind her. Good. One less to worry about. He took a moment to load his revolver, then slipped it in his back waistband. Leading with the point of his rifle, he warily headed into the passageway that led to the wheelhouse.

As soon as he opened the door, bullets rained down the passageway. Rafferty pulled back into the captain's quarters.

"Mr. Rafferty," a familiar voice called. "What good fortune to have you aboard. I thought you'd still be in a jail cell."

"Diplomatic immunity, Evans, or had you forgotten?" Rafferty scanned the room, looking for another way out. The sitting room had an outside door that led to small deck. If he remembered correctly, the deck tied to the outside steps that led up to the wheelhouse.

"Is your pretty little wife with you? Lady Arianne? A passionate little number, that piece of skirt. I heard the two of you. The whole bloody house did."

He was trying to bait him to come out into the passageway. If he kept on about Arianne, it might work.

"Briggs, are you all right?" Rafferty called, trying the outside door. It hadn't been used for years. Briggs always complained that it made his quarters cold and was unnecessary. Well, it was necessary now. It resisted his first tug, holding its seal.

"So far," Briggs replied. "Don't let Jane come up."

He tried again. This time the door opened, allowing him to step out on the deck. The *Irish Rose* had cleared the harbor and was heading for the middle of the bay. Rafferty crept to the end of the deck, then climbed the exterior stairs. He crouched low to stay out of sight.

He chanced a look through the windows. Evans still watched the passageway. Briggs stood at the wheel, guiding the ship into deeper water. He spotted Rafferty and motioned for him to stay down.

"What are you doing?" he heard Evans snarl.

"We're losing pressure," Briggs answered. "I'm sending a signal down to the boiler room."

"Make it quick."

Now that Briggs had mentioned it, the *Irish Rose* wasn't forging ahead with her earlier power. A good sign that Ben had gotten the engine crew to the stern lifeboats. The controls for the engine room were located next to the bridge door. Briggs pushed it open while moving the levers to signal for more steam. Rafferty took advantage, stood, and aimed his rifle.

"Put your hands up, Evans."

Evans had one gun aimed down the passageway and another aimed at Briggs. "Don't threaten me. You'll lose the good captain." His lips turned up at the corners. He shifted one gun from the passageway to Rafferty. "I see you found me guns. Did you find me money as well?"

"*Your* guns? I thought you were behind the Garfield . . ." Pieces of the puzzle clicked into place. There was only one person who would orchestrate both the smuggling and the assassination attempt. "Toomey," Rafferty said. "It is you, isn't it?"

"In the flesh, lad." He grinned. "And let me say what a pleasure it has been using your ship to transport the means for an uprising the likes of which have never been seen. Heads will roll. Blood will be shed. Hopefully, Ireland will be free, but I'll be a rich man either way."

"Rich? This isn't just about home rule?"

"The Americans are a generous people. I've collected enough for guns and a bit more for my efforts."

"What about the bombings? Was that for profit as well? Or for the blood in the streets?" Rafferty asked. He should just shoot the bloody bastard, but Briggs was still in Toomey's sights.

"Ack. I'm sorry about your family, lad. It wasn't personal. They were causalities of war. But you . . . your demise will be sweet. You, I take personal."

Briggs made a quick lunge. Toomey fired and ran down the stairs. Rafferty fired as well, but too late. Footfalls pounded the passageway. Rafferty dashed over to Briggs. "Are you hurt?"

"He got my arm."

Rafferty took a look. Blood seeped from Briggs's arm but didn't pump in a gushing flow. "Do you keep medical supplies about?"

"In the kitchen, but I'm not sure where."

Rafferty got him to his feet. With Rafferty in the lead, they followed the passageway to the dining saloon. Rafferty grabbed a bottle of whiskey from the sideboard and poured it on the wound.

Briggs hissed between his teeth. "Waste of good whiskey."

"The burn will do you good, old man," Rafferty said. He grabbed some dinner napkins from a drawer and fashioned a bandage. "You'll be able to impress the ladies with your scar," he said while wrapping the bandage on his arm.

"Only Jane," Briggs replied.

Rafferty handed him the loaded revolver. "Now take this and find your wife. I've sent everyone to the stern lifeboats. Once you're in, cast away. Get as far away from the boat as you can."

"What about you?" Briggs asked.

"Toomey's not going to get away again, and his guns aren't going to make port. It's personal between us." He smiled and extended his hand to Briggs. "You've been a good friend. I'm glad you found Mrs. Summers in your sunset years. Living to be lonely is no life, I'm thinking."

Briggs shook his hand. "I'm proud of you, lad, but don't be stupid. Get off the *Rose* as soon as you can."

"Aye, that I will." Rafferty grabbed a couple of napkins and his rifle, then started after Toomey.

For a small steamer, the *Irish Rose* was too big to search for a single man floor by floor. Rafferty had the advantage of knowing the ship inside and out. He figured Toomey had three choices: the guns, the money, or a lifeboat. If he were Toomey, he'd go for the money first.

Rafferty took the stairs cautiously, descending into the belly of the ship, mindful that a bullet could fly at his ears at any time.

As he approached the hold, he could hear Toomey talking to himself. "Which one, which one. Here it is. Miss Mary O'Sullivan." A light shone from the hold; he must have taken a lamp in there with him. Then he heard the sound of prying wood. A sound he was very familiar with after having opened so many coffins himself.

Rafferty struck a match and lit the cloth napkin until it crackled. He threw the rifle into the passageway, followed by the flaming napkin. Then ran like the devil himself up the steps. He cleared his way to the top deck and was running toward the rail when the cargo in the hold exploded. He was propelled into the air, over the rail, and into the peaceful waters of the Chesapeake Bay.

· Twenty-Nine ·

ARIANNE WAS STANDING BY THE EMPTY BERTH IN the Baltimore Harbor when she heard the explosion.

Everyone stopped and looked toward the horizon, toward a distant plume of black smoke. "Phineas!" she said, alarm catching in her throat. "What was that?"

He shook his head. His Adam's apple rose and fell, then he turned toward her, desolation in his eyes. "Maybe he wasn't on board."

But they both knew. If the *Irish Rose* had indeed left without Rafferty, he'd be standing right there beside them. Given the time the *Rose* had departed, the ship should have been in the vicinity of that explosion. For anyone on board that vessel, the likelihood of survival was slim.

Her heart fell to the bottom of her rib cage. Her throat constricted. Breathing the hot July air was nearly impossible. Her vision became unfocused. He couldn't be gone. Not Rafferty, not . . .

Her world turned black.

Vile ammonia fumes burned a path up her nostrils, waking

her with a start. Phineas knelt beside her, patting a moist cloth to her cheeks. He smiled. "Better now?"

"What happened?" She was sitting on the ground, propped against the wall on the shady side of the customs building.

"You fainted, most likely from the heat . . . and the shock."

The shock. Oh yes, she remembered that. Rafferty was gone. She was better off unconscious.

A man on a high platform with an expanded telescope called out. "There's a boat! Two boats! No, three lifeboats!"

Survivors! With Phineas's help, she scrambled to her feet. Dear Lord, let Rafferty be safe.

TWO HOURS PASSED BEFORE THE LIFEBOATS WERE TOWED back to the harbor. The tugboat, *Shadow*, had set out immediately to search for survivors. After transferring the passengers and crew from the lifeboats, the tug's captain had surveyed the explosion area looking for more survivors—one in particular— but none were found.

Arianne studied the passengers on the deck of the *Shadow* as it pulled into port. Spotting Mrs. Summers immediately, she raced to her old chaperone as soon as the passengers were released. If anyone would know if Rafferty survived, she would. Even before Arianne could ask, however, she knew the answer by the red-rimmed eyes of her friend. Rafferty had not been found. He had saved them all by getting them to lifeboats in time to escape the blast, she said, but he himself was not so fortunate.

As Phineas noted, neither was Toomey. He'd learned in New York that Evans and Mary O'Shay's gentleman friend were one and the same. Captain Briggs confirmed it when he told his version of the events. Rafferty had temporarily saved England from a violent uprising and satisfied his own goal of revenge for Toomey at the cost of his own life.

The consolation offered by her chaperone, that Rafferty had spoken of his love for Arianne, was of little comfort. She knew he loved her. It was the reason he let her go.

She had been so miserable yesterday without him. William wanted her to pack to return to London, but everywhere she turned she was beset by memories. His words replayed in her mind. *This is your home. This is sanctuary.* Suddenly, it occurred to her that he wasn't speaking of the legation, he was speaking of himself. And he was right. Rafferty was her sanctuary. It didn't matter if he had a title. It didn't matter if he had property. She loved him for him alone. When Phineas returned from New York, she insisted he take her with him to the harbor, but the *Irish Rose* had already sailed.

Now Rafferty would never know how much she loved him. He would go to his eternal rest believing he wasn't good enough—which was so very, very wrong. He was the best man she knew, would ever know. She'd been a fool not to marry him. She'd been a fool to believe property was as important as the possibility of living with the one you love. She'd been a fool with no hope of redemption.

A MONTH LATER, ARIANNE STILL WORE BLACK.

William had tried to convince her that she was not a widow. Two weeks was ample time to be buried beneath oppressive black veils. No man would approach her while she was in such deep mourning.

What he failed to understand was that she didn't particularly want anyone to approach her. She didn't wish to speak to anyone. She didn't care to witness the enthusiasm of the other passengers embarking on a trip to London. She didn't want to think at all about her wardrobe, or her manners, or her brother, or her life for that matter. She'd lost Rafferty without any hope of ever seeing him again. She'd never hear his soft brogue in her ear or hear his talk of selkies and mermaids. She'd lost everything in life that mattered.

William thought that as long as she planned to shut herself away in isolation from the world, she might as well do it in London instead of swamp-ridden Washington. It didn't matter to her. Nothing mattered to her. Kathleen packed her clothes away in trunks. William sent a cable to Lord Henderson that they were leaving, and suddenly they were on this ship, this four-stack new luxury liner, bound for England.

William even booked passage for Mr. and Mrs. Briggs in hopes that Mrs. Briggs could lift her spirits. Arianne could have told him the futility of that occurrence. There was only one thing that sparked her interest on this voyage. She wanted to have the opportunity to say good-bye to Rafferty.

She stood at the rail as the liner left the harbor. Amazing how the water no longer held a claim on her. Without an inclination to live, she had nothing to fear in death. She brought a bouquet of forget-me-nots laced with ivy sprigs. Touching the delicate blue flowers, she remembered the night Rafferty wore them on his lapel to her state dinner. Did he know then that the flowers meant true love? She remembered chuckling to herself, thinking how inappropriate he looked—yet she was the inappropriate one. Even then they were fated to be together. She'd just been too caught up in class issues to recognize it. A tear gathered in her eye, and she brushed it away. She hoped Rafferty would recognize the sprigs of ivy as the symbol for matrimony so he'd know, if he could see such things, that she had said yes to his proposal.

Captain Briggs promised to tell her of the spot where the *Irish Rose* exploded. After silently telling Rafferty of her everlasting devotion, Arianne tossed her bouquet into the water, saying good-bye to her true love.

"I still can't accept that he's gone."

Arianne's heart lurched. "Phineas!" She lifted the veil from her hat. "Where have you been?" Tears, never far from her eyes these days, fell again in well-worn tracks down her cheeks. She grasped his hands in her black gloves. "I've missed you so."

He smiled into her eyes. "I had some matters of unfinished business to attend to. Rafferty would have wanted to make sure the boys were taken care of."

"Yes. He would have wanted that." She sighed. "I should have seen to that myself."

He squeezed her hand. "You were too distraught. Sometimes, just breathing in and out is enough for one day."

Tears flowed anew. He was the only one who understood. He placed her hand in the crook of his arm and guided her toward the bow of the ship.

"I can't believe you're on this crossing," Arianne said. "I never got the opportunity to thank you for all you did for me that day. Once you delivered me to William, you just vanished."

Phineas shrugged. "Rafferty would have haunted me to the

end of my days if I hadn't seen you safely home. North German Lloyd is the only line sailing from Baltimore to England. I suppose we both decided at the same point it was time to get on with our lives." He stopped their promenade and faced her, his voice sober. "I probably shouldn't say this, but Rafferty loved you more than I believe he thought was possible. I had never seen him react the same way, or care as deeply, about anyone as much as he did you."

She dropped her gaze. "I know." A teardrop fell to her bodice. She plucked a handkerchief from her reticule and glanced back up. "I loved him too. Only I discovered too late how very much. I wish . . ." She looked toward the water. "I wish I could turn back time, do it all over again. I would have said yes to his first proposal." She laughed lightly and dabbed her eyes with the handkerchief. "I should have insisted he marry me when we met in Lord Henderson's office. Wouldn't he have been shocked then?"

Phineas smiled down at her. "That's good to know." He patted her hand, then raised his voice to normal tones. "I'm not traveling alone, you know. There's a gentleman here who I think you know." He spun her around.

"Lord Henderson!" She clasped the handkerchief to her lips a moment and smiled. "This is a surprise. When did you arrive in America? Why didn't you come to the legation?"

He kissed her cheek in greeting and patted her hand in sympathy. "I arrived about two weeks ago. I left England the day I heard that Rafferty had been implicated in President Garfield's attempted assassination." He grinned. "I knew Rafferty had some unique methods of solving mysteries, but I couldn't believe that allegation had merit. Still, I thought a treason charge was serious enough for me to personally intercede." Like Phineas, he took her arm, and the three of them walked farther down the promenade deck.

"I'm sorry you arrived too late," Arianne said. "Rafferty would have appreciated knowing you believed in him."

"Obviously you believed in him," Henderson said. "You could have knocked me over with one of my wife's ostrich plumes when I received the cablegram that you were going to pretend to be his wife. I thought you cared too much about your reputation to become involved in such a public display."

"He asked me to marry him, you know," Arianne said with a soft smile. "I think Rafferty was more concerned about my reputation than I was." She was too concerned about property issues at the time. She gave herself a mental shake. She'd grown through this whole experience, but at a terrible cost.

The day proved to be a beautiful one to be on the water. The movement of the boat, coupled with a slight breeze, added comfort to the early August afternoon. Smaller vessels harnessed the wind in a dance on the water on both sides of the liner. People jostled for position along the rail to watch the harbor's retreat as they sped down the wide Chesapeake.

The breeze pushed at their backs as she and Lord Henderson approached the stern. A man in front of them left his coveted position at the rail. Her gaze was drawn to him, but she wasn't sure why. His left arm, encased in plaster and stabilized in a sling, wouldn't fit in his jacket; thus the loose material wanted to lift in the wind. He had to hold it in place with his right hand, which was bandaged as well. The poor man. She wanted to tell him to throw proprieties to the wind and not wear the contrary garment. He moved with a slight limp and kept his gaze down as if to watch his feet. His concentration reminded her of Rafferty. He'd had that same determination when he was learning to dance. So much so that . . .

The stranger stopped in front of her and sniffed. His head lifted. A smile spread on his face. Through the cuts and abrasions, she could see a light shimmer in his eyes. He cocked his head. "Hello, darlin'."

She froze, afraid to believe her eyes. She pressed her handkerchief to her open mouth. "Rafferty?" she whispered. Then her voice came out a little louder. "You're alive? How can that be?"

He squinted his eyes a little. His lips tilted in that half smile she remembered in her dreams. "I've asked myself that question a number of times, and all I can say is—" She crashed into him. "Umph! Careful, darlin', the bones are still mending."

She wrapped her arms around his waist and kissed his neck, his jaw, his cheek. His bandaged hand slipped along her jaw, before he tilted her chin and captured her lips. The kiss lasted longer than decent by society's standards, but she didn't care. It could have gone on forever. He pulled back and stroked the side of her face with his fingers. "I missed you."

Lord Henderson stepped beside them. "Lady Arianne, I'd like to introduce you to Sir Michael Rafferty."

"*Sir* Michael Rafferty?"

"It's not exactly official yet," Rafferty said. "I received this cablegram from the Queen." He fumbled in his pocket for a paper. "Something about gratitude and risking my paltry life for the good of the Crown. I believe there's some sort of presentation in store. You might have to help me with the proper etiquette."

"Why didn't you tell me?" Tears slipped from her eyes. "I thought you were dead."

"I should have been," Rafferty said softly. "They tell me the explosion threw me a long distance away from the lifeboats. They missed me in all that nasty debris. I held on to a life preserver long enough for a fishing boat to pull me from the water."

"He was unconscious," Phineas said. "They took him to St. Agnes. That's where I found him."

"You!" She should have brought her fan so she could have smacked him with it. Of course that would have meant she had to let go of Rafferty, and she wasn't ready to do that. "Why did you keep it a secret from me?"

"I don't think Phineas left Rafferty's side the entire time he was unconscious," Lord Henderson said.

"And then I told him not to tell you," Rafferty added.

That hurt. She glanced up, the question in her gaze.

"You were free. As a widow, there could be no questions of a certain nature," he said quietly.

She had a few words to share with him about this free business, but she'd do that in private. She turned to Lord Henderson. "How did you find him?"

"The explosion of the *Irish Rose* was in the Baltimore papers. I had planned to come to the legation to express my sympathies, but I was waylaid by young Ben, who took me to the hospital."

Miffed that everyone knew that Rafferty lived but her, she was too ecstatically happy to give it weight. She laughed. "I suppose that you're all on this same voyage is a grand coincidence?"

"That would be my doing," William said from his position at the rail.

"William? You arranged this?" Had anyone ever been so manipulated?

"I saw Ben hanging about outside of the legation. Once I caught him by the collar, he told me that Mr. Rafferty—"

"Sir Rafferty, if you please," Rafferty corrected.

William grimaced. "Sir Rafferty was alive and had asked him to watch over you. He told me Lord Henderson had come over as well, so I went to have a talk with these fine gentlemen." William took Arianne's hand in his. "Anne, I only want what's best for you. I wanted you to have a choice about your future and not be forced into anything. Part of being free is knowing what choices are available." He pointed his chin toward Rafferty. "As that one suggested, you can return to London as a widow to find a proper aristocrat. But you needed to know that Sir Rafferty was alive and available as well. So I told them of our travel arrangements."

"Thank you, William." She squeezed his hand. "Thank you for loving me enough to look out for my best interests. I've considered my options over the past weeks very carefully, and I choose the man I know is worthy of being married to the sister of a duke." She captured Rafferty's gaze and held it. "I wish to be Mrs. Michael Rafferty, if you'll have me."

Love and lust smoldered in his eyes, warming Arianne to the tips of her toes. "Oh darlin', that I will."

· *Thirty* ·

WILLIAM PUSHED HIS HANDS BETWEEN ARIANNE and Rafferty, separating them. "There will be no *having* or *willing* until after a valid marriage." He brushed aside the jeers and hisses from Phineas and Henderson. "Furthermore, there will be no public kissing of widows in full mourning, even if the man she's kissing looks as if he has one foot in the grave. Let us keep some sense of propriety."

"William!" Arianne scolded.

"Need I remind you that I am a duke—and your brother—which presents sound footing for pronouncements in this regard. I believe it is this very oversight that placed us in such extreme conflict in the first place. I insist that the legalities be completed."

"I agree," Rafferty said, to William's obvious surprise. "I recall espousing a similar position not too long ago." His gaze at Arianne started a familiar tingling in her rib cage and below. "Speed, however, is of the essence."

Captain Briggs and his wife, having witnessed the reunion at a respectful distance, joined the celebratory gathering. Mrs. Briggs hugged Arianne. "I'm so happy for you. I knew you would choose Rafferty, but your brother insisted you should be given a chance to consider otherwise. He must have never seen the way you two look at each other."

"Captain Briggs," William said. "I understand you are just the man we need. Can you marry these two before they surrender to scandalous behavior?" He puffed out his chest as if it were decorated with medals from past military campaigns.

Rafferty leaned closer to Arianne. "Your brother is a bit of a pompous—"

"Yes, I know," she replied, patting Rafferty's arm. "He means well, though."

"The thing is, Your Grace," Briggs said, a bit more humbly than Rafferty anticipated. "I can't really do that. I only have the authority to record a marriage, not actually perform one." He glanced about the crestfallen faces. "As I'm not the captain of this ship, I haven't even the authority to do that."

While the other passengers laughed and pointed at the passing scenery, a heavy fog of silence engulfed the group. "Can the captain of this ship . . . ?" Mrs. Briggs asked hopefully.

Briggs shook his head. "Not unless the laws are different in Germany. A British sea captain hasn't the authority. What you need is a minister or a justice of the peace."

"Phineas?" Rafferty asked with a raised brow.

He nodded and melded into the crowd of passengers.

Arianne gazed up at Rafferty. "It's all right if we have to wait. I wouldn't wish to be married in all this black." She held out her skirts. "The important thing is that you're alive and near. If we have to wait a little longer, I can do that."

The Duke's cheek tightened. "You wouldn't be getting married in black."

She turned. "I wouldn't?"

"Remember I said no man would approach you in all that morbid veiling?" He fluttered his hand over the excess of black lace and black crepe. "I instructed Kathleen to pack colorful clothes for the journey and to especially include that white dress you wore to the red, white, and blue ball."

"You did? William, thank you." She kissed his cheek. "Thank you so much."

"Now let us hope Phineas can locate someone." Mrs. Briggs sighed.

"Have no fear. We'll be married by nightfall," Rafferty said confidently. "Phineas will find a minister." He leaned over and murmured in Lord Henderson's ear. "Even if he has to impersonate one himself."

LATER THAT EVENING, BEFORE A GATHERING OF FIRST-class passengers in the ballroom of the SS *Koenig*, Lady Arianne Chambers, in her white ball gown accented with a white silk lace mantilla, loaned to her by Mrs. Briggs, repeated her vows before God and an Anglican minister on holiday. Sir Michael Rafferty placed a ring on her finger, binding her to him before various members of London society, family, and friends. There was no pretense, no false appearance, no masquerade. They were undeniably, truly married, though William had already insisted that they repeat the ceremony in Bedfordshire in the chapel at Deerfield Abbey for the sake of his wife, Nicholas, Emma, and Thackett. Two weddings had served him well, he'd said. It would do so for them as well.

Champagne flowed freely in celebration. The ship's orchestra played a waltz. And although Rafferty was not the most fluid or accomplished dance partner with his various injuries, those that saw Rafferty and Arianne didn't really notice. The intensity of their locked gazes spoke in volumes of elegance.

SOMEONE TAPPED HIM ON THE SHOULDER. RAFFERTY turned from his conversation with Bedford, Lord Henderson, and Phineas to see a vaguely familiar face—thin, weak chin, ridiculous mustache, but with poetic blue eyes. "I wanted to congratulate you, sir." He held out a gloved hand.

Rafferty's eyes narrowed. "Have we met?"

"I don't believe I have had the formal honor, though we have passed on occasion. My wife and I are returning home from our own honeymoon." His lips turned up in something of a sneer. "Needed the rest, you might say. I'm known, of course, to your wife." He clicked his heels and extended his hand again. "Baron Von Dieter, sir."

Rafferty exchanged a glance with Bedford. "Have you met my wife's brother, the Duke of Bedford?"

The man gushed. "Your Grace, this is indeed an honor."
Rafferty finished the introduction.

Bedford glanced at Rafferty. "May I?"

Rafferty gestured to his cast and stepped back. "With my
blessings."

Bedford delivered a punch to that weak chin that knocked
the Baron out cold and sent him flying backward to lie sprawled
on the floor.

Rafferty smiled his approval. "Well done, Bedford." The
two turned back to their conversation, letting some hysterical,
vacuous woman tend to her husband on the floor. Rafferty put
his good arm around Bedford's shoulder. "Have you never tried
pugilism? You've got a strong right. How's your left?"

ARIANNE IGNORED THE CONVERSATION AROUND HER,
focusing instead on her dear husband, who she loved with her
heart and soul, engaged in conversation with her pompous but
loving brother. Rafferty was indeed her sanctuary; her safe place,
her sacred place. She had no need of a refuge outside of the
home she shared with him. That familiar tingling nagged at all
again, this time more insistently. Christopher! She'd waited a
month; she shouldn't be expected to wait any longer.

She left the gathering of women and crossed to her dear
love. Using his shoulder for balance, she rose on the tips of her
toes to whisper in his ear.

"Rafferty, my dear, I'm ready. I believe it's time to negotiate."

Dear Readers,

While several of my novels are influenced by true events, this may be true more so for Redeeming the Rogue *than in my other novels. For the curious, I thought I might separate fact from fiction.*

Though I'm sure a murder did not precipitate the assignment of Lord Lionel Sackville to the British legation in Washington, D.C., in 1881, he was presented with the problem of finding a suitable hostess. American ladies did not attend functions where there was no hostess to receive them, and as Lord Sackville was unmarried, he needed someone to fill this role. His solution was to make his illegitimate French daughter his hostess. This bold move required the Queen's approval. She insisted a committee of the most important American political hostesses be formed to determine whether society would accept this young eighteen-year-old of questionable parentage as an important political hostess. They decided to give her a chance. Victoria Sackville proved to be a tremendous success.

While my characters are all fictional, the assassination of President Garfield is not. Other than the accusations against my hero, all the other information is factual. Vice President Arthur Chester was briefly accused as being a conspirator in the assassination of Garfield due to his Irish heritage. The charges were quickly dismissed. Guiteau did claim to shoot the president because he was denied a political position for which he was not qualified. He was executed in 1882 after the president's death. It is said that President Garfield did not die so much from the bullet that remained lodged in his chest as from the incapable doctors that attended him. Many probed his wound with unsterilized fingers, searching for the bullet. One even punctured Garfield's liver. The unsanitary methods led to blood poisoning, and at that time, there were no antibiotics to treat that condition. Thankfully, medical practices have come a long way since then.

Finally, I was surprised to learn that ship captains cannot perform marriages at sea, unless they are also a minister, a justice of the peace, a judge, or have a specific license that allows them to do so. I hope you enjoy the little complication that information provided.

May you enjoy Redeeming the Rogue *as much as I enjoyed writing it. I look forward to hearing from you at www .DonnaMacMeans.com.*

Donna

Turn the page for a sneak peek of
Donna MacMeans's next historical romance

THE CASANOVA CODE

Coming soon from Berkley Sensation!

PATTERNS. EDWINA HARGROVE RECOGNIZED THEM everywhere: in the design of the teacup on the table before her; in the ebb and flow of voices at the Crescent Coffee Palace; even in the grain of the wood beneath her feet. The order, the predictability of acceptable patterns formed the framework of her rather tedious life. But when the sequences in patterns were broken, forming new patterns requiring interpretation, that was when adventures began.

Edwina retrieved her brother's encrypted letter from her reticule and held it for a moment, savoring with eagerness the process of unlocking its secrets. Laughing softly, she scanned her table, realizing even she had a pattern for transcribing the code. Her journal sat to the left, the ribbon loosened and already opened to the next blank page. She'd inked the alphabet down the left side of the page in anticipation of the coded text. The right page remained blank, waiting for the transcription. Fragrant steam lifted from her teacup sitting on her far right, and in the middle, she'd placed her copy of *Treasure Island*. A favored novel of both hers and her brother's, it was used as the key to the letter's meaning.

The transcription process required concentration, the sort one would not expect in such a public setting. Nevertheless she paused, letting the ring of spoons tapping fragile porcelain and the blended voices of the patrons of the Crescent dissolve into the distant cry of seabirds and the thunder of the Caribbean ocean pounding a white sand beach. She mentally transformed the lingering scent of wood and aged spirits from the once popular gin palace, now a ward of the Temperance movement, into that of imagined casks of pirates' rum. Even the current generated by the sway of a passing skirt became a gentle island breeze. Thus solidly engrained in the world of the book, and isolated from familiar reality, she bent to the task of transcribing the letter's nonsense patterns into meaningful discourse.

Soon she was lost in the tale of her brother's recent trip to a Caribbean sugar plantation. Edwina sighed. How wonderful it must be to see such things, to know a little of the world outside of England, to have unlimited possibilities for future adventures . . .

"Another letter from your brother?" Faith Huddleston peered down a moment before slipping into the chair next to Edwina. "It would be so much easier if they used the King's English. I just don't understand why they make you decipher everything."

There was no explaining the unleashed joy of solving the mystery behind the coded letters, so she didn't try. She'd encountered similar skepticism and annoyance from her friends before. Instead, she slipped the letter into the relevant pages of *Treasure Island*, then set it aside, ready to turn her attentions to her friend.

Faith tossed a copy of the *Mayfair Messenger* on the table. "The publisher didn't run Sarah's article on the number of birds killed for women's hats." Faith pulled off her gloves. "She won't be pleased."

A cup and saucer rattled loudly as one of the Crescent's former barmaids placed it by Faith's elbow. The renovation of the previous gin palace into a tea-toting coffeehouse required more than just changing the gilt lettering on the windows. The barmaids had to take the Temperance pledge as well. The change had been more difficult for some than others. Faith smiled up into the woman's lined face. "The chamomile, please." The barmaid nodded and left.

Edwina quickly shifted through the *Messenger*'s pages, confirming the absence of Sarah's contribution, but then paused at the "Personal & Misc" listings in the classified advertisements. Coded messages often lurked amongst the forthright and sometimes humorous ads. Men sought women, women sought men, secret arrangements were established for illicit rendezvous, and star-crossed lovers exchanged messages of longing, all on the very public pages of the *Mayfair Messenger*. Edwina scanned the column for snippets of an awkward construction, or the use of numbers instead of letters, all signs of a hidden meaning. Breaking a code was as close to adventurous as her dull life got—would ever get, she supposed.

"At least he ran Sarah's column on the Abington party," Faith said, her eyes wistful. "She's so lucky that she's allowed to attend those upper-class affairs. The ladies must be lovely with their beautiful gowns and jewelry."

"She's not exactly invited," Edwina reminded her. "She goes as a reporter, and an undervalued one at that. She could write circles around the men reporters if old Ramsey wasn't so set in his conservative ways." But she had to agree with Faith's envy. It would be an adventure to see how the truly wealthy lived, even if from the outside.

Faith pursed her lips. "I'd still like to attend just once. Even if I were to go as a—"

"Look at this!" Edwina stabbed the newsprint with her finger. "It's in code. If you ignore every other word, the message really says: Husband suspects. Not tomorrow. Watch ads." She looked up, pleased with her accomplishment. "She's canceling a tryst."

"Let me see." Faith bent her nose toward the column. "How do you know to do that? The listing looks perfectly normal to me." Astonishment registered in her friend's eyes. "Why would you look at every other word?"

Edwina smiled, triumphant. "Patterns." She shrugged. "It's such a simple code, I'm surprised they bothered. Still, I wonder who sent it. Do you think Sarah would know? Whoever placed the ad must have done so through Sarah's station at the *Messenger*."

A bell tacked over the palace entrance, a recent annoying

addition by the Temperance Committee, jangled with a discordant tone. Sarah barreled into the renovated drinking parlor like a steam engine puffing out of Victoria Station. Just as a steam engine is unmindful of the cars behind, Sarah took no notice of the fourth member of their party, Claire, who followed silently in her wake.

Sarah dropped her satchel onto an empty chair before she slipped into another. "Ramsey doesn't think anyone would be interested in the vast quantities of birds sacrificed for women's fashion."

"I'm so sorry." Faith patted her friend's arm. "After all your research . . ."

"It's only because you're a woman," Claire insisted, moving Sarah's satchel to the floor before she lowered herself into the seat. "One of these days, Ramsey will recognize your value and remove you from the agonies."

"You know, I dislike that reference," Sarah scolded. "There's more to the personal column than sad lovelorn ads and letters written in torment." She smiled weakly and adjusted her glasses. "However, I hope you're right."

"But in the meantime . . ." Edwina hesitated. "Do you know who placed this ad?" She turned the paper so both Sarah and Faith could see.

" 'For my darling husband,' " Sarah read. " 'Who suspects tenderness, not neglect, tomorrow awaits. Watch praising ads multiply.' " Sarah grimaced, then released the newsprint. "It's not as well written as Faith's poetry, but Mrs. Bottomsly wanted a tribute to her husband."

Edwina exchanged a satisfied look with Faith, who retrieved the paper from the table.

"What?" Sarah asked, looking from one to the other. "We just print what we're paid to print. We don't edit the personal ads for content." She poured some tea from Faith's pot into the empty cup that appeared by her wrist. "No one wants to pay a few pence more for extra words even if urgently needed."

"Look at this one. It's so sweet." Faith sighed, then smirked at Edwina. "And it's not in code."

A refined gentleman, age 25, of wealth and education, seeks the acquaintance, with a view to matrimony, of a high-

*minded, kindhearted lady who prefers an evening of quiet
conversation to the lively demands of society. Address box
8 at the Mayfair Messenger.*

"He's not a gentleman." Sarah scowled and sipped her tea.
"Refined or otherwise."

"You know who placed this ad?" Faith asked, her eyes
widened.

Sarah looked about the room as if she were about to share
the Queen's secrets. "Ashton Carswell Bradford Trewelyn III."

The resulting collective gasp turned the heads of the other
patrons.

"Casanova . . ." Claire whispered with disdain.

"You saw him?" Faith asked, awe in her voice. "Was he as
handsome as they say?"

Sarah nodded. "I can understand an attraction."

"That man knows no restraint." Claire bent her head closer
to the others. "I've heard that because of him, five otherwise
decent women have been unexpectedly bundled off to the Con-
tinent for an extended stay." She hesitated. "All within two
months of each other."

Everyone gasped.

"My brothers told me he was tossed out of every school
in England on moral grounds," Edwina murmured, though
she had no knowledge of what moral grounds those had been.
At the time she had difficulty accepting that news. His name,
Trewelyn, so resembled the name of the noble squire from
Treasure Island that she had difficulty separating the two.
Even today, she felt as if someone had slowly stroked a
feather down the inside of her arm just at the mention of his
name.

"Didn't he leave the country?" Faith asked, pulling Edwina
from her reverie.

"I thought my brother said he joined the King's Royal Rifles," Edwina offered.

"He's returned, and he's even more handsome than before,"
Sarah said. "His years away have given him a harder edge, a
sort of dangerous quality that . . . well, I don't recall before."
She leaned forward. "Lately when I go to those dinners and
dances on behalf of the *Messenger*, the question is always if

Casanova will make an appearance. All the single women hope he'll be in attendance. Some of the married ones too."

Claire scowled, then turned the paper around so she could read the ad. "Why would London's most notorious rake advertise for a kindhearted lady who prefers quiet conversation—"

"And enjoyment of a good book," Faith added with a wistful gleam in her eye.

"Over the lively demands of society?" Edwina finished.

"I can think of only one reason." Sarah leaned back in her chair. Her sober face studied each of them in turn. "Debauchery."

"Sarah!" Edwina straightened. Faith merely mouthed the sinful word without giving it voice. "You don't know that."

"Think of it," Sarah insisted. "Gentle women, quiet women respond to his ad in pursuit of love and affection. He lures them to his lecherous lair and seduces them into trading their innocence for a life of scandal and degradation." Sarah rummaged through her reticule for a handkerchief and dabbed at her eyes. "That's how it happened with my sister."

"Ashton Carswell Trewelyn the third?" Faith's jaw dropped.

"No, not him," Sarah said with a shake of her head. "But someone like him. He got her in the family way and then abandoned her. My dear sister didn't live long enough to hold little Nan in her arms."

They all knew the sad story. Sarah was raising her niece as her own child and had sought her current position at the *Messenger* as a means for her support. As much as they derided Ramsey for failing to publish Sarah's serious articles, they were grateful he'd offered her employment in her time of need. The friends sat in silence to allow Sarah time to gather her composure.

Ashton Trewelyn III. Edwina remembered him from her own two failed seasons years ago, before she gave up the illusion of a man falling at her feet and pleading his undying devotion. Trewelyn had been dashing back then, debonair in his evening tails, and desired by all the young women. He had smiled at her once, but she hadn't the coquettish looks or the charm or the connections to draw men to her side like honey. She certainly hadn't the allure to attract Ashton Trewelyn III. After that brief moment, he'd returned to his wealthy friends . . .

and one beautiful woman in particular . . . What was her name?
She remembered watching them on the dance floor; they had
moved so eloquently, so full of grace, as if they were one
person. Edwina recalled the woman had the smallest waistline
she'd ever seen and a strange sort of laugh. Trewelyn didn't
glance Edwina's way again. He ignored her, just like so many
others.

"I wrote a poem about him once," Faith admitted. "I fancied
him an angel cast to earth."

"From hell, more likely," Sarah grumbled.

"We can't let this occur," Claire insisted. "We can't let him
take advantage of innocent women." Ever since Claire had
become involved with the Temperance Society, Edwina had
noticed her passion for platforms. Sometimes the cause didn't
matter, just the related call to action.

"How can we stop him?" Sarah asked. "I had to run the ad
even though I suspected it was a deception. I have Nan to
consider."

Faith patted her hand in sympathy. "Casanova's lecherous
actions are not your fault."

"Surely we can use your connections to the *Messenger* to
thwart his scheme of seduction," Claire said, gathering a head
of steam. "Think, ladies."

"Will you see the responses to his ad?" Edwina asked.

"Only the envelopes," Sarah replied. "I'm not allowed to
open them. I could lose my position."

"Some of those envelopes will have the return address on
the back," Faith said. "We could at least warn those women."

"He may not have his sights set on those women," Edwina
said thoughtfully. "It would be better if we knew which responses interested him the most and concentrate our efforts
there. Perhaps we should follow him about London." She brightened at the idea. "I'll follow him and foil any attempt he makes
to meet with innocent women."

"You can't follow Trewelyn around London," Sarah said.

"I can," Edwina protested. By far, this would be the most
adventurous feat she'd ever attempted. She imagined Jim
Hawkins from *Treasure Island* must have felt a similar twinge
of anticipation. "My father is so involved with the Perkins case,
he won't know that I'm not about. My mother is barely home

as it is with all her clubs and organizations. I could be Trewe-lyn's shadow, and he won't even know it."

"What about your Mr. Thomas?" Faith asked. "Won't he disapprove?"

"I don't know," Edwina replied, defiance in her voice. But she did know. Mr. Thomas would not approve of anything that involved risk or adventure. If it weren't for the fact that being in the company of the beau her father had handpicked from among his employees to escort her about town allowed her a freedom she wouldn't otherwise experience, she would have ended their relationship. "I do know that Mr. Thomas has bin-oculars that he uses to watch birds. I'm certain he will let me borrow them."

Sarah's skepticism showed in her eyes.

"I'll watch him from afar, Sarah. No harm will come of it."

"She could try," Faith said. "What is there to lose?"

"I don't know, Edwina." Sarah gave voice to her uncertainty. "I'm not certain this will work, and it could prove dangerous. Besides, your actions could anger Mr. Thomas. While you may not appreciate it now, security is nothing to gamble away."

Edwina took her hand. "If we save one woman from the fate of your sister, it would be worth the risk. I won't do anything outlandish, I promise."

Edwina held Sarah's gaze until her skepticism reluctantly turned to acceptance.

"And if we're successful, as I'm certain we will be," Claire said, "we can do this for other questionable personal ads as well. We'll protect innocent women."

"We'll be the Rake Patrol," Faith whispered.

"The Rake Patrol," Sarah said softly, testing the sound.

Edwina lifted her teacup, inviting the others to do the same. "To the Rake Patrol."

The four carefully clinked their cups, then grinned as their pact was formed. After each took a dutiful sip of the cold tea, Edwina replaced her cup on the saucer. "Now, ladies, let us plan how this is to be done . . ."

THE BASE OF ASHTON TREWELYN'S NECK TINGLED, A warning not felt since his service in Burma. He looked about the stark environs of the *Mayfair Messenger*'s office, suspecting he was under unfriendly scrutiny—and by someone in addition to the woman clerk behind the wooden counter, who kept glancing his way when she thought he wouldn't notice. He remembered her from when he initially placed the ad. One would have thought he hadn't bathed for a week based on her reaction to his appearance then. Under the circumstances, he waited patiently for a well-attired young lady to conclude the business of placing an ad. The *Mayfair Messenger* had become known for their personal ads, just as the *Pall Mall Gazette* was known for their coverage of social issues, or the *Illustrated London News* was known for their woodcuts. They each had their specialty, but Ashton had to admit, the *Messenger*'s niche appeared to be a lucrative one.

The young woman turned away from the counter. The instant she spotted him near the door, her cheeks flushed an attractive pink. After a moment's hesitation, she patted her hair and issued a seductive smile. Ashton opened the door for her, then tipped his hat as she passed by, just as any gentleman would do. Yet she paused, issuing a brazen unspoken invitation with her eyes. He remembered a time when he would have led the lady to a less public location and explored the pleasures her gaze suggested she wished. But today he slowly shook his head. She nodded, then continued on her way. Though he never understood why his appearance managed to elicit that almost universal reaction, it was what it was, and he'd become accustomed to it. He returned inside, removed his hat, then stepped up to the counter.

"The replies in box eight, if you please." He held the marker he'd been given to claim the responses to his search for a suitable companion for his friend, James. If ever a man was in need of a woman's company, it would be James. His friend, however, refused to exert effort in that direction and had instead taken up some unsavory practices that were bound to destroy his health. As Ashton had already lost close companions in Burma, he had no desire to lose more. James would surely cease his latest pursuits if he had a caring companion by his side.

Companions Ashton could readily produce. The stipulation that they be caring, however, posed a difficulty. None of Ashton's acquaintances would be suitable. That pack of hungry wolves could judge a man's finances by the tilt of his top hat, and his marriage availability by the caliber of his glove. No, those shallow, transparent women would have no interest in James, just as he imagined James would have no interest in them. A quiet, unassuming woman would be best. Someone with little interest beyond the hearth. Someone—

"Your ad met with success." The lady clerk smiled, an event so unexpected and transforming of her features that Ashton was taken aback as she stacked a small quantity of letters before him.

Strange. This very same clerk wouldn't spare him the time of day last week. Now she embodied the very symbol of co-operation.

"Do you wish to continue your ad for another week?" she asked.

"All this resulted from one ad?" There must've been twenty letters in that pile. "I had anticipated only one or two responses."

"London is filled with honest women seeking companionship," the clerk said, her eyes warm and helpful. He truly must have caught her on a bad day before. That, or the lady had a friendly twin. A particularly licentious memory from years ago brought a smile to his lips. He'd had some experience with twins.

Did a flicker of disgust just flash in the clerk's eyes? Or was that merely a reflection off the lenses of her eyeglasses? No matter. The clerk's demure smile obscured any ill feelings. "Responses are bound to be plentiful when the ad is placed by a refined and educated man such as yourself."

"You recall the ad?" he said, surprised. "Given the number of advertisements that must slide across this very counter, you must possess a remarkable memory."

"It is a consequence of my position to associate the faces of the advertisers with the ads they place." She hesitated a moment, then glanced up at him from beneath her lashes. "I assume you intend to interview the respondents."

"That had been my initial intention, yes." He ran his finger across the edges of the envelopes. "However, I hadn't planned on so many replies."

She brightened. "You may find that some are unsuitable

once you read their letters. The others . . ." She pushed her spectacles farther up the bridge of her nose. "If I may be so bold, sir, have you given any thought as to where you intend to interview the others?"

Ashton straightened. "I believe that's a personal matter—"

The clerk leaned forward. "I only meant to caution that an honest, respectable woman might have difficulty meeting a bachelor in his own quarters."

"That is true." His lips quirked. He should have considered this before.

"So you might want to consider arranging a meeting in a public spot. Are you familiar with the recently renovated Crescent Coffee Palace?"

He frowned. "Coffee Palace? I thought the Crescent was known for . . . beverages of another nature."

"It has something of an illustrious past," the clerk admitted. "However, the Temperance Committee has renovated the building, and it now offers a variety of wholesome food and drinks of a more genteel nature."

Teetotalers. He winced. "Have you been to this new Crescent?"

"I have, sir." She smiled. "It is the reason I can recommend the location as perfect for your purposes."

He hesitated, then nodded. The clerk certainly would have more experience and knowledge of such matters than he. He supposed she dispensed this sort of advice with some regularity. Perhaps the Crescent would be best. He began to stuff the envelopes into his pocket.

"And, of course, you'll need a method to identify the woman," the clerk continued.

"Identify her?" Another detail he hadn't considered. Who would have thought finding a woman for James would prove so difficult?

"Of course, sir. There will be many women of quality at the Crescent. You should employ some method to distinguish the lady responding to your advertisement from the other patrons."

It had been Ashton's experience that most women managed to recognize him immediately. Or, if an attractive, engaging woman had only recently arrived in London, he generally knew someone who could intercede with an introduction. This meeting of strange women was problematic.

"Ask her to carry a rose," the clerk said suddenly. "There's a florist near the Crescent. Acquiring the flower would not be difficult."

"A rose . . ." It was a romantic notion worthy of one of those Austen books. He could place a bud in the buttonhole of his lapel. A woman with a single rose should be easy to spot. "That's an excellent idea."

Delight spread across the clerk's face, again transforming her into a much younger woman. Obviously she hadn't experienced an easy life or she would not be employed in a newspaper office. Ashton briefly wondered if his own face carried the travails of his years in Burma. His aching leg certainly did.

"Thank you," he said, sweeping the last of the letters from the counter. He secured some in his inside pocket before stuffing others in his coat pocket. "You've been most helpful."

All should be fine as long as Caroline did not discover the letters. He'd planned to meet with her and young Matthew in Regent's Park after this stop at the *Messenger*. While two letters would have been easy to conceal, twenty or so might catch her attention. With her sharp tongue, she'd eviscerate any kind woman daring enough to respond to an ad. Caroline knew a thing or two about "daring."

Ashton removed a few shillings from his pocket and placed them on the counter. "For your assistance."

Color bloomed in the clerk's cheeks, but as he turned, he heard the scraping of metal across wood. As he suspected, times could be difficult. He left the office, leaning more heavily on his walking stick. A change of weather must be in the air.

The prickling at his nape resumed even as he left the newspaper office. Pausing a moment, he searched for the unseen assailant. He'd foolishly thought he'd left combat behind when he departed the Royal Rifles with a bullet wound in his thigh. Instead he'd returned to a household riddled with conflict. He hadn't sorted out all the issues as yet. No one really spoke except young Matthew, and his governess hushed him at every opportunity. One didn't need words to sense the powder keg of tension, or the feeling that somehow he might be the match to ignite it all.

Scanning the street, he noted nothing out of the ordinary, except a lovely young woman with hair the color of sunlight standing next to a bicycle. She angled binoculars toward a copse of trees. What on earth was she studying there—pigeons? It was not as if the grays of London were disturbed with colorful birds like those of Burma. A smile tipped his lips with the memory. Some of Burma's heat would be appreciated on this cool spring day as well. London may not have been the best choice for his recuperation, but at the time, he had thought it was the easiest. He'd been mistaken there as well.

He glanced back at the girl. Surely a comely bird enthusiast posed no threat, especially one that should be the object of study rather than some feathered creature likely to end up on someone's dinner plate. He couldn't imagine danger coming from that quarter. No, the warning must be something else. Something not visible, not yet.

He patted his pocket, feeling the neat packet of envelopes tucked there, then climbed into his waiting carriage. Caroline and her son were waiting. He'd promised Matthew he'd show him the tigers, at least the ones behind bars. If nothing else, Matthew had certainly been a delight in Ashton's homecoming. Perhaps as the boy matured, Ashton would be able to teach him how to spot the predatory tigers who didn't wear stripes to warn of their ferocity. Tigers that hid behind serene human faces but had the ability to carve one's heart with a single swipe. Tigers like Matthew's mother.

FROM THE *USA TODAY* BESTSELLING AUTHOR OF
Lady Isabella's Scandalous Marriage

JENNIFER ASHLEY

The Madness of Lord Ian Mackenzie

Most women heeded the warnings.
One woman was tempted by them . . .

It was whispered all through London Society that Ian Mackenzie was mad, that he'd spent his youth in an asylum, and that he was not to be trusted—especially with a lady. For the reputation of any woman caught in his presence was instantly ruined.

Yet Beth found herself inexorably drawn to the Scottish lord, whose hint of a brogue wrapped around her like silk and whose touch could draw her into a world of ecstasy. Despite his decadence and his intimidating intelligence, she could see that he needed help. Her help. Because suddenly the only thing that made sense to her was . . .

The Madness of Lord Ian Mackenzie

"Big, arrogant, sexy highlanders—Jennifer Ashley writes the kind of heroes I crave!"   —Elizabeth Hoyt,
New York Times bestselling author

"A deliciously dark and delectably sexy story of love and romantic redemption."   —*Booklist*

penguin.com

M847T0311

From *New York Times* bestselling author
of *Sinful in Satin*

MADELINE HUNTER

Dangerous in Diamonds

Outrageously wealthy, the Duke of Castleford has little incentive to curb his profligate ways—gaming and whoring with equal abandon and enjoying his hedonistic lifestyle to the fullest. When a behest adds a small property to his vast holdings, one that houses a modest flower business known as The Rarest Blooms, Castleford sees little to interest him . . . until he lays eyes on its owner. Daphne Joyes is coolly mysterious, exquisitely beautiful, and utterly scathing toward a man of Castleford's stamp—in short, an object worthy of his most calculated seduction.

Daphne has no reason to entertain Castleford's outrageous advances, and every reason to keep him as far away as possible from her eclectic household. Not only has she been sheltering young ladies who have been victims of misfortune, but she has her own closely guarded secrets. Then Daphne makes a discovery that changes everything. She and Castleford have one thing in common: a profound hatred for the Duke of Becksbridge, who just happens to be Castleford's relative.

Never before were two people less likely to form an alliance—or to fall in love . . .

M848T0311

*Enter the rich world of
historical romance
with Berkley Books . . .*

Madeline Hunter

Jennifer Ashley

Joanna Bourne

Lynn Kurland

Jodi Thomas

Anne Gracie

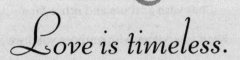

Love is timeless.

berkleyjoveauthors.com

M9G0610

Discover Romance

berkleyjoveauthors.com

See what's coming up next from your favorite romance authors and explore all the latest Berkley, Jove, and Sensation selections.

See what's new
~
Find author appearances
~
Win fantastic prizes
~
Get reading recommendations
~
Chat with authors and other fans
~
Read interviews with authors you love

berkleyjoveauthors.com

M1G0610